MW01172230

What Readers Are Saying About Dave Tevelin's Books

"As counsel for one of the defendants in US v Edmond, et al., I was impressed by Mr. Tevelin's mastery of the facts in this complicated trial and his ability to weave them into an exciting novel. I enjoyed Siege Of The Capital, but Mr. Tevelin stepped up his game with Murder On Morton." *Ernest W. McIntosh, Esq.*

"Although laced with fiction, Mr. Tevelin's Siege Of The Capital captures the essential elements of Hamaas Khaalis' takeover and the drama of those thirty-nine hours. He managed to make the complexity of the incident into a very readable story." *Earl Silbert, former U.S. Attorney for the District of Columbia*

"Dave Tevelin vividly captured the horror of the Khaalis slayings, and the drama of his takeover of the three buildings in D.C. He nailed Khaalis' voice, and compellingly laid out the web of factors that led to both the murders of his family and his actions four year years later. I recommend this book highly." *Henry Schuelke, former Assistant U.S. Attorney for the District of Columbia*

"Siege Of The Capital, a blend of fiction with real time events, is a great read! Its account brought back memories of a life-changing event for those involved in the 1977 hostage siege and the dramatic trial that followed. For me, as the federal prosecutor involved in the case, Dave Tevelin's account of those days – and Khaalis' back story – is well researched, vivid, and compelling." *Mark Tuohey, former Assistant U.S. Attorney for the District of Columbia*

"Dave Tevelin's Death At The Howard takes us back in time, recreating 1960s DC as few have been able to do, and, in the process, helps us understand the city we all live in now. And he does so with a good story compellingly told – a great read!" *Blair Ruble, Author, Washington's U Street, A Biography*

"Dave Tevelin weaves a taut drama filled with over-the-top characters in a fantastic series of events, all of which are based in fact. A terrific retelling of a bizarre chapter in Washington history that is both authentic and gripping." *Tim Murray, former D.C. pretrial official and Executive Director of the Pretrial Justice Institute*

"Dave Tevelin really tells it the way it was. I loved this book." *Greg Gaskins, guitarist for Elvis Presley, The Manhattans, and many others*

MURDER ON MORTON

MORTON

A Jake Katz Novel
Dave Tevelin

© David Tevelin 2020

*For J.D. Sprague, my 11th grade
English teacher,
who inspired me to be a reader and a
writer,
and who I was so happy to reconnect
with in 2019,
54 years down the road*

MURDER ON MORTON

November 23, 1987

"You got him?" Wallace said.

"I don't got him," O'Connell said. "Hold on." He squeezed the walkie-talkie under his neck and raised binoculars to his eyes.

"Where's he at?"

"Hold on, Detective," O'Connell said. "These things are for shit."

"You got the night ones, right?" Wallace said. "Tell me you got the night ones."

"I got 'em, man, I got 'em, but I might as well be lookin' up your midnight ass for all the good they're doin' me. Hold on, I'm gettin' closer."

O'Connell let the binoculars fall to his chest and squinted down Morton from 6th. Of course every streetlight was out. He zipped up his jacket to hide the goggles, slipped the walkie-talkie into his left pocket, and got up off his knees. He slid the billed Redskins cap out of his right pocket, tugged it low on his head, and double-timed up 6th to Orleans, turned right and went about 20 yards before heading back down an alley to Morton. He got back on his knees and scraped down a wall to the left until he could see most of the thin two-story dirty white brick house a few doors down and across the street. He kept as low and as far back as he could to stay out of sight of any spotters on the roof.

The walkie-talkie barked from his pocket. He fished it out. "What?" he whispered.

1

"Where you at, Patrolman?" Wallace said. "Don't leave me hangin' here."

"So sorry, just tryin' to do my job. I'm across the way, closer."

O'Connell brought the binoculars up again. "No one outside or on the roof, far as I can tell. What d'ya hear?"

"Wait a minute," Wallace said, and pressed his fat headphones as tight to his ears as he could. He heard what seemed to be footsteps on wooden stairs, but he couldn't tell if they were going up or down and he couldn't tell how many people were walking. They stopped and he closed his eyes to concentrate.

"Hey, you up? What's goin' on?" O'Connell squawked over the walkie-talkie.

"I can't hear nothin'," Wallace said. "What do you see? Any lights anywhere?"

"Yeah, upstairs, but there's shades down on all the — "

"Wait a second!" Wallace hissed. He heard a voice, then another, but he couldn't tell who it was. His man's was louder because the wire was right there, but he was just giving one-word answers. *C'm'on, man*, he thought, *don't wobble on me now. This is a big one.* There were other voices but they were softer, farther away. He heard someone laugh or maybe snort up close. "They're talkin'," he said, "but I can't make it out."

2

"Our man knows what he's doin'?"

"He knows." He'd been wearing the wire almost a year.

"You work with him before?"

"Yeah," Wallace said. "I know him, good. Hang on."

"Is that right?" he heard someone say. "That much?"

"That's what he said," the snitch said, louder and clearer.

"Huh. Way more 'n your usual, 'idn't it?"

"Didn't know I had a usual."

"Yeah, you do," another voice said. "And it's chicken shit. Now five hundred grams? Five-zero-zero? Nice big fat round number? Somethin' goin' on we oughta know 'bout?"

"Nothin's going on, man. Just a dude I know wants it is all. I said I might be able to make it happen. Didn't tell him nothin' about nothin'."

"Just some dude you know, huh? Is 'at what you tellin' me?" the second voice said.

"That's what I'm telling you."

"Well, that may be what you tellin' me," Wallace heard a lot closer, "but that's not what I'm hearin'."

"Oh shit!" Wallace said.

"Back off, man," the snitch said.

"Back off? You got a lot of balls, you pasty-faced white motherfucker, you know that?"

"What the fuck? I'm not – " Wallace heard a scuffle, then someone or something hit the floor, hard. A voice roared into his headset. "Say bye-bye to your boy, fuckheads!" Then he heard nothing.

"Shit! They made him, they got him!" he screamed into the walkie-talkie. "Tell me what you see!"

O'Connell jammed the glasses to his eyes. "Nothin'! I don't see nothin'!"

"Shit oh goddamned fuck shit!" Wallace screamed and flung his headset against the wall. "I'm sending a squad down there now! Don't lose 'em!"

O'Connell dropped the glasses and took one more look at the house. Still nothing. He walked fast to 6th, head down, and prayed no one was on lookout. He crossed the street and ran up the sidewalk to his civilian Pontiac. He jumped in the driver's seat, ripped the ignition on, and hung a quick left onto Morton, then pressed the brakes and crept down the street. He pulled to the right curb, his eyes fixed on the landing of the house. The night was chilly, but his face was bathed in sweat. Everything was still. He smacked the steering wheel with both palms, then gripped it tight, waiting for something, anything.

Headlights shone from an alley just behind him on the right. A black Lincoln pulled up to the street, paused, and turned his way, the only way it could go on Morton. O'Connell watched it pull slowly past. Two in the front, one in the back, all of them looking straight ahead. He waited for them to get further down the block, then eased away from the curb and followed them to the stop sign where the street dead-ended at 7th. He caught lights in the rear-view mirror and glanced up to see a beat-up minivan turning his way from out the alley. "Shit!" he muttered. *Which one had the snitch? What if neither of them did?*

The Lincoln pulled to a stop at the corner. He scribbled down the plate number. The rustbucket pulled too close behind him to read the tag. He couldn't make out a face or even a head. Neither car had a turn signal on. The Lincoln bolted left, squirting between cars running both ways on 7th. He pulled to the corner, keeping his eyes on the rear-view mirror. Still no signal behind, but he knew what was coming. He flicked a look up 7th and saw the Lincoln's brake lights flash as the light at Florida turned red. That gave him a shot to keep up so he swung left too and shook his head as he looked in the side mirror and watched the van peel out to the right. He grabbed the phone from the console and punched up Wallace.

"Where you now?" the detective said.

"I'm going north on 7th behind a Lincoln that pulled out the alley from behind the house."

"All right. I got cars headed for Morton."

5

"Roger that, but another car out the alley went south on 7th."

"Shit in my hat!" Wallace yelled. "What's that car?"

"Old bucket of a van's all I could see. Couldn't get the plates. DC's all I know."

"How 'bout the one you're on?" O'Connell read what he wrote.

"All right," Wallace said. "Stick with him and keep this thing open. I'll APB the van."

"Roger that." The light turned green. "We're movin'. Left on Florida, headin' for 6th."

He stayed far enough behind so no one in the Lincoln would think they had a tail, slowing enough to let a car cut between them as they crossed over 6th N.E. The Lincoln moved into the left lane. He waited till they crossed 4th before he did too. The light at New York two blocks ahead was green. They crossed under the railroad bridge just past 3rd, O'Connell's eyes trained on the light. Still green – then yellow a half-block from New York. The Lincoln sped up and he did too. He watched it blast through the red and stomped the gas to shoot through just behind, traffic pinching in on him from both sides. Brakes squealed and horns blared. He threw a middle finger up as both cars floored it up New York in tandem. He heard the faint wail of sirens behind him and hoped that was Wallace closing in on the van. Up ahead, the Lincoln was flying. *They know they have company now*, O'Connell thought,

6

and pressed the pedal down as they charged toward North Capitol. The light stayed green and he flicked a glance at the speedometer as he flew through the intersection into Northwest – 57 and climbing. He picked up the phone.

"Yo. We're bookin' it up Florida. He knows I'm here, no doubt about it now. Those sirens yours?"

"Yeah," Wallace said. "Squad car on Pennsylvania Southeast saw it go by two minutes after I put it out. We're closin' in."

"Roger that."

"You need backup?"

"Hard to know. All I got now's a speeder."

"Yeah. That and a corpse in the trunk."

"Detective," O'Connell said, "you tell me I got probable cause for that and I will pull him over and turn that thing inside out." He waited for the word as they zipped through the light at Georgia like O'Connell was drafting him at Daytona. Wallace muttered something he couldn't get.

"You say somethin'?"

"I said you don't have it, least not for that. He got an expired tag? Light out?"

"Shit, I could nail him right now." He flicked a glimpse at the speedometer. "61. In a 35."

7

"Your call."

"All right then," O'Connell said. "I'll let you know when." He groped behind him and pulled a portable beacon off the floor onto his lap. He slid the window down halfway as they made the soft left onto U Street way too hard. Traffic was heavier now, both lanes, so the Lincoln slowed down and he did too, right behind. He kept his left hand on the beacon as they crept down U to a red light at 13th. A couple of brothers crossed in front of him to join the late-night line spilling onto the sidewalk from Ben's Chili Bowl to his right. He made out a few bodies lying under the scaffolding at the Metro stop they were putting in just across the street. This was no place to pull anyone over so he kept the beacon on his lap as they crawled past 13th and 14th. O'Connell saw the driver's eyes dart back to look at him in the rear view mirror every other second. All he could make out was a dark knit cap, a puffy black face, a mustache, and a soul patch. The Lincoln came to a full stop at the stop signs at 15th and 16th, and the driver pulled to a stop at the red light at 17th. Then burst through it.

"Motherfucker!" O'Connell spat out. He flipped the beacon on, slapped it on the roof, banged his fist on the horn, and kept it there. He swerved his way through the intersection, then floored it to catch up to the Lincoln in the left lane maybe thirty yards ahead. The light where Florida curled back to meet U just before 18th was red. The Lincoln was pinned in, the second car back. Cars sat to his right. *Too much traffic coming their way off Florida to make a Uey,* he thought, then slapped his left armpit to make sure the Glock was there and pulled forward to about

8

ten feet behind the Lincoln when the light turned green. The car in front of it moved ahead but the Lincoln just sat there, brake lights on.

O'Connell edged forward, then slammed his foot on the brake when he saw doors burst open on both sides of the car, three dark forms flying out in different directions. The driver ran across the intersection and disappeared behind the lights of a car heading through it. O'Connell caught a glimpse of someone running up the pavement on the right side of Florida. He heard footsteps pound away from him up the other side, then fade into nothing.

O'Connell yanked the Glock from its holster and threw the car door open. An Oldsmobile swerved past him into the opposite lanes, horn screaming. He kept the gun trained on the Lincoln. The rear door on the driver's side was the only one shut. "Police!" he screamed. "Put your fuckin' hands up and get out of the car!" No one got out. He pointed the gun at the driver's seat and side-stepped slowly to just behind the rear door. The swirling reflection of the beacon light was the only thing moving.

"Get out now! Last fucking chance!" He edged a step closer, his back against the car, them heard something and froze.

You know it, you know, and the whole world has to answer right now.
Just to tell you once again. Who's bad?

Michael Effing Jackson. O'Connell swung around to fill the driver's doorway, two gloved hands on the gun he levelled straight ahead. The front seat was empty. He rotated right. Back seat too. He knelt on the driver's seat, flicked off the radio, and checked out the floorboards in front. Nothing. He leaned over the seat and saw a sea of empty Colt .45 cans on the floor. He batted them around but nothing else was back there. He spun back and slid into the driver's seat, wedged up tight against the steering wheel. He found the button at the side of the seat and watched raindrops start to dot the windshield as he slowly glided back. He sat still for a few seconds, then turned the car off and yanked the key from the ignition. He muttered a quiet "Fuck" and pushed himself out of the car.

He walked back to the trunk, put the key in, took a deep breath, and held it. He turned the key and the lid bounced up. A spare, a jack, some brown wrapping paper, and twine. He moved to the side so his lamps could light it up and knelt down to peer all the way back. That was it. No body, no blood, nothing.

He fell into the front seat of the Pontiac and picked up the phone. "Yo. Wallace. You there?"

"Yeah. What's up?"

"Guys ditched the car on U at Florida. Took off in every friggin' direction."

"You check it out?"

"Yeah, some beer cans, crap in the trunk. No body, no contraband, no nothin'."

10

"All right," Wallace said. "Impound it and call it a night."

"Will do. Where're you?"

"Chasing this goddamn van down P-A Av Southeast." O'Connell heard the sirens wail through the receiver. "You need backup?" he asked.

"We got it. Two units. Goddamn it!" Wallace yelled as the car took air going over the hill at Branch. Zimmer, the patrolman at the wheel, hit the brakes. Wallace reached forward and tapped him on the shoulder.

"No, no, no, Zim. Stick with 'im. Don't mind me."

"Getting' too old for this shit," Wallace said into the phone. "Let's talk tomorrow. 10-4." He handed the phone to a young black cop in the passenger seat, a kid he helped recruit named Jewelius Rodney. Zimmer slowed down anyway because they were at the van's bumper and cars in both lanes were pumping their brakes and pulling over to get out of the way. The avenue bottomed out and they climbed towards Alabama. The rain fell harder now. Zimmer sped up the wipers but the climb slowed the van down even more.

"I never been in a chase this goddamn slow before," Rodney said. "Friggin' bumper cars go faster."

Zimmer looked at Wallace in the rear view mirror. "We're in Maryland in probably less'n a mile," he said. "Should I call 'em?" He picked up the phone to let Wallace know what he thought. Wallace did the math. He

11

had a car coming down Pennsylvania behind him and another one coming up Southern chasing a van barely doing the speed limit that sounded like firecrackers on the Fourth of July and looked like it crashed onto earth sometime last century.

"No," he said. "There's enough of us already. Stand down." Zimmer laid the phone back in the console. They crested over Alabama and maybe it was just gravity but the van sped up, jets of water shooting off its rear wheels strafing the cruiser's windshield. Zimmer put the wipers on max and stuck to the van's bumper. Wallace heard another siren fire up behind them and turned to see flashers dancing on top of the cruiser racing up. He turned back to see they were coming to Southern, where D.C. turned into Maryland.

"See if you can pass him," he yelled to Zimmer, "box him between us."

Zimmer shot to the right and pumped the accelerator till he pulled even with the van. There were no windows on the side until the front seat and Wallace saw just the driver up there. The guy stole him a look and shot him the bird. Young, black, full beard, close cropped natural. Wallace motioned him to pull over. He took off. The cruiser kept pace. The light at Southern a hundred yards ahead turned yellow. Just past it, the road began a long turn left.

"Bust it!" Wallace yelled to Zimmer.

They raced through the red side by side. In the left lane no more than fifty yards ahead, a dark car's brake lights suddenly lit up the rain pouring down now. Wallace heard the van's brakes screech and watched it start to spin away from them. The cruiser shot past and Wallace whirled to see the van spin back the other way and skid across the right lane, carving ripples in the water till it hit the gravel on the shoulder and spun like a top into a thicket of trees. He heard a tremendous wham, then nothing but the wipers beating back and forth.

"Turn around!" he yelled, but Zimmer was already crossing the grass median and speeding back up Pennsylvania. The other cruiser was pulling to the shoulder where the van left the road. Wallace's car rolled up just behind it and he didn't wait for it to stop before he jumped out and ran to the edge of the trees. The headlamps and beacons lit the scene enough to show the van right side up, its rear wheels on the ground, the rest of it at about a thirty degree angle, impaled on a tree trunk. Both front doors were resting open against their frames, still quivering from the crash. The side door and rear door were shut. Zimmer came to Wallace's side. Rodney and two other cops fanned out to their right, guns drawn.

"Okay," Wallace said, "go ahead but take it slow. Don't want no surprises."

Zimmer took a step forward and waved his gun hand at the others to move ahead. They stepped forward slowly until they were within five yards of the back of the van. Zimmer motioned them to stop, then tipped his head forward to Rodney and they circled wide around the van,

13

Zimmer on the driver's side, Rodney on the other. The other two cops closed the gap with Wallace and knelt in place, their Glocks aimed at the van. Zimmer raised his left arm and motioned to Rodney to come closer. Wallace watched them edge closer to the van, each in a crouch, gun trained on the doors. Zimmer reached for the lip of the door and jerked it open all in one motion. The driver fell in a lifeless heap to the mud at his feet. A split-second later, Rodney threw the passenger door open and jumped to his knees up on the seat, both hands in a death grip on the gun, waving it back and forth at the empty back seat.

"No one else here!" he screamed, then slid back down into the seat and put his head between his knees.

Wallace slipped on a pair of latex gloves and walked to the driver's side. Zimmer backed off a step to let him kneel and get a good look at the body. Glass shards pockmarked his face and beard. His eyes, open and bulging, fixed their gaze somewhere over his shoulder. Blood dripped from a deep gash at his hairline down his right cheek and clung there. Wallace looked up and saw a huge ragged hole where the left side of the windshield used to be, red streaks striping the glass and the dash. The steering wheel was bent back and cracked open at the 12 position. Wallace pushed himself up and leaned into the front seat. The familiar stink of death drifted past him, mixed with menthol and alcohol.

Rodney raised his head and turned to look at him, licking his lips, his eyes rimmed red and wet. Wallace knew exactly what he was going through. He'd lived

14

through more than one nightmare over the past twenty-eight years on the MPD.

"So what do you see down there, my man?" he asked. Rodney looked back down at the floor and picked up an open pack of Salems. "Just this, detective." Wallace nodded and pushed himself back out the driver's side, then walked back to the rear of the van. Zimmer was there waiting for him. Wallace tipped his head to the van doors.

Zimmer nodded, gripped the handle on the right door, and pulled it open. He saw nothing but a big black plastic bag slide his way a little. He reached in over it to pull the latch on the inside of the other door and pushed it away from him. The bag slid out and spilled to the ground, landing with a heavy thud. A knot at the top kept it closed but the red ooze caked in a long ragged slit in the plastic told Wallace what to expect inside. He took his time squatting down, sucked in a deep breath, then ripped the slit open wide and peeled back the plastic. The face of a ghost stared back at him, its eyes open wide, its head barely attached to its neck, a thick coat of blood still glistening on his chest. Wallace fell back, stunned, sickened, the vomit rocketing up his throat. He lurched to his knees as it roared out, endlessly it seemed. When everything inside him was finally out, he bent over and buried his face in his hands. He mumbled something, too low and indistinct for anyone to make out. Rodney looked to Zimmer who could do nothing but stare, then got to his knees beside Wallace and threw an arm around him. He tugged the detective's sports jacket down and patted his back just to let him know he was there. Wallace was still mumbling the same thing over and over but Rodney couldn't make it out. He leaned down and whispered in his ear.

"Detective. What is it? What're you sayin'?" Wallace didn't change his position. He didn't raise his voice. But this time Rodney could make him out.

"Schein, Schein, shit, I'm sorry, I'm so sorry," he said again and again and again.

February 21, 1989

1

Katz popped open the styrofoam lid. LaVerne closed her eyes and lowered her face to let the tacos' aroma engulf her. "Oh man," she sighed, "that is heaven." She drew a long breath in through her nose, then sat back up and gave him a big grin. "Jake, thank you for turnin' me on to Antonio's. Seriously." She shook her head. "All those years I wasted at Popeyes."

Antonio's Mexican-Cuban luncheonette was a block farther from 5th Street than Popeyes but worth the walk, even on a chilly day like today. Katz had been going there since he was a cop and never did figure out what was Mexican and what was Cuban, but he really didn't care. Three crispy tacos, black beans, and rice was all he wanted pretty much every day he didn't have to meet a client for lunch, which was pretty much every day.

"How was court?" LaVerne asked.

"Superior, just one, but two Feds."

"All right then," she said. "We eat."

They both knew the code. D.C. Superior Court had appointed Katz counsel for one indigent defendant, but the Federal District Court assigned him two – and they paid better – so it was a good morning. He steeled himself to ask the question. "So?" he said.

"So." She handed him a pink slip of paper. "You know who, 12:05" he read. "Let me eat my lunch first, then I'll get back to him."

"That is a good plan," LaVerne said. "Maybe today's the day it'll actually work."

Katz grunted and walked back to his office, kicking the door shut so they could each enjoy a little privacy. He took three steps to his desk, a scarred walnut beauty he got cheap at a House of Representatives auction when he first opened shop, dropped his styrofoam box on it, then walked a step behind it to take in the traffic three stories down. Most of it was lawyers on the sidewalks heading to and from Superior Court two blocks to his right or District Court a block behind it. In another hour, he'd be down there with them, heading over for the arraignment of someone whose name he wouldn't know until he cracked open the file he threw right next to the tacos he was going to crack open first.

He filled a coffee cup at the bottled water cooler it cost him too much to fill every month, fell into his chair, and pulled the *Post* sports section to him. The Redskins signed Mike Tice. Katz remembered him playing for Maryland, which automatically disqualified him from ever being someone he would root for. He chomped a bite of taco a split second before the phone buzzed. He pushed the button.

"You know who," LaVerne sang.

"'ell 'im I'll 'all 'ack," Katz said.

The line clicked dead but he heard her mumble into the phone, then click back on.

20

"He wants you now," she said. No singing this time. "Says it's important."

Katz took his time chewing down the carnage in his mouth. "It's always important," he finally said. "Put his sorry ass through."

In the time it took him to wipe a napkin across his face, brace himself, and pick up the receiver, the whole flood of memories from their not-so-blissful five years together washed over his brain like it did every time Harry Alexander called. They had joined forces right after Hamaas Abdul Khaalis was found guilty after taking a hundred hostages in three buildings in '77. It seemed like such a good idea at the time. Katz' visibility would never be higher than it was after Khaalis' siege, and he was ready for a move. Harry'd been a Superior Court judge for ten years, he was a hero to big parts of the City's black community, and he could be – when he got out of his own way – a hell of a lawyer. Katz still carried the scars from his own battle with Harry on the stand about what he saw – or maybe didn't see – at the B'nai B'rith that March.

Katz worked for Harry as an independent contractor, leasing space in his office for a nominal fee. Respectful of Harry's status and experience, he agreed there'd be no profit sharing; each of them would eat only what he killed. Their independence also made professional sense because they could legally represent co-defendants in the same case without violating the code of ethics, a matter of concern to only Katz, as it turned out.

21

The business arrangement worked fine, but the personal relationship never did. Like Simon and Garfunkel or Sam and Dave, they made beautiful music together in public, but off the stage, it wasn't so much music as artillery fire. Katz grew from restive to vocal to pissed each new time Harry told him to drop everything to prepare or file a document he'd forgotten till the last minute, or his name showed up in yet another Board of Professional Responsibility decision. He went from pissed to gone one snowy afternoon when he had to cut a client conference short to drive someplace he'd never been in Virginia to appear before a Federal agency he didn't know existed to explain why Harry hadn't appeared at a hearing that morning that he thought he had filed a continuance for but, of course, hadn't.

There were way, way too many ethical misadventures to remember, but the Court of Appeals summed it up best – in their *two* opinions about whether Harry should be allowed to continue practicing law in the District. After using the terms "callous disregard," "inexcusable failures," "deliberate refusal," and "reprehensible" to describe his conduct, and "inherently incredible," "not worthy of comment," and "dissembling excuses" to describe his explanations, the court said simply: "We view neglect as the prevailing theme."

They formally ended their relationship in 1982, three years before the court finally suspended Harry from the bar for two years because of five instances of conduct prejudicial to the administration of justice, three of neglect, two of failure to obtain his client's lawful objective, one of deceit and misrepresentation, and most surprisingly of all to Katz, only one of failure to follow local custom, i.e., showing up on time and telling the truth when you do. Katz looked back on the two years that Harry was out of his life with great nostalgia. But they were long gone, as he was reminded now at least once every weekday. He took a deep sigh and picked up the receiver.

"And to whom do I owe the pleasure?" he said.

"Happy Presidents Day!" Harry said.

"That was yesterday, Harry."

"Then Happy Tuesday!"

"It was."

"Be kind, Jake. I was going to be nice to you, after Saturday and all."

"Okay. What happened Saturday?"

"Well, two things really. Hoyas crushed BC for openers. You mighta seen it. It was the headline in the Sunday Sports section. Made the front page too."

Katz hated Georgetown worse than he hated Maryland. They stopped playing his alma mater GW in b-ball in the '70s because the Colonials had a nasty habit of beating them. Harry went to Georgetown Law and became a huge fan right about the time they won the NCAAs in '84.

"I didn't notice," Katz lied.

23

"Is that right?" Harry said. "Then for sure you didn't notice that little box all the way down the corner on page E40 somethin', said your boys're now 1 and 23 after losin' to Rutgers? Didn't see that either, I guess, huh?"

"No," and that was the truth. He stopped looking for GW scores after 0-10. They somehow beat UMass by 26 points to finally win one but he couldn't bring himself to read even that article.

"What's your coach's name? Keister?"

"Kuester. OK, Harry, good talking to you. Gotta go now."

"Whoa, whoa, whoa, Jake," Harry said firmly. "I didn't call just to rub it in. Come on now. I got some business for you, could be big business."

"If it's so big, why don't you want it?"

"I will tell you if you'll let me start from the beginning."

Katz eyed the taco staring back at him. "Fine, go, start," he said, then tucked the phone between his chin and his left shoulder, wrapped his left hand around the mouthpiece, grabbed the taco with his right, twisted his head as far from the phone as he could, and raised it to his mouth.

"I got a call from Billy Murphy, maybe you heard of him?" So near and yet so far. He put the taco down and pushed it out of arm's reach.

"I've heard of him. Criminal attorney from Baltimore."

"'Criminal attorney from Baltimore.'" Harry laughed. "That's like sayin' Cal Ripken's a baseball player from Baltimore. He's the best there is, Jake. You ever hear of a guy named Charles Hopkins?"

"Harry, please, I'm beggin' you. Just tell me your story."

"Charles Hopkins was a fella who, back in the seventies sometime, was pissed off with Mayor Schaefer up there 'cause the city health department closed down his carryout joint. Mr. Hopkins had a mind to change the Mayor's mind – with a gun – at City Hall. Didn't find the Mayor, but he killed a councilman, shot a secretary. Sound familiar to you?" He had Katz' attention now. It sounded a lot like what Khaalis' crew did at the District Building in '77.

"You there?" Harry said. "Hello?"

"Yeah, it does. Where's Murphy come in?"

"He represented Hopkins when he went to trial – and got him off! Insanity! How d'ya like that? I thought about tryin' that with Hamaas but didn't think I could come close to pullin' it off even though he had some history with shrinks, as you know – but he went and did it! Guy's a hell of a lawyer."

"Okay. So where do I come in?"

"Hold on a second. So Billy calls me this mornin' and tells me a little bird told him that something big's going down here right now. You ever hear the name Rayful Edmond?"

"No."

"You will. According to Billy, the FBI thinks he's *the* drug kingpin in D.C. Got ties to L.A., brings in shitloads of cocaine, distributes it all over the city, etcetera, etcetera – allegedly, of course."

"So he wants you to represent him?"

"No, Billy's goin' to take care of Edmond, but he says a lot of guys're gonna need lawyers pronto. He thinks the Feebies mighta talked to some of 'em already, trying to get 'em to turn on Rayful."

"Anyone picked up yet?"

"He doesn't know for sure, but he's got the word from somebody that somethin's about to go down any day."

"Little vague, isn't it?"

"Jake, look, I didn't cross-examine the man. The point is that if it does go down, a lot of people're gonna be needin' some good lawyers and he wants me to start findin' 'em quick 'cause everyone's gonna be pointin' the finger at everyone else, so they're all gonna need their own lawyers, you know, with the ethics and all."

Katz bit his tongue, hard. "Right, with the ethics and all." Then he heard Harry sigh.

"Jake, my man, I'm just tryin' to pass a little business your way. If you don't want it, that's fine. Just let me know and I'll move right on down the rolodex."

Katz always could use more clients, but the little Harry had told him gave him cause for pause. Most of his clients were solo actors nabbed for B&Es or selling half a gram, not kilos. Maybe it was his days with the U.S. Attorney's office, but he always thought the hired guns who repped the big fish were as suspect as their clients. Did he really want to sully his own rep that way? On the other hand, this might raise his profile and generate more clients – plus it brought him back to his days on the MPD, which looked better every new day he trudged up the steps and wound up where he sat now.

"How long till I have to let you know?" he asked.

"Asap, Jake. You remember what Smokey sang, right?"

"The love I saw in you was just a mirage?"

"That too, but the one I'm thinkin' of's 'beggars can't be choicey'."

Then it hit Katz. He knew exactly who'd give him the straight scoop on this Edmond and what he'd be getting into, with no b.s. on top. "Let me make a call, Harry. I'll get back to you soon as I can." He hung up without waiting for an answer, then picked the receiver back up and dialed the number. He eyed the taco box, then pushed it away. He heard the other end pick up.

"Detective Wallace, please," he said.

2

When he hit the corner at 5th and D, Katz did his usual Metro math test, where the right answer depended on whether he valued his time more than his money. If he turned right and walked to Marrocco's, it'd take him 20 minutes and cost him bupkis. If he turned left to take the Metro, he'd be out a buck-ten but it would probably save him five minutes. A close call. He looked at his watch. 6:35. They were meeting at 7. He turned right.

As he drew closer to the restaurant, he tried to think of the last time he saw Wallace. They'd bumped into each other briefly at the FOP a few times after Katz left the MPD, and once at a Bullets game out at the Cap Centre, but the only time he remembered clearly was Andy Scheingold's funeral, which, he was stunned to recall, was over a year ago. He remembered feeling more sorry for Wallace than himself because Wallace was the one who had to make the call to tell him Schein'd died of an overdose. When Schein died, they were both forty and they'd known each other for more than half their lives. He was Katz's first friend to die, and that may be why he broke out bawling at the cemetery, or maybe it was seeing Schein's parents for the first time since graduation and remembering how happy they all were celebrating at Blackie's that night. He focused on the *Walk* signal to clear his eyes, then picked up the pace.

It was somehow right that Wallace gave him the word. He knew Schein almost as long as Katz did, starting from that day in '68 when he picked Katz up off the floor of the D.C. Coliseum during a Smokey Robinson and The

Miracles show. Katz had been kicked and beaten to within an inch of his life when Wallace carried him and pushed Schein – a/k/a "yo' fat friend" to Wallace forever more – to safety. Over the years, every time Schein got busted for selling weed or buying speed or some other small-shit dope deal, the usual drill was for him to call Katz from his house the next morning – or, after they started denying him bail, from jail that night – then Katz would call Wallace to see if he could help him out yet again. It was more than a little weird to realize that Schein was why they were in contact so often over the years. Maybe tonight'd give them a new reason to stay in touch.

Wallace was waiting for him at the corner of 20th and L. Before Katz could get close enough to shake his hand, Wallace jerked a thumb back at the glass and steel office building behind him.

"Why we meetin' here, man? One of us givin' a deposition?"

Katz laughed, shook his hand, and threw an arm over his shoulder. "You ever eat at Marrocco's? On Pennsylvania near 19th?"

"Okay, yeah, townhouse, big guy give you a lot of bullshit at the counter."

"Right. They're here now. It used to be almost a hangout for me and my crowd at GW, so I try to come here when I can for old time's sake."

"All right. 'Long as they brought the kitchen with 'em, it's okay by me."

They headed in and poked the button for the elevator. Katz stepped back and scanned Wallace head to toe. The hair was still a full natural. Flecks of silver shone at him around the sides but the 'stache and beard trimmed close to his face were both jet black. The barrel chest and the thick middle were just as he remembered. "You're lookin' good," he said. "Still at your playing weight."

Wallace gave him the once over and jutted out his lower lip. "You too," he said. "Maybe even lost a little?"

"Starvation'll do that for you." The elevator doors opened and they got on.

"Really?" Wallace said. "Any regrets about leavin' Harry?"

"None. I'd rather starve than commit suicide – or murder." Wallace barked a laugh. They got out on two and headed for the restaurant. A tall beefy man at the reception stand waved them forward.

"Big Eddie! Still here!" Katz said.

"Heeeeey!" Eddie said. Before they could even get to the stand, he wrapped Katz in a hug. "So good to see you again!" Katz patted his back, then swept an arm back to Wallace.

"Eddie Marrocco, Tom Wallace."

They shook hands and Eddie reached down for two menus. "Been a little while, huh?" he said to Katz. "How you been?" Before he could answer, Eddie crooked a

31

finger to follow him and led them to a table for two next to a pillar that separated them from the rest of the dining room. "This okay, gentlemen?"

"Perfect, Eddie," Katz said. "How'd you know we wanted a little privacy?"

"Hey, you know that's my job." He swatted Katz on the back. "Great to see you again." He nodded to Wallace, then headed back to the front. Wallace waited for him to leave, then turned to Katz.

"He has no fucking idea who you are, does he?"

"None. But it's a hell of a show, isn't it?"

The waiter brought some bread. Katz tore off a chunk and pushed the basket to Wallace. "So," he said, "how's business on your end?"

Wallace shook his head. "City's drownin' in coke, man. Shit is everywhere."

"I remember it was all the rage back in the seventies," Katz said. "It's worse now?"

"Worse? Man, it's a thousand times worse. Back then, guy scored a little coke in Baltimore or New York, sold a gram to one of his buddies down here, it was a big hairy deal. Now, man? It's nationwide, worldwide. Huge amounts coming in from LA, Mexico, Colombia, all over, every week, maybe every day. More than we know, that's for damn sure."

"I was actually going to ask you something about that. You ever hear of a guy named Rayful Edmond?"

Wallace cocked his head and looked at him like he couldn't be that stupid. "Are you serious, man?" he said. "There ain't a cop in this city don't know who Rayful Edmond is."

The waiter came to take their drink orders. Katz went for a carafe of red. Wallace asked for some fizzy water, whatever they had.

"I never heard of him till this morning," Katz said when he left.

"And how'd you come to hear of 'im this morning?"

"Harry told me a huge bust was about to go down and he was the guy they were after."

Now Wallace looked at him in disbelief. He leaned in and whispered angrily. "And where the fuck did Harry hear that?"

Katz lowered his voice too, though he wasn't sure why. "He said he heard it from Billy Murphy, Edmond's lawyer, from Baltimore."

Wallace slapped his hands on the table and sat back in his seat. Katz saw veins pop on both sides of his forehead. After a long moment of staring through Katz, Wallace drew his hands down his face, shook his head, and bent closer to him than before.

"There is some sorry, sorry shit goin' on here, Jake. I could tell you some things you wouldn't believe in a million years, but then I'd be just as bad as these assholes leakin' shit they shouldn't be leaking to anyone, much less Rayful Edmond's effin' lawyer."

"You're not leaking talkin' to me, man. I'm not telling anyone anything. You know that." Wallace drummed his fingers on the table. The waiter dropped off Katz' carafe and a large Pellegrino for Wallace.

"Let me ask you this 'fore I say anything. You know *why* Harry was talkin' to you about Rayful Edmond?"

"He said Murphy was giving him a heads up so he could start lining up lawyers for a bunch of guys in D.C. who were going to be arrested any day now."

"Uh-huh. He say how big a bunch of guys?"

"No, just a lot." Wallace sat back again and laced his hands behind his head. Katz could practically see the wrestling match going on in his head.

"Tom," he said, pouring himself some wine, "forget I asked. I'll figure out what I ought to do. Really. Forget about it."

Wallace rested his arms on the table and leaned in close enough this time that Katz could hear his whisper clearly. "Jake, I'm gonna tell you this just so – the next time you invite me out for dinner? – you won't cuss me out for not tellin' you what you were gettin' into."

"Okay. Tell me what I'm gettin' into."

"Just know this, okay? A couple months ago, right before Christmas, we were ready to make an undercover buy from some dude who used to be a high muckety-muck in the Virgin Islands, but we had to back off at the last minute."

"Why?"

"Because some other high official – and I do mean high – from right here in D.C. was in his hotel room at the time."

"How high? An official, I mean."

"High as they get."

Katz had to think about that a minute. George Bush was on his way out, Bill Clinton on his way in. Either of them would be unbelievable. But then he had another thought that was just as unbelievable. "Mayor Barry?"

Wallace backed away and threw up his hands. "You figure it out – and I'm only tellin' you this just so you know: You get involved with this guy Edmond, you're gettin' into some mighty deep an' dirty water."

Wallace poured his Pellegrino. Katz watched the fizz bubbles pop and settle over the ice, and felt a small twinge of guilt, thinking back to that sunny spring day Schein passed him his first nickel bag inside the back pocket of a three-ring notebook on the quad behind the Hall of Government, both of them grinning like monkeys. He

35

took a sip of wine and waited for Wallace to put his glass down.

"It's crazy, man, isn't it?" he said. "How did it get from me and Schein smokin' a little weed in our apartment, to him dyin' from an overdose, to all of this? Who knows, man, maybe if all of us jerkoffs at GW hadn't bought grass from him way back when, he wouldn't've wound up like he did. I think about that, man, I do."

Wallace sat quiet for a minute before he said "Man, you have no idea what guilt feels like."

"What do you mean?" He saw Wallace deep in his own mind again, reeling in the years, and the thought came to Katz just as Wallace cleared his throat and said it out loud. "Marcus, man, you know."

Katz nodded and remembered what Wallace told him just once. Marcus Morris was his patrol partner with MPD back in '59. They were off-duty one night trying to find a parking space on Capitol Hill, Marcus driving his Lincoln, when some dude ran a stop sign and plowed into them. Marcus jumped out of the car and so did the other guy and they started whaling on each other. Wallace grabbed his service gun and came out of the car too, yelling at the guy to stop, but he didn't, so Wallace cuffed him on the head, and the gun went off. The bullet went through Marcus' eye, killing him on the spot.

"Right," Katz said. "Sorry to put you through that again."

Wallace's eyes welled up.

36

"You want something a little stronger?" Katz said, pointing at the Pellegrino.

Wallace took a deep breath and shook his head. "Not these days," he said. "But I'd be lyin' if I said I didn't want to."

"Really? You stopped?"

"Yeah, for good this time," he sighed. "Been about fifteen months now."

"That is great, man. Good for you."

They raised their glasses and Wallace took another sip. "So, let me ask you," he said, "how would you go about gettin' these guys to be your clients?"

"The usual way, I guess. Once they get busted, I'll go over to Superior Court, or better yet, the Federal Public Defender, depending on whether the locals or the Feds picked them up, and see if they can throw some my way."

Wallace nodded. "Okay, then I suggest you go over to the Fed folks tomorrow morning, nine a.m., earlier if they're open. They'll have more'n a few waitin' for you – and again, you didn't hear it from me." They clinked their glasses.

"Hear what?" Katz said.

3

At 8:11 the next morning, Katz blew through the door to his office. LaVerne shrieked and dropped the coffee pot she was about to fill to keep their one real plant on life support. Katz skipped over the skittering pot as he hustled back to his desk.

"Good Lord, Jake! Why you here so early? Checkin' up on me, or what?"

"You? Never!" he called back. LaVerne followed him as far as the doorway and looked at him with quizzical eyes as he grabbed the phone and dialed up the Federal Public Defenders, a number he knew by heart.

"May I speak to Mr. Dodell, please?" he said. "Tell him it's Jake Katz."

He covered the mouthpiece and said "I got a tip they got a lotta folks needing counsel this morning. Big cocaine —"

She held her hand up. "No need for more. That's all I got to hear. You go and take care o' your business, cause your business is my business." She pulled the door shut behind her. He put the phone on speaker and took a seat.

"Hello, Jake," he heard. "I was wondering when I'd start hearing from my brethren in the bar. Kudos to you, you're the first."

"Good morning, Harvey. I heard a rumor you might have more business than you can handle today."

"That's no rumor. It's true, big time."

"What d'ya got?"

"Right now, they're all just papered for possession, some misdemeanor, some felony, but I gotta believe that's just a holding charge for most of 'em. I'm betting we're gonna see a lot of conspiracy to distribute interstate, RICO, all kinds of shit dumpin' on 'em real soon."

"When can I come over? I'm ready any time."

"Pretrial's still putting the files together, but I'll give you what we got. You get there first, you get the pick of the litter. Go straight to lockup and tell them I said it was okay."

"I'm on my way." Katz hung up the phone, grabbed his briefcase, and headed out the door. "I'll be back sometime," he told LaVerne.

"With clients, right?" she yelled, but heard nothing back but the fading banging of his shoes down the stairs. Jogging all the way, Katz made it to the courthouse in five minutes. He took the steps to the second floor and made his way to the holding cell behind Courtroom 4. A black U.S. Marshal and a scowling long-haired white guy gleaming in sweat and carrying a wad of file folders turned to face him when he came through the door. Katz knew them both. He liked the Marshal.

"Marshal Gaskins," he said, extending his hand. "It's been a while."

Katz first got to know him during the trial of the murderers of Khaalis' family three years before he went haywire and took over the buildings. Hamaas sat in the front row of the courtroom right behind the prosecutors' table where Katz couldn't see him seethe, but the Marshal could. He kept Katz posted during the breaks about whenever he thought Hamaas was ready to explode so that Katz could try to calm him down. It worked every time but one, when Gaskins and every other Marshal in the courtroom had to drag Hamaas out of the courtroom, sputtering and screaming at the defendants in a blind rage. Their bond had lasted ever since.

Marshal Gaskins gripped Katz' hand with both of his own and chuckled. "Mr. Katz! I've seen you flittin' around here from time to time, doin' your thing. How've you been?"

"Great, I've been great," Katz said and turned to Allan Peterson, a guy he loathed when he was an AUSA because Peterson's mission in life was to paper him – and every other AUSA – to death in every case he tried. When Katz saw Peterson was the public defender assigned to represent the accused, he knew he'd get a full smorgasbord of filings, no matter how small the charge, because the asshole knew that he – and everyone else at the USA's – would sooner or later submit to a crappy bargain just to avoid dealing with him one second longer. For obvious reasons, he was known throughout the Office as "Petty," a term that Katz greeted him with every previous time they met. But now that Peterson was responsible for doling out the Public Defender's overflow to private counsel like Katz, he shook his hand and heard himself say "Allan! How have you been?" as effusively as he could. He promised himself to gargle – with salt – later.

"Oh, just terrific," Peterson said, waving his arm at the cell crowded with alleged perps behind him. "Business is sensational today. And you're here because?"

"Because Harvey said I could come over and start thinning the herd for you."

Katz saw the shadow of doubt flash across Peterson's face, replaced in an instant by the flood of anxiety he saw when he first came in. "Fine," he muttered, "anyone in particular?"

Katz glanced back at the cell. All black men of a mix of ages, no one he'd had the pleasure to represent before. He turned to Marshal Gaskins. "Any recommendations?"

The Marshal twisted his head to scan the crowd of listless men sleeping on the seats or the floor or propped up against the bars, then looked back at Katz and shook his head. "A few," he said, "but it really doesn't matter. You'll have a hell of a time with any of 'em, if what your old buddies are sayin' is true."

"Okay," Katz said, pointing at the files weighing Peterson down. "Pick me a winner."

Peterson dropped the pile onto the counter next to him and slid one after another off the top. He stopped about eight in and handed it to Katz, who couldn't help but take it warily.

"This one may be interesting for you," Peterson said.

Katz kept it closed. "'Interesting' covers a multitude of sins, doesn't it, *Allan*?" he said, doubling down on the name to let Petty know friendliness had its limits, and they were dead ahead. "What makes this one so interesting?"

"Jake, really. I'm distressed to know you still think so little of me. Take a look at the tab. Turn it over."

Katz looked down at the folder and read the name scrawled in pencil: Cleopatra Salome Smythe. "Okay. Who is she?"

"I have no idea, but she's a rare bird here, the only one of the female persuasion I've come across yet – and, anticipating your next question, I have no idea what she's here for, other than the mandatory possession and conspiracy to distribute b.s. I'm giving you the opportunity to get to the bottom of all of it. Good enough? It's not like we got a boatload of altar boys in here."

Katz flipped open the folder. No picture yet, no list of priors, just the charging document. He gave it a quick scan and didn't see anything other than what Petty said. Unlike times past, it was hard to know if he was screwing with him.

"She in or out?" he asked.

"In. Magistrate posted five hundred K bail on her last night, right after she was brought in."

Katz tilted his head in disbelief and picked up the charging sheet just to make sure he hadn't missed anything. "Five hundred K? Little steep, isn't it? What's he know we don't know?"

"Don't get too worked up about it," Peterson said. "He put at least that much on everybody after your office – excuse me – *ex*-office told him that this was such a big, bad, criminal enterprise, worldwide, blah, blah, blah. She could just be a mule or someone at the wrong place at the wrong time. Like I said, you'll find out. In or out? What's it gonna be?" Katz didn't have to think about it. He was here, she was here, the money was here. He tucked the folder under his arm.

"In," he said. He nodded to Petty, saluted Marshal Gaskins, and turned to the door, then pulled up short. He looked to the Marshal. "Hey, where is the ladies' lockup? I don't believe I've had the pleasure before."

Gaskins threw Peterson a look. "The Jail Annex," he said.

"Where's that?" Katz asked. "Attached to the jail?"

Gaskins sighed. "Not quite."

"Please, allow me, Marshal," Peterson said, grinning like a jackal. "Lorton. Virginia." He looked at his watch. "You leave now, you can probably get there in an hour – if you know where you're going."

"Thanks so effing much, Petty," Katz said. "As ever."

"You're welcome, Jake," Petty said, turning back to his files. "Always happy to tell you where to go. Best of luck with Cleopatra."

4

Katz returned to his office, watched LaVerne find Lorton on a map, and hustled back down the stairs. In twelve minutes, he was off. In an hour and fifteen minutes, he was there, and five minutes later, he was sitting at a long wooden table in the Attorney Conference Room at the Annex, yellow legal pad and pen at the ready, waiting for Cleopatra Salome Smythe.

He heard steps shuffle up outside the door and looked through the square window to see a black face and a white face looking down at the keys turning the lock. The black lady had processed hair pinned up high. The white's was spiky blond, nearly as pale as her skin. When the white face glanced up at him, his first thought was: You are way too hot to be a prison guard. When he saw her pale green scrubs, he knew she wasn't. The guard guided her to the plastic chair across the table from Katz. He reached over to shake her hand.

"Ms. Smythe. Jake Katz."

She gave him a quick shake, fell into the chair, shut her eyes, and slid down till her neck rested against the thin curve at the top. The guard rolled her eyes at Katz and pointed at him. "Thirty minutes." she said. "That's it, sleepin' or up."

"Got it," he said with a sloppy salute, and waited for her to close the door before he turned back to Ms. Smythe. Her eyes opened a slit at the sound of the key turning in the lock and when she turned his way, slivers of crystal blue gleamed at him through streaks of red.

"Been a real long night," she mumbled and pushed herself slowly back up to seated. "Or a real short one, depending on how you look at it." She yawned and dropped her head on her crossed arms. Katz glanced at his watch. Twenty-nine minutes and counting. When he was just about to speak, she raised her head and turned his way. "It's Smythe, by the way," she said with a flat accent he couldn't place. "With a long i, like scythe."

"Forgive me," he said.

"No problem." She shrugged. "Call me Cleo anyway."

"Then Cleo it is." He flipped open the file.

"So who made you my lawyer?" she asked.

"No one," Katz said. "You're not my client and I'm not your lawyer if you don't want me to be. It's totally up to you."

"Right, I get that," she said, "but I meant *why*'re you here?"

"Public defender gave me your file, that's it." Harry and Petty flitted through his brain, but he kept smiling.

"Anybody tell them to do that?"

Now Rayful Edmond flew through, but he said "No, just the luck of the draw."

She mulled that over a second, her eyes locked in on his like magnets. "So whatever I tell you is confidential, right? Just between you and me?"

He slid the top sheet in the file over to her and spun it around so she could read it. "It is, the second you sign that. 'Til then, anything you tell me I have to tell a judge, just like anyone else you tell anything to – except your husband, of course."

"No husband," she said and rolled her eyes. "That's all I'd need."

She pulled the paper closer and started to read it. While she did, he checked her out. Thin and drawn, but she had every right to be. Hard to guess her age, maybe twenty-five give or take, but even with all the stress and without any makeup, he didn't have to guess she was pretty. The piercing blue eyes and a short scar etching her right cheek gave her a little mystery, but not as much as the mystery about how and why she was caught up in all this, whatever it was. Allegedly, he reminded himself.

"I've handled a lot of drug cases, Cleo, from every side," he said. "I used to be a cop in D.C., then I was an Assistant U.S. Attorney, and now I'm on the defense side, so I have a pretty good feel for how these things go. You'll be in good hands, I promise you."

She looked up only when she finished. "I borrow the pen?" He handed it to her and she signed in big, bold strokes, then slid the sheet back to him with the pen on top.

"Okay, now you're my lawyer. Now what?" Katz picked up the pen and pulled the yellow pad to him.

"First, let's talk about what you're in for. The only info I have is they booked you for possession and conspiracy to distribute cocaine. Does that sound right?"

"It does."

"Okay, so the Federal statute on that requires you to plan to sell at least fifty grams of cocaine. Do you have any reason to believe you had that much? Keep in mind a gram is like two-thousandth of a pound so fifty grams isn't a whole lot, like maybe a tenth of a pound?"

She smiled at him like he'd said something funny. "I'll keep that in mind."

"So did you have at least a tenth of a pound?"

She leaned back, crossed her arms in front of her, and fixed her eyes on his. "If we're going to do the math, let's do it for real. A gram is actually point oh oh two two oh four six two pounds, and every brick I cut, measured, and bagged that night was five hundred grams – on the nose – which means each of the two bricks I was holding when they pulled me over was one point one oh two three one pounds, so, yeah, I think I might been holding more than a tenth of a pound. Does that sound right to you?" Before Katz could answer, she smiled at him again. "It's

48

what I do, Jake. Or did. Ray was an excellent math teacher, let me tell you. Every speck was money to him, man, so you just learned it."

"Ray is Rayful Edmond, right?"

"He is. You know who he is, right?"

"I'm just starting to," Katz said. "Tell me how you got to know him."

She snorted a laugh. "How much time you got?'

Katz looked at his watch. "Twenty-three minutes, but we'll have more. Take all the time you need."

She nodded and he waited for her to make her way back to a time when she was just starting to know who Rayful Edmond was too. "Okay, back about two, three, years ago, must've been nineteen-eighty . . . six, I used to have two jobs." She paused. "Let me back up. I'd come to D.C. waitin' for a government clearance for some file clerk job with the Army at Fort Belvoir, but it dragged on and on and I needed to be making some money, so I started waitressing some joints in Dupont Circle, Georgetown, you know, and I was at the Pall Mall then, on M Street, you know it?"

"I know it."

"Well, this other waitress there was a little sweet on me, I think, but that's not my thing – anyhow, she says to me," laying on a real backwoods Virginia accent, "'you know, darlin', with that smokin' body you got, you oughta be dancin' at one a them titty bars.' I said no, that's not my thing and even if it was" – she grabbed her breasts – "these ain't no forty-four double D's or whatever they're lookin' for."

Katz looked just long enough to see they were exactly what anyone at a titty bar would be looking for, then dropped his eyes to follow his hand writing faster across the page.

"But she said, 'Honey, you got that look they're payin' for, a lot more'n this shithole' so it got me thinkin' about it, and one day, I went to this place – Archibald's? On K, right near 16th? – and I did a little dance for the guy there, thought I was gonna pass out, I was so embarrassed – but he said, when can you start, and I said right now and he said you're hired and that's when I started makin' what I thought was some real money – "

"Till you met Rayful?'

"Right. Till I met Rayful."

"And you met him there, at Archibald's?"

"No, I didn't meet him till the Florida Avenue Grill."

"So why are we talking about Archibald's?"

She dropped her jaw and flashed him a look of disbelief. "Excuse me, but didn't you tell me to take all the time I needed?"

He groped for the right response until another smile brightened her face again. He smiled back and held up his hands in surrender.

"I did. Keep going. Sorry."

"I didn't meet Rayful till the Florida Avenue Grill – but he'd seen me at Archibald's and remembered me when he saw me at the Grill, get it?"

"Got it. Continue."

"Okay, so that was my second job, my day job, waitressing there at the Grill, mostly at lunch time because it was hard for me to drag my butt out of bed most mornings because I was working Archibald's at night. And so I'm waiting on Rayful's table one day, and he tells me he knows me from the club and blah, blah, blah. I figured he was just another horny brother comin' on to me, but then at the end of the meal, he lays a fifty-dollar tip on me for a half-smoke and some fries or something, and that got my attention, you know, and he was like that with me every time he came in."

"How often did he come in?"

"Maybe once or twice a week most weeks."

"So as far as you knew, he was just a big tipper?"

"That was it, plus, there was never any come-on or anything like that. Just a real nice guy, could talk about anything, the kind of guy who knows a lot about a lot, you know?"

"And I take it the customer-waitress thing changed at some point?"

"Yeah. So one day he writes down his beeper number on a little piece of paper and tells me to keep in touch. I probably lost it right away and didn't even think about it till one day I'm driving up Connecticut Avenue and I hear all this beepin' from across the way and I look up and somebody's wavin' from this red Porsche zippin' past. I don't know who it is and I don't know who he's wavin' at so I keep going – until I hear these tires screeching behind me and I look in the rear view mirror and I see them makin' a U-turn and there's Rayful wavin' at me!"

"Was he driving?"

"No, he hardly ever drives. Tony Lewis was driving. Rayful was ridin' shotgun. So I pull into this little shopping center somewhere up past the zoo and they pull into the space next to me, with Rayful on my side, and he says 'Hey, why didn't you ever call me?' I say 'I lost your number' and he says 'You got a piece of paper?' And I take down his number and I give him mine, and he says 'Later' and they pull out."

Katz was racing to keep up. It didn't help that he printed everything because he couldn't read his own writing, but one of the best things he learned in law school was to print just consonants once he figured out that 'njnctn' could only mean "injunction" and 'mlprctc' could only mean "malpractice". Even so, she was testing his speed limit, not that she noticed.

52

"So the next day, I think it was," she rolled on, "he calls me and asks me to meet him at his aunt's house."

"Where was that?" Katz asked, head down.

"407 M Northeast. I see him standing with Tony and a guy I later knew was Dave McCraw and I pull up in front of the house and he gets in, and we ride to another house a couple of blocks away and we go inside, and there's no one there, so I get a little uptight about that, and he must've noticed 'cause he says 'Relax, this is just a business meeting' and we sit down at a breakfast-like table and he asks me if I can rent an apartment for him, in Crystal City, right down by National." Katz finished 'bsnss mtg' and looked up.

"Okay. Why'd he need you to rent it?"

"That's what I asked him, and he said he needed a place to entertain people, without his mother being around."

"No. I meant why did he need *you* to rent it for him? Why didn't he do it himself?"

"'Cause he didn't want his name on anything that had anything to do with his business. So I tell him my credit's not so hot so that might be a problem, but he says 'Don't worry about it, I'll give you the cash for the deposit and the first month's rent – plus five hundred to fill out the application' and I think to myself 'that's a lot of tips,' even Rayful-size tips, so I said sure. So the next week he calls me to say they got the apartment and that I need to sign the lease, which I do and I meet up with him to give him the keys and he tells me to make a set for myself first. You gettin' all this?"

"Keep going," Katz said.

"When I give him the keys the next day or two, he gives me two big fat manila envelopes stuffed with cash and asks me to go to Family Furniture out in Hillcrest Heights or somewhere to buy some furniture and have it delivered to the apartment – and oh, yeah – get him a wide-screen TV too."

"How much cash are we talking about?"

"Maybe five thousand, a lot of hundreds and fifties, but some fives, tens, twenties too."

"Are these all crisp and shiny from the bank?"

"Hell, no," she laughed. "Most of it came out of the pockets of the guys buying his stuff. They unfolded it maybe, but that was it. No banks ever saw any of this money, trust me. We'd haul suitcases, duffel bags stuffed with cash, ridiculous amounts – "

"Okay," Katz said, rolling his left hand in the universal sign for 'speed it up', "lest we digress."

"So for a couple of months, the only time I see or hear from him is when he wants to give me the money for the rent. Then, one day, he gives me a call and says to come over to the apartment to help him count some money. I knock on the door and Nut – Columbus Daniels, a little guy, that's why they call him Nut – he looks through the

54

peephole and lets me in, then signals me to come on back with him. I follow him into the bedroom and there's Rayful laying across the bed, with money spread out all around him, like mounds and mounds of it."

Katz' mind must have shown up on his face because she squinted her eyes and said "He had his clothes on, Mr. Katz. It wasn't like that, whatever you're thinkin', ever."

"I'm not thinking anything, Cleo, honestly," he said dishonestly.

She shook her head. "I told you, it wasn't ever like that so put all that b.s. outta your head."

"It's gone. I believe you, I swear."

After a long stare, she went on. "Anyway, there was fifty thousand dollars there if there was one – and there were plenty of ones and fives and tens this time, all the way up. I helped him and Tony put it in piles, then gave it to him to run through the money machine, so he'd know exactly how much he had."

"And he paid you for this too?"

"Oh, yeah, and he got more and more generous as time went by. After I'd shown him he could trust me, he asked if the money was okay. It was, and I told him that, but I also mentioned that since I stopped the dancin' and the waitressin', I needed somethin' else to do all the times he didn't need me. So he asked if I had anything in mind, and I told him I wanted to open up a nail salon and get it incorporated, and he said he'd take care of it, just let him know how much and when, and he straight up did it."

"He must've been pretty grateful to you."

Cleo shook her head again, this time like she couldn't believe what she had seen. "It was just a drop in the bucket. There was so much money – cash money – you couldn't believe it. And that's all they spent, never checks, credit, anything that could be traced. Like that red Porsche I told you about that Tony Lewis was drivin' him around in? Some jerkoff buddy of his'd stopped paying the note on it even though Rayful gave him the cash for it every month. He knew he could trust me to not do nothing crazy or stupid with it so he asked me to start payin' it."

Katz looked up to see the guard with the beehive buzz back through the door. "Time's up, counselor," she said.

Cleo stood up before he did.

"Ms. Smythe, it was a pleasure to meet you," he said, extending his hand. "Can I set up another time to come out and continue our conversation?"

She left his hand hanging out there between them.

"I gotta know you believe me when I tell you things, Mr. Katz," she said. "There was nothing going on between Rayful and me."

He dropped his hand. "Cleo, I believe you, but it's my job as your lawyer to put things together in a way a jury will believe too. Sometimes I have to be – " he caught himself before he said 'the devil's advocate' – "I might come across just a little skeptical, but that's the only reason why."

"Ahem," the guard said, holding the door open.

"I believe you, Cleo," he said. "That's the bottom line. When can I come back so we can keep talking?"

She looked at him hard with those ice blue eyes. "I'll let you know," she said and walked out the door.

5

The next morning, Katz dialed up Rosa Washington, his old secretary at the U.S. Attorney's Office. It'd been twelve years since he left, but she was at her post every time he had reason to call and he was especially happy to hear she still was today.

"Rosa, it's Jake! How are you?"

"Well, hi, Jake. I'm good. You still miss us?"

"Not all of you, but you specifically? Always."

She laughed. "What can I do for you?"

"I want to talk to whoever's been assigned to U.S. v. Smythe, a possession case that just came in." He spelled it for her and she put him on hold. He hoped it had already been papered and the AUSA was somebody he had a little history with who'd be willing to play Let's Make A Deal. The wait was interminable. Finally, she clicked back on the line. "Say 'Thank you, Rosa'."

"Thank you, Rosa."

"You're welcome, Jake. I just helped them make up the file. These children today are so slow."

"It's the video games rotting their brains. But seriously, thank you. Who'd they assign it to?"

"Ron Hutchison. You know him?"

"I don't. He must have come in after my time."

"Tell you the truth, just about everyone here's come in since you left. Only the appellate guys seem to stick around."

"That's 'cause they're the smart ones," Katz said. "Hang in there till you're fifty-five, get the pension, put your feet up, eat Mallomars, and watch TV all day. Your day's coming, just as soon as you hit the magic number."

Rosa laughed, hard this time.

"Jake, you are so crazy and so sweet. I passed that number about four years ago. I can't afford to retire, what with the grandchildren and all, much as I'd like to."

When did all that happen? Katz thought. What was it Satchel Paige said? Don't look back, something might be gainin' on you? He got back to business.

"Okay, you're the best. Can you ring Mr. Hutchison up? See if he's got any time to talk with Ms. Smythe's lawyer today? Work your magic!"

"You are so crazy. Hold on." She put him back on hold, then clicked back on in a few seconds. "Can you stop by now?"

"I'm there. Thanks again, Rosa, a million times. I'll stop by you too." He grabbed his briefcase and headed through the reception area.

"Mo' business?" LaVerne asked.

"Mo' business," Katz said.

59

"Mo' business is good business!" she yelled as he took off down the steps.

After checking in with Rosa and finding where Ron Hutchison sat, he told the secretary that he was expected. He watched her press the red button and heard the familiar buzz through the closed wooden door behind her.

"A Mr. Katz is here to see you?" she said.

Katz heard a chair creak behind the door and pictured, for the first time in a long time, the ten-by-twelve-foot drywall cage that used to hold him just down the hall, the chipped sickly green walls, the pink phone slips, the olive case folders strewn across the desk, the yellow legal pads – and tried to calculate whether it was nostalgia or nausea flooding over him. The next second, Ron Hutchison popped through the door, black, smiling, hand extended. *Was I ever this young in this place?* he thought, then let it go and squeezed Ron's hand.

"Mr. Katz, a pleasure to meet you in person. I've heard a lot about you."

"Uh-oh. And you're shaking my hand?"

Hutchison laughed and guided him back to his office. Katz stopped at the doorway and took it in. "Bring back memories?" Hutchison asked.

"It does. I'm doing my best to stifle the tears."

Hutchison pointed him to what looked to be the newest chair facing his desk, a faux walnut beauty with a thin brown cushion and four metal legs. Katz took a seat. Hutchison took his, then pushed his chair back and stretched his legs onto the desk. "So" he said, still smiling, "you're Ms. Smythe's lawyer?"

"It's Smythe like scythe," he said, then thought about her last words and shrugged. "At least till she tells me I'm not."

"Okay," Hutchison laughed. "I won't go there, unless there's something else you want to tell me."

"No, let's let it go at that."

"And may I ask how long you've been her lawyer?"

"Public Defender appointed me yesterday."

"Wow. You piss somebody off over there?"

"The name Allan Peterman mean anything to you?"

"Ow!" Hutchison winced. "Petty strikes again."

"Yeah. We go way back."

"So you had no prior involvement with Ms. Smythe, representing her, any time before this?"

"No, and not with Rayful Edmond either. I feel like my learning curve on him has gone straight up in the past twenty-four hours."

Hutchison brought his legs down and wheeled his chair back to the desk. He crossed his arms on the desktop and leaned in towards Katz, no smiles now. "Okay, then

61

you're probably getting a good sense of what we're dealing with here."

Katz shrugged. "It seems pretty big."

Hutchison pushed himself back upright and did his best impression of a nuclear bomb blast. "Boom!" he boomed. "It's fucking huge, Jake! Bigger than anything I've ever seen here and I bet anything you ever saw."

"Okay, it's bigger than big. That's great, but where does my client come in? I spent some time with her over at Lorton yesterday and from what she told me so far, she's just a pawn in the game."

Hutchison gave him a long stare for a minute, then pushed himself up out of his chair and came around the desk to perch himself on the corner closest to Katz. "Let's start on what I think we can agree on," he said. "We both want to get her on the street, okay? Are we on the same page?"

"I'm right there with you."

"Good. And we both want her out there as soon as possible."

"I do. She does. But why do you?"

"So nobody connected with Edmond misses her or suspects anything." Hutchison jabbed a finger at him. "And, we're even willing to waive the five hundred thousand bail even though we could make it twice that, I'm betting."

"I saw that," Katz said. "Who do you think you're dealing with here, Patty Hearst? That's crazy!"

"Jake – may I call you that? – the two pounds of shit she had with her was more than enough to justify it, but even without that, we have every reason to believe your client is way high up in the CCE Mr. Edmond is operating."

Katz shook his head. A CCE was a Continuing Criminal Enterprise. If the USA's office could prove Rayful Edmond was running one, they had the biggest sledgehammer available under Federal law: Life behind bars without parole, ever.

"Okay, Ron, if I may. Let's play make-believe that my client is this fearsome drug kingpin or queenpin or whatever you say she is. What do you want in return for all these great favors?"

"Three things. First, she pleads to one count of conspiracy to possess with intent to distribute under 21 USC 846."

"Okay," Katz said, scribbling it on his pad, "by which I mean 'Okay, understood' not 'Okay, we accept'. Second?"

"She lets us tap her phone."

Katz knew that was coming. The wiretap immediately became the Feds' favorite tool in big drug cases as soon as Congress okayed it back in the sixties, and they used it a lot more frequently once they got used to using it, pretty much like coke. All the law said they needed was three things: the okay of just one of the people on the call, a court order that only required the judge to find probable cause that someone on the call would be talking about a possible drug crime, and that "normal investigative procedures" either wouldn't work or would be too dangerous. It was like giving the home team as many downs as they needed to score. He hated it now that he was on the other side. But those had been the rules of the game since before he'd been a lawyer so he knew he'd have to roll with it, whether he liked it or not – but not quite yet.

"Okay ditto. And third?"

"She wears a wire."

Katz stopped scribbling. "With who?"

"Rayful Edmond."

"Ron, please, if I know something big's coming down, Rayful Edmond has to know it too, and won't he be a little wary about this white chick – who might not actually have as much to do with him as you think she does – suddenly wanting to have a nice long cozy chat with him? You're setting her up more than you're setting him up."

Hutchison shrugged. "He's the guy we're after, Jake. It's got to be him."

"But why not use her to go up the ranks till you find someone who lets you connect the dots directly to him?"

"We are going up the ranks, Jake. That's how we got to your client."

Katz shook his head. "Ron, with all due respect for you and this office, I don't buy it – and what do you think a jury in this city's going to think about you telling them this white chick who's been in town for a minute is a major player in a massive drug cartel where everyone else is black? You'll never get them to convict."

Hutchison stood up and walked back to look out the window behind his desk. Katz watched him watch the cars shuttle back and forth on Constitution Avenue for a good while before he turned back to face him. "I shouldn't be doing this," he said, "but I'm going to show you something I think might convince you I'm not just blowing smoke up your ass."

Katz opened his arms wide to show he was ready to receive. Hutchison stepped over to a tall gray metal file cabinet and pulled open the top drawer. He flipped a few files to him before reaching in one and pulling out a piece of paper, then walked back around the desk and handed it to Katz. "Take a look. See anyone familiar?"

Katz scanned a grainy Xerox of a photograph of five people arm in arm smiling at the camera, all decked out in their finest. Only one of them was white, a foxy blond lady who, on closer inspection, looked like a very dolled-up version of the person he interviewed yesterday at the Annex.

"I take it you want me to believe that's Cleo Smythe."

"I don't really care if you believe it, but that is Cleo Smythe."

Hutchison came around to look at the picture over Katz's shoulder and pointed to the rest of the crew one by one from left to right. "That gentleman is Rayful Edmond Junior, the father of the Rayful Edmond we've been talking about. Next to him is your client. Next to her is a gentleman named Tony Lewis. That's Constance Perry, Rayful's mother, a/k/a Bootsie next to Tony, and Robert Hardy a/k/a Fila Bob on the end."

"But no Rayful the third, I note."

"We expect the evidence will show he was taking the picture."

Katz scanned the picture again. "And where was it taken, may I ask?"

"A little event you might've heard of. Sugar Ray Leonard, Marvin Hagler, Las Vegas, April '87? These folks were there live, no pay-per-view, no party chippin' in with the neighbors. Caesars Palace, baby, with your girl smilin' with the whole damn family. Get the picture a little clearer now, Jake?"

Katz had to admit this guy was good. Now he knew that little wave he felt before was nostalgia. He loved being the guy holding all the cards. Hutchison waited till Katz looked up at him before gently removing the picture

66

from his hand, walking back to the file cabinet, and sliding it back into the file.

"Okay," Katz said, "let's just presume she's everything you say and let's also presume she does everything you ask her to. What's in it for her?"

"I'd have to talk to the brass about it, but my best guess is we'd knock the charges down to whatever it takes under the guidelines to come up with a sentence around five years – at some cushy minimum security community college campus they call a prison these days, of course."

"Five years, plus putting her life on the line with a wire? That's total bullshit. I won't even take that to her."

Hutchison raised his hands with another shrug. "It's your call, Jake. You know as well as I do that five years is a slap on the wrist under the guidelines these days."

Katz stood up and walked to the door. "And you know as well as I do that's not going to do it. You want Rayful Edmond, not Cleo Smythe, and if she's the way to bring him down, you're going to have to do a lot better than that, i.e., no years. You want her to literally put her neck on the line for you, she's got to walk. Period."

"You're her lawyer, Jake. You tell her what you think best. But just so you both know: This is a limited time offer. Her usefulness to us ends if we hold her too long and no one on Edmond's crew can account for her whereabouts. You know they'll smell a rat and do God knows what to her to find out what's up. That's out of our hands, okay?"

Katz knew exactly what he was feeling now. "I'll get back to you," he said, and waited for the bile to slide back down before he slammed the door behind him.

6

By the time he made it back up to his office, it was lunch time and LaVerne was out. A small stack of upside-down "While You Were Out" messages sat next to her phone beside a steno pad with a jagged written note he couldn't read. He hung up his coat, then walked behind her chair. "Just so you know what I put up with too," he read. A slashing arrow pointed to the pink slips. He turned over the first one.

"Harry" it read. 9:15. He must have just missed him. Oh shucks. He turned over the next one.

"Harry!" 10:01. He turned over the third one.

"YOU KNOW WHO!! Come back!!" 10:38. He reached for the last one.

"Gone to lunch – forever!!!" 11:00.

Katz looked at his watch. 12:19. Maybe he gave up. The phone rang. Maybe not. Katz carried his briefcase back to his desk and slumped into his seat. He tried to stare the phone into submission, but it would not stop. He picked it up and prayed it would be a pleasant surprise, like a crank call, or a ransom demand.

"Hello?" he said quietly.

"Where the hell have you been?" Harry thundered.

"Avoiding you. What else?"

"When're you going to get a car phone like everyone else?"

"I have a car phone, Harry."

"Then why the hell don't you pick it up?"

"I do, Harry. But I couldn't reach it because I was *at the courthouse* and they wouldn't let me bring *my car* in."

"You're a real comedian, Jake, a regular Johnny Carson. You down there for anything havin' to do with Rayful Edmond?"

"If I tell you the truth, will you get off the phone quicker?"

"Just tell me, man, and stop bustin' my balls."

"I got a case assigned to me by the Federal Defender, one of Rayful's crowd."

"Who is he?" Harry asked.

"It's a she," Katz said. "Cleo Smythe. You know anything about her?"

"Never heard of her. Only women I've heard hooked up with him're relatives. She related to him?"

"Uh, no."

"You don't sound too sure about that."

"I'm sure she's white. That good enough for you?"

"Are you shittin' me?"

"Harry, it's the truth. No bullshit."

"How well's she know Rayful?"

"I'm not sure yet. I've only talked to her once."

"She in the can?"

"Yeah, out in Lorton, the Women's Annex."

The line was blessedly quiet. Katz waited a full second. "Okay, we done?" he asked.

"No, we ain't done, Jake. I'm just thinkin' it through a minute. Let me just lay this on you so you understand exactly what's involved here, okay?"

"Lay it on me, Harry."

"You know as well as I do the government's going to try to get some of the little fish to turn on the medium-sized fish so they can get those folks to save their asses by rattin' out the bigger fish."

"I'm a little lost in the animal kingdom there, Harry, but I think I get it."

"So my question to you is have any of your old buddies asked your girl to flip?"

"Harry, I know you were out that day in law school when they went over the whole ethics thing, so I'll just make this as clear as I can: I'm not going to tell you what the government has done or not done as it concerns my client."

"Maybe you misunderstood my question, Jake, so I'll repeat it real slow. I didn't ask what your client told you, I asked what the government told you."

"Harry, I heard you and you know I'm not going to tell you that. All discussions between me, my client, and the government are confidential. Period."

"Jake," Harry said, his tone as blunt as Katz ever heard it, "you need to stop this fuckin' around, okay? There's one reason and one reason only that Billy Murphy asked me to get the best lawyers I could down here: To protect Rayful Edmond. Period. End of sentence, end of story. I put my own ass on the line for you 'cause I told him you were someone I could trust, okay? So your job, whether you like it or not or whether it's in some code of ethics somewhere, is to protect Rayful Edmond too, all right?"

"Harry –" Katz said, but Harry talked right over him. "So, get it straight. Your girl Cleo ain't playin' any horseshoes or makin' any pancakes here, okay? Ain't no flippin' in this game."

He had his attention now. "Harry, you can stop now. I know the game we're playing. You told Billy Murphy I was a good lawyer and I am, so let me do my thing with my client, and it will all work out."

"Jake, I hear you, but just let me tell you, you don't want the wrong people mad at you in this deal, trust me."

For the first time in a long time, Katz did.

7

The next morning, he was back at Lorton setting up his cassette recorder when the guard walked Cleo in. She stopped short and pointed at the machine. "What is that?"

"Tape recorder," he said. "Just making sure I get everything right."

"Uh-uh, no way. No tapes."

The guard looked from Katz to Cleo and back again. "I'll leave you two lovebirds alone," she said. "Thirty minutes." She locked the door behind her.

"Cleo – " Jake started but she waved a finger in his face. "You turn that thing on, I'm out of here. Whatever we say is just between us, that's what you told me, right?"

"I did, but if this is anything like the last time, I – "

"Look, man, it's bad enough you're takin' notes. Anyone gets their hands on a tape?" She shook her head. "That ain't happenin'."

Katz started to say something but thought better of it. He picked up the recorder and put it back in his briefcase.

Cleo held her ground. "And it's off, right?" she said. Katz gave her a long look, then reached back down into the briefcase and handed her the recorder. She didn't take it but looked at it long enough to make sure the wheels weren't turning. When she nodded to him, Katz put it back and motioned her to take a seat. She slumped into the chair. "So where did I leave off?"

"We'll get to that, but we need to talk about a few other things first. Like, do you still want me to be your lawyer?"

"Why're you asking? You want out already?"

Katz shook his head. "I'm positively thrilled to represent you, Cleo, but when I left here last time, you seemed a little uh, let's say hesitant about it, so I just wanted to get that straight from the get-go. You say no, I'll be on my way and you can enjoy the rest of your day. You say yes, we'll keep talking."

Now she fixed him with the long look, then threw up her hands. "Might as well be you. What the hell."

Katz couldn't help but laugh. "Well, thank you so much, Cleo. That'll be my next ad." He held up his hands to frame the sentiment. "'*Jake Katz. Might as well be him. What the hell.' That's* what I should have taped."

"I didn't mean to insult you, Mr. Katz. I'm not in the best frame of mind, okay? I want you to be my lawyer. Good enough?"

"That's fine. And as long as we're pals now, call me Jake."

"Jake. Fine. What else do we need to talk about?"

"I met with the guy who's been assigned your case in the U.S. Attorney's office, to talk about bailing you out of here."

Cleo leaned forward. "Okay."

"He said they're going to ask for five hundred thousand bail."

Cleo slapped the table and glared at him. "Five hundred thousand? That's fucking crazy!"

"That's exactly what I told him," Katz said. "He also offered you a deal that'd reduce your sentence to no more than five years."

"And that's fucking crazy too! For what?"

"They seem to think they can get you on a lot of charges just for basically being a big fish in Mr. Edmond's operation, but as part of the deal, they'll knock everything down to one charge of possession with intent to distribute."

Cleo shook her head. "Five years is a hell of a long time just for that, isn't it?"

"Cleo, under the guidelines the judges have to follow these days, you can get five years for crossing against the red. The Feds hold all the cards now, more than ever. It's not fair, but that's the way the game is played today. I already told them there's no way you're going to do any time for what they want you to do."

"And what do they want me to do?"

"Let them tap your phone."

Cleo's look grew even darker. Katz steeled himself. He paused "And –"

"*And?*" she said. "And what?"

"Wear a wire."

Cleo pushed her chair back from the table, the legs screeching against the concrete. "No fucking way! I don't want *you* to tape me, you think I'm going to let them? And wear it in front of somebody that'd kill me if he saw it? You must be shittin' me."

"Cleo, don't shoot the messenger," Katz said. "I'm telling you what they said so I can tell them your reply."

"Okay," she said. "You can tell them my reply is they can shove it up their ass sideways."

Katz's pen jerked across the paper. "S-i-d-e-w-a-y-s," he said. "So noted."

"Who do they think they're dealin' with?" Cleo said.

"Like I said, the prosecutor thinks you're a big fish."

"Why'd he say that? Somebody talkin'? Somebody already wearin' a wire?"

"That they didn't tell me, but," Katz said with a shake of the head and a laugh he rehearsed on the drive over, "they did show me a picture that was supposed to make me cringe in my boots."

The look on Cleo's face showed him he had her undivided attention now. "Picture?" she said. "Of what?"

"You. With someone he said was Mr. Edmond's mom and dad and another couple of guys."

"I never took any picture with his parents. And who were the other guys?"

Katz had memorized the names but he made a show of checking his notes to give Cleo a little time to start thinking things over. "Hold on. Okay, uh, Tony Lewis who I think you mentioned the last time I was here, and, uh, Robert Hardy a/k/a Fila Bob, I hope I'm pronouncing that right, like the sneaker? Or maybe it's filet like the fish, I'm sorry, I don't know." When he looked up, she was deep in thought, staring at the wall behind him. "He said it was taken in Las Vegas at the Hagler-Leonard fight. Sometime in 1987."

Cleo squeezed her eyes shut and cupped her face in her hands. When she picked her head up, Katz thought he saw a weakness he hadn't seen before and when she turned to look at him, he knew it. He flicked a glance at his watch and did a quick calculation.

"Hey, you know what?" he said. "We only have about twenty minutes left. Let's come back to this, okay?" He took his time flipping the pages on his pad until he got to where they'd stopped. "So last time, we got up to where

Rayful was trusting you with his cash, paying for the Porsche."

Cleo was still somewhere else, somewhere she didn't want to be. He cleared his throat and she looked at him like she was surprised to see him in Vegas or prison or wherever she thought she was. She pulled her hands down over her eyes and kept them there, shaking her head. When she was done, she slumped back in the chair and looked up at the ceiling. Katz was just about to open his mouth when she cleared her throat. "That was the first time I actually talked to Tony, out in Vegas."

"How about Mr. Hardy?"

"Fila Bob – like the sneaker. I'd met him before, back in D.C., and at the apartment in Crystal City."

"And Rayful's parents?"

"I had met them a few times at his aunt's house over on M Street."

"Okay. What's the aunt's name?"

"Armaretta. She's Bootsie's sister."

"And Bootsie's what they call Constance, Rayful's mother?"

"Yeah. How'd you know that?"

"The prosecutor told me, when he showed me the picture, from Vegas."

Katz saw the cloud pass over her face again and laid his pen on his pad. "Cleo, I'm not playing any games with you, I promise. I don't know who anyone is unless you told me or he told me, okay? There's a lot I need to know, which is why I brought the tape recorder. I'm not going to use it, I promise, but, the thing is, you have got to trust me on everything – period – or we're done before we start."

"I don't know what to think or who to trust anymore, Mr. Katz – Jake. My brain is fried."

"I know it must be, Cleo, and I don't have point one percent of the information you have. I can come back or you can go on, it's totally your call."

She took a deep breath, sat up straight, and picked up right where she left off. Katz took it all down as fast as he could, but the prosecutor piece of his brain couldn't keep from thinking she was as high up as Hutchison said she was. *Why did she know Bootsie and Armaretta? Why was she in Vegas? Why was she in the picture?* He glanced down at his notes to see what the rest of his brain had been telling his hand to write.

"So when we got back from the fight," he heard her say, "Rayful said he had something else for me to do. So a couple of days after that, Niecey and Dave and Minor –

"Hold on," Katz said. "Who're they?"

"Sorry. Niecey is Rayniece Hillman, Rayful's sister, and Dave McCraw is her boyfriend. Minor is James Minor, who *was* a friend of Dave. So they came to my place with three kilos of cocaine, that was like so much

80

more than I'd ever seen before, it absolutely blew my mind. I mean it was like a mountain of snow sittin' on top of the dining room table! Anyhow, they showed me how to bag it, with the scales and the spoons and the baggies, and I got five hundred for each kilo, so fifteen hundred for sitting at my kitchen table for a couple hours? That worked for me."

"Was that a one-time thing, or was there more?"

"A lot more. I kept at it, at first with Niecey, and Dave and Minor sometimes, then with whoever showed up with the stuff."

"And what would you do with it when you were done?"

"Early on, Niecey or Dave would take it, or someone would come over to pick it up but after a while, I'd drop the bags off at Bootsie's house or over to Rachelle's place off Suitland Parkway in P.G., Upper Marlboro."

"Who's Rachelle?"

"Rayful's other sister."

"This sounds like quite the family affair."

"Oh, yeah," Cleo said. "But there're a lot more than them too."

Katz's prosecutorial juices bubbled again, but they served him well on defense too because they showed him just where his case was weak. If the USA's office knew she knew everyone at the top of the food chain, why

81

wouldn't they think she was up there too? He filed the thought with the others.

"And how about the money? Did Rayful let you handle that cash too?"

"Oh, yeah. Once I showed him I could be trusted with the rent money and the car money like I told you, he let me handle as much as he could give me. After a while, I'd be holding ten, twenty, twenty-five thousand dollars in cash in paper bags, waitin' for him to tell me where to take it. Once, I gave 'em to him right in the middle of Georgetown Park."

"The mall?"

She nodded and smiled at the audacity of it. "Hide in plain sight, right? That was how we did."

"And that's what you've been doing for him right along?"

"That, and a few other things."

"Any things your lawyer should know?"

"No, let's just say he knew he could trust me."

"Because?" Katz lifted his hand, inviting her to finish the sentence.

"Because I proved my loyalty to him, okay? Let's let it go at that."

Katz made himself circle back to the eight-hundred-pound gorilla still filling the room. "Okay," he said, "let's come back to the deal they offered you."

"Yeah, right. Some deal. Here's my counter-offer: N-O fucking way."

"That's what my advice would've been, Cleo, and that's what I'll tell them, but – just doing my job – I need to tell you the rest of the offer."

"Oh, there's more?" she snorted. "I don't have a first-born, sorry."

"They tried to put the squeeze on by saying they'd take it off the table if we didn't buy it right away."

"Fat effin' chance."

"It's just the way they do business," Katz said. "Believe me, I know."

Cleo shook her head, with vigor. "If even the whiff of any of that got back to Rayful, I'd be dead the next day. If anyone knows how he operates, I do. Believe *me* on that. *I* know."

The swirl in Katz' head started to gel. The picture. The evidence Hutchison had to have to back up the charges but couldn't show him. The stiff terms of the deal. Edmond knew he could trust Cleo. She knew she'd be dead because she knows how he operates. Maybe, just maybe, Hutchison wasn't as full of shit as he thought and maybe, just maybe, Cleo was letting him know in her own way that the negotiation was starting.

"Okay," he said, with another glance at his watch. "Just hear me out on this. I'm betting they won't make you wear a wire against him. They'd cream in their jeans if you agreed to wear one against someone lower they really wanted to turn on him, someone who might even know more than you know." She was paying attention now, so he pressed his advantage. "So, if it's not totally off the table, I want to keep the conversation going, talk to them about one, finding another target besides Rayful, and two, getting their so-called offer down to zero jail time. We can always say no to anything more than that. Just tell me if you want me to keep on talking."

The door knob turned and they both looked up to see the guard's face in the window. Cleo stood up, but before the guard could escort her out, she turned back to Katz. "Keep talking."

Katz nodded, stuffed his pad into his briefcase, and followed them out. In the good old days, prisons let him use their phones because he was on the same team. Now he knew better than to even ask so he headed for the car and got off 95 the first exit he saw a phone sign. He wheeled into a Texaco station and found the pay phone hanging on a side wall next to the rest room. He pushed a quarter into the slot, dialed the number for the U.S. Attorney's Office, and told the operator to tell Hutchison who was calling. The line picked up on the first ring.

84

"Good morning, Jake," Hutchison said. "How's your day going?"

"Just super. And yours?"

"Hard to tell yet. You going to make it better or worse?"

"That depends. Let me start with something to put you in the right frame of mind."

The door next to the phone opened and a guy with a frizzy red beard and a biker helmet pushed through, followed immediately by an odor that crossed Katz' eyes. He waited for the biker to leave, but the aroma lingered.

"You there?" Hutchison asked.

"I'm here," Katz coughed. "Sorry, fighting a cold. My client is willing to do what we talked about."

"Just so we're clear," Hutchison said. "You mean wear a wire, right?"

A woman bigger than the biker turned the corner toward Katz and threw a titanic hip into him before turning into the rest room. He waited for the door to lock.

"Hello? Katz?"

"I'm here, I'm here. I'm calling you from the road and I don't want anyone listening in. Yeah, what you said. She'll do it – for the right price and on her terms." Katz remembered many a call when he sat where Hutchison did when the next thing opposing counsel would hear was a laugh followed by a click. If he didn't hear either, he knew he had a shot.

"Okay," he heard Hutchison say. "You've got balls, or she does. Let's hear the price first."

"Like I told you yesterday, no jail time. She's putting her life on the line if she –"

Now he got the laugh. "Jake, spare me," Hutchison said. "I know the rest by heart. We're talking about wearing it with Rayful, right?"

Katz heard a blast that sounded like a flat bugle hooked to an amp. He did not want to be around for the smell.

"That's a no."

Another blast, only this time from a bassoon.

"Then who the fuck needs her?" Hutchison said. "He's the one we're after, in case you missed it."

"He's got a big family, all of 'em in it up to their eyes, according to her. She'd have a much better chance of sitting down with one of them without somebody getting suspicious."

"Name names – and don't tell me his fourth cousin on his stepdaddy's side or this call is over."

"Maybe Bootsie? That name ring a bell?" The only thing he heard now was a flush. Thank God for small favors. "Okay," he said. "You think about it. I gotta go.

I'll be back in my office in an hour. I so look forward to your call."

He enjoyed being the one to hang up first, but once he heard the lock rattle open next door, he didn't linger to savor it.

8

At 6:57 the next morning, Marshal Gaskins flipped
the light switch and extended his arm to welcome Katz into
the lawyers' conference room just off one of the
courtrooms on the fourth floor of the District Court. A
particle board conference table with a scratched laminated
walnut top and dinged aluminum legs filled the room,
complemented only by four plastic yellow chairs on each
side and a cockeyed wall clock.

"Man, I have never been here this early," Katz said,
"never mind on a Saturday. You?"

The Marshal shook his head. "Not 'til recently, but
now they're shuttlin' people in and out o' here all the time,
every day, all hours. Old man like me starts to creak up
with all the overtime."

"Sorry they're working you so hard."

Marshal Gaskins shrugged and smiled. "When I see
the check, I forgive 'em. This have anything to do with the
lady your friend Mr. Peterson gave you?"

"It does. Her willingness to cooperate, as a matter
of fact."

"Ah. Seems to be a whole lot of that goin' on too –
" Gaskins cut himself off and held up a finger to Katz, then
disappeared. In a second, he was back. "Looks like they're
here. Good luck."

He backed out of the doorway and offered the wide sweep of his hand to what sounded like a small army approaching. A form wearing a dark poncho with the hood up, a black ski mask, and sunglasses turned into the room first, followed by a taller square-jawed man in a black jacket with a U.S. Marshal's patch and a name tag that read McDermott. Katz didn't know him and didn't know who or what the other person was either. Behind both of them, two uniformed men, one black, one white, flanked the doorway. The most noticeable thing about them was their fingers on the triggers of the M-16 automatic rifles they held tight to their chests. Marshal McDermott spoke first. "Your name, sir?"

"Jake Katz." Neither of them offered a hand. "I'm waiting for Cleo Smythe, my client."

The Marshal nodded and turned to the specter to his left. When it whipped its shades off and pointed them at Katz, he knew who it was the split second that unmistakable glare of wet red and electric blue sizzled back at him. "That's him," Cleo said through the mask. "Can I get out of this shit now?"

Katz' jaw dropped. When he recovered the power of speech, he said "What the hell, guys? Is this really necessary?"

"It's for her protection, sir," Marshal McDermott said.

Katz barked a short laugh. "Really? I know Rayful Edmond's supposed to be the next coming of Al Capone,

89

but do you really think he's got someone hangin' around Lorton all day just waitin' to take a potshot at her?"

Now the Marshal's stare flamed at him. "With all due respect, Mr. Katz, is it? You don't know jack shit about Rayful Edmond or Lorton, never mind all the dudes locked up there who can – and do – get word to him. You also might have noticed this is the District of Columbia, where a lot more dudes who ain't locked up might be waitin' to get a piece of her. You got any other questions?"

Katz let the fire in his cheeks die down before he answered. "Yeah, just one. Can I be alone with my client now?"

The Marshal nodded curtly and turned to Gaskins. "We got it now," he said. "I'll post out here in the hall and they'll be down the ends. You can stand down."

Gaskins nodded and turned to let his gaze linger on Katz a beat longer than it had to, but just as long as Katz expected. He closed the door behind them and Katz turned to see Cleo yanking away the mask, eyes still blazing. "Jesus Christ!" she spat out. "I told them 'What is this, fucking Halloween?' A-holes're just jerkin' me around."

Katz shook his head and gave her costume the once over. There were bulges where he didn't expect them. Cleo caught his look. "That's another thing!" She tore the poncho up and off, and threw up her hands. Katz hadn't seen a pair of football shoulder pads since high school. "Look at these!" she screamed. "They supposed to stop a bullet? I don't think so!"

90

He knew she knew they were really supposed to disguise who was under all that, so he just stood in silence watching her claw behind her back, groping at some way to take them off. After more than a few seconds of curses and grunts, she fixed her lasers back on him.

"You think you might give me a hand?"

He walked behind her and pulled the slip knot in the strings, then lifted the pads over her head. "There you go," he said.

She shook her head and ran her fingers through her hair, then spun her head in search of something. Katz was pretty sure he knew what, but kept his counsel.

"Christ! No goddamn mirrors?" Cleo said. "I must look like shit."

You look damn fine, Katz thought, but he kept that to himself too. He took his seat and waited for her to calm down. When she blew out a deep breath, he pointed to the seat next to him. "If you're okay, we need to talk before they get here." She did her usual flop into the chair and motioned him to start already.

"So I'm hoping we have some leverage here," he said. "First, they're meeting with us on a Saturday, which tells me they want to get a deal done asap – and second, they didn't hang up on me when I said what we wanted."

"And what exactly did you say we want?"

91

"Just what we talked about: You serve no jail time, and you don't wear a wire with Rayful."

"And they're okay with that?"

"We'll see. They are definitely going to want to tap your phone and if they give in on you talking to Rayful, they're definitely going to want you to wear the wire with the next best thing. You know who that is better than me." He watched the minute hand on the wall clock slide past 12. "Cleo, we don't have a lot of time. Who's the one they'd most want besides Rayful? His mom? His dad?"

She snorted. "No, not his dad. He thinks he's all that, but he ain't. They don't let him any nearer to Rayful – or more to the point, the money than they have to."

"Who's 'they'?"

"Bootsie, mostly."

"Does she know enough to make the Feds interested?"

"She knows everything, Jake, *everything*. She runs the show almost as much as Rayful."

Katz heard an elevator ding around the corner. "That's gotta be them. Do you feel comfortable talking to Bootsie with a wire on? She won't think it's strange you're chatting her up about the business?"

"No," she said, "we talk a lot, about everything. But –" She paused and shook her head.

"But what?"

"But, if *she* suspects anything, Rayful's way more likely to hear about it – and in a heartbeat, man – than he would from anyone else."

Katz heard footsteps drawing nearer. "Who else could you" – he swallowed 'give up' – "talk to that these guys might go for?" He heard a knock on the door and turned to see Hutchison through the window, palms up. Katz held up a finger and turned back to Cleo. She cupped a hand over her mouth so only Katz could see it, and whispered her words. "Armaretta, her sister, Rayful's aunt."

Katz shielded his mouth too. "Then that's Plan A, okay?" She nodded. "You ready?" he whispered. She nodded again. Katz turned and waved Hutchison in.

Hutchison held the door open for another man, white, curly black going on gray hair, maybe ten years older, a few inches taller, and forty pounds heavier than Katz. Katz tried to imagine him, younger and thinner, from back in his own days in the USA's office, but couldn't. Hutchison did the introductions.

"Jake Katz, Charlie Madden. Charlie's the Chief of Criminal."

They shook hands. "Sorry to intrude on your weekend, Mr. Katz," Madden said.

"The cause of justice heeds no calendar," Katz said, expecting to see the eye roll he got.

"I understand you used to be one of us," Madden said.

"Yeah, but it's been a while now. Been gone twelve years."

"Let's see, that'd be 1977, right? I was just a few years in at Criminal in DOJ then. I came over here in '80." Madden stretched his hand to Cleo, still in her seat. "Ms. Smythe," he said. She eyed him but didn't move a muscle.

Madden smiled tightly, then moved around the other side of the table to take the chair opposite her. Hutchison sat next to him across from Katz. They each set their standard government issue hard black briefcases on the floor. Hutchison opened his, pulled up a notebook, flipped it open, and clicked his pen. Madden let his be.

"So Ron's told me where things stand right now," he said, "but let me lay out my understanding just to make sure we're all on the same page. First, I understand that Ron has asked your client to wear a listening device when she talks to Mr. Edmond, and you've asked if she can wear it with someone else. Do I understand that correctly?"

"You do," Katz said.

"Second, he told you we want to tap her phone, but he's not real sure you gave him an answer on that. Do you have an answer for us?"

"Not yet. Let's see how the rest of our conversation goes first."

94

"All right, and, third, Ron told you that if Ms. Smythe agreed to wear the device, the government would present a plea bargain to the court that would reduce her sentence to no more than five years. Do I have that right?"

"Let's see, how do I put this?" Katz said. "It is right, but only in the sense that you are correct. In any other sense – like, say, moral, or just – it's anything but."

"And so you told Ron that you think Ms. Smythe should not serve any time at all, correct?"

"Correct. And she gets witness protection, of course."

"Of course." Madden turned to Hutchison. "Have I left anything out?"

"You have not," he said.

Madden nodded and turned back to Katz. "Okay, so let me give you my perspective on this. First, not only do we have probable cause to believe that Ms. Smythe is one of Mr. Edmond's closest and most trusted colleagues in his drug enterprise, we have absolutely no doubt about it."

"Really?" Katz said. "That's a pretty big jump from being in a picture with some of his relatives in Vegas."

Madden curved his mouth into a smile his eyes didn't share. "That's just a very small part of the evidence, Mr. Katz, and, as I know you well know, we can't show you any of it until trial."

"Actually, assuming you somehow come across any evidence that might actually exculpate her, you probably have to."

"Mr. Katz," Madden said with a smile, "I'll be more precise from now on, I promise. My point is that your client is very highly placed in Mr. Edmond's organization and we have substantial evidence to prove it, far more than just the picture."

"Uh huh, and do you have enough evidence to prove to a jury beyond a reasonable doubt that she committed specific actual crimes while in this supposed high position?"

"Again, you know I can't tell you that, Mr. Katz. All I can say is we're all officers of the court with a duty to tell the truth, and that's what I'm telling you. At this point, you'll just have to trust me on that."

Cleo snorted, loudly. "Right," she muttered. Katz laid his hand on her forearm.

"I know the drill," Katz said, lifting his hand, "but I think Ms. Smythe is in the best position to know what the evidence will actually say about her role in this so-called criminal enterprise, and she's just given you her opinion." Madden looked from him to Cleo, then back again, his smile a memory.

"Mr. Katz, your client faces a long, long term of imprisonment, and I am telling you that as truthfully and with as much certainty as I can. There's an indictment sitting in my in-box that runs for pages, listing crimes that you, Ms. Smythe, have committed both individually and as a ranking member of a criminal enterprise. Those crimes include multiple counts of felony possession of controlled substances, the sale of controlled substances, the laundering of the money paid for those substances, RICO violations, extortion, and conspiracy to do all of the above, including murder."

"I never killed anyone!" Cleo cried out.

"Cleo!" Katz said, slapping his hand on hers this time. "Not another word!" She yanked her hand out and pointed a trembling finger at Madden. "That is a fucking lie!" she yelled.

"Cleo! Enough!" Katz said as firmly as he'd said anything in his life. She seethed, those eyes riveted on Madden, then slapped the table with both hands and stared at Katz, then Hutchison, then the clock, and finally her clenched hands.

Madden waited for the air to settle. "If you were a partner in a felony that resulted in someone's death, Mrs. Smythe," he said, "you can be charged for that person's death whether your finger was on the trigger or not." He turned to Katz. "All it needs is my signature and my boss's. Once his pen leaves the paper, we've got nothing more to talk about."

Katz literally felt the pressure. He longed to jerk his tie off, rip open his shirt, and head for the Bahamas, but he willed his pulse to slow down while he sat back, picked up his yellow pad with both hands to steady his grip, and stared intently at a blank sheet of paper. He forced himself to focus. *If she really is all they think she is, her testimony is a valuable commodity,* he told himself, *and the tap and the wire just make her more valuable.* He looked at Cleo intently, but she was still smoldering, so this was no time to ask for a break to talk to his client. He turned the pad face down, and stepped back into the batter's box.

"Okay. Let's leave the particulars out of it and just presume you're right about her exalted place in the food chain." He pointed his finger at Madden. "You want to buy her cooperation, you gotta pay for it. If she testifies against Mr. Edmond, she gets no jail time and she gets witness protection."

"You've conveniently forgotten about the phone tap and the wire, Mr. Katz," Madden said. "Those are indispensable parts of the agreement: No tap, no wire, no deal."

"We'll talk about all that after you talk about the sentence."

"You're not running the show, Katz, you got that?" Hutchison spit out. Now Madden laid his hand on Hutchison's arm. "This is an important case, Mr. Katz," he said, "and Ms. Smythe is an important part of it, for the reasons we already discussed. Let's set witness protection aside for now, because that's ultimately not our call, but — if she lets us tap her phone and she wears the wire with Rayful Edmond, we'll ask the judge for no jail time."

"We appreciate the offer, Mr. Madden," Katz said, "but there's a problem with her having a conversation with Mr. Edmond. To the best of Ms. Smythe's recollection, the two of them have never had a one-on-one conversation." He was winging it now, so he went for it. "Yes, they have talked in group conversations, like at the Vegas fight, but that's it. If all of a sudden, she's wanting to have a personal chat with him, he is definitely going to think something's up, especially now, when he has to know the walls are pressing in."

"How do you know he knows that?" Hutchison asked.

"If I know it, he knows it, that's how – and Ms. Smythe knows it – and not because Rayful told her, by the way, but because they're buzzin' about it all over Lorton. You guys know jack shit about what's going on there – with all due respect." He gave the Marshal in the hall a silent tip of the hat.

"Mr. Katz," Madden said, "Rayful Edmond is the top of the food chain, as you put it. If she can't help us put him away, forever, we can't help her."

"But that doesn't mean she has to be on the wire with *him*, does it? How about someone else who wouldn't smell a rat if they talked?"

"Like who?" Hutchison asked.

Katz looked at Cleo. She nodded the shortest of nods. He turned to Madden. "Like I said yesterday, Armaretta. Rayful's aunt. Ms. Smythe has a close

99

relationship with her, and she – allegedly – knows a lot about the enterprise."

Madden and Hutchison exchanged glances. "Give us a minute to talk," Madden said. He got up and Hutchison followed him out of the room. Katz waited till the door clicked shut behind them, then turned to Cleo.

"I never fucking killed anyone!" she hissed.

"I hear you. I'm sure you didn't. But, like he said, the law's clear that if you were in control of an enterprise and one of the guys under you killed someone, you can be charged for murder too."

She sunk back in her chair and covered her eyes with both hands. He tugged his chair closer to her. "Cleo, take a deep breath. We need to talk about our options here. They may come back and say it's Rayful or nothing. If they do, I might be able to get witness protection out of it, but if you say you absolutely won't talk to him and they say no to Armaretta, we're going need to give them someone else. We talked about Bootsie – "

Cleo threw up her hand to block the view from the hallway. "No Bootsie!" she said. "She's been a friend, a *real* friend, Jake. I can't sell her out."

"Cleo, listen, they just want her for the same reason they want you – to get Rayful. If you do give her up, they're going to offer her the same deal they give you, which probably means no jail time for her either."

"No!" Cleo said behind her hand, now more a fist. Jake looked to the hallway. Madden and Hutchison had their backs to the door, still talking. He leaned close to Cleo, their heads almost touching. The wisps of her hair tickled his forehead.

"Cleo, think of it like this," he whispered, "you're doing her a favor in the long run. If you don't wear the wire with her, they're going to bring everything they can against her, and if they convict her of anything, I can guarantee you she'll never see daylight again."

Cleo turned her head away but not before Jake saw her eyes well up. "This is some fucked-up game we're playing," she muttered. "Everybody loses."

Katz heard a knock on the door. When he turned to look, Madden was framed in the glass. "You ready?" he asked.

Katz held up a finger, then turned back to Cleo. "I'll push for Armaretta as long as I can, but if it's Bootsie or nothing, that's got to be your call, okay?" He waited for a response, but when it was clear none was coming, he turned and beckoned Madden back in. Hutchison followed him to their seats. Cleo spun in her chair so her back was to them and kept her eyes trained on the empty hallway.

"Armaretta's not good enough," Madden said. "It has to be Rayful."

"I've already told you she won't wear it with him," Katz said. "What the hell were you talking about out there, the weather?"

Madden smiled and stood up. Hutchison did the same, without the smile. "Enjoy the rest of your day, Mr. Katz, Ms. Smythe." Madden looked at his watch, then at Hutchison. "I may be able to make that tee time after all."

Cleo spun to look at Katz. He saw nothing but fear in those eyes now. He turned to Madden. "I know all the theatrics, Mr. Madden. I get the point. Why is Armaretta not enough for you? My client says she knows everything and won't suspect a thing if Ms. Smythe calls her up to talk."

"Because she doesn't know everything, Mr. Katz," Madden said. "There's only two people who do: Rayful Edmond and his mother, Bootsie." Hutchison was staring at the same empty hallway Cleo found so fascinating a minute ago. Now Katz knew what they were talking about. "So Bootsie would be acceptable to you?" he said.

Madden nodded. "She would – and we tap the phone."

"And the same deal – no jail time and witness protection."

"We will ask for both, but you know the judge can always do what he wants, no matter what we agree to, and we can't guarantee witness protection on our own either. It's got to go through a whole DOJ process – but, if you ask for it, yes, we will support your request."

Katz turned to see Cleo staring back at him, eyes wet, skin pale, shaking. She jerked her hand up to shield her face and closed her eyes shut as if to keep herself from seeing the silent 'Okay' she mouthed to him. Katz waited for her to open them again just to make sure. "That's a yes?" he whispered behind his hand. "Yes," she muttered through quivering lips.

Katz turned back to Madden. "It's a deal."

Madden nodded. Hutchison stood up. Madden didn't. "I'll have to run it past the USA, of course," he said.

Katz lifted his head to the clock over Madden's shoulder. "It's 7:30 on a Saturday morning and it's forty degrees," he said. "I'm betting his tee time can wait too. Let's get her back home, for everyone's good, okay?"

Hutchison didn't need the cue. He was out the door before Madden stood up, no smile on his face now.

"Talk amongst yourselves," Madden said and left them alone.

9

Cleo put her face in her hands and sobbed, hard, her whole body convulsing. Katz reached out to stroke her hair, then thought better of it and leaned down to whisper in her ear.

"Cleo, I can't tell you it's all going to be okay, I can't promise you that. But when it's all said and done, this is going to be a good thing, you have to believe me."

She shook her head, still buried in her hands. "If I fucking live through it."

"Cleo, you're going to have so much protection from the cops and the Feds, you will live through it, trust me on that. You're their prized possession – and you're one of a kind. You're their Hope Diamond!"

She kept shaking her head, but when she lifted it from her hands and turned to him, her face was flushed and streaked with tears, her hair matted, tangled, and unflattering in every way possible, but the trace of a smile was on her lips. "You sure know how to flatter a girl, Jake."

"You look great," he heard himself say, so sincerely he realized he actually meant it. He made himself focus on why they were there. "Cleo, this is all part of the game they play. It's the only way they know to play it."

"What more can I goddamn give them?"

Katz shrugged. "They may take one more shot at having you sit down with Rayful –" He caught the look in her eyes. "I'm just telling you, they're going to let us both sit here as long as they want just to jerk us around, and when they finally do come back, don't be surprised if they try to up the ante again."

Especially if the USA sides with Hutchison, he thought. He knew the look in his eyes first hand. It was the same look every AUSA had when he thought his boss was pussying out on him. On the other hand, if the USA backed up Madden, it would only take a minute to white out "Rayful Edmond," type in "Constance Perry," and come down with the same agreement. But either way, they'd still make them wait. It's just how they do. Cleo drew her left sleeve across her face to dry her eyes. She caught him looking at her and laughed her harsh laugh. "Quite the sight, huh?" She stood up and posed for him, hands on hips. "And how about the outfit?" She twirled around for him in her orange jump suit, finishing with a goofy come-hither look. Even then, he knew why the guy at Archibald's hired her on the spot. If he was at a table there, he knew what he'd holler, but he said, "Just needs a pair of shoulder pads, then it's perfect."

She laughed and gave him a mock curtsey and a genuine smile he'd never seen before. He knew he had to stay all business, but he couldn't think of a single business thing to say, so he just smiled back and hoped it wasn't too creepy.

"Jake, thank you for everything you're doing for me. I know I don't show it too well or too often, but I do appreciate it. I want you to know that."

"I appreciate that, Cleo, but don't thank me yet. Let's wait and see how it all turns out first."

Her eyes welled up again and she shook her head. "Man, all I've been thinking is why didn't I just stay at Fort Belvoir? Why didn't I throw away his number? Why didn't I have the good sense to just take off once I saw what I was getting into? Why was I so stupid so many times?"

Katz knew the correct answer to every one of those questions was spelled m-o-n-e-y, but he said "Don't beat yourself about it, Cleo. What's past is past. Let's just try to make your future – "

"Worth living?" she said.

"I was going to say 'the best you can make it'."

"Yeah, right," she said and slumped forward, elbows on her knees, staring at the ground, and shaking her head. *The hell with it*, Katz thought, and reached over to pat her hair gently, then slid his hand down to massage her neck. In a few seconds, she turned and smiled the wannest of smiles. She reached up to press his hand for a quick second before she sat up and took a deep breath when she saw McDermott pull the door open to admit Madden, accompanied by only his briefcase. He looked at Cleo. Katz kept his eyes trained on him and held his breath.

"If you consent to the phone tap, and you wear the wire when you talk to Constance and Armaretta Perry in person," Madden said, "and that gives us something we can use to convict Mr. Edmond – and you testify at the grand jury and at trial, and you do not take the Fifth Amendment," he turned to look at Katz, "we'll give your client what you asked for – no jail time and support for her request for witness protection." Katz exhaled as slowly as he could manage and turned to Cleo, whose puzzled look let him know she didn't think this was the total victory he did.

"What's that mean?" she said to Madden. "'Something we can use to convict Mr. Edmond'? What if I get her to open up about him, but the jury lets him go? Where's that leave me?"

"Cleo – " Katz started, but she waved him off. "Uh-uh. I want to hear it from him."

Madden thought it over a second, then bent down to pop open the metal snaps on his briefcase. He reached in and pulled out three manila folders. He handed one to Cleo and one to Katz, and flipped open the third one. "Let's go through this together," he said. "If you or Mr. Katz have any questions at any point, I'll answer them then, okay?"

Katz spoke before Cleo could open her mouth this time. "I think that's a good way to go, Cleo." He turned to Madden. "And if either of us wants to talk to the other about anything, I'm sure Mr. Madden will leave the room and let us do that too, correct?"

"Correct," Madden said, and waited for Cleo to turn back to him. "Shall I proceed?" She flipped open her folder. "Okay. The sections at the top are pretty much boilerplate. Number 1 says that both parties agree that this agreement will be placed under seal until we need to disclose it in the event of your appearance at trial, Ms. Smythe. In the real world, that means if we decide to put you on the stand and we need to refer to a transcript of, say, a phone conversation, we'll have to show it to Mr. Edmond and his lawyer to let them prepare their cross-examination of you."

Cleo looked to Katz. "That's standard operating procedure," he told her. "They have to do it, just like they'd have to show it to you if you were the defendant."

"Which I'm not, right?" she said to Madden.

"You are pleading guilty to the crime we discussed, Ms. Smythe. That's spelled out down below. But like we discussed – and unlike how we deal with almost every other person guilty of a crime – we're going to do our best to keep you out of prison, not in. Should I go on?"

"Sure, why not? I love reading my own death warrant."

"All right. Section 2 just says you've read the agreement and reviewed it with Mr. Katz, and section 3 lists the general conditions that apply, basically that you're not going to lie about anything you tell us. No perjury, no false statements, no false declarations, no obstruction of justice. Section 4 says that we can prosecute you if you do lie, but I don't expect it'll come to that, so I'm not going to waste your time by going over it. There are other kinds of standard provisions in there, like surrendering your passport and getting our permission to leave the D.C. area, that you and Mr. Katz can read when I'm done walking you through this, but let's go over the one that deals with payments. Take a look at section 9."

Cleo's look at him was somewhere between quizzical and hostile. "Payment? Who's paying who?"

"We're paying you. We fully understand that your decision to testify against Rayful is going to have some financial consequences for you – "

"Oh, you think?" Cleo cut him off. Madden continued. "We offer you two choices. The one that most people choose is the one you've told us you're interested in, witness protection. If the Department winds up approving it, you'll receive about fifty thousand dollars a year for five years, which we've found is enough time for you to find work that will let you support yourself."

"Uh huh," Cleo said, "and what do the other people do?"

"Some people – not many, but a few – decide not to go into witness protection. Those people receive a one-time sum substantially higher than fifty thousand, but when they do, that's the end of the government's protection. No relocation, no more money, you just become a regular citizen again. It is a much riskier proposition."

Katz started to offer the same opinion, but Cleo didn't wait to hear it. "So what's the higher sum?" Madden glanced back down at the agreement. "That number isn't filled in," he said, "because, like I said, almost everyone likes the idea of getting fifty grand a year for five years while they figure out how to start their life over."

"I heard you the first time. I get all that," Cleo said, "but what if I don't need five years to get myself started again, and took my chances staying right here. What would I get?"

Madden shrugged his shoulders. "My guess is we'd be like a bank. You'd probably get some kind of smaller amount up front, but the boys in the green eye shades would have to give you the exact number."

"I don't expect they're around this morning," Katz said.

"They're not, but if you're serious about this, Ms. Smythe, I will get a number to you on Monday."

"Oh, I'm serious," she said.

Madden pulled out a pen, put an asterisk on the blank line, then wrote next to another asterisk at the bottom of the page. He held the page up to them. Katz read out loud "$ amount to be provided Monday 4/24." He looked at Cleo. "Okay with you?"

She gave a quick nod.

"Then consider it done," Madden said. "Anything else before we move on to what I think is the heart of the deal?"

Cleo shook her head.

"Okay, so please look at section 10. Ms. Smythe, that is your agreement to plead guilty to one count of violating section 846 of Title 21 of the U.S. Code for conspiring to distribute, and possessing with intent to distribute, more than 500 grams of cocaine."

"Okay, and where's my 'get out of jail free' card?" Cleo asked.

"I'm coming to that. Section 11 spells out the four conditions you need to meet to cash that card. First, you have to tell us everything you know – again, truthfully. Second, you have to wear the wire as we designate. The agreement specifies the two people we've discussed, but we retain the discretion to require you to wear it with others too."

Cleo pounded her fist on the table. "I am not wearing it with Rayful! That's not happening. How many times do we have to go over that?" Katz started to speak, but Madden held his left hand up and wrote on the agreement with his right. "Excluding Rayful Edmond," he said out loud. Katz said nothing. Madden continued on like he didn't take Cleo's muttered "Motherfucker!" personally.

"Third, you have to testify at the grand jury and the trial of Mr. Edmond without invoking the Fifth

Amendment, and, fourth, the evidence you provide through either the wire or the testimony has to be useful to the government. That's what you need to do. Any other questions before I continue?"

"So the first question my client asked still needs to be answered," Katz said. "Tell us what 'useful to the government' means."

"It means we're not interested in hearing Ms. Perry talk about the weather or the Redskins or how nice your client looks today or anything other than criminal activity that ties back to Mr. Edmond."

"And what if you don't think I give you whatever you need?" Cleo cut in. "Then what? You lock me away? That's a lot of bullshit, man."

Katz couldn't have said it any better, so he waited for Madden to answer.

"Ms. Smythe, I can guarantee you we're going to give you every chance to succeed. We will coach you on specific things we want you to talk about, and believe me, if it takes more than one conversation, then so be it. We're willing to wait for what we need. Within reason, of course."

"Yeah, right," Cleo shot back. "It sounds pretty shitty to me. I gotta hope what she says gives you guys what you want, and that she says it before you say 'time's up'? You guys can fuck me up any time you want. What kind of deal is that?"

Madden looked to Katz for some help but Katz wasn't about to give him any. He sat quietly, waiting to hear what Madden had to say.

"Ms. Smythe," he said, "it's a good deal for you and for us, but both of us have to do our part. As we say in the next section, we will ask the judge to impose no prison time, and recommend you for witness protection if you want it – and get you out of harm's way during the grand jury and trial – but if we're going to do all that, you've got to give us something substantial we can use to make our best case to get these people behind bars."

"And if you don't," Katz added. "They'll put you out of sight in a Federal prison for the rest of your life, or try anyway. That's the part that usually goes unsaid, so I just thought I'd say it. Do I have it right, Mr. Madden?"

"You have it right, Mr. Katz," Madden said, closing his folder. "That's the deal – and as you pointed out, if we're going to agree, we need to do it today, now, for all our sakes. Your unexplained absence, Ms. Smythe, will cause Mr. Edmond to be concerned the longer it goes on. The more he suspects you, the less he trusts you." He sat back. "And that's not good for anyone."

Katz couldn't have said that any better either. He looked at his client. "Cleo, do you have any other questions?" She was slumped away from him, her left hand kneading her forehead, eyes closed. If she heard him, he couldn't tell. He turned to Madden and gave him his own tight smile. "Can I have a little time with my client?"

113

Madden stood up, looked at his watch, and looked back at Katz. "You can have ten minutes. After that, the store's closed, except for the accountants filling in the dollar amount. Once that blank is filled in, this is the best deal your client's ever going to get, Mr. Katz. Tell her to take it."

Before he could leave the table, Cleo raised her head to look at him. "I'll take it," she said, with as much weariness as Katz had ever heard in anyone's voice. He couldn't be sure why she took it. Because she really did everything they said she did? Because, even if she didn't, a jury might believe she did? Because the next fifty years in prison was too much to even contemplate? *You're not her psychiatrist*, Katz reminded himself, *you're her lawyer. Get with it.* "Cleo," he said. "Let's take – "

She waved him off. "No, Jake, no. This is how it's going to be, so let's get on with it. I made my deal with one devil, I can make it with another one."

"Counselor," Madden said, "just for the record. Do you want to take some time to talk to your client?"

Katz took one more look at Cleo. She shook her head, emphatically, exhausted, her eyes pleading for – what? – mercy, rest, peace? He couldn't put his finger on it, but in that moment, he didn't feel like her psychiatrist, or her lawyer. Whatever he was, he just wanted to give her whatever she wanted.

"No," he said. "We'll take the deal."

10

Less than two hours later, Katz was back in the Attorney Conference Room at Lorton. Hutchison was there too and apparently in no mood to talk because after they exchanged the briefest of nods when Katz arrived, he was finding all the outside stimulus he needed in the *Washington Post* he held up between them. Katz couldn't see if Hutchison was really reading or just seething behind it, but he was starting to wonder if that sectional sofa in the Woodies ad filling the back page might actually fit in his living room when the door popped open and Cleo came through, followed by the guard with the Diana Ross do and a black man he'd never seen before.

Cleo was carrying a white Wilson gym bag and wearing what they must have picked her up in, a burgundy Redskins sweatshirt, black sweat pants, and lime green Nikes. She threw the bag on the table and started rifling through it. She shunted aside a swim cap, a bathing suit, a towel, flip flops, a bottle of Dasani, and a hair brush until she found what she was looking for: a thick black wallet with a brass buckle. She turned to Katz to shield everyone else's view, unclasped the buckle, and plucked a fat wad of currency from the billfold. Katz caught a few portraits of Hamilton and Jackson riffle by before a lot more Grants and Franklins. Cleo tucked them all back in and stuffed the wallet deep into the bag. When her quick nod let him know all was in order, he rose and extended his hand to the black man who followed Cleo in. They were about the same height and age, but he was a lot handsomer, Katz allowed. They gave each other a quick shake.

"Marion Strickland, Mr. Katz. I'm the Superintendent here."

"Sorry to intrude on your weekend."

"I'm told this is important business for everyone, so no need to apologize."

Hutchison slipped the *Post* into his briefcase, clicked it shut, and kept his mouth shut too. Strickland didn't even turn to acknowledge him. Katz guessed they'd done this more than once, and neither of them needed to say a word for Strickland to know Hutchison was not happy that Cleo was on her way out.

"So," he said to Katz, "your client is free to leave, and as far as anyone except us knows, she's never been here. There's not a piece of paper that shows her coming or going, she's been in solitary since she got here, and there's not going to be any fanfare about her leaving – no escorts, no Marshals, no nothing. Do you have any questions or concerns, Mr. Katz? Ms. Smythe?"

Cleo looked at Katz and shrugged. Katz looked at Strickland. "That pretty much sums up my views," he said.

Strickland nodded. "Once you leave the grounds, of course, Ms. Smythe is no longer my concern. You'll have to deal with the USA's office about anything going forward."

They all turned to look at Hutchison. He looked to Cleo. "We need to make sure that if anyone's noticed you're missing, you have a very good reason why. Can you think of anything they'd buy, no questions asked?"

Katz followed Cleo's eyes to the clock. 10:35. "You said this was Saturday?" she asked him.

"It is."

"And I was picked up when?" Katz turned to Hutchison.

"Monday," he said, "just about this time, as a matter of fact."

"Jesus Christ!" Cleo said. "Five days of my life just fucking gone?"

"That's why you need to get back in the mix asap," Katz said.

"And why you've got to come up with a plausible story to explain why you've been out of touch," Hutchison said. "So I ask you again, do you have any good ideas on that score?"

It didn't take long for Cleo to answer. "Yeah, I do," she said.

"Okay," Hutchison said. "What?"

"I had a woman's problem."

"A woman's problem," Hutchison repeated.

"Trust me," Cleo said. "No man wants to hear anything after that. Do you want me to go on?" Hutchison started to say something, then shut his mouth again. "Exactly," Cleo said.

When Hutchison turned to him, Katz raised his hands. "All I need to know, thanks." Hutchison rubbed his temples. "And the other women – Bootsie, Armaretta – they're not going to think that's bullshit?"

Cleo shot him a look. "They'll buy it, believe me. There ain't a woman alive who wouldn't." Katz almost felt a twinge of sympathy for Hutchison, lost at sea without a compass, but he got over it.

"Okay," Hutchison said, "fine. You had a woman's problem. We also need to let you off somewhere inconspicuous, somewhere you can just get back in the swing of things where nobody'd think it's strange to see you."

She held up the gym bag. "Then drop me at the pool. On North Carolina. That's where I was heading when you grabbed me."

"And from there?" Hutchison asked.

She shrugged. "I'll walk home like I usually do."

"I'll drop her at the pool," Katz said. "No one we care about knows me or my car."

Hutchison stewed on that quietly, then turned back to Strickland. "Okay," he said, "then that's the plan."

"So, Mr. Katz," Strickland said, "go get your car and follow the signs around to the loading dock. We'll bring Ms. Smythe there, in a DOC parka with the hood pulled up –" "No ski mask!" Cleo interrupted. Strickland smiled. "No ski mask," he said and turned back to Katz. "After she's in the car, just follow the service road and look for the signs to 395. That's it."

"And if you see anything funny on the way back," Hutchison said, "somebody you think's trailing you, whatever, let me know – seriously, no bullshit. We need to keep her safe."

"Yeah, right," Cleo said, "until you get what you need from me. Then you could give a shit."

"I'm sure Mr. Madden told you we'll back your request for witness protection." That drew a sharp hack of a laugh from Cleo. "That's not worth the effing paper it's printed on," she spat back.

Katz turned to Strickland. "I'll get the car." A few minutes later, he watched Strickland lead Cleo down the steps from the loading dock, her face down and shrouded by the parka hood. He rolled down his window. "Mr. Hutchison take off?" he asked.

"Out the door right after you," Strickland said. He opened the passenger side door for Cleo and waited for her to slide into the seat, then closed her door and walked around the back of the car to Katz' side. He bent down and pointed straight ahead. "Just follow this to the end and hang a left and you'll be right at the ramp."

"Many thanks."

"Good luck," Strickland said, "and good luck to you too, Ms. Smythe."

"Let's get the fuck out of here," she said from somewhere deep in the parka.

Katz headed for the highway. Cleo flipped back her hood and sighed. "That douche bag Hutchison wanted me to wear some sunglasses but the only ones they could find were some really hideous wraparound black frames like the people with glaucoma wear."

"So what'd you tell him?"

"I'd rather be shot." She laughed, but not her usual bark of a laugh, more of a sweet and satisfied "that was a good one, wasn't it?" kind of laugh. Katz laughed too but kept his eyes focused on the road. Inside a minute, he was on the highway, heading back to D.C. Cleo rolled down the window and let her face bask in the sunshine. "Aw, man," she said. "That never felt so good."

The chill rush of air didn't feel quite that good to Katz. The dash told him it was 42 degrees outside. He cranked up the heat and pushed a vent his way, then stole a look at the rear view mirror. Only a few trucks and a pickup. He stayed in the right lane anyhow just to make sure no one got a good look at his passenger. Her head was resting on her hands on the car door, eyes closed, face bright and smiling in the sunshine.

"So," he asked, "where's the pool?" If she heard him over the wind, she didn't show it. He let his gaze linger, then re-focused on the traffic ahead. In a bit, she rolled up the window and fell back in the seat, eyes still closed, mouth still smiling. Then she turned to look at him.

"What kinda car is this, you gotta crank a handle to close the window?"

Katz barked the laugh this time. "Sorry, Cleo. My brand of law's not quite as lucrative as the drug business. I'm saving up for my Porsche though. Another hundred years or so, I might be able to buy the very one Rayful was tooling around in."

"Sorry, Jake, didn't mean to touch a nerve."

Katz was sorry she was sorry. "Nah," he said, "no harm taken. So, the pool?"

"It's on North Carolina, a little behind the Capitol. Get off at 6th Southeast, I'll show you." They passed a sign that said "Washington 20 Miles."

"You want the radio on?" Katz asked.

"No, this is good," she said. "Man, I'm beat." She closed her eyes again. Gentle snores reached his ear within a minute. When he crossed the 14th Street Bridge about fifteen minutes later, he reached over and rubbed her shoulder. She awoke with a start and looked out her window, then at the roadway, in total confusion. Only when she looked at Katz smiling back at her from the driver's seat did she seem to remember where she was, and why. She rubbed her eyes roughly and covered a gaping yawn. "Oh, man," she said, "how long was I out?"

"Not long enough, I bet."

She stretched. "I am racking out as soon as I get back from the pool, I'll tell you that. Oh man!"

"Okay, but while you're still awake, tell me where I'm going."

"Get off at 6th and make a left off the ramp."

"Got it." She let her head fall back onto the headrest with a grunt, then turned to look out her window. "Well, Margaret Ann, you sure did it this time," she muttered.

Unless one of them was hallucinating, Katz knew she wasn't talking to him, so he asked "Who's Margaret Ann?"

She said nothing until he got on the exit ramp, then sighed and shook her head. "It's just what I call myself when I get depressed. Make a left here."

He headed up 6th. "I don't get it," Katz said. "Why Margaret Ann?"

"It's the name my momma stuck me with."

"So Cleopatra Salome Smythe is not your real name?"

She found this really funny and had trouble calming down enough to talk. "Now, really, Jake," she finally croaked out, "what mother would lay that on her baby? Even my mother had the good sense not to cripple me from the get-go. She and darling Daddy did a great job of it eventually, but it even took them years and years."

The light ahead at Pennsylvania turned yellow and Katz rolled to a stop. Cleo, or whoever she was, turned to him with a wisp of a smile. "I just wanted something as far away from my real name as possible, so I picked something exotic, something fun. I think it suits me, don't you?"

"What was your real name, the whole name?"

"We don't know each other well enough, yet."

Katz had trouble coming up with a cogent thought after that, until she said "Uh, it's green." He crossed through the intersection at C Southeast. She pointed to the North Carolina street sign coming up. "Make a right here. The pool's down this side." Katz pulled to a stop just before the main entrance of the William H. Rumsey Aquatic Center and made himself concentrate on the matter at hand.

"Okay, tell me what you think of this," he said. "Go on inside and wait a few minutes, then come back out and take a quick look over here. If I saw anything out of the ordinary out here for whatever reason, I'll flash my brights and you go back in. If everything's cool, I won't do anything and you just make your way back home like it's any other day."

"But how're you going to know what's ordinary? You don't know who might be one of Rayful's people."

"That's true," he said and pondered it a second. "But you do, so before you come out, take a quick look around. If you see anyone or anything weird at all, just don't come out. If you're not back out here in fifteen minutes, I'll come in and we'll figure out Plan B."

She thought that over a bit, turned to pull the door lock up, then turned back to him. "Okay, I'll go into the locker room, then I'll come out into the foyer there and hang around for a minute. If it's cool, I'll head home."

"Which is where?"

"Fifth Street, Northeast. Just before D. If it's not cool, I'll go back inside and wait for you way over to the right, by an exit sign over some stairs no one ever uses."

"Sounds like a plan."

She pulled the rear view mirror her way and tousled her hair. "Ugh! Jesus Christ!" She leaned over to give him a quick kiss on the cheek before he had a chance to react. "Gotta keep it real. Wish me luck!"

She popped out the door and walked briskly to the Center, like anyone else on Capitol Hill looking forward to a swim after a tough week's work. Katz watched her disappear through the doors and looked at his watch. 11:55. He hoped he'd be done thinking about that kiss by 12:10. At 12:08, he saw her come out the door and walk past him back to 6th. If she even glanced his way, he didn't see it. Her hair was straight and wet now, just like it would be if she just came out of the pool. *Probably the Dasani or maybe a sink*, he thought, but either way, he was impressed by her attention to detail. In the rear view mirror, he watched her cross North Carolina and head north up 6th. He waited a few minutes after he lost sight of her, then made a right on Independence and a left on 8th. At A St., he made a left, rode the short block down to 7th, then tried to see if he could catch her crossing at 6th. It was too far to make out anyone, so he crept slowly down the block and pulled to the curb about halfway down. In a minute, he saw her cross, head down, gym bag in her right hand. He waited another minute, then made a right on 6th. She was moving out pretty good, he thought, given how beat she was in the car. He waited till she crossed the next block at Constitution and followed slowly behind, pulling over twice when he thought he might be getting too close. When she crossed Massachusetts Avenue and cut through Stanton Park, he waited till she was out of sight, then drove up the east side of the park. He was happy to get the light at C and took his time moving out when it turned green. He circled around the far side of the park, ready to pull over if he saw her, but he didn't so he kept moving to the light at 5th, slowing enough to be the second car in the right lane when it turned red. When he got the green, he slowly made the turn just in time to see her crossing the street to the sidewalk on the left about fifty yards ahead of him.

He slid into a parking space on the right and sat there until he saw her take four steps up to the landing of a gray brick two-story townhouse. He waited till she fished her keys out of the gym bag and let herself inside, then counted to sixty and headed up 5th. As he drew near, he saw the windows on the ground floor were covered by bushes. He read 312 next to the door, and looked up to see two windows on the top floor. When the shade on the one on the right slid up, he saw Cleo smile and throw him a kiss as he drove by.

He pushed open the office door and did a double take at the sight of LaVerne sitting behind her desk, arms folded, fixing him with a questioning stare. "Well, looky who decided to roll in after all! I was just about to split."

He looked at the clock over her shoulder. Eleven fifty-five. He pointed to it. "Is that right?"

LaVerne seemed very concerned. "You okay? You fall down on the way up here? Bang your head on the steps real hard?"

Katz stepped over to the reception area and fell back into the chair. He let his head flop back and enjoyed the prospect of keeping his eyes closed for a very long time, but the second he shut them, the relentless swirl of the morning's memories forced them open. He lifted his head to check one more thing with her. "And it's still Saturday, right?" he asked.

"That's right," she said slowly. "The day you pay me time-and-a-half to come up here in the morning, get you squared away for next week? You remember that part, don't you?"

"So let's see," he said, "I got up, got showered, got dressed, got out of the house, and over to the U.S. Courthouse before seven. I went two rounds with the USA's office there, then I drove out to Lorton – for the third time in four days, if you're keeping score at home – got my client out, drove her back to DC, dropped her off at a swimming pool on North Carolina, trailed her home to make sure she made it back in one piece, then came here and – hey! – it's still Saturday morning! What do I win, Johnny?"

LaVerne thought about that a moment, stood up, and reached her hand out to him. "You get to buy us lunch at Antonio's."

"Deal," he said, and fished a twenty out of his wallet.

She came around the desk and took it, then disappeared out the doorway before she stuck her head back in. "Oh, and like you say, it goes without sayin', but I'll say it anyway, you need to call your boyfriend back. He don' take Saturdays off neither, I guess. Some crisis you need to attend to. Now. Pronto. As soon as possible – man, I can't remember all the ways he said call back right away – oh, giddyap, that was another one – but you get the point, right?"

He waited for her steps to fade away before he pushed himself up and out of the chair and headed slowly for his desk, taking the time to consider whether he wanted to prolong his misery by subjecting himself to Harry, or just fall into a coma at his desk and let LaVerne wake him up with the sweet smell of lunch. He slumped into his office chair and decided to get his troubles – his *tsuris*, his mother would have called it – out of the way so he could eat his tacos in peace. Harry picked up on the first ring.

"Judge Alexander."

128

"Wow. Answering your own phones these days? Or is it 'phone'?"

"Katz! It's about time. Where you been?"

"What's it matter, Harry? I'm here now. What can I do for you?"

"You been spending time with your client, whatever her name is?"

"Smythe, but I give you two points for remembering it was something you couldn't remember. Good job!"

"Whatever the hell her name is, we're not the only ones talkin' about her," Harry said. "She seems to be real popular these days."

"What do you mean, Harry?"

"I mean Billy Murphy's been askin' about her. That's what I mean."

Katz' grip on the receiver tightened. "What's he asking?"

"What do you think he's askin'? Is she gonna give Rayful up? That's what!"

"Harry, let's not go down this road again – "

"Jake," Harry cut him off, "I know what you told me, but I'm tellin' you what Billy's tellin' me."

"Which is . . . ?"

"Rayful's crowd, a bunch of 'em, are tellin' their lawyers to watch out for her – for whatever reason, I don't know –"

"You don't know?" Katz cut in. "You don't think it maybe has something to do with her being of the Caucasian persuasion – or the female one? She's white, Harry – and she came to the party late. They're black and they go way back with him. That's what it's all about." He almost persuaded himself, but he didn't persuade Harry.

"I don't know why they're sayin' it," he said, "and I don't care – and neither should you. The fact that someone's sayin' it at all's what you oughta be thinkin' about, for reasons I shouldn't have to explain to you."

Katz wasn't ready to concede the point. "And what's his client Rayful say – not his boys, him?"

"Billy says he's the only one who trusts her."

"Okay, then what's he worrying about?"

"He doesn't want to take the chance that all these folks're right and Rayful's wrong."

"Harry, I'm sure Billy Murphy's smart enough to know that the government's case isn't going to rise or fall on who says what about his client. He knows they think they have enough hard evidence – drugs, money, guns, prints, whatever – to put Rayful away forever."

"He says Rayful told him if everyone stands up and does the time, he's convinced he can beat whatever they charge him with."

That made Katz laugh. "Harry, he's delusional. They're going to be loaded for bear. You've seen it – from the bench, and from the defense table – even on a routine case. Billy needs to be thinking about a plea, not getting him off."

Harry sighed. "Jake, I know you're a clean-cut kid 'n all, but let's not be totally naive. How 'bout I put it to you like this? He doesn't think a jury of his peers will put him away."

That made Katz sit up a little straighter. "What're you saying, Harry? That people are going to be too scared to say he's guilty?"

"Back up a couple of steps, son. You think anyone's going to want to even sit on that jury? You think anyone's going to want to have their name out there that they're even on that jury? *Then* you throw in whether they think it makes any sense to say he's guilty. Then you think about whether all twelve people in that box are going to have the balls to do all that. Now you understand why Rayful would say that and why Billy would believe him? This startin' to sink in?"

Katz's mouth was dry. It was all sinking in, like a cave-in. Even the familiar sweet smell wafting in from the stairway wasn't enough to rescue him.

"I'm late for lunch," he managed to get out and hung up without a goodbye.

12

Katz was profoundly grateful for the small mercy of an open legal parking spot right in front of his townhouse at 1524 East Capitol. He grabbed his briefcase and the taco bag, shoved open the car door, and planted his feet firmly on the street while he gathered the strength to push himself up and out. It'd been a long day by noon, and his chat with Harry only motivated him to take his bag out of LaVerne's hand and call it a day for both of them.

He headed up the walk to his front door, now the one above ground. Until about seven years ago, his door was the one to the basement he rented from Mrs. DeCarlo, the widow who lived on the top two floors. When she passed away in '82, her kids had no interest in moving back, the neighborhood was suffering from a high crime rep, and he was still making good money with Harry, so the place was available at a price he could afford and he grabbed it.

Even though his financial state of health was declining in recent years, he kept resisting the urge to rent out his old subterranean digs. The growing flood of out-of-state immigrants coming to find work in the new Congress and the Bush Administration was already driving the rents up, but every time he started to reconsider – like now – he conjured up the ghost of Marty McAdoo, usually pressed up next to him in that queen-sized bed they crammed into what passed for a bedroom down there.

It'd been twelve years since she picked up and left him, but he still saw her lying in that bed, smiling that smile waiting for him to slide next to her under the sheets. There'd been a few one-night stands since then, even a couple of extended stays that he thought might take his mind off her, but it was still Marty he saw lost in thought combing her long blonde hair in the bathroom mirror. He held out a faint hope that there'd be someone else he could make a life with, but every time he tried to picture that someone, it was Marty's face that beamed back at him with what he stupidly thought was love.

In the time it took him to scold himself *It's twelve years already, give it up!*, he sped up the three steps to his landing and through the door. His closest love these days loomed right in front of him: A floor sample deep-padded phony brown leather recliner he got at Marlo's in Forestville for 99 bucks. It was love at first sit. He threw his jacket, tie, and lunch on the nubby red Goodwill sofa he'd bought just to fill some space, and sank into the chair with a loud and deeply satisfying groan. He fished the *Post* Sports section out of the splintered wicker basket he'd had since GW days, but he didn't even make it to page two before he slid into a loud and deeply satisfying sleep.

When he came to, strips of fading light shone at him through the blinds. His watch told him it was 3:19. He looked to see who was playing what on the tube tonight, but before it was 3:20, he figured out that unhappy fragrance enveloping him was coming from the Antonio's bag that never made it to the refrigerator. He staggered to his feet and tossed it in now, hoping that a late chill was better than none. He carried the Sports section with him into the bathroom with every intention of foomphing back

134

into the chair but when he came out, the vision of his bed changed his plans.

When he woke up this time, it was 7:17. He'd slept through dinner time, but maybe not dinner. He stretched and headed for the fridge, slipped the taco box out of the bag, and popped it open on the counter. The smell was almost gone. *Good enough*, he thought, and scarfed one down standing there before tossing the box onto his card/dining room table and grabbing a Carling from the refrigerator. He retrieved the Sports section from the floor next to his bed and checked out the TV listings.

The offerings were pretty poor. Mike Tyson was fighting Frank Bruno on HBO, which was out for two reasons: one, it had to be a dog if it was on cable for free, and two, he didn't have cable. The Caps weren't playing, but the Bullets were. He flipped back to the front sports page, where an article told him they'd won three in a row, including the last one over the Knicks with Patrick Ewing, who he of course hated because he went to Georgetown. *Okay, maybe*, he thought, and walked over to flick the tube on, click the top dial to UHF, and spin the other one to channel 20.

He winced at the first thing he saw: a closeup of John Williams kicking a rebound out of bounds. Typical Bullets luck: two John Williamses were in the draft a few years ago and they picked the wrong one, in the first round. The Cleveland Cavaliers took theirs in the second. That John Williams quickly became a crowd favorite; he was 6'11", reed thin, and so quick they called him "Hot Rod." The Bullets' John Williams was officially listed as 6'8" and

135

235, but anyone who saw him in the heaping flesh knew the scale was just getting started there. Because his greatest talent was obviously eating, Bullet fans called their John Williams "Hot Plate".

The rest of the team wasn't much better, but Katz tried to stick with them until a Derek Harper 3 put them down 82-64 at the end of three, He pushed the button off and headed for the bedroom, but the jangle of his phone stopped him short. He glanced at his watch to confirm it was indeed almost 10 o'clock, then turned back to pluck the receiver off the cradle. Before he could say hello, he heard "Jake, it's me, Cleo. I am freaking out!"

"What's the matter?"

"Every time the phone rings, I know somebody's listenin' in and I'm watchin' every word I say to the point I can't even talk – and I am scared shitless that anyone I do talk to'll know I'm being tapped. What the fuck, Jake? Is this what I signed up for? Good God Jesus Christ Almighty, send me back to Lorton now!" She was yelling now, but not at him, at the phantoms on the wire. "You hear that? Come get me! Now! I surrender!"

"Cleo, Cleo," he finally wedged in. "Calm down. Let's talk about this a minute."

"Calm down. Right. You're not the one they're tappin'."

"Come on now. Take a deep breath and just hear me out, okay?"

Now he heard nothing. "Cleo?"

"You said you wanted to talk, so talk."

"All right. First of all, you are absolutely right: They are listening in to every one of your phone calls, incoming, outgoing, it doesn't matter."

"That is so reassuring, Jake. Thank you so much."

"But, just because they are doesn't mean you're giving up your right not to incriminate yourself, so anything you say can't be held against you, whether they hear it or not."

"It is so great to know that, Jake," she said, then yelled, "because we all know how you can always trust the cops!"

Katz rubbed his free hand over his eyes, then tugged it down his face. "Cleo, even if they do hear it, no judge will allow it in as evidence against you in court. All that was spelled out in the agreement you signed back at the courthouse." He waited for another dose of sarcasm, but when it didn't come, he went on. "And, they also can't listen in to this call or any calls between you and me, because they're protected by the attorney-client privilege, and guaranteed to be confidential."

"Yeah, right. And they're the ones guaranteeing it. Nice fucking setup you've got goin' here!" she let the specters know.

"Cleo, they're gone," Katz said, hoping he was right. "Just trust me if you don't trust them, all right? Nothing from any conversation you ever have with me will come back to haunt you. The courts will throw it out. They call it the fruit of the poisonous tree."

"I call it bullshit. Thanks a lot for nothin', Jake!"

The slam of her phone made him wince again. He stood there, trying to make some sense of the call, the day, the case, his life – until he realized he was a man holding a phone, listening to a dial tone, staring at a blank television screen. Before he read too much into that, he reached over and turned the TV back on. Now it was 92-64. He tried not to read too much into that either, turned it back off, hung up the phone, and headed for the bathroom. He'd just about wrapped up his ablutions when he heard the phone in the bedroom ring. He perched himself on the side of the bed, took a deep breath, and picked it up. He got out "Hello" this time.

"Jake, it's me. I just got a call, from the FBI – but first I want to tell you I'm sorry. I really am. I had no business – "

"Cleo, you don't owe me any apologies. It's okay."

"But I feel awful. The second I hung up, I knew I fucked up. You've done a lot for me, Jake, and I want you to know I really appreciate it."

"Cleo, thank you, but that's what I'm here for. I'm your lawyer and I want you to tell me what's on your mind so I can help you sort through it."

"God, that sounds more like a shrink!" she laughed.

"Vell," Katz said, "the doctor is in at any time. So what'd the FBI want?"

"They're sending somebody over here tomorrow afternoon – some guy who's going to look like a plumber or something – to sit with me when I make my first call."

"Okay."

"And I asked him if my lawyer could sit in too."

"Did he have a problem with that?" Katz asked, just to give himself a minute to think. He had every right to be there, but the thought of sitting with a cooperating witness on a tapped call did tighten his bowels a bit. He knew he had to say yes, if only to assure her she could count on him, but that didn't loosen his sphincter one iota.

"He didn't seem to. Can you do it, Jake? It would mean a lot."

"Absolutely," he said with the most confidence he could muster through clenched teeth. "We're in this together."

"Thank you, thank you, thank you!" Cleo said. "I mean it."

"When's he going to be there?"

"He said like mid-afternoon sometime."

"All right. I'll plan on getting there around two. Just one thing though, how do I get in without anyone noticing? My plumber outfit's at the cleaners."

Cleo took a second to think about that. "You know where I live, right?"

He remembered her smiling wave one more time. "Yep."

"Well, come up the sidewalk on 5th and just before my house, there's an alley that leads back to a bunch of parking spaces and a lot of other houses, so no one'll think you're coming to my place. Make a right off of that into the first alley and go in the second door, which'll put you on my patio. I'll leave the back door open for you."

"That's another good plan." Katz tried hard not to think there was any connection between her talent for subterfuge and her – alleged – crimes against the republic. "I will see you tomorrow."

"Thank you again, Jake. I'm so glad you can be there – and I won't call back, I promise! Get some sleep. You earned it."

"Good night, Cleo." He hung up, turned out the lights, slipped under the sheets, and closed his eyes. This time it wasn't Marty's face he saw smiling back at him.

13

Just after two the next afternoon, Katz pushed open Cleo's back door to see her leaning against the refrigerator across from him. Legs crossed, a cup of something in her hand, the sweet smile he imagined really beaming back at him, she made a gray U.S. Army sweatshirt and bright blue spandex pants tapering into grungy sweat socks look damn good. She gave him the once over too, shaking her head and coughing that laugh.

"What's so funny?" he asked.

"You always look like this when you go see a client?" Katz looked down at the XL field jacket he picked up at Sunny's Surplus hanging over his ripped jeans and high black Chucks, then back at her. "I shaved."

"Well, that does make up for everything else, no question." She gave her head one last shake. "Can I get you something while we wait for 'the plumber'?"

"What're you drinking?"

"Cocoa, straight up."

"Works for me."

She motioned him to sit at the small table against the wall to her right. He checked out the premises as best he could through the doorway to the living room. Plush light blue sofa with step tables on both sides, a couple of high-backed ornate wooden chairs, stereo system on shelves above a big black Sony TV/VCR combo. He tried not to think how she came by all of it, but couldn't help but think he really did need some new shit. She set a steaming cup in front of him.

"This is really nice," he said.

Cleo shook her head. "You should see the upstairs, what the fucking Feds did to it."

"They searched it? When?"

"Had to be while I was in Lorton. I sure as hell didn't leave it like that. Drawers on the floor, papers all over, bed ripped up. It's all I've been doing to straighten everything up since I got back. Bastards!"

"Did they take anything?"

"Probably. I haven't gone through all the papers yet, just scooped 'em up and stuffed 'em back in my desk so I could walk to the goddamn bathroom." She started to sit down, then turned to grab an ash tray and a pack of Kools off a counter. "You mind?"

"It's your house, Cleo."

She shook one out and pushed a matchbook out of the pack's plastic wrapper. She lit up, sucked down a deep drag, and took her seat. "I was trying to quit – really, and when they locked me up, I actually thought that might be the one good thing to come of it but, uh-uh, only made it worse. I mooched one off a guard every chance I could. They fucking hated me." She inhaled again and kept it all in again. "Since you dropped me off, I must've smoked two packs, no shit. It sucks but I can't help it. Sorry."

"Don't be sorry. You're under a lot of stress."

"Tell me about it." She pulled another drag in.

"You own the place?" he asked.

"No, Rayful. But he lets me live here rent free, so I can afford to dress it up a little."

"And what is it, two bedrooms?"

"Two upstairs, and another – "

A phone ringing in the living room cut her off. She jumped out of her chair like it was an ejection seat. "Oh my Good God Jesus Christ! What am I supposed to do? Where's that goddamned plumber?"

"Cleo," Katz yelled over the ringing, "what do you normally do, answer it or let it go to the machine?"

"Answer it!" She lurched toward the side table where the phone sat, then back again. "Ray don't allow messages." The phone cried out again. "Shit!" she shouted.

"Okay," Katz said, "then answer it, just like normal. Can you put it on speaker?"

She nodded yes and he pointed at one of the high-back chairs.

"I'll sit over there, just to listen in and give you any help I can."

"Okay, okay," she said and pitched herself onto the sofa. She reached for the phone, then turned to Katz and pointed a trembling finger at him, grimmer than he'd ever seen her. "Do not make a fucking sound!" she spat out. He held up his hands, then made a motion to hit the speaker button. She took a quick breath, blew it out, then jabbed her quivering finger at the phone until the speaker light came on.

"Hello," she said, but it sounded more like a question. Katz spread his hands to calm her down but she was focused on the phone.

"Yeah. What's up?" a man's voice on the other end said. Cleo looked at Katz like she wasn't quite sure who she was talking to, but she said "Hi."

"What's happenin'?" the man said.

"Who is this?"

"This is Ray, baby. What's up?"

"This isn't Rayful."

"I got somethin' in my throat," he said.

"No, it is not Rayful," she said and shot Katz a worried glance. He'd stopped breathing when she punched up the phone and couldn't think of a reason to start now.

"Yes, it is, Cleo."

"No, it is not," Cleo said, her voice tightening.

The man laughed. "Ha! You got me. This is Tony. What's up?" Cleo fell back on the cushions and put her hands over her eyes. She pulled herself together in an instant and looked at Katz. *Tony Lewis* she mouthed, then leaned back to the phone. "I knew it wasn't Ray. Baby, how you doing?"

"Good, good," Tony said. "Say, where you been? Been trying to reach you the last few days."

Cleo looked at Katz while she answered. "Woman's business, Tony. You don't want to know. Couldn't even get out of bed till yesterday and last thing I wanted to do was chit-chat on the phone with anyone, believe me."

"Oh, I believe you." They heard him talk to someone in the background. "Ray say he definitely don't want to know either." Katz threw her a salute and resumed breathing.

"So what's up?" Cleo asked, holding her eyes steady on him.

"Ray wants to know if you ever got the Range Rover."

Now Cleo breathed a sigh of relief. "No. You know they closed at six the last time I went."

"Yeah, he knows that. Nothin' since then?"

"Naw, baby, I've been laid up like I said. He want it today? I'll go get it."

Something outside the window behind Cleo caught Katz' eye – a fat guy holding a fat tool box heading up the front walk. He bolted from his chair and raced past Cleo, hearing her "What the – " and Tony's "You say something, girl?" as he opened the door. The plumber stopped dead at the sight of him, a very quizzical look in his eye.

Katz heard Cleo say, "No, baby, just clearin' my throat," before he pulled the door shut quietly and approached the plumber with a big grin on his face.

"Hi!" he said, offering his hand. "I'm Ms. Smythe's lawyer and I know you're not a plumber. She just got a call that's probably going to go better if we don't make any noise 'cause the guy on the other end might get suspicious, I'm sure you'll agree." The plumber, a pale white guy probably younger than Katz, reached up slowly, his broad blank face trying hard to compute exactly what was happening. Katz grabbed his hand, still smiling, and swept his arm to the door. "Let's just walk up the steps and chat outside till she hangs up, okay?"

The plumber looked him up and down, then tipped his head to the side. "You're a lawyer?" Katz heard the door pull open behind him and turned to see Cleo, mouth smiling but eyes glaring.

"Oh hi, Mr. Plumber," she said. "Sorry I couldn't come to the door – but I was on the *phone*? Please do come in." She held the door for both of them.

"Everything go okay?" Katz murmured as he passed her. "So far," she said. "He said they'll call back about the car."

The plumber dropped his box by the door and waited for Cleo to close it. "You Miss Smythe?" he asked but didn't wait for her answer. "Joe Mazerski, FBI." Then he nodded to Katz. "And he's really your lawyer?"

"He is," Cleo said.

"Also known as Jake Katz," Katz said. "Sorry about all that outside. Just trying to protect my client."

"O-kay," Mazerski said and turned back to Cleo. "So, was that your first call today?"

Cleo hacked out a laugh. "You don't know? You are wiretapping me, right?"

"I just set it up, Miss Smythe. I don't do the listening."

"So who is?" she asked.

"Before I get into that, did you tell Mr. Katz these people were going to call you back?"

"I thought you didn't do the listening."

"Miss Smythe, if they are calling you back, I need to set up quick to make sure everything's working before they do. So, again, are they?"

"Yeah, but I'm not sure when. And what's all the gear for? I thought the phone was already bugged."

Mazerski flipped open the hasps on his toolbox and lifted the lid.

"Your actual phone's not bugged," he said. "It's on the telephone pole out there."

He brought out a small metallic tripod, pulled out the legs, and set it up against the wall next to the window behind the sofa, then dipped back into the box to pull out what looked like a tiny black earphone poking up from what looked to Katz like a black poker chip with a screw attached. He screwed the chip into the top of the tripod, then took out a brown headset with cushiony brown earpieces and put it around his neck. A cord from one of the earphones led to a gizmo in his hand that looked like a cheap transistor radio.

"So here's the deal," he said. "Ordinarily, we'd do a test call to make sure we're getting the signal loud and clear, and the tape's working. But if they're calling you back, that's an even better test."

"This shit's not gonna stay here, is it?" Cleo asked.

"Just for the call. When I go, it goes. So, what you asked, about who's listening? There's a bug on your line up on a telephone pole, which is really a little radio transmitter just like the one on the tripod here, set to the same frequency, and just like I can hear it, someone's listening to it at the Bureau around the clock."

148

"Twenty-four hours a day?" Cleo asked.

"Twenty-four hours a day. Anytime somebody says something on it, incoming, outgoing, it doesn't matter, somebody's there hearing every word."

"No matter who?"

"No matter who," he said, "but – if they hear you talking with Mr. Katz, they'll hang up and wait for the next call. But understand, those guys're sitting on your line because they don't want to miss something they might hear too late, like, say, somebody talking about killing someone, okay?"

"Okay," Cleo said. "So let's go back to the telephone pole. What if some good citizen walkin' his dog saw you up there in the middle of the night and called it in – or maybe some not so good citizen saw you and put two and two together? Then what?"

A case Katz had a few years ago popped into his mind. His client was – allegedly – a small-time drug dealer who couldn't believe he got busted. He told Katz he saw someone shinnying down a telephone pole when he was coming home stoned from a party one night around four in the morning, but chalked it up to a drug hallucination and didn't think about it again – until he was busted a few weeks later. Katz told him he was just paranoid, but after he made a few inquiries of his former colleagues, he knew the guy was probably right, even though he couldn't prove it.

"Ms. Smythe," Mazerski said, "that could happen, but if MPD gets a call like that, the drill is they say 'thank you sir, we'll check it out,' then let us know they got the call. But that's as far as it goes. No one checks it out. No one even logs the call. If the citizen calls back, they tell him they checked and it was just a C and P guy putting in some overtime."

"Jesus Christ. And I'm the criminal! What a fucking racket!"

"As far as the not-so-good citizen, I don't think you –." The phone cut him off. He pulled his headphones up over his ears, then pointed to Cleo and gave her a thumbs up. Katz sat back down in his chair and Cleo sat back on the couch. She punched the speaker and said hello. A man's voice said "Hey, Cleo, how you doin'?" It didn't sound like Tony, or Tony trying to sound like Rayful either.

"Jerry, that you?" she said.

"It is, sugar. What's happenin'?"

"Nothin' much. Ray talk to you?"

"Yeah, he says you can pick up the car anytime this week, whenever works best for you."

"Aw, he's a sweetie. I'll go after I get back from the pool." Katz heard him mumble something to someone else. Cleo stole a look at Mazerski, who took his hand off a dial on the gizmo to give her another thumbs up.

"He says that's cool," Jerry said. "Also, he just wanted to know if you know a judge or something in Virginia, that could look out for my man."

"Who, Ray?"

"Naw, Dave."

"Dave? What happened to Dave?"

"He got locked up."

"When?"

"Yesterday," Jerry said. "We think."

Cleo looked at Katz with a questioning look. He mouthed *Lawyers yes, judge no*. "Uh no," she said, "wait, yeah, I do know somebody I think, but he's a lawyer, not a judge."

Katz heard Jerry again with whoever was there with him. "She says she knows somebody, a lawyer, not a judge. . . . I just told her. She didn't know till I told her. I told her. She says she knows a lawyer. . . . Yeah." Then he was back on the phone with her. "Yeah, he says he wants you to."

"Does he want me to call him?"

"Naw, he wants you to call Dave." The guy in the background was talking now. "He's in the D.C. jail."

"Okay."

"Okay," Jerry said, "he's gonna get Rachelle to call you and tell you everything. He's gonna call Rachelle right quick."

"All right," Cleo said. "I'll wait on her to call me."

"All right. You wait by the phone then. Bye bye."

The phone went dead. Katz and Cleo both looked at Mazerski. He dropped the phones around his neck and said "Perfect. Clear as a bell. Even picked up most of what the dude in the back was saying. Good work. One minute so I know the tape worked." He pulled a fat black mobile phone out of the toolbox and punched the numbers in on his way into the kitchen.

Cleo fell back into the sofa and shook her head. "I got a real bad feeling about this."

"You sounded completely natural to me, Cleo," Katz said.

"Yeah, maybe, but now Dave's picked up. The walls are closin' in, man. Someone's going to know someone's turned, I'm telling you."

"But maybe they'll think it's Dave, or whoever's picked up next. Or maybe whoever got Dave busted – and you really sounded surprised when you said you had no idea he got picked up. They heard that too, I bet." Cleo fell back and kept shaking her head at the ceiling.

"All right," Mazerski said. "I'm out of here." He folded up the tripod and threw his headphones into the toolbox. "The tape worked fine so no worries there."

"No worries, right," Cleo said. "You can let yourself out." He did and Katz got up to watch him go down the walk, then turn right down the sidewalk to a patchy gray van with a ladder clamped to the top, an empty blue bucket hanging from it. No name on the side, no phone number, no nothing except an ordinary D.C. plate on the back. He watched it pull away and head down 5th, then scanned the street for another thirty seconds or so just to make sure nothing seemed too weird. Nothing did, so he turned back to see Cleo, still on the couch, her eyes covered with both hands.

"Who's Jerry?" Katz asked.

"He's Rachelle's boyfriend or maybe husband, I don't really know."

"And Rachelle's Rayful's sister."

"There you go," Cleo said. "You're keepin' up."

"And the guy in the background, was that Ray?"

"Yeah, he always – ". The phone rang again.

"Wow," Katz said. "You are a popular person."

She rolled her eyes and waited for him to sit back down before she punched up the speaker. "Hey, Cleo," a woman's voice said. *Rachelle*, Cleo let him know.

"Hey, Rachelle."

"Jerry told you they picked up Dave, right?"

"Yeah."

"And did he tell you the police raided him and Niecey's house too?"

"No!"

"Well they did, and they took all her reefer, her phone bills, papers, her pictures too. You know they gonna go after everybody in there, you know, who this, who that."

Cleo thought a bit about that before answering. "You talking about the ones in her living room, the holiday pictures?"

"Oh yeah."

"Shit! I'm in there."

"I know you are, honey, and so am I. Art says they gonna try and get everyone on a conspiracy thing with Dave." Katz waved his hand and Cleo turned to look at him. *Art?* he mouthed. *Who's Art?* She held up a finger, opened a drawer under the coffee table, and pulled out a pad and pencil. She scribbled on it while Rachelle went on.

"They talked to Kathy too. She say she don't tell nobody her business an' I don't either. I told her, I already started burnin' everything in my fireplace – receipts, records, money – I don't care, everything."

Cleo held up the pad. He leaned forward and read "Art Reynolds – 1 of Ray's lawyers, business shit." He knew Art Reynolds by reputation, some of it good, some of it not. He gave her the OK sign. "Shit, I'll do that too," Cleo said.

"You got to. And Dave, shit – when he got busted? – he told Jerry and Ray and them he'd been robbed and was cryin' at 'em to come on over there with their guns and shit, get these motherfuckers. And he's carryin' on, screamin', all boo-hoo saying they beat him bad and everything, tellin' 'em they gotta come and get their shit."

"Did they go?"

"No. And you wanna know why? 'Cause the number he left? I looked it up – it was the Airport Police!"

"Are you shittin' me?"

"Oh no, I ain't. And Ma called him back!"

"What, to that number? The Airport Police?"

"That's right, and from my house! And look what she did. She say 'Can I speak to Dave?' They say 'He's busy, who's this?' Ma say 'A friend. Who's this?' They say 'A friend' and I hung the phone up so they couldn't trace it back, 'cause the police always tell you they're a friend when they raid something, so I hung it right up."

"Holy shit!" Cleo said. "That's scary, Rachelle!" What was scary to Katz was how well she was playing her part. No death grip on the phone, no tremble in the voice,

155

just as cool as can be. If he didn't know it, he never would've guessed she was wired, so there was no way Rachelle would ever suspect.

"Yeah, it is," Rachelle said, "but what made me really worry, Cleo, was the business with the news. That scared me." Cleo threw Katz a quizzical look. He threw one right back.

"Where?" she said. "On TV?"

"Yeah."

"I didn't see it. I don't know nothin' about it."

"It was real small," Rachelle said, "a small thing sayin' the cops seized 35 pounds of cocaine. But I said 'Wait a minute, that's big shit', to get 35 pounds of coke, right? It just didn't register why this shit wasn't all over TV. So I told Ray and them 'Dave was trying to get you out there,' holdin' all that shit right out there for them to come out there and get it. They was gonna close their investigation right there!"

"And what'd they say?"

Katz waved his hand to Cleo and motioned her to hand him the pad and pencil. She did and he sat back and scribbled his own note, then handed the pad back to her. She read it while Rachelle was talking.

"Ray say 'Naw, Rachelle always worried'. But Tony, he say 'Well, I'm listenin' to her. I ain't goin' no motherfuckin' where like that.' And then come to find out, he was with the police, just like I tol' 'em!"

"Wow!" Cleo said, glancing back at the pad. "So wait, back up a minute. How'd they get Dave to begin with?" Katz gave her the thumbs up.

"Police lady caught him in the elevator out there in that hotel by the airport carryin' all that shit, that's how."

"What?"

"They was on the elevator."

"With the shit?"

"With the shit. He was in 310 and the police was in 309. She come off the elevator with him and when he opened the door, this bitch go right in with him."

"Are you fucking kidding me?"

"I told 'em. I said 'Dave oughta know you don't ride in no elevator with no people when you got that shit on you.'"

"Why are they even messin' with these people from California, Melvin and them? Isn't that really just kinda dumb?"

"Daddy told Rayful 'Do not mess with these people.' He said 'Leave that shit alone because they already connectin' you with that, just go on about your business,' but Rayful just go right on behind Daddy's back. *Now* he sayin' 'I know I shouldn'ta done it, but I was doin'

157

it for Tony.' Oh! And Dave got Melvin locked up out in LA too because he ratted him out, so now everyone in the shit."

"How 'bout you?" Cleo asked, with what Katz couldn't help but feel was totally genuine concern.

"Like I say, I'm burnin' everything up," Rachelle said. "Police come at me, I'm gonna tell 'em 'That's my brother all right but I don't associate with him like that, you know. We grew up, he had his family, I had mine. We see each other holidays and that's it.' Plus I have never personally seen Rayful and my father do anything, so even if they called me to say something, all I'd be doing is assuming or insinuating – "

"That's exactly what I'm gonna say too, it comes to it. I've never actually seen him do anything."

"But they got some goddamned reliable source, Cleo. Do you hear what I'm tellin' you?" Katz waited for Cleo to shoot him a look, but she didn't. She just went on, as natural as ever. "I think they're just following everybody, Rachelle," she said. "I mean, they're gonna get all this stuff if they're following people – "

"I don't know. Somebody talkin' And once somebody start talkin', everyone gonna start rattin' everyone else out, save their ass – they think."

"Well, I'm going to do just what you're doin'," Cleo said. "Won't be a thing here links me to anyone, anything."

"You go do that, girl. Hey look, I gotta run. You gonna call that lawyer, right? Help Dave get his sorry ass out?"

"Yeah, I'm on it."

"Okay then," Rachelle said. "Keep your head down."

"You too, baby," Cleo said and hung up the phone. She fell back onto the cushion and clapped her hands over her eyes again.

"Cleo," Katz said, "I don't know how you did that, but you were fantastic. She had no idea you were, you know – "

"About to get 'em all put away for life?"

"That's not exactly what I was going to say."

"You didn't have to." Cleo tipped over to fall on to the couch, her hands still shielding her eyes, covering everything but the tears running through her fingers. He came to her side and started stroking her hair, just like he did that day in the courthouse when she signed up for all this. He started to say something, then thought better of it. In a few seconds, she pulled her hands down and let them fall on the cushion. "Oh shit!" she said and rolled her eyes at the ceiling. He saw her eyes burning red and wet and couldn't help himself from running the back of his hand down her cheek until she finally looked up at him and smiled. Then he couldn't help himself leaning over and kissing her gently on the lips. She kissed him back, then ran a hand up his cheek and pulled back to look at him, a sweet smile belying her sad eyes. "Jake?"

"Yeah, Cleo?"

"You need to go."

14

Despite the chill, Katz decided a brisk walk to work Monday morning would give him time to wrestle with a legal question he never had to face before: Was he ethically permitted to screw a client – not the way Harry screwed his – but the way men and women had always done it, lawyers or no? He'd hoped the crispness of the air and the length of the walk would help him sort it out, but he realized in less than a block that the answer depended solely on what D.C.'s Rules of Professional Conduct said, and not only did he have no idea what they said, he couldn't even remember where he put them.

The walk turned out to be just a long cold extension of the mental masturbation he hadn't engaged in since high school: Did Cleo really like him, or was it just an act? Was she telling him the truth, the whole truth, and nothing but the truth, or was she just using him? And if she was using him, for what possible purpose? And why did she tell him to go – because she was afraid he wouldn't be able to contain himself, or because – he was really pushing the edges of his imagination now – she was afraid she wouldn't be able to help herself? And, oh yeah, was she really just a pawn in Rayful's game, or a queen? By the time he got to his office, the only thing he was sure of was that he should have driven. He was frozen – and more confused than when he stepped out the door.

He hoped LaVerne's smiling face might snap him out of it, but there was no smile on the face that turned to him, just wide eyes that frightened him until she tipped her head to a face that scared him worse. Harry rose from the folding chair, a little larger, older, and even unhappier than Katz remembered him. "Katz!" he said, barely containing something – rage, frustration, acid reflux? "We need to talk."

"Okay, Harry. Can we do it back in chambers?" He gestured to his office and Harry grabbed his briefcase and strode in ahead of him. Katz looked at LaVerne, whose eyes followed Harry through the door, then flicked to him. "I might take an early lunch," she said. "Like now."

"Stay here, please," he begged. "I may need a witness. And take notes. You'll hear him just fine." LaVerne sighed and flipped open her steno pad. "Okay," she said, looking up at him. "And if you need any help? I promise you I will go get some."

When Katz closed the door behind him, Harry was standing in front of his desk, arms folded across his chest, until he aimed a large index finger straight at him. "Your client needs to start losin' anything she's got that ties her to Rayful, pronto," he said. "Like yesterday."

Katz had already heard that from Rayful's sister, but he wasn't about to let Harry know it. "Why? What're you talking about, Harry?"

"The shit is about to hit the fan, Jake. Hell, it's already hittin' the fan. People are getting picked up and you know's well as I do that everyone's gonna start turnin' on everyone else. She needs to get rid of everything that connects her to him – phones, guns, drugs, anything she can burn or shred, everything, man!"

"Who got picked up?" Katz asked, trying to act as natural as his client.

"The name Dave McCraw mean anything to you?"

Katz pretended to think about it, then said "No, I don't think so. Who's Dave McCraw?" He held his breath to see if he could actually shit a shitter.

"He's one of them the cops picked up." He could.

"Where? How?" Katz pressed his luck.

"Out in Virginia somewhere, near the airport, National."

"Was that the thirty-five pounds I heard about?" The squint in Harry's eyes told him he'd pressed too far. "Where the fuck did you hear that?" Harry said, giving Jake just enough time to remember where Rachelle said she heard it.

"TV," Katz said, hoping Harry didn't catch the sudden whiff of sweat he did. "It was on the news a few days ago."

"The TV, huh? The TV tell you anything else?"

"No. That was it. It was a real short piece, but it caught my attention, for obvious reasons."

"Uh huh. Just the TV then, not your client, huh? What else she tell you an' who else she tellin' it to?" Katz couldn't remember if Mao Tse Tung or his high school football coach said the best defense was a good offense but he was grateful one of them did.

"You know, Harry, I could ask you the same question."

"What? You think I'm representin' a rat?"

"I don't know who you're representing, Harry, and I don't care, but you said it: Somebody's talking. How do I know it's not whoever your client is?"

Harry held up his hands. "Jake, take a step back, okay? Ain't no sense us pissin' all over each other about this, at least now. Let's stick to what I came here to tell you. Your client needs to get rid of anything that's going to point to Rayful, asap."

Katz realized he was still standing in his overcoat, still holding his briefcase. He walked behind his desk, dropped the briefcase, took off the coat, and folded it over the back of his chair. He survived one trip to the edge, so he thought he'd take another one. "Who told you to do this, Harry? Billy? Rayful?"

"Didn't need nobody to tell me nothin'. This is what you do, Jake."

"No, this is what *you* do, Harry. I know who I'm dealing with." He tried to ignore his own little ethical issue tapping at the base of his brain.

164

"Listen to me," Harry said. "This is no time to worry about ethics or any airy-fairy bullshit other than what's best for your client, Rayful – and you!"

"Am I being intimidated, Harry?" Katz asked, now trying to ignore his speeding heartbeat.

"You're being informed, Jake," Harry said, now close enough to jab his finger in his chest, "reminded, okay, about what you already know. Your client Goldilocks has got a right not to incriminate herself, period. The other side's got all the fucking tools they need – Wiretaps! Warrants! Police! If they got a case, let 'em prove it! They don't need our side to give 'em a helpin' hand."

And I don't need to get disbarred by destroying evidence, Katz thought. He was just about to show him the door when it occurred to him that Harry might actually be able to give him a helping hand. "Okay, Harry, message received. Now I'll ask you something my client asked me. I don't know if it's for Dave McCraw or anyone else, but do you know any Virginia lawyer who might want to get involved in this?"

"Oh, now that *you* want something, you tell me what Goldilocks says, is that how it goes?"

"A guy I called out there couldn't do it, but he mentioned Art Reynolds' name," Katz confected. "You know anything about him?"

"Art Reynolds? Yeah, I know him, but he practices in DC and Maryland. I don't know if he's even licensed in

165

Virginia, plus he's already involved. Maybe a little too much."

"What do you mean?"

"I mean he doesn't always take his pay in cash."

"And that's how he's involved?"

"That, and he's representin' Rayful too, not on the criminal side, more civil stuff."

"Anyone you know in Virginia that might want to get involved?"

"Yeah, some guy named Whitestone, Whiteside, something like that. Call me when I get back to my office, I'll get it for you." Katz weighed the costs and benefits of calling him and surprised himself by saying "Okay."

"All right," Harry said, "but for right now, you just get missy to get rid of her shit, okay? Now."

"Understood, Harry. Message received." He circled the desk and Harry, and opened the door. LaVerne spun away from them to roll a piece of letterhead through her typewriter. "Anything else?" Katz asked. Harry stewed on that a minute, then said "Yeah. Pick up the goddamn phone when I call you so I don't have to drag my ass up here again."

Katz followed him out and watched him throw the door open so hard it banged against the wall and slapped back shut. He waited for the thunder of Harry's footsteps to ebb to a low rumble, then turned to LaVerne with mock outrage. "I told you to put the man through whenever he called. Now see what you've done?"

"That is one angry black man," she said.

"I don't know. He might be more scared than angry."

"Are you okay?" He took inventory and was surprised to see he was. "I think so, but – new policy – whenever he calls again, I will take it, at least till this thing's done."

"All right," LaVerne said, "but that means you're going to have to let me know where you are when you're not here. Oh, and speakin' of that, I got a call from Mr. Madden while you two were goin' on in there."

"Oh, right," Katz said, remembering Saturday's asterisk. "Did he leave a number?" "Yeah," she said, and read "207,106 dollars and 23 cents" off her pad. "He wouldn't tell me what it was, but I made him repeat it and whatever it is, that's it. He said you'd know what it means."

"I do. Give it to me again." He wrote it down, and now remembered something else. "Next order of business. Do you know where the code of conduct is, the thing the D.C. Bar puts out?"

"I do." She walked into his office, turned to the file cabinet to her right, reached into the third drawer down, riffled past a few folders, pulled one out, and handed it to him. He saw the tab said Code of Conduct.

"LaVerne, what would I do without you?"

"That is a good question. Cry? Starve? Get your own lunch?"

"All of the above." He took his seat. "Close the door behind you, thanks."

When it was shut, Katz opened the file and pulled out what he quickly realized was a previously unopened booklet entitled Rules of Professional Conduct. He found the Conflict of Interest section in the index, thumbed to it, and scanned down the list of prohibitions. He was just about to declare victory when he tripped, two words before the finish line. The last subparagraph prohibited a lawyer from representing a client in any matter where:

> The lawyer's professional judgment on behalf of the client will be or reasonably may be adversely affected by the lawyer's responsibilities to or interests in a third party or the lawyer's own financial, business, property, or *personal interests*.

He ran his finger down the Comments section that was ten times longer than the rule until he came to a passage under "Situations That Frequently Arise" that said:

> A lawyer might not be able to represent a client vigorously if the client's adversary is a person with whom the lawyer has longstanding personal or social ties.

There was his escape hatch. No one could say the week he knew Cleo was a "longstanding" tie. He shook his clenched fist and muttered what he thought was a quiet "Yes!" until he heard LaVerne call in. "Jake? Everything all right?"

"Perfect," he called back, "great!" and kept believing that until he opened the folder to put the booklet back and saw a stapled article ripped from the D.C. Bar's magazine. When he pulled it out and saw that it was from the July issue, he remembered ripping it out for future reference. The Bar was requesting comment on a new set of proposed rules. The print was so small he could barely read it, but he managed to find the conflicts section and skimmed it to see if he'd still be able to ethically violate Cleo.

The 'personal interest' section looked identical to the old one, so he mentally crossed his fingers and scanned down a Comments section that was now probably twenty times longer than the rule. He made it through a full thirty-six comments before he found what he hoped he wouldn't, buried in the middle of one entitled "Sexual Relations Between Lawyer and Client". He squinted to read it.

> A sexual relationship between lawyer and client can involve unfair exploitation of the lawyer's fiduciary role and thereby violate the lawyer's basic obligation not to use the trust of the client to the client's disadvantage.

He dropped the article back in the file and slapped it shut. His defeated brain was capable of only two thoughts. One, the rules in place now would let him off the hook, so if he made his move quick enough, he'd still be able to at least claim he was ethical. Two, he understood for the first time why Harry didn't give a damn about ethics.

15

Katz had never been one for too much introspection because he never saw the value of exploring his inner depths, much less figuring out why he didn't. Maybe that's why practicing criminal law appealed to him: It didn't matter what was really true, or why. It only mattered what the jury – or if you were a defense attorney, just one juror – *believed* was true.

He'd also never seen the point of figuring out why he turned out to be a pretty good criminal lawyer. Was it because he had a natural gift for the mental gymnastics and theatrics it required, or because he'd learned to be good at it, through studying, watching, mimicking? Whatever the reason, things were what they were, period, and that was always more than enough to deal with anyhow.

He remembered way back, when he had to choose between the work his heart wanted him to stick with – staying on the MPD – or the work his brain knew he'd be good at – becoming a lawyer. He followed his brain, not because it was telling him the right thing or his heart was telling him the wrong thing, but because all the forces in his life at the moment he made the choice compelled him to. A moment of clarity, he'd called it then, but twenty-two years later, he still couldn't explain to himself why it was so clear. At that precise moment, it just was.

Unfortunately, everything in his life since that moment lacked clarity all the time. His inability to conjure up a satisfactory answer to why Cleo'd pushed him away was only the latest exhibit. Maybe she was just shocked by it. Maybe she didn't like him 'that way'. Maybe she had more than enough to deal with without dragging an affair with her lawyer into the mix. A million more maybes led his trained legal mind to a million more dead ends.

In the deep recesses of his brain and his heart, he clung to what he hoped was the best reason: She knew that kiss could only lead to complications that might wind up killing her. Any sign of him at her place – or in her company anywhere other than his office or a courtroom – would only raise questions in the minds of Rayful's crew that had no good answers, only fatal ones. As grim as that calculation was, it let Katz hold on to the faint wisp of hope that if they ever did somehow manage to make those complications disappear, she might actually come to like him that way. For now, though, both his head and his heart were telling him the same thing: Move on. If that was the clarity he was looking for, he hoped it was only temporary.

The fact was that anything he could do for her now could be handled by phone, even if the Feebies were hanging on the line, or by mail, which had the side benefit of letting Cleo tell Rayful with a straight face that she was getting rid of anything that connected her to him. He didn't have to know she was sending it all to Katz so that he could go through it and copy anything that might protect her from the Feds before he handed it over to them.

She called every day or two at first, mostly to let him know who she'd talked to or what they'd talked about, or to get his advice on what to say or not to say on any call she knew was coming up. He called her only if he had something substantive to tell her, which meant he didn't

172

call too often. The only one he remembered was the first one, the day he called her to give her the number Madden had passed along.

"That's a lot of money," she said. "Not Rayful money, but still, a lot."

"Yeah, the only problem is you might not live to spend it."

"I get it," she said, then went quiet before she added "Just something to think about."

Over the last week or so, even her calls had stopped. He told himself that what used to scare the shit out of her was now routine, so no news was good news. The last time they talked, she said she'd call him if she needed him, but apparently she didn't, because that was four days ago. All that changed when LaVerne buzzed him. He picked up the receiver. "Yeah?" "Ms. Smythe is on the phone, and she seems a little, uh, excited?"

"Like happy excited?"

"No, more like totally losin' her shit excited."

"Put her through." At the click, he said "Cleo, how are you?"

"Out of my goddamn mind, that's how I am."

"Why? What's going on?"

"The fucking Feds want me to wear a wire."

"With who?"

"Bootsie."

"Cleo, that's what we bargained for."

"Well, it's a fucking bad bargain and I want out."

Katz nearly bit through his tongue before he said "Cleo, listen to me. Out is the last place you're going if you back out of this deal. They'll throw you back in Lorton – or somewhere worse – for a very long time."

"Damn it, Jake! Why'd I ever let you talk me into this?"

Katz let that steaming pile simmer a while too. "Tell me exactly what they asked you to do," he finally said.

"They said they want me to call her to have lunch or dinner somewhere and get her to talk about a bunch of stuff that I really stopped listening to. I freaked and I'm still freaking!"

Katz sighed. "Who called you?"

"Somebody at the FBI, I have no idea who."

"Okay, let me call the U.S. Attorney's Office. Once I know what's what, I will call you back and we'll talk it through, okay?" He waited for her okay, but the slam of her phone told him he could stop waiting. He put the receiver back and looked up to call out to Laverne, but she was in the doorway.

"That as bad as it sounded?" she asked, but Katz was already lost in thought, trying to decide if he should call Hutchison or Madden to get the straight scoop. Hutchison was the line guy he ought to call, but Madden would probably be a lot easier to deal with and have the final say anyhow, so he won on points.

"Can you buzz up Charlie Madden in the U.S. Attorney's Criminal Division? Tell him it's really important I talk to him now." She scooted to her desk. A minute later she let him know he was on the phone.

"Counselor," Madden said, "what can I do for you?"

"My client tells me the FBI wants her to wear the wire with Bootsie. Is that right?"

"It is, and, as I recall, that should come as no surprise. Is there a problem, Mr. Katz?"

"No, but I just want to make sure she gives you exactly what you want. So here's my question: What exactly do you want?"

"It's really what we want from Bootsie."

"Which is?"

"I don't have a bill of particulars, Mr. Katz. You know what we're after, anything that helps show that she – Bootsie, not your client – was up to her eyeballs in this enterprise."

"I get that, but I also don't want Cleo to make her smell a rat." *Bad choice of words*, he thought after the words left his mouth.

"Look, we just want her to act how she usually does when she's with her – only maybe guide the conversation a little."

"To what? I don't want her to miss the mark and put her life on the line any more than she has to. You don't have to put your case on the table, just tell me where you want her to guide it."

He heard only silence, then a sigh. "Okay, grab a pen so I don't have to go through this again." Katz pulled his pen and his pad to him. "Okay, go." "We need to connect the dots between Bootsie and Rayful, and Bootsie and the operation, okay? So anything that ties her to specific people in the enterprise or specific events connected to moving the shit will help, especially anything about moving it across state lines." Katz scribbled his notes, racing to keep up.

"Plus," Madden went on, "anything she's doing now to help them get rid of stuff, like money, cars, furniture, anything that shows they've been making a hell of a lot more money than any W-2's going to show, or that they're obstructing justice, that's good too."

"This isn't exactly lunch-time chit chat."

"That's why your client may need to guide it a little. All it usually takes is to open the door just a crack. It is truly amazing the stuff that comes out once they start. This is what they really want to talk about, especially with each other, because there's no one else they can talk to about it. Tell her she'll do just fine. She's done great with the phone calls."

"With all due respect, Mr. Madden, those phone calls weren't face to face," Katz said. "She's scared shitless."

"What can I tell you, Mr. Katz? That's our deal, the one she signed, okay? I'm sure you can persuade her why she needs to honor it. I gotta go. Anything else? Are we done here?"

"Yeah, for now. If she comes up with anything else, I'll let you know."

"I look forward to not hearing from you," Madden said, followed by a click. Katz called out to LaVerne to call Cleo.

"Yeah?" he heard a ring later.

"It's me, Jake."

"That was fast."

"He gave me what I needed. Are you still freaking or can we go through it now?"

"I can do both, trust me."

"All right, but it's probably better you don't take notes just in case you have some unexpected company."

"That's Rayful's drill too, Jake. I can handle it. Shoot."

Katz read his own notes and tried to distill it down. "Okay," he said, "basically anything that ties Bootsie to Rayful is what they're after, especially moving the coke or the cash across state lines."

"Across state lines? Like from California? Like from Melvin and them in L.A.?" Cleo replied.

"That, or even between Maryland, D.C., and Virginia. That counts too."

"Okay. What else?"

"If Bootsie's getting rid of anything like money or cars or furniture or anything else, that'll help make the case too. That's it. What do you think?"

Cleo sighed, or maybe groaned. It was tough for Katz to tell. "Fuck," she said, "it's the shit we wind up talkin' about anyhow."

"There you go. Just do like you do? Isn't that how it goes?"

Katz heard her laugh but didn't know if it was with him or at him. "Yeah, Jake," Cleo said. "That's how we do. Just like that. Man, you are somethin'." Katz didn't want to know exactly what, so he changed the topic. "Okay, so is there anything else you want me to ask them?" He waited while she thought about it.

"Yeah," she said. "How do they put the wire on me?"

"How do they put the wire on you?"

"Yeah. Do they stick it to me or wrap it in bandages or attach it to somethin', or what?"

Katz hesitated, hearing himself ask that to Madden. "Is that really such a big deal?" he asked her.

"Yeah, it is, Jake. We always hug each other when we meet and when we say goodbye too. She feels some bug inside my top somewhere, that's all she wrote. So if that's part of the deal, man, it's off. They can send me to Leavenworth or wherever. I'm not takin' that chance."

"Okay, Cleo. I will call him back, right now."

"And this is no bullshit, Jake. You make sure he tells you exactly what's what, okay?"

"Okay. I will let you know as soon as I know." He hung up the phone but before he could ask LaVerne to call Madden back, she yelled in, "I'm gettin' him right now."

"You were listening?" Katz asked.

"Door was open, baby. I wanna know how they put it on her too."

He got up and walked to the door. "Buzz me when he's on." He pushed the door shut. "Spoil sport," he heard her yell. The phone buzzed a minute later.

179

"Mr. Katz," Madden said, "I thought we were done."

"My client had one more question."

"Okay. What's her one question?"

"How do they put the wire on her?"

"How do they put the wire on her?" Madden repeated this time.

"Right. It's important because if they hug each other, she doesn't want Bootsie to feel it, so she wants to know how they put it on her."

Madden laughed. "They clip it inside her bra and put a little pad against her, uh, skin so it's as comfy as possible, they tell me. They can hug, put their arms around each other, whatever they want – as long as she keeps her bra on, okay? Think she can handle that, or is there something about their relationship I don't know?"

"I expect she can handle it."

"I really do have to go now, Mr. Katz. But thanks for making my day."

"Do I have to ask you to call her back?" Katz called through the closed door. "Ringin' her now," LaVerne said. Katz picked up right before Cleo.

"So here's how they do it," he said. "They clip it inside your bra and put some cushion between you and the bug, so as long as you keep your bra on, she'll never know."

"Okay," Cleo said. "And who's going to put it in there? You? The plumber?" Katz opened his mouth to speak and hoped that a moment of clarity would present itself before the words came. It didn't. "I will call him back," he said and hung his head before he hung up the phone.

"Whoo, this is getting' good now," he heard through the door.

16

Every time Katz stepped to his filthy office window to look at 5th Street Northwest three floors down, he remembered Zero Mostel in *The Producers* splashing a cup of coffee on his grimy window and yelling at some Manhattan swell exiting the back seat of his Rolls, "That's it, baby! When you got it, flaunt it!" But no swells ever exited a Rolls on 5th Street, only commuters stepping off Metrobuses, or, today, splashing off. In March, D.C.'s usual humidity spilled over into rain, and this morning was wetter and grayer than most. Katz hoped his work would be less depressing, and slumped into his chair.

As was its annoying custom, his daily calendar informed him he was free all day, so he reached for the short stack of case folders recently bestowed upon him by the Superior Court. A quick flip through the files showed him they were all misdemeanors, which made the chances of going to trial – and, more to the point, cashing a check worth cashing – remote. He flipped open the top folder, but it only took him a few seconds to realize he wasn't reading the file anymore. He was thinking about Cleo, again.

Their last conversation of any length had been weeks ago, right after she filled him in on her brunch with Bootsie and told him she was worried sick that she'd shut her down too soon and would have to wear that frigging bug again and again until they finally had enough or she'd killed herself. Katz told her he'd call the U.S. Attorneys and stay on them till he heard something, but he hadn't heard a thing, so their calls had grown fewer and shorter until he just stopped making them to spare them both.

He roused himself to walk to the doorway. LaVerne was paging through *Essence* and listening to something with a beat but no discernible tune coming from a portable radio on the floor.

"Busy?" he said. She jumped in her seat and slapped both hands to her chest. "Jesus Christ, Jake!" she shrieked. "You scared the bejeebers outa me!"

"So sorry," he said, "but when you get a break, can you try the USA's again?" She muttered something dark to herself, threw an even darker look at him, then picked up the phone. By the time he was in his seat, Madden was on the line.

"Mr. Katz, how are you?"

"I'm fine, thanks, but I'm more concerned about how my client's doing."

"Then I suggest you hang up and call her. She probably knows better than me, don't you think?"

"Let me be more precise then. When I first started calling you a couple of weeks ago, it was to see if you got what you needed from her chat with Bootsie. Now, I want to know if you've got what you need from her, period."

"What's she told you?"

Katz thought how he could improve on "Nothing".

"That she's done more than enough," he decided. "And no phone call or meeting's going to give you anything more anyhow. In a word, she's done."

"That's good to know," Madden chuckled. "Too bad that's not her call."

"Mr. Madden, you didn't pick up the phone this time just to bust my chops, right?"

"I did not, but don't bust mine either, okay?"

"Okay, deal. So where do we stand?"

"We're very happy with what she's given us so far. She's holding up her end of the bargain."

"And from here on out?"

"Well, there's the little matter of her testifying at the grand jury and the trial."

"She fully intends to do that – truthfully, I might add. So is that all you need now?"

"We're not pulling the tap on her phone, Mr. Katz, if that's what you're asking."

"I'm not asking for that. But wearing the wire, face-to-face, can I tell her she can stop worrying about that? That's the thing she wants most."

"You know I can't give you a one hundred percent confirmation on that now, Jake."

"Now" and "Jake" gave him hope.

"We're off the record, Charlie," Katz said to his new best friend. "Nobody's tapping this call, right? I'm just asking you to give me something to let her know she's going to be rewarded for all this at the end of the day. That's in both our interests, isn't it?"

He heard Madden sigh, then talk a shade quieter. "Reserving the right to have her talk to anyone we think is going to be helpful, we have no present plans for her to wear a wire, and if she tells the truth at the grand jury and in the courtroom, she will not have to do any time, okay? And if anyone asks, you didn't hear any of that here. Are we clear on that too?"

"We're clear on all of it," Katz said. "I am now going to hang up and get out of your hair. Enjoy your day, Charlie, and thanks, very much." If Charlie uttered anything more than a grunt, Katz didn't hear it. He hung up and lifted two fists in victory.

"You got what you wanted, I'm guessin'?" LaVerne asked.

"I believe I did. Can you call Ms. Smythe now?" LaVerne dialed her up, then pointed to Katz and waited for him to pick up. He motioned her to shut the door, and she did just as Cleo picked up and mumbled something close to "Hello".

"Good morning, Cleo. How's your day going?"

"What?" she said sleepily. "My day? What time is it?"

185

Katz threw a look at his wall clock. "Twenty after nine. A.M."

"Jesus Christ, Jake. I'm still in bed."

"Late night?"

"No, lousy night, like all of 'em since I signed that goddamned agreement."

"Well, I think I have some very good news for you."

"Okay," he heard a shade more brightly, "I'm ready for that. Shoot."

"I just got off the phone with Charlie Madden, the chief – "

"I know who he is," Cleo cut him off, fully alert now. "What'd he say?"

"He said they're very happy with what you've given them. That's number one."

"And number two?"

"If you tell the truth at the grand jury and the trial, you will walk."

"Uh huh," she said, "and wearin' the fuckin' bug? What about that?"

Katz decided on the spot not to be too fine about it. "You're done. They've got enough."

"Are you for real? Are you serious?"

"I am. They're as happy as they can be with what you've given them."

"Oh my God, Jake! I feel like the weight of the world's off me, no shit! I could fucking cry!"

"I'm happy too, Cleo. The only tiny little grain of bad news is they're going to keep listening to your phone calls."

"Shit, Jake, I don't even think about that any more. I'm numb to it."

"That's good too. And Rayful and everyone, they're still calling you, business as usual?"

"Yeah, nothin's changed, thank God."

"And business is business as usual too?"

"Jake, I'm not lyin' to you," Cleo said. "Unless they're all great actors." *Like you?* Katz decided not to ask.

"Oh, man," she said. "I am dyin' to go somewhere no one's doin' business, no one's listenin' in, just have a normal conversation with a normal person."

"Like who?" he decided to say.

She paused, then said "Shit, you might be the only normal person I know anymore."

That made him laugh for the first time all day. "Wow! I feel so special."

"Oh, God, Jake, I didn't mean it like that," she said. "I'm sorry."

"No apologies needed. But thanks for the laugh."

"So, how 'bout it? You want to sneak out somewhere, just someplace to eat, maybe even have a glass of wine? What d'you say?" He ignored his legal instincts as soon as a small quiet restaurant in Alexandria sprang to mind, one he discovered when he had to stop for a cold one after one of his jaunts into Virginia to bail out Harry. Once he discovered the food was even better than the beer, the stop became mandatory every time he had to cross the river to cover for his so-called partner.

"Ever hear of a place called Stardust, in Alexandria?"

"No."

"The food's great and it's out of the way, kind of tucked into a residential area between D.C. and Old Town."

"I love it already."

"You know, I'd love to pick you up but I'm a little worried that if –"

"Say no more," Cleo said. "I'll cab it. Just give me the time and place and I'll meet you there."

"Sounds good. We can talk about your grand jury testimony."

"Wow, Jake, you really know how to romance a girl, don't you?"

17

The hostess greeted him like he was an old regular, even though he hadn't set foot in the place for years. She checked for his name on the list. "Looks like you're the first to arrive," she said. "Would you like to sit at the table or wait at the bar?"

The open stools at the bar behind her were too inviting to pass up. "I'll wait there, thanks," he said, slid onto a stool between two empty ones, and ordered a Johnny Walker Red on the rocks with a splash of water, the drink his dad Sam always ordered before he literally disappeared right before his bar-mitzvah. The last place anyone saw him was making his rounds in Trenton, collecting whatever people could afford to pay down their bills at E.J. Korvette or one of the other department stores that paid him to squeeze the customers. They'd talked on the phone just before whatever happened to him happened, and then he was gone, forever. He must've replayed that talk in his head a million times, always searching for some clue, some hint of why his dad vanished, but he never came up with even one that made any sense to him. Even now, as a grown man – a lawyer who knew too well how the world really worked – nothing added up.

In its own circuitous way, his father's disappearance led him to where he was right now. From the minute it happened, he wanted to be a cop, so he could solve the mystery and end all Sam's so-called friends' chatter that he faked his death to run away with some *shicksa* or, worse, the department stores' money he must have been stashing away somewhere nobody knew. Katz never believed it and his mother didn't either. She dropped them all from her life, and God too, so she'd never have to see any of them anywhere ever.

It was only after his marriage to Lisa began crumbling, right after he graduated from GW, that he had his moment of clarity and decided to go to law school and leave the MPD behind. Even now, struggling to pay his bills, he knew it was the smart thing to do, the thing that let him put his best talents to use, but he also knew he'd always miss the unpredictability, the rough and tumble, the rush of immediate gratification he loved on the beat. In time, he got over the nagging idea that he was somehow selling Sam out by leaving the force. Now, it was a moment like ordering his dad's drink that kept their bond alive. When the bartender put it in front of him and Jake lifted it in salute, the bartender lifted his own hand too, but it was Sam's face Jake saw smiling back at him.

Cleo's appearance in the doorway brought him back to the here and now. He started to wave to her, but laid his hand back down to take in a Cleo he'd never seen before. She was stunning. Her honey blond hair was longer than he remembered, falling softly on the fur collar of her dark jacket. The face was as pretty as he remembered, but there was something more defined, more striking about it than he'd ever noticed before. He didn't know much about makeup but whatever she'd done made her even more beautiful. When those pale blue eyes spotted him and crinkled, all he hoped was that he was worthy of her.

She pointed him out to the hostess, then made her way back to him, her smile lighting the way. He stood up to greet her and they hugged each other tight. She backed away first and took him in, shaking her head and hacking that laugh. He stole a look down to make sure his tie was straight and his zipper up.

"Wow!" she said. "I guess clothes do make the man. You look great!"

"You look fantastic!" he couldn't help but say, even before she slid out of her jacket and showed him how really fantastic she looked in a black silky sheath, he thought it was called, that snaked around her from neck to mid-thigh. "And you dress up nice too." She gave him a mock curtsey and slid up onto the stool he pulled out next to his.

"Last time I saw you," she said, "you looked a little more, uh –"

"Homeless?"

"Casual, I was going to say. But – homeless works too."

Before Katz could signal the bartender, the hostess came by to tell him their table was ready and walked them into a cozy dark dining room lit only by the glow of a fireplace to their left. She led them past it to the last table and pulled out a chair for Cleo. When they were both seated, a waiter appeared to drop off the menus and take her drink order.

"Vodka gimlet, neat," she said and he left them alone.

"So," Katz said, "how've you been?" She thought about that a while, eyeing him the whole time. "You remember when I told you I was numb to that thing on the phone?"

"I do," Katz said.

"I think the truth is I'm just numb to everything now."

The waiter came back with her drink and took their orders for two linguini pescatores. When he left, they raised their glasses to each other.

"Here's to getting past numb," Katz said.

Cleo clinked his glass and threw down a long swallow. "That was a good start," she said.

"So should we get business out of the way?"

"Ugh. Do we have to?"

"Five minutes tops, I promise. I just want to hit the high points of what you can expect at the grand jury, so you're not surprised by anything when you get there – and more importantly, you give them what they want."

"But you'll be there to keep me on track, right?" she said.

"No, Cleo, I won't. The grand jury's like a prosecutor's playground and the only people allowed to play on it are you, him, the court reporter, and twenty-three grand jurors whose only job is to decide if there's probable cause to find Rayful – or whoever – committed a crime. And believe me, they will give the government whatever it wants. The old joke is a prosecutor can indict a ham sandwich if he wants, except it's not a joke. It's just how it is."

Cleo shook her head. "Rayful's no ham sandwich, Jake. No one in D.C. who's ever heard of him – and that's anyone who knows anything about the street – will tell the government anything that'll get in his way. His guys will do whatever it takes to take care of business, including getting to those twenty-three people, believe me. I know."

"Cleo, I know he's supposed to be bigger than Al Capone, but the government's bigger than he is, and they've been doing this a long time." He listed the reasons on his fingers. "First, a grand jury meets in secret, with no press or anyone else around, only witnesses, and they're only there when they're actually testifying. Second, even their names are kept confidential – and third, in a big case like this one, they're put up in a hotel that not even their family knows, with U.S. Marshals protecting them around the clock. Outside of the President, no one gets more protection than a grand jury. Trust me on that."

The look on Cleo's face told him she didn't. "Jake, you don't know Rayful or his operation, okay? He gets the word about everything from people you wouldn't believe – cops, lawyers, people filin' shit in offices – they're everywhere, Jake, and they tell him ev-er-y-thing, everything! He is just totally wired, man. Shit, he probably knew the names of the grand jurors before the government did."

194

Katz uncomfortably remembered Harry telling him pretty much the same thing. He downed some more Johnny Walker to flush the memory out of his brain, then looked at Cleo, staring down at the glass she was clutching in both hands and shaking her head. He didn't know what was going on in his own head, how could he possibly know what was going on in hers? She broke the silence first. "Let's talk about something else, okay?"

Before he could answer, the waiter delivered their pescatores.

"I got an even better idea," Katz said. "Let's eat."

"And keep drinkin'," she said, rattling the cubes at the bottom of her glass at the waiter.

"Absolutely," the waiter said. "And you, sir?"

"By all means," Katz said, "except make mine wine. Anything red will do."

"A Merlot?"

"Red enough." The waiter nodded and left. They dug in, in silence, until he came back with the drinks and left again. When Katz reached over to clink her glass with his own, that brought the smallest of smiles back to her lips.

"So what do you want to talk about?" he said.

She twirled some linguini onto her fork and speared a calamari ring before she answered. "Since you know everything about me by now, let's talk about you." Katz buried the thought that he still knew next to nothing about her, and gave her the headline version of his back pages. When he got to the part about being married in '67 and divorced in '68, she nearly choked on a shrimp and held up her hand to make him stop. "Whoa, whoa, whoa!" she finally got out. "Now this I want to hear about. What was missy's name, first of all?"

"Lisa, Lisa Rubin from Cherry Hill, New Jersey, right outside of – "

"I don't care about that. What'd she look like? Was she hot?"

"Of course, what would you expect?"

"Oh, just that, of course," she laughed. "And since 1968, no one else?" *Only one that counted*, he thought, and let Marty's fine face flit through his synapses in excellent focus. "I've had my share, thank you," he said, "but a gentleman never tells." She seemed to buy that.

"And you?" he asked.

"Now?" she asked. "What man would want any piece of this?" Before Katz could decide exactly how to answer that, she made it easy on him. "The life I got now is not what you'd call real – what's the word? – conducive to romance, you know?"

"I don't want to know who you dated or married as much as I want to know who you were before you were Cleo Smythe. I seem to remember you called yourself Mary Margaret or something – "

"Margaret Ann, counselor. Get it right."

"Margaret Ann Smythe?"

She reached back into her purse and came back up with a pack of Kools and a lighter. "You mind if I smoke? Actually, I don't give a shit if you mind 'cause I'm going to smoke – and drink – if you really want me to do this." She lit one up and flipped the lighter on the table.

"Cleo," he said, "I was just curious. Talk about whatever you want. I'm just happy to be here." He went back to his linguini and tried to ignore the cloud of smoke wafting past him.

"Mahoney," he heard. "Of the Williamsburg Mahoneys."

"The lady Margaret Ann Mahoney of Williamsburg. That sounds very posh. Were you posh, Margaret Ann?"

"Let's stick with Cleo, Jake. We're talking about who I used to be, okay?"

Katz raised his wine glass to her and took a sip. "And your folks?"

"Daddy was a lawyer – a partner, excuse me – with a firm that had a lot of big fat cat clients."

"What was his specialty?"

"Scotch mostly," Cleo said. "What you ordered, in fact, except his had to be the Black. Oh, he loved him his JWB." She lowered her glass till it almost touched the

197

floor. "Here's to you, Pops," she said, then lifted it back up and threw down a long swig.

"He's dead, I take it?"

"Yep, and if there's a hell, he's deep down at the bottom of it."

"Okay. And Mom?"

"Jane. Jane Louise Dalton Gibbons Davis Mahoney. There may be more now, I don't know. That's the last I knew."

"She's still alive?"

"Last I heard."

"You don't keep in touch?"

"I did, sort of, when I first got up here – till I got hooked up with Rayful, then I didn't see the point of it, plus she was starting to lose it and it really got to be no fun going over everything five times every time we talked."

"What do you mean, she was senile?"

"Then, not totally. But by now, yeah, probably."

"How old is she?"

Cleo thought about that. "Let's see, she married Wally – "

"Wally?" Katz said.

"Daddy darling," Cleo said. "Wallace Herbert Mahoney – the Third. How's that, huh? I don't really think she wanted a kid with him – but I happened somehow, really late, so whatever, she's maybe sixty-nine or seventy now? I haven't thought about her too much lately, so, sorry, can't do much better'n that."

She threw down the last of her latest gimlet and Katz let her fiddle with her linguini a while before he asked, "So when was the last time you actually saw her?"

"That I can tell you exactly," she said. "June 28, 1984. And I can tell you exactly where too. On the first tee of the Golden Horseshoe Golf Club. I was on my way out of that burg for the last time –"

"Wait a minute. Did she know you were leaving?"

"Nope, no clue. But I had had it and I knew she'd be at the club all day like she usually was, her being the ladies' champ three years running once upon a time, blah, blah, blah – don't get me started, that I still know by heart. I knew her tee times too, so I knew exactly when I could get the hell out of there and never have to see her or Daddy Dearest again. But – I'd forgotten I'd be driving right past the club, so when I got there I actually stopped and pulled into the parking lot and I walked behind the clubhouse so I could see her and her little foursome on the first tee, but they couldn't see me and she was in her little lime green outfit, all trim and pretty even then, and I waited till she drove it – straight down the middle, by the way – and then I said 'Bye bye mama' to myself and I was up here before she putted out on eighteen."

The waiter came by and asked Katz if he could take his plate. When he looked down, he was amazed to see it was empty. Cleo was still working on hers. "Sorry," she said. "Guess I'm doin' most of the talking."

"Leave it," Katz said. "I'll wait for her to finish." The waiter nodded and left. Cleo raised a forkful of linguine to him. "Thank you, Jake. Very gallant of you."

"Anything for Lady Mahoney," he said. "So, back to your mom. Did she try to get hold of you?"

"I don't know, but good Catholic girl that I was, I called her that night from the motel I found up here somewhere. Didn't want her to worry, you know, about her little eighteen-year-old girl that just up and left. I wasn't thinking straight, you know, but I just had to get out and deal with everything else later."

"Why? Why'd you have to get out?"

Cleo shook her head and fired up another Kool. "I just couldn't stay anymore, that's what it came down to. I hated my life, I hated her, I hated Wally, and if I didn't go right then, I woulda killed all three of us."

"And when did your dad die?"

"I don't really remember. Two years after I got up here? Three years? I found out by seeing his obituary in the *Post*, just like by accident."

"Your mom didn't call you?"

"Nope. There was no way she could have. I never gave her my number or my address or anything. I wanted out, Jake – Out! Period! So I just cut the cord. If we ever talked, it was gonna be my decision, not hers."

"So did you call her after you read about it?"

"Nope, and didn't go to the funeral either. Fuck. Him." She sucked one long drag out of her cigarette then ground it out in the ashtray till every last spark was dead. Katz was still debating whether he should ask the obvious question when Cleo gave him the answer. "My dad was shitfaced drunk at least part of the day, every day, seven days a week, for years, okay?"

"Your mom too?" Katz asked. Cleo reached over and patted his hands. "Jake, you want to hear my story? Let me tell it."

"Sorry, it's the lawyer in me. Go."

She sat back and sighed. "To answer your question, when I was a kid, never – but by the time I got to be twelve or so, maybe just to deal with him, she just started getting in the bag more and more. She never let him lay a hand on me though, I will give her that. He'd cuff her around every time she'd get in the way of him going apeshit anywhere near me and she gave it right back till he finally got the picture and left me alone whenever she was around."

"But when she wasn't?"

"Until this story that you won't let me tell you, he'd always back off. It was more mind games with him, you know – he's in control and I have to do what he says. So that's what I did, not to please him, but just to show him it didn't mean squat to me. 'Make me some soup!' So I did and I brought it to him. 'You didn't ask me what kind I wanted!' he'd go. 'OK, what kind do you want?' He'd tell me something different than whatever I made, so I'd go make that and bring it to him, and this went on for months, years maybe, who knows now, on and on and on."

"God, Cleo, that's fucking horrible!"

"Yeah, it was. I'll spare both of us all the gory details and cut to the end, or at least the beginning of the end."

The waiter came by and picked up her empty plate. "Would either of you like to see the dessert menu?" "Do you have tiramisu?" Cleo asked. "We do," the waiter said and turned to Katz. "Tiramisu for two," he said. The waiter scrawled it down and left.

"So, the very short version is that one day after school – when I'm fourteen, ninth grade – I'm waiting for Wally to come home, all dressed up and ready to go with him to the mall because, in one of his rare sober moments, he said he'd take me – just me – to the mall after he got home from work to walk around and eat somewhere, you know, just like real daddies and daughters do. But he comes home drunk off his ass as usual and starts dragging himself up the stairs with me crying and screaming at him." She was back there again, eyes watering, skin flushing, until she somehow willed herself to keep going.

202

"I'll spare you the battle royale too, but cut to he finally grabs me by my shoulders and pushes me right down the stairs. It was all in slow motion, you know, like I'm falling all over myself and feeling and seeing everything, every bump and bruise, and by the time I finally roll to a stop down in the foyer, I knew that was it – Game Over! Finished! Done! So I picked my ass up and ran out the door and never looked back."

"Good God! He didn't come after you?"

"I didn't look back to see. I ran right across the front lawn to our neighbors, the Evers, and started banging on the door. Mr. Evers, bless his heart forever, opened it up and I ran past him down to the basement and hid behind a couch they had there. I'm waiting to hear Wally smash down the door and come down and get me, but all I hear is Mr. Evers and Mrs. Evers talking to each other real low, and then they come down the steps and she finds me and he bends down and he asks me what's going on and it just all pours out of me and I'm crying and snotting and he finally says 'That's enough. I'm calling child welfare.' Just like that. I remember it like it was a minute ago."

"And did the child welfare people come get you?"

"No. They told him because I was only fourteen, they'd have to send me back home – unless I was somewhere they couldn't find me, hint hint, so it became like three whole days of me being driven from one house to the other – my grandparents, my aunts, friends' houses, I don't even remember where, until the cops" – she made air quotes – "'couldn't find me' and the child welfare people had to go to court and have a hearing before a judge to figure out what to do with me."

"Wow again. So what did the judge do?"

"He gave my grandparents – Jane's folks – custody of me."

They watched the waiter set down their tiramisus. Katz took a bite but Cleo sat there, rigid, until she looked down and pulled a tissue up from her purse and pressed it to her eyes. When she took it away, all he saw was heartbreaking. "Sorry, I haven't told anyone that story ever." She cracked a small sad smile. "You should be honored."

"No." He reached for her hand. "I'm just so sorry for you. The whole thing is so sad." She stared at their hands and shook her head, her eyes clouding.

"They were really great to me, they were, but they were getting older and I was getting older so as soon as I got out of high school, I just decided to split for D.C. for no real reason than it was the nearest big city, right? Ha! How'd that fucking work out?" She sat back up and squeezed what was left of the tissue to her eyes. Katz grabbed his napkin and reached over to touch it against her elbow. She took it and cried into it softly.

"Cleo," he said, "it took a lot of guts to go through what you did and come out on the other side as well as you have." He heard a snort from behind the napkin. "Oh, yeah, I've got it all now, don't I?" she said. "Sittin' on top of the world!"

He leaned in. "Hey, you've got a good shot at coming out the other end of this – of all that – in pretty good shape." She put the napkin down and looked at him in wonder through the tears. "Careful now, Jake. Hope has a way of turning to shit with me."

"I know the feeling," he said. "I haven't been through one millionth of what you have but I know what it is to be disappointed and unhappy, and I don't want to feel that way ever again." He couldn't stop himself. "And I don't want you to either."

She slid her hands across the table and laid them on top of his. Her eyes beamed in a way he always hoped to see in Lisa's or Marty's but never did.

"Let's get out of here," she said.

18

He paid the bill and walked her out the door towards his car, then stopped. "You know, I probably ought to get you a cab," he said.

"Why?"

"Same reason you took one out here. Just to be on the safe side with your old crowd. We don't want to risk someone seeing you with me and starting to put two and two to – "

"I tell you what, I give you a waiver – isn't that what they call it? You're not responsible for whatever happens. How's that?"

Katz didn't know if it was the cold night air, the drinks he couldn't count, or that he was starting to fall in love with his client, but for some reason Cleo's argument made as much sense to him as it did to her. He pointed to his car just down the block. "Okay, you win. I will drive you home."

"Mine or yours?" she smiled, and leaned into him. He felt the world spin a little faster.

"Let's take that under advisement until we make it back across the bridge."

When they got to the car, he dug into his pocket for the keys. "Oh my God, Jake! This is your car?" she laughed. He ignored that, then opened the door for her and tried to ignore the squeak.

"It's a Nova, a Chevrolet Nova, I'll have you know – and you were in it, the day I got you at Lorton." She got into the passenger seat and gave it the once over, shaking her head the whole time. "Really? Wow! You'd think I'd remember this. I must've really been out of it."

"As I recall, you were a little more concerned with catching some z's than checking out your ride." He tried to surreptitiously push a ripped piece of cloth ceiling cover dangling over her head back in place but she caught him.

"Good lord, Jake! Are we going to make it back to D.C.?" "Quiet, woman," he said and pushed the door shut, watching the cloth flop back down to an inch above her hair. When he got in the driver's side, she was still laughing.

He turned the car on, raced the engine to make sure it wouldn't stall, then headed up Montgomery and made a right onto the right lane of the GW Parkway. She reached across the gearshift between them and caressed his ear.

"I'm sorry I laughed, Jake. This car's as cute as you are."

"Is that a compliment or an insult?"

They pulled to a stop at the light at Slater's Lane, the last light they'd see till they got into the city, and she dropped her hand to his neck and gently rubbed it. He smiled at her, then watched a few cars turn through the intersection on their way towards D.C. until a black Mercedes slid into the left lane next to him. He felt her hand stiffen, then slide off his shoulder. When he turned to look at her, her head was practically wedged between his seat and the console, her face turned away from the Mercedes.

"Jake, that's Tony Lewis' car. I know, I bought it for him."

Katz turned back as casually as he could to look at the other car. The tinted windows made it impossible to see who was inside. He slowly turned back to look straight ahead. "Cleo," he said, "that could be anybody. There're a lot of black Mercedes around D.C."

"Does it have D.C. plates?"

The light turned green but Katz paused to let the Mercedes pull ahead of him. The other driver was in no hurry either so Katz had to drop his speed to 20 to get a look at the rear plate. He was never so depressed reading "District of Columbia/No Taxation Without Representation". "Yeah," he said, creeping along, praying for the other driver to speed up. "You remember the number?"

"Shit, I'm not sure." "It's 979-203," he read. The Mercedes pulled into the right lane ahead of him. "Christ, I don't know. Maybe."

Katz wasn't ready to believe Tony Lewis had mystically appeared next to them on the GW Parkway, but his grip tightened on the wheel even before his brain told him why. He'd mentioned Stardust on his call with Cleo. If the FBI was listening in, even though they weren't legally allowed to hear them, and if someone on their end

208

really was hooked in to Rayful – like Cleo and Harry would have him believe – then maybe, just maybe, it was possible. But could they move this quick? The KGB, maybe, but was Rayful that good or was he even better at paranoia? He remembered the joke that it wasn't paranoia if they were really after you, but it wasn't one bit funny this time.

His lights flashed on the sign to the Potowmack Landing Restaurant up ahead to his right. He did the calculations quickly. He could turn in and wait a while before getting back on the Parkway, but the Mercedes could do a uey across the grass median and pin him in up there if he did. He kept going.

"Why are we going so slow?"

"I wanted to see the plates." Katz looked in the rear view mirror. It was clear to his left. "Hang on!" He veered sharply to his left and passed the Mercedes, not bothering to glance over. He tried to calm himself down. That could be anybody. He shot a quick glance at the rear view mirror. Then why was he speeding up too? *Maybe he was just daydreaming and lost track of how slow he was going till he saw a Chevy Nova shut him down and sped up,* Katz thought. *Or maybe he was Tony Lewis and he knew Cleo was in the car.*

Katz bolted a little further ahead until cars leaving National Airport made him slow down. He tried to keep his eyes on the Mercedes but now he wasn't sure whose lights were whose. "Is he still there?" Cleo asked.

"Hard to tell. Keep your head down just in case. I'm going to turn onto the bridge in a second."

"Fuck, Jake! Don't take him to my house! He's probably on a burner right now telling 'em to wait for me there." It didn't take Katz a second to figure out he didn't want the welcoming party waiting at his house either. He cruised up the ramp to the 14th Street bridge, watching to see who else was coming up behind him. Every car looked black behind their lights so it was impossible to tell. He sped up past the merge from the other side of the Parkway and slid into the right hand lane on the D.C. side.

"What's happening, Jake?" She sounded like she was being strangled. "Where are we?"

"We're on 295. I have no idea where he is, but he's not going to stick with us, trust me."

"How can you be so fucking sure?"

"Hold on." He moved back over into the second lane from the right as the right lane turned into a Right Turn Only lane for 12th St., N.W. downtown. A car about twenty-five yards behind him moved over too. No one was making a right turn onto 12th St. this time of night. Just as he crested the hill, Katz drew almost even with the exit, then shot across the right lane and sped off down the ramp, tires squealing all the way. Cleo screamed "Fuck, Jake, fuck!" Once he banked through the turn, Katz looked in his rear view mirror and prayed. His prayers were answered. No one was behind them.

"I think we lost them, Cleo, if it even was them," he said.

"We cannot go to my place, Jake."

"Cleo, let's not panic any more than we have to, okay? Stick with me on this. I've got you this far, right?" He heard a muffled "Shit!" in return, then took another look in the rear view mirror as he merged onto 12th St. Still nothing. No one ahead or next to them either. "Okay, the coast is clear, I promise. You can sit up now." She picked her head up high enough and long enough to see they were coming to a stop at the light at Constitution, then slipped back down against his leg.

"So where are you taking me?" she asked just as a semblance of a plan popped in his head.

"Let's take the long way around to your house, make sure no one's joining us on the ride, then come in from the other direction and see if everything's cool on your block. If it isn't, I'll drive you directly to the nearest police station and we'll take it from there. Sound like a plan?"

He took her grunt as a yes, and wended his way back and forth through Northwest, taking slow laps around a few traffic circles before he crept slowly down 5th St. N.E. past E heading for D. The only other cars on the street were parked.

"Cleo, we're a block from your house. Sit up and tell me if you see anything funny."

She sat up slowly and peeked over the edge of the dashboard. "No, it looks like it always does."

"How about your house?" He pointed to the far right corner of the intersection ahead of them. "Are the lights how you left them?" He watched her take in the stoop light and the light behind the drawn curtain upstairs.

"Yeah, they are," she said, then sat up and took in a deep breath. She patted Jake's thigh and left her hand there. "You did a great job, Jake. I owe you big time – just not tonight, I hope you understand."

"No problem. I'm happy to take the rain check."

She bent over and kissed him on the cheek, then lifted her hand to his other cheek and turned his face to him. They kissed each other long and hard, their tongues driving their passion on, until she laid a hand on his chest just like the first time and he pulled back to take her gorgeous face in. "Till the rain check, okay?" she said softly.

"Till then. I'll wait here till you get in safe and sound."

"Are you always such a gentleman?"

"With a Lady, always."

She gave him a smiling peck on the cheek, then pushed open the door and shut it. When she bent down to see him pushing the cloth ceiling back in place, he heard her laugh through the window. She tapped her goodbye on the glass, and he watched her cross the intersection and head up the stoop. Only then did he see a car door open at the curb behind her and a large black man step out onto the pavement.

"Cleo!" he cried out but she couldn't hear him. He whipped out of the car and she turned at the sound of his door slam, then saw the man behind her, and an even larger black man getting out of the driver's side of a white Ford.

"Jake!" she yelled and he rushed past both of them to block her, his pulse pounding. She held the back of his arms tight.

"She Cleo Smythe?" the one closest to them said.

Cleo leaned to her right and watched the guy tug on his police hat.

"I am."

"We need you to come with us, ma'am," he said, "right now."

"I'm her lawyer," Katz said. "What's going on?"

"We're busting Rayful Edmond and his crowd all over the city tonight," he said. "She's going into protection, U.S.A.'s orders."

19

Katz'd always been an early riser. When he was a kid, his father once caught him sitting by the front door in his pajamas around 6 o'clock on a Saturday morning. "Afraid you're going to miss something?" he asked. Then, he'd been waiting for the Inquirer so he could find out if the Phillies wound up winning the game he fell asleep listening to on his transistor. Today, he was waiting on the Monday *Post* to get up to speed on the Edmond busts.

The MPD guys who scooped Cleo up Saturday night wouldn't tell him anything, and the reports he saw on the local news yesterday just told him drug raids like the one they filmed on M St. Northeast were going on all night, which probably explained why Sunday's *Post* had nothing on them. When he heard today's paper slap on the walk, he scrambled down the steps to pick it up and there it was, in big bold type across the front page: "16 Linked to Drug Gang Arrested in Area Sweep".

Sixteen seemed low to him, but MPD Chief Maurice Turner said more were coming, and the rest of the numbers were staggering. Thirty homicides were tied to the Edmond gang just in the last year. More than a hundred DEA, FBI, and MPD agents carried out the raids, at least four residences were seized, and the police estimated that more than four hundred and forty pounds of cocaine were sold every week, not just in D.C., but the suburbs too. Rayful was responsible for most of it, allegedly.

He flipped to the continuation and read the rest walking back in. A lot of the names were familiar to him.

Besides Rayful, they picked up his sister Rachelle and her husband Jerry Millington, who was on the phone with Cleo that first day, Bootsie and her sister Armaretta, Niecey and her husband Jeff Thompson, and Tony Lewis, among a long list of others he didn't know, at least by their names in the paper.

The article said the FBI originally planned to start the busts Monday morning but moved them up because a lot of the targets had gotten word they were coming. Katz was not stunned to read that, and he wondered if the TV crews who just happened to be hanging out on M St. at one a.m. Sunday had been tipped off by the same people. His first thought was that D.C.'d gotten a lot leakier since he left the government, but his second was maybe he never had cause to know just how leaky it was even then.

He flipped the paper onto the sofa and cranked through the TV channels to see if anyone had anything newer. They didn't, so he headed upstairs to get ready for the day. When he came back down, Bruce Johnson was live on Channel 9, standing in front of a mob of people outside the Federal Courthouse. Katz walked over to turn up the sound just as the picture flicked to Jay Stephens, the U.S. Attorney for D.C., standing at a lectern bearing the DOJ seal, a cluster of microphones pointing up at him.

"This is the most significant law enforcement operation here directed at a cocaine distribution network," he said. *So why isn't Chief Turner or some muckety-muck at the FBI or DEA standing there?* Katz thought. He didn't know Stephens at all, but he did know that Earl Silbert, his

USA, wouldn't be caught dead grandstanding in front of a microphone before a case'd even started. Bad form.

"This is the principal case," Stephens said. "Based on our intelligence, Edmond's group distributed twenty to fifty percent of the cocaine coming in. It was a closely knit family organization with enforcers, runners, lieutenants, and money counters." Katz listened to him drone on a while he dug into his bowl of Honey Nut Cheerios. When Stephens was through, someone asked if anyone wanted to comment on why Mayor Barry had said yesterday that the arrests would only make a "dent" in the market. Chief Turner edged in to take that one.

"I don't agree with that," he said. "We've taken down a major distributor in the city. That sends a message to the community that we are serious – that we are going to close this drug distribution market down."

Was that message really for Barry? Katz thought, thinking back to Wallace telling him at their dinner at Marrocco's just how high a D.C. official he really was. He'd heard enough. He pushed the TV off, scarfed down the last of his cereal, and headed out the door.

On the way to the Nova, he found himself wondering what side he'd really done more good on in the drug cases he'd handled. When he was an AUSA, he never wondered – he knew he was on the side of truth, justice, and the American way every time. But once he went over to the other side and had to really focus on how and why his clients got hooked so he could persuade a judge to reduce their sentence or put them into rehab rather than jail

216

– or worse, Federal prison, once the new sentencing guidelines multiplied the length of every term – he started to have his doubts.

Schein was a perfect example. It'd taken him no time to graduate from being slapped on the wrist for carrying pot to facing long, hard time for selling coke. He ducked prison only because Katz managed to get his old buddies in the USA's office to knock the charge down to possession on the promise he'd go to rehab. It turned out that going to rehab was easy for Schein – the hard part was staying. The second time Katz drove him there was the last time the Feds said they'd offer it. Schein cried all the way, swearing he'd clean up, thanking Katz for everything he'd done for him. At the gate, they hugged for a long time and he swore he'd make Katz proud. He still remembered the last words he ever heard Schein utter: "I will call you the minute I'm out, man, and we will go out and celebrate however straight people celebrate, I swear."

But he never got the call, and never even heard about how he was doing until Wallace told him he'd o.d.'d. When he cleared his eyes and his head, he saw he was at the light at 5th and D Northwest, a block from his office, with no clue how he got there. He found a space and fed the meter, then headed down the street and up the stairs. LaVerne greeted him with a brighter smile than he'd seen her flash in a long time. "Good mornin', Jake!" she crowed.

"Good morning, LaVerne!" he crowed back. "Why are we so happy?"

217

She held up a blank pad of "While You Were Out" notes. "'Cause your special friend hasn't called six times already, and he didn't leave no messages either. Oh, it's a happy day."

He gave her a high five, but something was making his stomach churn. Why no calls from Harry, today of all days? Because he already knew Cleo'd gone over to the other side, or was it just something innocent, like he was in court or with a client? With anyone else, Katz'd buy that, but he knew from bitter experience that when Harry was involved, the innocent reason was never the right one.

"I'll withhold judgment on that for a while," he said. "Anyone else?" She picked a pink note off her desk and handed it to him. "Mr. Madden? From the USA? Said you need to call him back soon as you get in."

"Ring him up," Katz said and closed the door to his office behind him. By the time he was in his seat, jacket off, pad out, LaVerne buzzed him. He picked up the receiver.

"Mr. Madden, I didn't expect to hear from you so early, after all that overtime you and your boys put in on Sunday. Quite a day's work, according to the *Post*."

"Wasn't me out there, Jake. I slept in, to tell you the truth. Anyway, I'm calling to let you know what you already know. We want the grand jury to hear from your client."

"I recall hearing something about that."

"As her lawyer, I'm giving you the courtesy of letting you know we're scheduling her to appear tomorrow afternoon. She'll probably go on right after lunch and be up there the rest of the day and probably most of Wednesday, too."

"That is so nice of you, Charlie, so let me give you the courtesy of reminding you she has a constitutional right to talk to her lawyer before she takes the stand – unless, of course, you're really calling to promise me you're never going to prosecute her even if she lies and doesn't give you everything you laid out in our agreement."

"Oh, we still expect her to do just what she promised," Madden said. "Don't worry yourself about that."

"I didn't think I had to worry about it one bit, so if she's still at risk of you guys coming after her, I need to prep her and make sure she's living up to the agreement, for everyone's sake. When and where should I go?" He heard a muffled conversation. With Hutchison or Stephens, or maybe a Marshal or a Feebie? Whoever it was, Katz took some pride in knowing Madden had them there because he expected him to push back.

"Come to the conference room outside the grand jury room," Madden said. "We'll have her there as early as you want her. How long do you think you'll need – I mean, really need?"

"Depends on what you're going to ask her."

"We're going to ask her a lot. How she came to work for Rayful, what he had her doing, who she did it with, where, when, the phone taps, the meeting with Bootsie – like I said, a lot."

"And do I get to see the transcripts of the taps?"

"You do not, as you well know."

"I do, but for the record, let me say my position on that has done a complete one-eighty since I left your office."

"So noted," Madden said. "Here's the bottom line: We'll give the two of you a quiet place to talk all morning but no later than two o'clock Wednesday afternoon, she's going on the stand."

"One morning is not enough time, Charlie, come on," Katz said.

He heard Madden's sigh. "Jake, the only advice you need to give her is 'Tell the truth, Cleo'. You want more time than I just gave you, you can take your chances filing some kind of bullshit motion with the court, but before you do that, you might want to take a little more time to think about just how much that's going to piss off her only other friend in this world now – i.e., me."

"Okay, I get it, but if it goes more than one day, I need to have some time with her every morning before she goes back, an hour at least."

"An hour," Madden said, "at most."

Katz sighed this time. "I'll be there at eight tomorrow. Have her there." Madden's click told him the conversation was over.

20

Katz sat down with Cleo at 8:04 Tuesday morning. By 11:13, they'd covered everything on his pad. He thumbed through the sheets again until he was looking at a blank page. "Okay," he said. "I got nothing else. You?"

"God, no." She pushed herself off her straightback metal seat. "I'm already worn out. How am I going to get through two days of this? Jesus Christ!"

"Well, the chair in there's more comfortable, so you got that going for you."

She arched her back, hands on hips, and threw her head back. Katz took in the view. Face and neck beautiful, even without the glitzy makeup he still remembered from the last time he saw her. More to the point, in her black suit over a white blouse – cotton, not silk, so they didn't get the wrong idea, or the right one – she looked just like any other professional woman anyone on the grand jury might see on the streets of D.C. any time of day. She patted her jacket and tugged it down, then pulled herself up straight and looked at him.

"So, how do I look?" *Gorgeous*, he thought. "Credible," he said. "Should I let them know you're ready?"

"They let you smoke in there?"

"That would be a no."

"Then not yet," she said, and picked the pack of Kools off the table. She torched one up and walked away from him, then back, inhaling so deep there was scarcely a trace of smoke in the air.

"You want me to buy a little more time?" Katz asked. "Maybe go down and bring us up some lunch?"

"Like a last meal for the condemned man?" she said with a grim smile, then took another drag and flicked an ash onto a pile of butts filling a metal ash tray. "No, let's get this show on the road. If they're ready, I'm ready." He nodded, opened the door, and poked his head out. A white Marshal too young to be that heavy filled a chair next to the doorway. He rolled his head to look up at Katz.

"She's ready," Katz said. The Marshal nodded and reached for the wall phone just above him. "Lawyer says she's ready," he said into it, then grunted "Uh-huh" and hung up. "They'll come get her," he said, then crossed his arms and his legs, and resumed his vacant stare at the bank of elevators across from him.

When Katz turned back to tell Cleo, he saw the bathroom door closing, so he stepped back into the lobby and helped the Marshal watch elevator doors open. When the one on the far right did, he saw a few Marshals guide a handcuffed prisoner out, followed by a familiar form and face striding across the lobby just behind them. "Is that who I think it is?" Katz called out.

All four of them turned his way, but Wallace was the only one who smiled at him. He made a quick comment to the Marshal closest to him, then strode over to Katz, hand extended. The Marshal in the chair glanced up at him, then got back to work. Katz shook Wallace's hand and they gave each other a quick half hug. "My man!" Wallace said. "What're you doin' here?"

"Just finishing up a meeting before my client goes before the Edmond grand jury. And you?"

"Escorting another bad boy up to do the very same thing. Business is boomin', I'll say that."

"You weren't lying at Marrocco's that night. This thing is as huge as you said."

"Huger, if that's a word." Wallace said. Katz watched the crowd he left the elevator with disappear around a corner. Wallace swatted him on the shoulder and took off in pursuit. "When this shit ever settles down, man, let's get together an' trade horror stories."

"I'm not waitin' that long," Katz yelled, then turned back to the conference room and saw Cleo in the doorway just as he heard another elevator door open and watched two more Marshals step out and come their way. One of them was Marshal Gaskins. He shook Katz' hand.

"Mr. Katz, we meet again," he said with a warm smile, then turned to Cleo. "I recall our first meeting, Ms. Smythe." Katz flashed back to the day she arrived at the courthouse in ski mask and shoulder pads to hammer out her plea agreement. It seemed years ago now.

"We're going to escort her to the grand jury room," Gaskins said. "I'm not sure how long she'll have to be there, but – well, you know the drill. You can hang out here as long as you like, but the only way you're going to know when she's done is to call the U.S. Attorney's Office, and I bet you know the number."

"I do." Katz turned to Cleo and put a hand on her elbow. "I'll be right here till they excuse you today. Remember, I can't go in there but you can ask for a break to talk to me any time you want, okay?" She nodded and squeezed his hand, then headed to the elevator with the Marshals. When the doors started closing, Katz yelled "Call me if you have to!" If she heard him, she gave no sign. "I'm going to wait here in case she needs me," he told the Marshal at the door, who gave him the same response.

Katz pulled a copy of the *Post* from his briefcase. He'd barely unfolded it when the phone on the wall next to him rang. He figured it was a wrong number and let it go till the sixth ring persuaded him he had to make it stop.

"Hello?" he said.

"Is this Mr. Katz?" a young female voice inquired.

"Yes, but how did you – "

"One moment please."

Katz sat baffled until a man's voice came on the line.

"Mr. Katz? This is Billy Murphy. How are you this fine day, sir?"

"A bit confused, actually. How did you get this number?"

"Judge Alexander gave it to me." Murphy went on over Katz' sigh. "I just want to make sure I got the right information from him. He said you're representing Cleo Smythe. Is that right?"

"He is correct, but just to make sure you have it right too, Harry's no longer a judge – if we're talking about the same Judge Alexander." Katz heard a soft chuckle on the other end.

"We are talking about Harry Alexander, the one and only. I'm sorry, it's kind of our own private joke, Mr. Katz. I was a judge up here in Baltimore the same time he was down there so we call each other "Judge" just as a term of mutual respect, I guess. I'm aware he's no longer on the bench."

"Did he also tell you we shared office space for a while?"

"Oh, you're being a bit modest, aren't you, Mr. Katz? Harry told me you were partners." Katz shook his head at the reminder that Harry would say anything to anybody if it was in his best interests. He had no idea why making him his partner served Harry well but he did know he didn't care.

"So, getting to the business at hand, what is it?"

"Well, I'm contacting all the lawyers who I know are representing defendants caught up in Rayful Edmond's alleged operation to see if we might get together in Washington sometime in the next few weeks to start thinking about how we can work together to protect everyone's best interests." Katz knew he was really trying to find out who'd turned – and he also knew Harry would've told him Katz would know that's what he wanted to know so Billy would have to be slick about it – but Katz knew that too and he wasn't falling for it.

"I'm not sure that's going to be possible, Mr. Murphy."

"Call me Billy, Jake. And why is that?"

"Come on, Billy. You know better than I do. Everybody's going to be pointing their finger at everyone else. It's every man for himself now."

"And every woman?"

"Would I be doing my job if she wasn't?"

"No you would not, you most certainly would not. But what you fear is not what I have in mind."

"So what do you have in mind?"

"Just that everyone gives a quick summary of what they expect their client's testimony to be," he said, "so that each of us is prepared to craft our best defense not only to the government, but to help each other, so that ultimately as many of our clients as possible go free." *This guy is good,* Katz thought, *but not good enough.*

"Billy, I get where you're going," he said, "but what our clients testify about isn't really up to us, is it? It's up to the government, and they don't usually give us many hints about what they've got and where they're going, do they?"

"But you'll be ready for them, won't you." Murphy said it more like a statement of fact than a question. "If you're anything like me, Jake, you'll have interviewed Ms. Smythe to a faretheewell and you'll have your cross-ex ready to go, augmented by anything you need to address from her testimony on direct, right?" *And he sure knows how to lead a witness.* "Yeah, that's right," he conceded.

"So that's what I think we can talk about – what we each expect to hear from the government and how we each expect to respond to it. I don't want anyone to tell anyone else who they're pointing the finger at. We'll all know that anyhow, I suspect," Murphy said, again with the soft chuckle. Katz wasn't quite sure how he meant that. More to the point, he wasn't sure if Murphy already knew Cleo was playing for the other side and just wanted Katz to confirm it by ducking his little confab. On the other hand, if he said he'd go, Billy might be more inclined to think Cleo was still in Rayful's corner. Going would also require a huge set of brass balls, and that settled it. "Okay," he said, "let's do it."

"Excellent. I'll get back to you with some times after I hear from everyone else. I'll be in touch. I look forward to making your acquaintance in person very soon."

"Yeah, same here."

When Katz hung up the phone, it was quiet all around him. He tried to enjoy it but couldn't. What he felt instead was pressure, from all sides. Harry. Billy. Cleo. Even Schein in his own way, from above. He took his bearings and remembered that where he was sitting now was one floor below that ten foot cube he felt so trapped in when he was an Assistant USA. At least then, the walls weren't closing in.

21

At ten to nine on Wednesday, Katz got off the elevator on three, just in time to see the Marshal who encumbered the chair yesterday escorting Cleo into the conference room. He followed them in. "Good morning, Cleo, Marshal," he said. The Marshal turned and looked through him on his way back to the door. He deposited himself in the chair with a thud and a grunt, then pawed the door closed. Cleo fell into Katz and held herself to him tight.

"Jake, do I have to go back in there? Can't you work your legal magic and make them stop? Please?"

He had a pretty good idea this was coming, after he saw what she looked like after five hours on the stand yesterday, and their monosyllabic conversation when the Marshals put him on the phone with her last night. He squeezed her tighter.

"I wish I could, Cleo, but those are powers I don't have. Don't hate me." She let him go and walked down the table to fetch the ash tray and fire up a Kool. "If you need a break today," he said, "remember, you can tell them you need to talk to me. At least that'll give you a break."

"I thought about it yesterday, but I wanted to get it over with as soon as possible even more." She held up the cigarette. "And I needed one of these too, believe me."

"So anything come to you last night we need to talk about now?"

She blew out a long ribbon of smoke and shook her head. "No, I can handle it, but the thing that bugged me the most was my voice on those tapes. I didn't even recognize myself. Am I really that whiny?"

"No," Katz laughed, "your voice is like music, a flute."

She rolled her eyes. "You going to be here all day too?"

"As long as you are."

She stubbed out the cigarette. Katz held up a finger and leaned out the door to the Marshal. "Excuse me, do you know when they want her?"

The Marshal lifted his wrist and looked at his watch. Katz read 9:09. "9:15 the latest, they said," he said. In a burst of initiative, he looked up at Katz. "She ready now?"

"She's ready."

The good news was she was done by lunch time, which gave Katz the rest of the day to enjoy a walk to Antonio's in the spring sunshine, return calls, review old files, create new ones, and absorb himself in all manner of distractions until he was ready to call it a day and head back home. He planted his briefcase on LaVerne's desk at 4:45. "I'm out of here," he said. "May I escort you to the door?"

"'Less I beat you to it." She gathered her things up in one swoop while he held the door for her. At the sound of footsteps coming up the stairs, they turned to each other.

"You make an appointment I don't know about?" she said.

Katz shook his head, then turned to see a light-skinned middle-aged black man in a steel gray suit make the turn at the landing below them. Katz couldn't see his face, only a high forehead with dark wavy processed hair behind it falling to just above his shoulders. When he looked up and smiled at them, he also saw a gold tooth shine from where his right front tooth should've been. He reached his hand out to Katz at the doorway.

"Mr. Katz?" he said. "I'm Billy Murphy."

"Very nice to meet you," Katz said, shaking his hand, "but I don't recall scheduling a meeting with you now."

Murphy smiled. "You didn't, and if you're heading home, I can make other arrangements. I just need to take a call before I get on the road back to Baltimore and yours was the closest address in my book."

I don't recall giving you my address either, Katz thought, but he decided to see where Murphy was going. "Of course, sure," he said, "happy to oblige."

"Do you have a spare office I can use?" Murphy looked at his watch. "I'm supposed to be on the line at 5 sharp. It should only take a few minutes."

"The only spare office is mine," Katz said. "Just give me one minute." He walked back into his office, closing the door enough to keep his desk from Murphy's view, then flipped quickly through everything on it that had anything to do with Cleo. He threw what he found into a drawer of the standup steel cabinet next to the window and locked it, then straightened up the other files scattered on his desk, and pulled the door wide open. "All right, much more presentable now. Please come in."

Behind Murphy's back, LaVerne pointed to the door with pleading eyes. When Murphy passed him, Katz mouthed "I owe you" and pointed to her desk. LaVerne rolled her eyes. Katz closed the door and heard her bag hit the desktop like it was a bowling ball. Murphy waited for Katz to take his seat before he sat down.

"Reminds me of my first office," he said. "If you're as sharp as Judge – Harry says you are, you've got a lot to look forward to."

"Is he representing anyone in this?" Katz asked innocently.

Murphy shrugged. "I don't know, but I don't care anymore either."

"Why's that?"

"Once he decided not to be part of the meeting I talked to you about, I decided he wasn't going to be part of our team either."

Katz was more than a little surprised to hear that. "Did he tell you why he wasn't coming?"

"He did not. Maybe he wanted to be in charge, maybe he didn't want me to know his client would be laying everything at Rayful's doorstep, but whatever the reason, he's out – and the meeting's off."

"Why?"

"After talking to you and Harry and a few other lawyers, I think it might be best for all concerned to wait till the grand jury's handed down its indictments, so we know who to invite – and who no longer needs to be invited."

"Because they weren't indicted?"

"That, and maybe more importantly, *why* they weren't indicted."

Katz kept a poker face until he thought he'd waited long enough to persuade Murphy he'd finally figured out what he meant. "Oh, I get it," he said, "because they might have rolled."

"Precisely, Mr. Katz."

"Do you know if anyone has?"

"Has your client made you aware of someone named Deborah Phillips?"

"No," Katz said truthfully, "who is she?"

"Well, it seems that after she was arrested for her involvement in Mr. Edmonds' so-called enterprise, the government apparently made her an offer she couldn't refuse." He stopped, still smiling. Katz waited him out. "So she made her deal," Murphy went on, "and started testifying before the grand jury early last week, as a matter of fact." He stopped again.

"Okay," Katz said, "and?"

"And apparently her deal required the Attorney General to sign off on it."

"How do you know that?"

"Because instead of sending the final agreement to him in one of those inter-office envelopes, someone screwed up and put it in a real envelope and mailed it."

"To the AG?"

"Nope. To her. At her home address." Another pause. *This guy must put on a hell of a show for a jury,* Katz thought. Murphy finally let the other shoe drop. "Where she lives with Emmanuel Sutton, better known as Mangie Sutton – who also happens to be Rayful Edmond's half-brother."

"Oh Jesus! Is she still alive?" Katz said before he could stop himself.

"Barely, it seems. She was shot and then given a huge overdose."

"Courtesy of Mangie?"

"If it was, she's not saying. When she regained the power of speech, she told the police somebody she didn't know shot her, on the street."

"And shot her up with drugs too?"

"She said she was so sick about deciding to cooperate that she tried to kill herself by o.d.ing on pills – and taping her mouth shut so that she couldn't vomit them up."

Katz barked a laugh at that. "You don't believe any of that, do you?"

Murphy gave him the smallest of smiles. "Jake, it's probably best for everyone that I withhold further comment – except that she must be pretty important to the government because they're putting her back before the grand jury, maybe even today I hear."

Was that who Harry was representing? Katz thought. *And is that why he backed out of the meeting?* He looked up and felt Murphy was looking at him now like he was a specimen under a microscope, his thoughts on full display. "Wow," he got out, "that's some story."

"So, that's a long answer to your question why we're waiting on the meeting." He looked back at his watch. Katz glanced down at his too. Two minutes to five. "My call's supposed to be any minute," Murphy said. "Would it be better if I take it out there or – ?" He let the question hang there long enough for Katz to get up and point to his chair.

236

"Please," he said. Murphy nodded and came around the table. He laid his briefcase on the desktop, unsnapped the hasps, and pulled out a folder. Katz read the name on the tab.

"Are you calling Rayful Edmond?"

"No. He's calling me."

If this was a fight, Katz would've taken a standing eight count. A call *to* your client behind bars was something he had experience with, but a call *from* your client, at an appointed hour, to a random number? When his head cleared enough to formulate a question, he tried to start with the most basic one he could conjure up. "He's in custody, right?"

"Yes, he is." Murphy flipped open a manila folder. Katz saw a color picture of a young black man's face clipped to the side he opened.

"Then how do you know he'd be able to call you now?"

"Jake, let me just say this: When Rayful Edmond wants to make a call, they let him make a call."

"And call you here?"

"I took a shot." Murphy shrugged. "If it didn't work out, I figured you'd just say you wouldn't accept the charges. But it did and I thank you for your hospitality."

Was Murphy really letting him know Rayful knew where he worked too? Katz thought. *Or was this just business as usual for high-caliber criminals and their lawyers?* Every answer raised another dozen questions, but the ring of the phone on LaVerne's desk made them all academic. Billy glanced at his watch. Five on the dot, Katz saw.

"That's probably him," Murphy said.

Katz pointed to the picture clipped to Billy's folder. "Is that him?"

"It is indeed." Murphy slid it out of the clip and held it out across the table. Katz took it. "Hold on one minute," he heard LaVerne say, then turned to see her put her hand over the phone. "A Federal correctional institution has a collect call for William Murphy? Does he work here now?"

"It's okay. Tell them you'll accept the charges." "Okay," she said into the receiver, "we'll accept them. Please hold a minute for Mr. Murphy." The phone on Katz' desk buzzed and he headed for the door.

"You're welcome to stay, Jake," Murphy said. "It's your office." Katz knew that wasn't happening. "No, thanks. That'd just make me a witness, which means they can force me to tell them anything I hear. Just let me know when you're off." Billy nodded and waited till he left to pick up the phone. Through the closed door, Katz heard "Hello, Rayful! How's it going?"

He took the seat in the visitor's area, then pointed to LaVerne's radio. "Crank that up enough so I can't hear

238

them, please." She made it loud enough that he could only hear Young MC bust a move.

"Seriously, Jake, what is goin' on? This dude's talkin' to Rayful Edmond? Here? Do I need to take out some life insurance? Good lord!" Katz looked down to see Rayful's picture was still in his hand, then came around behind LaVerne and handed it to her. "Okay, here's a trivia question. Who's that?" He looked at it with her. Slender face. Medium dark skin. Neat short natural hair. Wide-set eyes, full lips – and young.

"That the dude in there? When he was in like eleventh grade?"

"No," Katz said. "That is Rayful Edmond."

"Get out of here! This cat looks like he's the captain of the math team or somethin'."

"I know. Not what I was expecting either." That was something on the order of Mean Joe Greene, only meaner.

"This is him now though?" LaVerne said. "I mean, maybe it's from high school? Dude looks like Arsenio's kid brother! Seriously." The door to Katz' office popped open and Billy strode through. "All through," he said, then smiled when he saw her holding Rayful's picture.

"So how old is he?" Katz asked.

"Twenty-four," Murphy said. "Pretty young for public enemy number one, wouldn't you say?" Katz handed him back the picture. Murphy tucked it inside his suit pocket, then extended his hand to Katz. "Thank you for the use of the room and the phone, Jake."

They shook, Murphy nodded to LaVerne, and left. She waited till his footsteps faded, then picked her things back up and headed for the door before looking back to Katz, still standing, lost in thought, behind her chair. "Jake? You okay?"

He wasn't sure. There were so many unanswered questions bobbing and weaving through his head. *Why was Murphy really here? Why did Rayful call here? Did Harry take himself out of the meeting because he was representing Deborah Phillips, or am I adding two and two and getting five?* When he looked up to answer LaVerne, she was gone.

22

Early Monday morning, Katz took a call from a Marshal whose name he didn't get and whose voice he didn't know. "Is this Mr. Katz?"

"It is." In a second, a very familiar voice sang through the line. "Jake, it's Cleo!"

"Hey! How are you? What's up?"

"I told 'em I wanted to talk to my lawyer."

"Okay. About what?"

"Nothing," she said, softer. "I just wanted to talk to you." He was speechless, but she filled the void. "I miss you, Jake." He struggled for a response. "I've never heard a client say that, Cleo," he finally came up with. "I miss you too," poured out unbidden.

"My nannies tell me you're the only person in the world allowed to be here," she said. "You got some time to visit me, please, pretty please?"

He checked his calendar to make sure it was as empty as he remembered. His memory was good. "I can make time," he said. "When's good for you?"

"Uh, now?" she laughed.

"How about lunch? Will they let me bring you something to eat?"

"Hold on a second." He heard a door pop open and a few mumbles before she came back on the line. "They said okay, but they're going to have to pick you up and bring you here."

"Okay. When and where should I be?" Another set of muffled mumbles, then "Where's your office?" "410 Fifth Street Northwest." He heard her repeat it, then repeat what they told her. "Be out front at 11:30. They'll be in a black Lincoln with US plates."

"Where are you?"

"I'm not allowed to tell you."

"Okay," Katz said, "so I'm also guessing they're not going to serve us a catered meal, so what can I get you to eat?"

"Anything that's easy for you."

"You like tacos?"

"Love 'em."

"How about the nannies?"

More mumbles. "They say thanks, but they're good."

"I will see you at lunch," he said.

"I can't wait."

At 11:30, Katz rounded the corner coming back from Antonio's and saw a black Lincoln with government plates double-parked in front of his building, flashers flashing. When he drew near, he raised his taco bag. The tinted window on the passenger side slid down to reveal a thin balding white man about his age. A U.S. Marshals badge gleamed from the pocket of his blue sport jacket. "Are you my ride?" Katz asked.

"Are you Mr. Katz?"

"The taco bag's not good enough?"

"Sorry," the Marshal said, "I need to see an official ID."

Katz set down the bag and his briefcase, and flipped open his wallet to show him his driver's license. The Marshal took a quick look, then stepped out of the car and held his hand out. Katz shook it and read Kravitz on the badge.

"You been through this before? Visiting a cooperator?" Kravitz asked.

"I have not."

"Okay, let's get in the back seat and I'll give you the drill." Katz grabbed his bags and got in. The woman at the wheel nodded at him in the rear view mirror.

"Good morning, sir," she said. "I'm Marshal Bykovsky."

"Pleased to meet you," Katz said as Marshal Kravitz slid in next to him, closed the door, and held up what looked like a ski mask, except the eyeholes were lower and smaller. "This is the drill," he said. "You can't know where we're taking you, for your protection and hers." He held it out for Katz to take, but he didn't. "What's with the little eye holes?" he asked.

"They're not eye holes. They're nose holes." Kravitz pressed the mask to Katz' chest. Katz declined the opportunity again.

"Mr. Katz," Kravitz said, "you can put this on or you can keep talking to Ms. Smythe on the telephone. It's your choice." Bykovsky turned off the ignition and bounced a high-beam glare back at him. Katz took the mask and tugged it on. Kravitz helped him line up the nose holes. Katz found the mouth hole on his own. "I feel like I should be holding up a bank," he said, "if I could see it."

Bykovsky put the car in gear. Katz groped in front of him till he felt the back of her head rest. "Wait one second," he tried to say. "Just tell me she's somewhere in the tri-state area. If she's not, you can let me off here."

"We'll be there soon enough," Kravitz said. "Might be a good time to catch up on some shuteye."

Katz sat back and sighed. He remembered seeing some grade Z movie where Robert Young was locked blindfolded in the trunk of a car but could trace the route afterwards because he remembered every turn. Katz felt them make a left onto D, but after that he was lost. *Robert Young would be so ashamed* was the last thought he remembered. The next thing he knew, a firm hand was shaking his shoulder. He opened his eyes to see nothing.

244

"Give me your hand," he heard Kravitz say, "and duck your head." He did as he was told, then felt a lighter touch on his other elbow. "Just walk with us," Bykovsky said. "We'll be there in a minute."

He stepped stiffly across something hard for a few seconds, then heard Kravitz say "Okay, three short steps," and managed to climb them without falling on his face. He heard a door swing open and let Bykovsky lead him through into warmer air. He summoned his inner Robert Young and counted twenty-two steps until he stopped and heard a key in a lock and another door open. Bykovsky's arm dropped from his elbow and Kravitz pushed him gently inside wherever they were. The door shut behind them. "All right, Mr. Katz, well done," Kravitz said. "You can take the mask off now."

Katz pulled it off and looked straight into Cleo's smiling eyes. She shook her head. "I thought I saw every version of Jake Katz there was to see, but this one beats 'em all." She reached over to her pocketbook on a dresser and pulled out a comb. "Here," she said and gestured to a mirror over the dresser. "You might want to use this."

Katz took it and turned to Kravitz. "Is it okay if I look at myself now?"

"Knock yourself out," Kravitz said and laid Katz' briefcase and taco bag on a small round table between the door and the double bed to his right. "We'll be right outside," he told Cleo. "Just knock on the door when you're done."

"Will do."

They went out the door. Katz watched Cleo's reflection smile at him trying to comb the static electricity out of his hair, then turned to see the real thing, even more gloriously radiant than he remembered. When she reached both arms to him, he took her hands and let her pull him away from the mirror and into the bathroom. She put a finger to her lips, reached around him to push the door as shut as she could without making a noise, then threw her arms around his neck and squeezed him tight. He squeezed her back, helpless to resist, then kissed her welcoming lips long and hard. He felt her breasts press into his chest and reached down to push her skirt up over her waist. She pulled her panties down and kicked them off, then pulled his cock out and felt its growing stiffness. She fell to her knees to suck it hard but he pulled her up and kissed her with a desire he forgot he had and feared he'd spend too soon. He grabbed her ass and hoisted her up till she was propped on the edge of the sink and sank himself into her. It only took a few seconds till he stifled a cry into her shoulder and only a few more till she buried her head in his chest to muffle her moans. They clung to each other, rocking back and forth, sweating, stunned, and silent until a tune that matched their rhythm popped into his head.

"Dum dum dumby doo dum," he whispered in her ear. She pulled her head back and looked into his eyes quizzically. "Dum dum dumby doo dum," he whispered again, then sang "Come softly to me, come softly to me."

She threw her head back and choked, quietly, on her laugh. "I always wondered what that song meant," she whispered.

"And now we know," he whispered back. A rational thought struck him for the first time since she grabbed his hands. "It's probably a little late to ask this," he said, "but – "

"IUD," she smiled, "so no worries." She rocked with him again before she kissed him again long and deep. When they parted, she laid her head on his shoulder. "I'm going to need a minute," she whispered. "Do you mind taking care of yourself out there, while I – ". She left the rest unsaid.

"Not at all," Katz said. "Take your time."

They kissed again before he pulled up his pants. She pulled the door shut, but left it open just enough to wink at him through the crack. He got himself together next to her bed and looked around for a matchbook, some stationery, a card, any sign of where on earth he might be, but found nothing. He had no idea how long he'd been asleep in the car, but the clock on the night stand read 12:45, so he figured it took him about an hour to get here, but even that was suspect because the Marshals might have taken the long way around. He walked over to the window and pushed the curtain back, but the only view was the back of the units behind hers. He counted three floors, none giving away any clues where he might be.

When he heard the toilet flush, he took a seat at the table and waited. Cleo opened the door a few seconds later, but stopped in the doorway, pointing first to the door to the hall, then her ear, her eyes narrowed. "Nothing," Katz said. "Don't worry. Your reputation is still intact with the Marshals Service."

"I don't know," she said, crossing to him, then kissing his cheek silently. "Things get really wild here, especially when they break out the Mad Libs."

"How's that?"

She slid a hard pack out of the Kool carton on the dresser next to him, popped the top open, and pulled one out. "Everything's dick, balls, and pussy with them, even her. They think it's a riot. 'The pussy licked his dicks' was a real showstopper. They're still laughing at that one."

"Seems you're all bonding very nicely."

"Eh, they're all I got so I gotta make the best of it."

He pulled the taco bag to him and opened it, wallowing in the aroma. He looked to Cleo. "Taco?"

"Not now, but go ahead."

"Nah, I'll wait for you," he said, rolling up the bag. "So what else do you do here?"

"Not much. Read. Watch a lot of TV, videos – anything that passes the time. Shit, I can practically recite *Batman* to you." She lit the cigarette and took one of her long puffs. "And this. A lot of this. They'll be lucky if I make it to the trial – if they indict him."

"I've heard some other people doubt that," Katz said, "but between what they seized and what you and a lot of other folks are telling them, I don't think that's going to be a problem."

She took the other seat at the table and flicked a long ash into a nameless ashtray. "I hope you're right. And that's makin' me think about one other thing."

"What?"

"Witness protection."

"What about it?"

"If I want it."

Katz was stunned. "Are you serious, Cleo? Why wouldn't you want it? That's crazy!"

"It ain't crazy to think about two hundred thousand dollars from where I sit, Jake. That's what it is, if I take it all at once, right?"

"Yeah, but that's not the crazy part. What's crazy is thinking you're ever going to have a chance to spend it if you stay in D.C. You remember that'd be part of the deal too, right?"

She shrugged. "So maybe I'll change my name again. No one found me last time."

Katz reached out to hold her free hand tightly. "Cleo, last time – no offense – the only person looking for you was your mother. This time, there's going to be a lot more people, armed and dangerous people, plus Rayful."

"Rayful? Rayful's in jail, Jake, in case *you* forgot that part," she said, "and I seem to remember you and beaucoup other people tellin' me that once this all works out, he's never comin' out. Am I right about that – or is there something going on I don't know about?"

There is something going on you don't know about, Katz thought, thinking back to Rayful's on-the-dot phone call to Billy, *but there's no good reason you have to know about it either. I can be scared shitless enough for both of us.* "Cleo," he said, "you know a lot better than me that even if he is locked away forever, there are still going to be plenty of people out on the street – or coming back to the street – who are going want to pay people back, and you're going to be their grand prize, I'm sorry to say."

Cleo pulled her hand from his and stabbed her cigarette out until each spark was dead. She raised her eyes to Katz', angry now. "And if I'm such a big fucking prize, then why am I worth only two hundred-some thousand measly dollars for what I'm giving 'em? Without me, they got no case, Jake! Is someone else givin' 'em anything close to what I'm givin' 'em? Anyone? Shit, without me, Jake, they're dead in the water." She sprung to her feet now and slapped the ashtray onto the carpet, cigarettes, matches, and ashes flying in every direction.

Now Katz knew there was one more thing she did to fill up all the dead time. She'd dug so deep into her own head that she managed to convince herself that not only could she survive in a city where a lot of people would love to kill a person named Cleo Smythe or whatever she changed her name to, but that she deserved a bigger reward for daring to do it. Katz had to concede there was a twisted logic in all of that, but only if she didn't mind that the price of being wrong was her funeral. He heard a knock on the door.

"Everything okay in there?" Kravitz called in.

"Yeah," Katz called back, "I just knocked the ash tray off the table. We're cleaning it up."

"Okay. Got any idea how much longer you'll be? No hurry, but we got to let the next crew know." Katz turned to Cleo, who had her back to him, her face buried in her hands. "Just a few more minutes, thanks," he said.

"No problem. Just knock on the door when you're ready."

Katz put a hand on Cleo's back and walked around her. He tried to lift her face to look at him but she was having none of it. Tears trickled down her fingers. It was only when he hugged her tight that she dropped her hands and hugged him back.

"Jake, I am so sorry. You're the last person I want to upset, especially after – "

251

"I know, I know. It's okay." He felt her tears dampen his shirt. "Oh now, look what you've done," he said, pulling back to show her. She took a look and cracked a smile through the tears. "I've made you wet again," she said. "Will you come back and see me if I promise you'll stay dry?"

"Wet or dry, I promise I'll be back." She kissed him, then pressed her cheek to his. He knew he had to let go sometime, but was in no hurry. When he finally did, she let him tilt her chin up this time.

"And about the witness protection thing?" he said. "Let me talk to Madden and see what he might be willing to do. I will be your advocate, I promise."

"Okay, Jake," she whispered. "We can talk about it the next time." She nuzzled deep into his neck. "I really liked talking to you."

"And I loved talking to you." They kissed deeply, long enough for Katz to develop a new taste for menthol. Cleo broke first and straightened herself up in the mirror, then went to the door and tapped on it. "Okay, guys, we're done."

Marshal Kravitz came in, mask in hand. Katz held up the bag. "Tacos?" he asked. "We never got around to them."

"Pass," Kravitz said before he heard Bykovsky clear her throat in the hall. "On second thought, I'll trade you."

Katz handed him the bag and took the mask. "It's okay. I could use a nap." He turned to smile at Cleo. "I look forward to talking to you again soon," he said, then slipped on the mask and let the Marshals take him away.

23

Madden returned his call late the next afternoon. "And what can I do for you today, Mr. Katz?"

"I actually want to circle back to something we've talked about before."

"Let's see, we've talked about so many things. She's worn the bug enough, so I'm guessing it's not that. Is it whether we need her for the grand jury again? Am I getting warm?"

"No, but now that you mention it – "

"We don't, I'm happy to tell you, but if you want to know if that means she's going to be released from protective custody before the trial, the answer to that is no too. The indictments just need Stephens' signature and when that happens – as I'm sure you remember – the next step is to get a judge appointed, then start ramping up for trial."

"But that's going to be a long ramp, isn't it?" Katz asked. "Unless I'm seriously mistaken, you're going to have multiple defendants with multiple counts, which means multiple lawyers with multiple motions. It could be months till you get a jury ready to hear this thing."

"Wow! I hadn't thought about that, Jake! Thanks for the call!"

"Charlie, no bullshit. Does she really need to be kept out of sight for all that time?"

"Is that really why you called me?"

"No, but maybe it should've been."

"Sorry, Jake, but we're not going to risk losing her – and her testimony – at trial. I realize she's being inconvenienced, but it's better than being dead, right?" He didn't wait for Katz to answer. "So please, Jake, the suspense is killing me. Tell me. Why did you call?"

"Okay, you remember we discussed her not going into witness protection."

"Yeah, and I gave you a dollar figure."

"Let's talk about that."

"What, the number?" Madden laughed. "Are we negotiating now? What do you think this is, the NFL? Cleo Smythe is not a fucking free agent, Jake. She's a cooperating witness and she's being treated very well for it."

"Charlie, Cleo's not dumb. She knows how valuable her testimony is and she knows you know how valuable it's going to be at trial. She just wants to be fairly compensated for it."

"Two hundred-some thousand dollars is fair compensation, Jake!" Madden yelled. "She wants more, she can take it in installments like pretty much every other snitch – and if she really wants to live to spend it, she needs to go into witness protection. No amount of money's going to change that."

"She knows she'd be putting her life on the line, but that's going to be the case whether she goes into protection or she doesn't. You know that Rayful Edmond is doing anything he wants anytime he wants to, right? He's got people inside the prison, MPD, everywhere, feeding him all kinds of information, doing all kinds of shit for him."

"Tell me something I don't know," Madden spit back.

"The point is, if he wants her found, she's going to be found. A little more money would just maybe give her some better options, that's all I'm saying." Katz waited to hear something back until he started to wonder if Madden had hung up on him. When he finally heard him, the strain in his voice made Katz wonder if he was passing a kidney stone.

"You say you're client's not dumb, Jake? I beg to differ. The only reason she'd get a lump sum is if she declines witness protection – and that's the definition of dumb. I seem to be more concerned with her living than either one of you and, honestly, the only reason I give a damn is 'cause I do need her at trial. After that, if she gets what she deserves? I could shit care less."

"Charlie, I'm representing my client, okay? She asked me to explore it with you and that's what I'm doing. What's the problem with asking the Department to sweeten the pot a little? Let's see what they say."

"Uh huh, and if they say no, what's she going to do, clam up on the stand? Number one, we can impeach the shit out of her with her grand jury testimony anyway – she's already waived her Fifth Amendment rights in case you forgot – and number two, the agreement says her testimony has to be 'useful to the government'. You remember that part, don't you, Jake? You sure as shit don't want me saying it wasn't, trust me."

"Charlie, I know we're asking a lot, but you are too. Let's just try to keep your star witness happy."

This time, Katz didn't have to wonder if Madden was still on the other end. The slam was conclusive proof. Katz laid the receiver back in its cradle to sort out his thoughts before he dialed up Cleo to tell her – what? – that he gave it a shot? That Madden hung up on him? That the whole idea was crazy, not just to Madden, but him too? But if it was so crazy to them, why wasn't it crazy to her, the one whose life actually was on the line? Was keeping her made-up name so important? Or was staying in D.C. really so much better than starting over fresh somewhere else? She had no legitimate business prospects unless she was hankering to go back on the titty bar circuit, and everyone she knew here was about to go behind bars for the rest of their lives anyway, so what – or who – could be the big draw?

He could only come up with one name. His. But that was the craziest thought of all. He was just her lawyer and they'd only known each other a minute. And yet. He couldn't deny how he felt about her, and their little bathroom encounter might've been a tipoff that she felt the same about him – but it also could've been just the volatile mix of two pent-up doses of lust going off.

Or maybe she was just using him. That was the least crazy explanation by far but it also posed a key question he still couldn't answer: For what? The ring of the phone on LaVerne's desk mercifully derailed his train of thought. In a second, her voice pierced through the door.

"Surprise, surprise, guess who?" she called. "Says it's *real* important."

For the first time he could remember, Katz welcomed Harry's interruption. "Greetings, counselor," he said. "What's so important this time?"

"How about the indictments against Rayful Edmond and his crew? Would seein' them maybe interest you a little bit?" Katz thought nothing Harry said could shock him anymore, but he was wrong.

"What? Are they out?"

"No, they ain't out. They're not even signed yet."

"Then how did you get them?"

"Fax. Right now."

"That's not what I meant. Who sent them to you? I literally just got off the phone with someone who told me they were waiting for Stephens' signature."

"Then you know I ain't lyin'."

"So who's the leak? Someone in the USA's office?"

"You don't need to know who, Jake, so don't worry about it. I just thought you might be interested to know your client wasn't charged." That was no surprise to Katz but he didn't see the point of letting Harry know that. "Well, that's good news," he said.

"Yeah, well, I'm not so sure a lot of other people're gonna think that's such good news. They're going to be a lot more concerned about why she wasn't."

"Uh huh. And is your client on there?"

"Who says I even got a dog in this fight?" Harry asked.

"Billy Murphy, as a matter of fact. He said you declined his invitation to a little get-together of everyone's lawyers."

"That don't mean shit!" Harry barked. "I got my reasons."

"The same reason you think Cleo Smythe's name's not on there?"

"Goddamn it, Jake! Why you got to do me like this? You want me to fax this over or don't you?"

"Shit no, I don't want it, Harry," Katz said. "Always a pleasure." Especially the hanging up part. Katz tried to prioritize what he ought to do next and was happy that calling Cleo about his talk with Madden came in second. He dialed up number one.

"Gaskins," he heard.

"Marshal Gaskins, Jake Katz."

"Well, howdy, my friend. To what do I owe the honor?"

"In the last ten minutes, I've had two sources – one reliable, one not so much – tell me that indictments are just about to come down in the Rayful Edmond case. Any truth to that rumor?"

"That does track with the scuttlebutt going around here, but I haven't seen anything official. Either of 'em say anything about your lady?"

"The unreliable one did, but I think he might actually be right for a change. No charges."

"That's good. Now I did hear one other rumor I hope is wrong, for a lot of people's sake, including yours."

"What's that?"

"You ever try a case before Judge Richey? Word is he's gettin' this one."

Katz' stomach turned cartwheels before all the reasons why flooded back to him. Nixon appointed Charles Richey to the bench in 1971, the same year Katz started at the U.S. Attorney's Office. He only appeared before him at a couple of hearings before leaving the USA's, but heard all about the twists and turns of one of the biggest cases Richey presided over, the Government's criminal prosecution of the Church of Scientology, over drinks with his old crew at The Man In the Green Hat. At the heart of the charges was the Church's massive effort to infiltrate its members into the workforce at Justice and the IRS so they could steal records about those agencies' plans to sue it. The Church's attorneys were merciless to Richey throughout the case, insulting him daily, filing all kinds of chickenshit motions and interlocutory appeals, and finally driving him over the edge by planting a story with Jack Anderson saying he'd been patronizing call girls during the case. Richey wound up in the hospital a few days later with a pulmonary embolism that nearly killed him.

Katz didn't know if that case was why Richey was so erratic – if he was being kind – or manic depressive – if he wasn't – ever since, but it was a reputation he earned. His law clerks, court staff, and lawyers on both sides felt his warmth, then his wrath within the same minute. He would yell at all of them, brutally, in open court. Out of court, he was notorious for calling lawyers at home in the middle of a trial to talk about the day's events and tell them what motions he'd grant or deny. The USA's Office did everything it could to get him to stop – begging him, calling the Chief Judge, complaining to the Committee on Judicial Conduct – but nothing worked. The thought of Richey presiding over this monster of a case made him pray that Harry was right that Cleo wasn't going to be anything more than a witness. Katz summed up that firehose of memories in two words to Marshal Gaskins.

"Uh oh," he said.

24

The next morning, the *Post* confirmed Harry's scoop: The Edmond grand jury had issued its indictments. Katz parked himself at the kitchen table and skimmed the article quickly to see if either of Cleo's names popped up, and exhaled only when he saw they didn't. Then he took his time reading about everyone else's *tsuris*.

As he expected, Rayful took the hardest hit: fourteen counts of murder, assault with intent to kill, racketeering, gun violations, and using juveniles to distribute drugs. Each count had a mandatory minimum sentence of twenty years in prison and eight million dollars in fines. In all, twenty-nine people were indicted, every one of them hit with conspiracy to distribute more than five grams of coke, some with more, but the conspiracy charge alone was enough to guarantee that the judge could give them life without parole, so the rest was really just to show the public how tough Jay Stephens was. Uncharacteristically, he gave no quote and neither did Billy Murphy.

The last thing he read was that Richey would be doing the arraignment, a sure sign he'd be doing the trial too. Score one for Marshal Gaskins. He wanted to give Cleo the good news but had no way to reach her. He glanced at the clock on the stove. 7:35. Now that the grand jury was over, the Marshal wouldn't be at his post that early and neither would anyone else, so Katz took his shower, ate his Cheerios, and came through his office door an hour later. LaVerne hadn't made it in yet, so he didn't have to fear seeing one of her pink love notes warning him

Harry had called. Two good things before nine o'clock. That was as close as Katz ever got to being on a roll, so he pushed his luck and tried the Marshal's number now.

"Marshals' office," he heard. "Gaskins."

"Marshal, Jake Katz."

Gaskins chuckled. "You read the Post, I take it."

"I did. You were right on the money."

"I wish I wasn't, for your sake and everyone else who's gonna have to deal with him. He's gonna be a handful. But I'm guessing you didn't call just to talk about him."

"No, I need to talk to my client to let her know she didn't get indicted, but I don't know how to reach her because I have no idea where she is. Any chance you might be able to put me in touch with the Marshals who're babysitting her?"

"You got any idea who they are?"

"I do. A guy named Kravitz and a woman named Bykofsky, at least that's who was with her the last time I saw her."

"Hold on a minute," Gaskins said and put him on hold. Katz tried to think of anything but the last time he saw Cleo, but couldn't. He was just about to plant her on the sink again when the Marshal curbed his enthusiasm.

"The guy's name is Gibson," he said, "Lee Gibson. He's the Deputy who supervises both of 'em. If they've rotated off her, he'll tell you who's on her now." Katz' enthusiasm grew a mite again, but he forced himself to focus.

"Great," he said. "You have his number?" The Marshal gave it to him, they wished each other luck, and Katz dialed it up. When he heard "Gibson" on the other end, he told him he was the lawyer for Cleo Smythe. "If the name doesn't ring a bell, she's a cooperating witness – "

"I know who she is, but I can't let you talk to her."

"I think I mentioned I'm her lawyer. That gives her a constitutional right to talk to me."

"I'm sure she does, Mr. Katz, but it's not my call. The word came down from on high."

"From who?"

"Judge Richey."

"Why would Judge Richey care if I see my client?"

"Don't take it personally, Mr. Katz. He's not letting any of you talk to any witness that's turned. For their protection."

"Okay, I'm officially lost. Give it to me in words of one syllable or less."

"There've been some threats made," Gibson said. "That's all I can tell you. And now everyone's in a high state of alert, starting with Richey. He's basically afraid bad guys might follow you or anyone else who's meeting with a cooperator to find out where they are and do something to make sure they won't testify."

"Okay," Katz said, "and how long is this supposed to last?"

"No idea, sorry."

"And I have no idea where she is, which means I can't talk to her or see her. Judge Richey have anything to say about that?"

"I'm no lawyer, Mr. Katz, but I know they file some kind of papers when they're not happy about something. I think they're called motions?"

Katz knew sarcasm when he heard it, but decided not to napalm the only bridge to Cleo. "Thank you for that information, Marshal Gibson," he said. "I'll keep it in mind. In the meantime, can I ask if you might let her know I'd really like to talk to her as soon as possible and arrange for her to give me a call? She has my number."

"I'll get right on that" were the last words Katz heard before the dial tone. Two days and six hours later, LaVerne let him know Cleo was on the line.

"Cleo, it's great to hear from you. How are you?"

"Oh, super, when I'm not bored to death watching TV or playing 500 Rummy or smoking two packs a day or packing my suitcase every fifteen minutes."

"I'm going to assume you're joking about that last part."

"Not so much, Jake. Every night, it's a different place. I feel like a goddamn hooker."

"Did they tell you why they're moving you so much?"

She groaned. "Yeah, and I get it, believe me. They ain't wrong. But hey, the Marshals told me the indictments came down. Is that right?"

"It is, and did they tell you you weren't charged with a thing?"

"They did, but I wanted to hear it was for real from you."

"It's for real. They held up their end of the bargain. You hold up yours, you get to play your get out of jail free card." She didn't say anything. Maybe she was thinking about what was on his own mind: Then what? His brain knew the ethical thing was to tell her just what he already had: Be smart. Go somewhere far away from here and become somebody else, forever. But then she'd be gone from him, forever. His heart had another opinion: Beg her to stay. "*We'll figure out a way to make it work,*" he heard himself say to her. "*Let's give ourselves a chance.*" He'd roll his eyes if he heard anyone say that in a movie, but

266

now that the words were on his own tongue in real life, they sounded like the truest words he'd ever utter. She took him off the hook.

"I miss you, Jake."

"I miss you too." *Good enough for now.* "Is one of your babysitters around? Let me see what I can do about seeing you."

"Okay, hold on." He heard a door open and some mumbled conversation, then Cleo again. "Jake, I'm putting Marshal Kravitz on. Do your thing."

"Good morning, Mr. Katz," Kravitz said. "What's on your mind?"

"I'd like to see my client, Marshal. Can you make that happen?"

"If it was up to me, Mr. Katz, no problem. But it's not."

"So who is it up to? Richey?"

"You got it."

"Look, Marshal, I know this case involves a lot of really scary guys and I know Richey can freak out for no reason, but I also know he knows he can't keep clients from seeing their lawyers. What's the point of making me and everyone else file stuff to make him do what he knows he has to do?"

Kravitz paused, then said "Can I call you back?"

"Marshal, with all due respect, I waited two days plus for Cleo to call me after your boss said he'd get right on it. Can you – ?"

"Give me your number, Mr. Katz, and I will call you back in two minutes."

He did and Kravitz did. "Mr. Katz, me again. I just needed to get away from Cleo – Ms. Smythe – if I'm going to be able to talk to you about this. She doesn't need to hear it."

"Okay, so what's the deal?"

"You didn't hear this from me, either, okay? If any of this comes back to me – "

"Marshal, you have my word." Katz heard him sigh.

"So just the other day, maybe a day after Richey gets the assignment, one of his clerks brings a letter *he* got at home into the office, no stamp, no postmark, no address, no nothin' – except the only thing that's inside the envelope: A floor plan of his fucking house." Katz tried to make some sense of that, but before he could, Marshal Kravitz filled the blanks in for him. "One of Rayful's guys dropped it in his mailbox, let him know they knew where he lived, where he and his wife slept, where his kids' bedrooms are, get the picture?"

"Oh, Jesus."

"So that's all Richey had to see. You think not being able to see your client's a big deal, you have no idea the rest of the bullshit that's going on here. Once the trial starts and they start picking a jury and the public's in here, this place is going to be locked up tighter than a max prison, man. Wait'll you see. It's going to be unbefuckinglievable!"

Katz weighed his options. He could file some motions but they'd only piss Richey off, and he'd be in no hurry to rule on them anyhow. Then he could ask the Court of Appeals to jump in, but not only would that would piss him off even more, by the time they ruled on it, cooler heads might have already prevailed, and all he'd have accomplished was turn Richey against him – and, more importantly, against Cleo. His only other choice was to call Madden and see if he'd help him persuade Richey, but given their last chat, he was even more doubtful anything good would come of that either.

"Okay," he said, "let me think about it. In the meantime, can she call me maybe every day or two? We'll forget about the meetings until we see how things go with Richey."

"I think that's a good way to go. We'll ask her every day. If she wants to talk, we'll call you and put her on, no problem."

"Thank you, Marshal. Can you put her back on now?" In a few seconds, he heard a door click, then Cleo. "What was that all about?" she asked.

"He just wanted to fill me in on what to expect from Richey, off the record. He didn't want you or whoever's else there listening in. He just told me what I already knew." He hoped she'd buy that.

"So, when are you coming to see me?" She did.

"He thinks we should wait a little, just till all the indictment noise dies down a little and everyone's comfy that no one's looking for you too hard."

"And what do you think?"

"I could give you a lot of legal mumbo-jumbo, but the bottom line is he's probably right. I think it's best if we hold our fire a little while." When he heard her sigh, he said "Hey, look at it this way. It just gives us something to look forward to a little longer. He said he'll ask you every day if you want to talk. If you say you do, he'll put you right through."

"And actually seeing you? When's that going to happen? When I wave at you from the witness stand?"

Katz laughed. "We'll see plenty of each other, Cleo, no worries."

"Well that's something to look forward to too." Before Katz could figure out exactly how she meant that, her giggle told him all he needed to know. "Bye, Jake," she said. "Sweet dreams."

25

Over the next few months, Katz' confusion about his relationship with Cleo was matched in intensity only by the anger and envy that surged through him every time another legal bombshell burst in the Edmond case.

The target of his anger was Petty, always and only Petty. If that prick had assigned him a real live defendant, he'd've been up to his ears in so much action, he'd never have time to envy all of his 5th Street buddies who were getting that action with every new development in the case, and there were plenty of developments. In June, the grand jury handed down a superseding indictment full of new charges, and Stephens ordered the forfeiture of four houses and three cars – a Corvette, a Mercedes, and a Jaguar. In August, Richey made his first major ruling, breaking the case into two trials. All the violent crimes and weapons charges would be heard first, the conspiracy and drug charges next. The ripples from those blasts would cause every lawyer assigned to represent an accused to spend so much time on the case, they could actually generate a living wage from the invoices they sent the Federal Defenders' Office. They'd be plumbing the depths of law libraries, drafting motions to suppress, sever, and dismiss, arguing them in court, interviewing their clients constantly, prepping them how to answer the government's lawyer on direct, framing their own questions for cross, and cashing checks for all of it. Missing out on that left him with just the usual array of plea bargains and appearances, barely enough to cover the monthly nuts on his townhouse and the office. Lunch at Antonio's was starting to be an extravagance.

Katz's confusion about Cleo only grew whenever he thought about her, which was constantly. It was a never-ending closed circuit that could be triggered by almost anything. The route in from Petty was a perfect example. Every time Katz thought of him, he actually forgave him just a little because he realized that if it wasn't for that asshole, he never would have met her. Which he hoped was worth something, but couldn't be sure. Cue the confusion.

He'd no sooner persuade himself that her legal issues were first and foremost in his mind than he'd start thinking – dwelling? obsessing? – about whether she was – what? His girlfriend? Just a one-time thing? The damsel he'd rescue and marry happily ever after? Then he'd think about why he didn't know what she was. For a mind that didn't tolerate any introspection, that was already way too much, but one other little wrinkle baffled him most of all. He knew he could confect any number of legitimate reasons to visit her, but none of them was worth putting her life on the line, so he kept his pledge not to call her. But why didn't she call him?

Maybe the explanation was the obvious one: Her life was the one at risk and she had every reason not to put it in even more danger by having someone somehow connect the dots from Katz to her. He didn't know anything more about her than what she told him that night at Stardust, but the little he did know made it crystal clear she knew how to survive. She survived mommy and daddy by escaping Williamsburg, somehow survived being part of Rayful's murderous empire, and now was doing whatever it took to put it all behind her and somehow start a fresh life with serious money, a new name, and – if she wanted it – a new address far, far away. But why did she want to stay in D.C? That's when he'd hop back on the merry-go-round, wondering if it had something to do with him, then dismissing the whole idea as his own crazy fantasy, then letting himself hope, if only for a second, that it may be, might, just possibly, could be, true. But the carousel never ended, so he kept spinning, and clinging to the hope that it would finally stop whenever he got her alone and heard her answers to all his questions face to face. For now, he was happy just hearing LaVerne put it all on pause.

"Jake" she called in, "Charles Madden, U.S. Attorney's Office." He hadn't even heard the phone ring over the calliope in his head. He picked up the receiver.

"Mr. Madden, what an unexpected pleasure. Finally got a number for me?" Madden either cleared his throat or barked out a laugh, Katz couldn't tell. "I just told Hutchison you would start with me on that," Madden said. "You did not disappoint."

"I'll try not to be so predictable from now on. So, do you?"

"You really are a case, Jake. Let's just say we're still working on it."

"So what do have to talk about?"

"Your client's testimony. You might've heard the trial's coming up."

"I did. Do we have a trial date?"

"Richey's looking to start jury selection right after Labor Day." Katz glanced up at his wall calendar. That was two weeks away. "So, we'd like to get together with the two of you, go over the questions we expect to ask, talk about her answers, prepare her for cross-ex, all that." The cross-ex part gave Katz cause to pause.

"How many defendants are there?" he asked.

"Eleven."

"So that's eleven lawyers who're going to cross-examine her?"

"Theoretically, yes, but we're going to ask Richey to limit it."

"How're you going to do that? They've got a constitutional right."

"Yeah, but not to ask the same questions over and over. We're going to file something on it, see what he says, or maybe it'll just drive the defense guys to work something out with us, we'll see what shakes out." Katz was glad it was Madden's problem now, not his, and even passed a silent thanks to Harry for giving him the chance to represent one person at a time rather than all the People of the District of Columbia. That was two moments of forgiveness in the space of fifteen minutes for two people he'd long thought were beyond forgiveness. Maybe he was finally having a growth spurt.

"You know who's on the other side yet?" he asked.

"Not all of them. Billy Murphy's on for Rayful – "

"That I know."

"Along with James Robertson, you know him?"

"No."

Madden grunted. "He's another piece of work. About six, seven months ago, the Fourth Circuit suspended him from appearing down there. For a year."

"For what?"

"I don't know all the details, but it had something to do with him filing notices of appeal in a bunch of cases, then letting 'em sit, ignoring their notices, all that kind of stuff. Fined him pretty good too."

"So why does he get to represent Rayful here? Isn't there some kind of reciprocal deal, you're out of luck there, you're out of luck here?"

"Our benevolent disciplinary board just gave him a public censure," Madden said, "no suspension." Benevolent was not a word Katz usually associated with the D.C. Board of Professional Responsibility. "Why?" he asked.

"They felt sorry for him. His medical condition was to blame, you see."

"Okay, I'll bite. What was his medical condition?"

"He said he had some weird kind of cancer, got all kinds of treatments, supposedly went into a coma for a while, who knows, but it worked. They gave him a pass."

"Wow. This thing has some cast of characters," Katz said.

"Oh yeah, and we haven't even talked about Sol Rosen, of course, your patron saint." Sol Z. Rosen was the King of the 5th Streeters, lawyers like Katz who depended on appointed counsel fees to pay their rent, but he was also a poster boy for attorney malfeasance, on a scale much bigger than what Madden told him about Robertson. Katz recalled that Sol would have been the only lawyer who was ever suspended, reprimanded, or otherwise disciplined by D.C., Virginia, and Maryland, except Maryland let him resign from their bar rather than pile on.

"I thought he was still on double-secret probation from somebody," Katz said.

"Nine months, from D.C., but it just ended so he'll be at the party with all the other A-listers. You'll see them on the pleadings. So, enough about all your esteemed colleagues. When can we get together?"

"I'm fine any time, but it's really going to be up to the Marshals, isn't it? You know they've been moving her pretty much every day, right?"

"I do. I just wanted to check your schedule first, so let me call them and I'll get back to you with the when and where."

"And the how," Katz said. "The last time I saw her was like something out of a spy movie, with the mask and the hidden location. I'd really appreciate being spared all that. Plus, I want some time with her alone first."

"Anything else? Wake-up call? Room service?"

"I'm not trying to be difficult," Katz said.

"So it just comes naturally? All right, fine, I'll call the Marshals and try to make it all happen to your liking, Jake. Don't make any plans you can't break in the next few days. I'll get back to you."

Katz hung up the phone. Now Madden was bringing him to Cleo. *Three people to forgive in one day? Unbelievable.* But was that a good sign or a bad one? It was hard to think over all that music banging in his head again.

26

Eleven o'clock the next morning, LaVerne told him Madden was back on the phone. "Do we have a plan?" Katz said.

"We do. Get to the Mayflower Hotel around 12:30 – take Metro or a cab, no driving your own car, no walking – and take the elevator down to the basement. When you get out, a Marshal will be down there and he'll take you to see your client."

"There? Or are we going to another undisclosed location?"

"Hutchison and I are going to meet you at 1:30, Jake, and the Marshals won't even tell us where we're going until we take off, so I honestly don't know what they're planning to do with you and your client. See you then, wherever."

At 12:25, Katz got off the elevator in the basement and saw Marshal Kravitz leaning against a gray cinderblock wall waiting for him.

"Good to see you again, Marshal," Katz said.

"You too, Mr. Katz. Follow me." Kravitz led him to the elevators and they rode up to nine, one below the top floor. Kravitz got off first and pointed down the hall to the right, where a young black Marshal Katz didn't recognize was slumped back in a metal chair, arms folded, legs crossed, a folded-up newspaper on the floor next to him. He managed to turn his head to give Katz the once-over but otherwise didn't move. Katz remembered his portly minder at the courthouse. *They must teach listlessness at the Marshals School*, he thought.

When Katz showed him his bar card, the Marshal nodded and slid a card into a slot above the door handle. A light above the slot turned green and he pushed it open. Katz walked into the room and took it in. The Mayflower was a hell of a step above wherever Cleo was the last time he saw her. A long black leather sofa and two matching chairs framed a walnut coffee table to his left, facing a fat TV sitting on a large console against the wall. A King-sized bed filled the wall across from him, and a round pedestal table matching the coffee table sat to his right, circled by four black leather and shiny metal chairs. Three of the last hotel's rooms could have fit in this one, with room to spare. Only one thing was missing. Cleo. Then he heard her, from somewhere off to the right of the bed.

"Jake, is that you?"

"It is. Where are you?"

"Back here. Come on back." He saw an open doorway to the bathroom and there she was, even prettier than he remembered, in a cream silk blouse and a brown skirt that stopped about halfway down the thighs of her crossed legs, perched on the marble counter next to the sink.

"I've been waiting for you," she laughed. He was as lost as he usually was when it came to figuring her out, but he stopped thinking altogether when she hopped down to throw her arms around him and hold him close. He held her closer still and they rocked back and forth slowly, neither in any hurry to let the other one go.

"God, I missed you," she murmured into his tie. He lifted her chin to take in those eyes and that smile before kissing her longer and deeper than he remembered ever kissing anyone before. Whatever it was between them, it never felt more real than it did now. When they needed air, he said "I've missed you too, Cleo. A lot."

She slid her hands under the back of his coat and pressed him even closer to her. "You didn't have to tell me," she giggled, and kissed his neck. "I'm on the rag, honey, but I'd be more than happy to – " He smiled and laid a finger on those full lips.

"I'd be even happier," he said, "and if we stand here another five seconds, you won't have to do a thing." She laughed again and he ran his hands down the side of her face and neck until they reached her shoulders before he found the will to gently push her back a few inches. "But let's try and stick to business today. There'll be plenty of time to celebrate after, if everything goes right."

She closed the distance between them again, kissed him softly on the cheek, then stepped back to look him square in the eyes, shaking her head slowly. "You are a good man, Jake Katz," she said. "Why couldn't we meet like normal people, years ago? Jesus, things would've been so different."

Katz conjured up the vision and the sound track of his mother telling him if he ever wanted to kill her, the easiest way would be to marry a *shicksa*. Fanny Katz and Margaret Ann Mahoney? Not happening. Still, he appreciated the sentiment. "If you'd met me years ago, Cleo, let's just say you might not've had such a good opinion of me. I've always been kind of a work in progress."

"And humble too," she laughed. "I think I coulda shaped you up just fine."

"And I would've been happy to let you, believe me." He made a show of looking at his watch. "But they're going to be here in less than an hour and there's some stuff we need to talk about they don't need to hear, so maybe we ought to get started, okay?"

"Okay, counselor. Have it your way." They sat next to each other on the sofa. Katz parked his briefcase on the coffee table and pulled out the pad with the questions he scratched out after Madden hung up on him. "First of all, you told me about the custody hearing, but have you ever testified in a real trial before, with a judge or a jury?"

Cleo shook her head no. "Closest thing was the grand jury."

"Okay, not to say that was a stroll in the park, but except for sitting in a chair and answering questions, being on the stand in a trial is a completely different thing."

"'Cause Rayful's lawyer will be asking me questions too, right?"

"Right, but it's not just his lawyers – he's got two of them, by the way – it's everyone else's too."

"So how many is that?" He tried to make his answer sound more like a question, hoping that might make it sound a little less overwhelming. "Could be as many as eleven, twelve maybe, if the judge lets both of Rayful's cross-examine you."

"Twelve fucking lawyers? Are you shitting me?" It didn't.

"The government's going to try to get the judge to knock the number down, that's the best I can tell you. I know this is a lot to take in, Cleo, but – "

"I can call time out and talk to you though, just like with the grand jury, right?"

"Not really. It doesn't work that way in a trial."

"Christ! This is another fucked-up game, isn't it? Just like the goddamned plea agreement."

"Cleo, some of what goes on is up to the lawyers and the judge, but this isn't. It just is what it is." Watching her fume, he hesitated to bring up the thing he was sure would set her off, but, on the other hand, how much more pissed could she get? In for a dime, in for a dollar, he went for it. "Including whether I can even sit where the lawyers usually sit while you're up there."

"Say what now?"

"You're not a defendant, so I can't be at the defense table and I'm not a prosecutor so I can't sit at their table either without his say-so."

"Even though you know more about their supposed star witness than all of them do combined? You can pass them notes or whisper in their ear, can't you? They're always doing that shit on L.A. Law."

"I'm going to bring it up with Madden today," Katz said, "see what he says. If he gives us the wrong answer, I'll file something with Richey on my own. It's just going to take a little time to work out, that's all."

Cleo's eyes fired at him. "Right," she spat out, "just a little time to decide which of 'em's going to fuck me over. Jesus, it never stops!"

He looked back at his watch. He needed to let this pot simmer a while before Madden and Hutchison showed up.

"Cleo, I got a good idea," he said. "I haven't had a thing to eat since breakfast. How about you? Want me to get us something to eat?" She threw her head back and covered her eyes with both hands, muttering something he couldn't hear but didn't need to. He tossed his pad and pen onto the coffee table, slumped back, and let the blank TV screen fascinate him until he felt her hand on his shoulder.

"Jake," he heard her say, "forgive me. I didn't mean to shoot the messenger. None of this is your fault, it's all mine, I know it, believe me I know it. I'm just really overwhelmed and screwed up – and scared shitless, to tell you the truth."

He reached his hand back to pull hers down and clasp it in both of his, then turned to her. "Cleo, you have every right to be every one of those things. I don't know how you've kept it together this long. I couldn't."

She squeezed his hand and turned to look at him. "Too much time to fill, man, that's what it comes down to. You start thinkin' about things you never would otherwise."

"Like?" he asked. She started to answer, then stopped, her eyes blank and distant. Katz had no idea where her head was taking her, but it was somewhere far, far from the Mayflower. "There's just shit I know, Jake, okay?" she said.

He leaned closer to her. "Cleo, I'm your lawyer. Whatever you tell me stays between us, period. If it's something that can help – "

That seemed to make up her mind. "It won't, Jake, believe me. It'll only make things worse. Let's change the subject, okay? Please."

"Okay," he said, and picked up his pad to look for what would make the best use of their time. "So, the indictment lists a lot of murders that Rayful is supposed to have ordered. The Feds're going to eat up any information you can give him on any of that. Do you know anything that would link him directly to any of them?"

She seemed to zone again, then refocus, and shook her head. "All these people Rayful supposedly took out, almost all of 'em were done by guys who thought that's what he wanted, but he didn't, Jake. You really need to understand him, man. He was running a business, a big business, organized like a business is supposed to be – lines of authority, round-the-clock shifts, controls on the money, everything. But to these guys supposedly protecting him, it was just a big gang, with all the shit that goes on with that."

"I'm not sure I get where you're going."

"Okay, I'll give you an example. Ray put this guy Ike in charge of enforcing things when it needed to be done, but that was all Ike knew, so any screwup, no matter how big, how small – in his head, it always needed enforcing."

"Okay, when all you have is a hammer, everything looks like a nail. Got it."

Cleo squinted at him. "Whatever. So like a year and a half, two years ago, Ike goes to this go-go club off South Capitol Street, and shoots up a couple of bouncers over selling some drugs on Ray's turf. Okay, bad enough, right? Then – like six months later – he goes back there again and shoots up seven more dudes! Ray told him 'Look, man, you think you're helping me, but you ain't, you're hurting me.' All he was doing was drawing the cops' attention to something that put the whole operation at risk, and for what? Some bug shit operation didn't mean anything? Fucking ridiculous. But see, that's how they think."

Katz remembered hearing something on the local news a while back about some shootings at another club in Southeast. "Did Ike – or Rayful – have anything to do with that thing at Chapter Three?" he asked.

"Hah," Cleo hacked, "*thing*? There were two things there too. Nut killed some guy on the sidewalk right outside the place last year, then a couple months after that, some poor girl who had nothing to do with anything got caught in a shootout with some guys down from New York who actually were trying to horn in on Ray's action. But that was all Ike too. Thanks for reminding me, Jake. You see what I'm saying? I'm fucking toast!"

She pointed a trembling finger at him, her eyes wet now, but not wet enough to put out the flames raging at him. "You want more? One of the Marshals let it slip what they did to Deborah Phillips, how they fucked her up for doing the same thing I'm doing – only now I'm doin' 'em worse than her even – then I go back to that goddamned Mercedes that scared the shit out of me that night with you – and you start thinkin' 'Jesus Christ, I am a goddamned sitting duck'. And it doesn't even matter if Rayful doesn't want me dead, if Ike or Nut or anyone else does. It doesn't even matter if the Marshals move me every twenty minutes. They put their minds to it, call whoever they got inside everywhere, they will find out where I am, man. They just will. I am dead meat, man, who's kiddin' who?"

Katz winced inside, thinking of the things she didn't know that would freak her out even more, if that was possible. The letter Richey's clerk found in his mailbox. Kravitz telling him how unbefuckinglievable security was going to be at the courthouse. Billy Murphy showing up at his office out of the blue. He shot a look back at his legal pad. The only other major thing on there was the 'should she stay or should she go' question, but even he could sense this was not the time to start up on that again. He got up and circled behind her, put his hands on her shoulders, and massaged them softly.

"Cleo," he said, "I'm sorry about all this, I really am."

She didn't say anything but he felt her shoulders relax. He kept kneading them. "Can I get you something to eat before they get here?" he asked. "They could be here a few hours."

She swayed a little, eyes closed. "The Marshals won't let you, Jake. They'll get it. They're used to it, trust me."

"Okay, what do you want?"

"My usual. Tuna on whole wheat, lettuce and tomato, no mayo – and a large coffee, black."

"Got it. Madden and Hutchison're probably going to be up here about the same time as the food, so if you need to get yourself together, this might be a good time."

She opened her eyes and took a deep breath, then reached back to pat his hands. He kissed the top of her head. "I'll be good," she said, "I promise," then got up and kissed him on the cheek before she headed for the bathroom. When she got to the door, she turned and gave him a wan smile, then closed it behind her. Before he could take a step, Katz heard her cry out and froze.

"Cleo, what's wrong?" he yelled.

"I look like absolute shit!" she said.

He exhaled. "I'll get us some lunch."

27

Ten minutes later, he heard a knock on the outside door. When he opened it, Charlie Madden handed him a white paper bag.

"You thought I was kidding about the room service, didn't you?" he said. "See how good I am to you?" Katz watched him and Hutchison come in just as Cleo came out of the bathroom. "Ms. Smythe," Madden said. "Good to see you again."

"Wish I could say the same."

"Cleo, the man brought us a free lunch," Katz said. "Let's cut him some slack."

Cleo parked herself in a chair. Madden and Hutchison took the couch, Katz the other chair. "So," Madden said to him, "have you told your client what she can expect?"

"Generally," Katz said, "but you're the only ones who know exactly what you want from her, so have at it."

Madden nodded and turned to Cleo. "First, I'm not going to lie to you, Ms. Smythe. You're the most important witness we're going to present, so it's extremely important that we know exactly what you're going to tell us and, maybe even more important, that we know what you're going to say when the defendants' lawyers cross-examine you."

"All twelve of them, right?" Cleo snapped.

"We're going to do our best to knock that number down," Hutchison said, "for all our sakes."

"No offense," Cleo said, "but I don't give one shit about your sake. I'm the one up there." Katz saw Hutchison's neck muscles tighten, but Madden stayed cool.

"You are exactly right, Ms. Smythe," he said, "and we're going to be filing a motion with the judge very shortly asking him to keep you from being asked about the same things by more than one lawyer. Of course, once we get in the courtroom, we'll object to any question asking about anything you've already answered."

"Can I see a draft before you submit it, give you some comments?" Katz asked.

"Absolutely," Madden said and wrote himself a note. "So, we have your grand jury testimony – and, by the way, we're leaving you copies when we're done here so that you and Mr. Katz can review it before you testify – but there are a few specific items we want to talk about with you today, just so we can see what we ought to spend our time on at the trial, okay?"

"How much time are we talking about?" Cleo asked. "I spent the better part of two days giving you everything you wanted at the grand jury."

"But it's not just us this time," Hutchison said. "It's them too. Until we get a feel for what their lawyers want to know and what Richey's going do to keep 'em under control, no one can tell you how long you're going to be up there." He saw the look on her face, then turned to see a close cousin on Madden's. "Hey, I'm just telling you the way it is," he said. "There's no use lyin' about it."

Madden jumped right back in. "So, Ms. Smythe, let's go back to the custody issue for openers. Anything we ought to know about things you did when you were having problems with your folks?"

"*I* did? Nothing! They're the ones who fucked up, not me."

"I have no doubt," Madden said, "but did you act out in any way to, you know, rebel? Shoplift, maybe, or get in trouble as a juvenile delinquent? Anything that Rayful's lawyers can try to use against you?"

"Hold on," Cleo said. "I thought all of the shit you do as a kid do was off limits."

"It is, no question, legally, but that won't stop Billy Murphy or any of the rest of them from asking about it, just to plant a seed with the jury that you can't be trusted because you've been bad from the get-go. We'll object, believe me, but the damage will've been done."

Cleo steamed on that a few seconds until Katz saw her eyes turn as hot and red as they did twenty minutes ago. He braced himself, but it turned out these tears were for something else, maybe something she hadn't let herself see for a long time.

"I did not do a thing wrong, Mr. Madden. The only person who did anything wrong in that house was my fucking father. He was a miserable drunk and he took whatever made him miserable on any given day out on me – and my mother – all the time. Maybe she was what they'd call an enabler now, but what choice did she have, really, huh? Whatever anyone might say she did wrong – turn a blind eye, a deaf ear, whatever – she did it because she thought it would make things better, for me."

Katz looked for a box of tissues but couldn't find one, so he fished into the bag of uneaten lunch for a wad of paper napkins and handed them to her. She pulled one free and dabbed her eyes. Hutchison turned to Madden.

"We might want to bring that in, you know?" he said. "Build a little sympathy for her."

"Fuck that," Cleo said. "I don't need their pity."

Madden scribbled a note Katz couldn't read, then looked back up at Cleo. "When we ran your name – names – on NCIC, the criminal information system, we found no prior convictions. Is that right?"

"It is," Cleo said.

"Okay, then tell me why you changed your name."

"I didn't do it on my own," Cleo said. "The judge did. It was completely legit."

"Were you hiding something?" Hutchison asked. Cleo fired her stare at him now. "All I wanted was to start over, Mr. Hutchison, fresh."

"I don't know," he said, "Cleo, Margaret Ann, whatever your name is, what kind of cruel, heartless kid would leave her mommy and daddy, and then change her name so they couldn't ever find her? Someone who'd do something like that might do anything, like lie to let someone else take the rap, don't you think?"

Cleo looked like she was about to leap off the chair at him. "What the fuck?" she screamed. Madden held up his hands.

"Ms. Smythe," he said. "Ron's just trying to get you prepared for how Billy Murphy and all the rest of them are going to come at you. I told you before that they're going to plant any seed they can with the jury and hope it takes root. Just know that at the end of the day, all they need is one juror to buy whatever bullshit they throw out there. If just one of them doesn't believe you for whatever reason, and decides he's not going to convict Rayful Edmond, that's a hung jury and if they hang, Rayful walks."

"Cleo," Katz said, "let me just add one asterisk to that. He won't necessarily walk, because a hung jury doesn't mean a jury acquitted him. If they can't reach a verdict, the government can try him again."

"Is that supposed to be good news, Jake?" Cleo asked, wide-eyed. "So, what, I gotta hide out in hotels and God knows where for another six months or a year or forever, wondering all the time when and if someone's going to take me out? Goddamn it, spare me! Take me out now!" Katz liked it better when she was spitting fire at Hutchison.

293

Madden tried to bail him out, even daring to lean closer to her. "Ms. Smythe, you made a good deal, believe me. All the options you had when you decided to take it were bad, trust me on that too. We had – and we still have – enough evidence to send you to prison for the rest of your life. Now, you have a good chance to live a free life with some money behind you and even a new name and a new place to live, if you want that."

"I was just trying to make sure you knew all the options, Cleo," Katz said as softly as he could yet still be heard. "I didn't mean to upset you. I'm sorry."

But she was somewhere else again. "So this Billy Murphy," she said, "or any of the lawyers, they don't have to tell the truth when they ask me a question?"

"No, they do not," Madden said. "They're not the ones under oath. And even if we object and even if the judge sustains it and instructs the jury to disregard it, they've still heard it and they can't unhear it."

"Jesus Christ!" Cleo said. "How does anyone get a fair trial in this country?" She turned to Katz. "Maybe I shoulda just taken my chances, huh? Let *you* poke holes in all *their* stories! What a goddamned racket!"

They all sat quiet until Katz spoke. "Cleo, think about everything we talked about before and everything they've told you. You've still got a very good chance of coming out on the winning side in this thing – but you can't explode every time they ask you a question you don't like.

You do that, you're only making it easier for somebody to vote to acquit him just because they don't like you."

She sat quiet, then sunk back in her chair and turned to look at Madden. "So I gotta be Miss Congeniality too, is that it?"

"That's about right," he said, "but the questions are going to be a lot tougher than 'What do you think about world peace?' They're going to probe everything, insinuate anything, do whatever they can to get that one vote. Your job is to answer only what Murphy asks. That's it. Don't volunteer anything. He wants anything more, he can ask for it – and you just answer that, okay? If he gets frustrated and pissed, that's his problem – and it'll just be more fun for the rest of us."

She looked back at Katz. "Couldn't have said it better myself," he said.

She blew out a breath, sat back up straight, and folded her hands on her lap. "Okay," she said to Madden. "Bring it on." Madden nodded to Hutchison.

"Did you have sex with Rayful Edmond?" Hutchison asked her. Katz watched Cleo's face flush and her hands clench. "No," she finally said.

"Never?" Hutchison asked. "Come on, you really expect us to believe that?" Katz thought he was enjoying this a little too much. "But you'll be objecting to that, right, guys?" he said. "'Asked and answered', right?"

295

"Right," Madden said, "but let him go on, okay? I want your client to know exactly what it's going to be like in there." Katz looked at Cleo.

"I don't care if you believe me or not," she said to Hutchison. "I didn't. Not once. Not ever. No fucking, no blow job, no hand job, no nothing. Okay? Clear enough?"

"Very," Madden said, his own face flushing now. "But that's probably a little clearer than we need. 'No sir, I did not' would do just fine." Katz looked at him intently, mostly to keep from looking at Cleo. Madden turned back to Hutchison.

"How much coke did you snort on any given day?" Hutchison asked her.

"None. Sir."

"None? You expect me to believe that when you had piles of the stuff around you twenty-four hours a day?"

"I don't expect you to believe me at all. I'm just telling you how it is. It's not my thing."

"So just selling it was your thing, is that it?"

"That's right," she said, shaking her head. "I saw what it did to people. I was screwed up enough already, didn't need that."

"And you only sold it for Rayful, that's what you're telling me?" Hutchison went on.

"That's what I'm telling you," she said.

296

"Never anything on the side?"

"No, sir, never," Cleo said. "Rayful paid me more than enough. I would never give him a moment to doubt me. I was loyal and honest with him from the get-go."

"Excellent," Madden said. "The jury will love that. Honor among thieves." Cleo let that go without even a blink. Katz marveled at how she could transform herself in a flash. *Cleo Chameleon*, he sang to himself. But it made him wonder. *Is that how she learned to survive her parents? Climb the ladder to get next to Rayful? Maybe even use Jake Katz?* He made himself focus on Hutchison again.

"Let me be clear on this, Ms. Smythe," Hutchison said, "just so there's no misunderstanding, okay? I'm not talking about just selling bricks, I mean never a gram or an ounce or a baggie or nothin', ever, is that your testimony?"

Cleo shrugged. "That's my testimony, 'cause it's the truth. That's what you want, right?" Now even Hutchison was impressed. "That's good right there," he said. "Work that in too, for sure."

The next two hours ground on, up the ladder to Rayful and back down, through every defendant, every incident, every plane ticket, every hotel receipt, every picture. Ever cut coke with her? Carry money there? Who's he, she, them? On and on they went till long after Katz was ready to snap, but Cleo maintained her cool through it all. She answered every question she was supposed to answer, wouldn't take the bait on anything she wasn't, and didn't volunteer one syllable more than she needed. Finally, Katz watched Madden flip to an empty sheet and look to Hutchison. "You got anything else?" he asked. Katz sent a stream of telepathic *No!s* his way.

"Wiretap transcripts," Hutchison said, but even he didn't sound too enthused about it.

"Next time," Madden said and pulled his briefcase up on the table with a grunt. He reached in with both hands, pulled out six thick binders of paper held together by long tin prongs, and laid them on the table. "Here's your homework, a copy for each of you of Ms. Smythe's grand jury testimony and her wiretapped conversations. Ms. Smythe, I'd greatly appreciate it if you could give them a good read before we get together again."

"I don't need to read it," she said. "I lived it."

"I'm well aware," Madden said. "And I'll be asking you to listen to the tapes too." He tucked his pad inside the briefcase and pushed himself off the couch. He stretched his hand out to Cleo.

"You did good," he said, "very good."

She gave him a perfunctory shake and ignored Hutchison's hand. "Good enough to get out of jail free?" she asked Madden.

He gave her his grim grin. "You do on the stand what you did here today, absolutely." He shook Katz' hand and Hutchison did too. When they got to the door, Madden turned back to her. "We'll talk again when we get closer.

Please do go over that stuff, especially the brunch with Bootsie. When you start testifying, we'll meet every night just to keep things on track the best we can."

Katz expected a cascade of curses, or at least a groan and a finger, but all he heard from her was nothing, all he saw was serene. She turned to him. "Don't you have something to ask him, Jake?"

She doesn't miss a thing, he reminded himself one more time. "I do, thanks, Cleo. When she's up there, you think I can sit at your table so I can slide you some notes, maybe suggest some questions on re-direct, just give you someone else to bounce things off of?"

Madden didn't waste any time thinking about it. "Absolutely," he said, "makes perfect sense."

"Will Richey have to okay it?" Katz asked.

"He shouldn't, it's our table, but – we probably ought to clear it with him just so he doesn't go off."

Katz turned to Cleo to see if she remembered anything else he didn't, but she was leafing through a volume of her testimony. She flipped it shut and looked at Madden. "Does Rayful get to see this?" she asked.

"Yes, but, under the rules, only after you testify."

All Cleo's cool evaporated in a flash. "Motherfucker!" she screamed. "You might remember you're not talking about a guy who plays by the goddamned rules. Shit, he probably got 'em before I did! Before you did!"

Katz' first instinct was to calm her down, but his first thought trumped it: *If Ray got it, Billy Murphy did too, and no doubt before his surprise visit.* He waited for the chill to scoot all the way down his spine before he looked back at Madden. "Charlie, back in my day, those transcripts were literally under lock and key, in a safe. It's probably even tighter now, right?"

Madden and Hutchison exchanged glances. The chill headed back up.

"Mr. Katz, Ms. Smythe," Madden said, "I'd love to assure you that we work in an ironclad vault where nothing ever gets out without our permission – but I can't. You might've had leakers and thieves back in your day, Mr. Katz, but the sad truth is it's worse than it's ever been, and this case is the worst of the worst."

Katz flashed back to his skirmish with the Scientologists but Cleo lasered in on the here and now.

"So Ray does have it," Cleo said. "Is that what you're telling me?"

"Like I said, I can't guarantee he doesn't," Madden said, "and I know what you must be think –"

"You have no fucking idea what I'm thinking," she said.

"Ms. Smythe," Madden said, "I can guarantee you this. That courthouse and that courtroom are going to be more secure than any courthouse in the history of the world and you are going to be more safe than any witness in history."

"Wow, Mr. Madden, that is so comforting coming from someone who's never promised me anything except that I'm going to prison if I fuck up in there," Cleo said, icicles hanging from every word. Katz tried a different tack.

"Can you explain that a little, maybe give her a reason to actually believe you?" he asked. Madden eyed the door for a second, then took a deep breath. "I can't tell you everything, okay, and what I'm telling you, you didn't hear from me, all right?" he said.

"Honor among thieves is right," Cleo muttered. "Go ahead, convince me how safe and secure I'm gonna be, I dare you."

"The courthouse and the courtroom are going to have metal detectors, like they have at the airports – at every door. No one is going to be able to bring anything in, period. Plus there are going to be more armed cops and marshals in the courtroom than there are out on the streets, and just in case all that's not enough, they're talking about putting up some kind of bulletproof shield between us and the gallery."

Cleo shot Katz a quizzical look. "Where the spectators sit," he said. She turned her hot gaze to Madden.

"Jesus Christ!" she yelled. "This is not making me feel better! I'll be lucky if I make it to the courtroom!"

"You've made it this far," Hutchison said, "for, what, six, seven months? That's a pretty damn good track record, I'd say."

"Right," Cleo said, "but all you gotta do is fuck up once and there goes your record – and, oh yeah – my life!"

Madden squared his shoulders, then pulled the door open. "Ms. Smythe, Mr. Katz. We'll be in touch. Mr. Katz, same rules leaving as coming here, okay?" Katz nodded and waited for them to close the door before daring to face Cleo. She grabbed a napkin and pressed it to her eyes. Katz forced himself to realize that the best thing for her was to take the money and run. He laid a gentle hand on her shoulder.

"Cleo," he said, "I'm going to head out, give you a chance to grab some sleep or a pack of Kools or whatever'll let you decompress a little, okay?" She nodded and walked him to the door, arm in arm, then planted a kiss on him that made him seriously doubt he knew what was best for either of them.

28

Four meetings, nineteen days, and eighteen sleepless nights later, Katz picked the Sunday *Post* off his walkway and flipped it over to read what he already knew: Jury selection was starting in the Rayful Edmond trial tomorrow morning, September 11. 9:30 a.m. sharp.

The second Madden told him that last Thursday afternoon, Katz promised himself he'd do whatever it took to keep from being anywhere near the frenzy that would engulf the courthouse Monday. By Friday morning, he started thinking that he may actually owe it to his client, a/k/a the prosecution's star witness, to scope it out so she was as ready as she could be when she took the stand. By Friday afternoon, he called Marshal Gaskins to see if he might pretty please be able to get a peek before show time.

At 9 Saturday morning, the Marshal pushed open a door on the Fourth Street side of the courthouse to let him in. He was wearing a hooded black USMS sweatshirt, an Orioles cap, faded blue jeans, and low black Chucks. It was the first time Katz had ever seen him not in uniform and made him regret that, except for a tie, he was in his. He handed Gaskins a brown paper Popeyes bag and a styrofoam cup of coffee with a plastic lid.

"What's this?" the Marshal asked.

"A token of my appreciation, the chicken and biscuits platter, without the platter. It was the only place open so if — "

The Marshal held up his left hand and took the bag with his right. "No explanation necessary, Mr. Katz," he said with a smile. "I appreciate the kindness."

"And I really appreciate you doing this for me, Marshal."

"They wanted me here bright and early today anyway, Mr. Katz. Might as well have a little friendly company."

"Let's make it Jake then. And I should know, after all these years, but I'm sorry to say I don't."

"Phillip, but to my friends, Jake, it's Phil." They shook hands and Katz followed him around the metal detector belts, through a glass door to the main corridor, and down a hall to the right to an elevator Katz didn't remember ever seeing. "I've never been down here before," he said.

"Oh, the fun's just startin', Jake. You're about to see stuff neither of us has ever seen here before." He poked the button for four.

"We going to the secure courtroom?" Katz asked.

"If that's 21, yeah, but now it's really secure, like Superman Fortress of Solitude secure. And they ain't done yet." The elevator stopped and Katz followed him back around the corner and down the broad central hallway. Just past the main elevators, Gaskins pointed off to the right to what looked like a door frame standing perpendicular to the wall just outside Courtroom 21, except there was no door in it, just a small wooden table sitting to its left.

"Is that another metal detector?" Katz asked.

"Yep." Gaskins said.

"But everybody's already come through the one downstairs, right? They think Michael Corleone's going to pull a gun off a toilet up here or what?"

Gaskins grunted a chuckle and set his breakfast bag down on the table. He nodded at two uniformed Marshals chatting just outside the double wood and glass doors to the courtroom, then turned to Katz. "You buckled in?"

He didn't wait for an answer and pushed the door for Katz to go through first, then joined him just inside the door. He pointed a finger at what Katz was already trying to come to grips with. "Ever seen anything like that here? Or anywhere else for that matter?" Five yards away, stretching from one wall to the other, a thick glass partition about ten feet high loomed over them. Katz had a flashback that dizzied him for a second.

"I have, believe it or not," he said. "In Superior Court back in '77, the Khaalis trial. Bulletproof too, right?"

"Oh yeah. Howitzer shell wouldn't crack it." Gaskins pointed to a chair facing them in front of a door-size opening in the middle. "Door's going in today, and one of our guys – armed to the teeth of course – will be sitting there all the time, scannin' the peanut gallery, making sure nobody goes through uninvited."

Katz looked to his left and right. Five oak benches sat on each side, each one big enough to hold maybe eight people. "Aren't there usually more benches?" he asked. "This seems small to me for some reason."

Gaskins nodded and pointed ahead to his left. "We had to pull out two rows to make room for them." Katz followed his finger to four long tables sitting behind each other that filled the space between the glass and the bench where Richey would sit. "Okay, for all the lawyers. I get it," he said.

Gaskins led him through the opening into the courtroom. Katz saw boxes overflowing with headphones and wires sitting on two of the tables.

"What's that all about?"

"Wireless headphones, 'cause they're afraid all of them up there won't be able to hear everyone else's questions when they're picking the jury, they tell me."

Katz looked to the right. One table for the prosecution faced the defense tables, the jury box behind it. "At least the jury's where it's supposed to be," he said.

"Yeah – but." Katz cocked his head and waited to hear the rest. "Richey's got some plans for them too."

"They're going to be anonymous, I hear," Katz said. "That'll be a first, at least around here."

"Right on both counts, and they're going to be sequestered too, of course."

"I'm sure. So all that seems normal enough."

Gaskins chuckled and kept his eyes on the box. "Remember that mask you and your client had to wear?"

"How could I forget it?"

"Well, you must've looked so good in it, Richey wants the jury to wear 'em."

"Are you serious?"

"Well, maybe not the part about you so much, but the part about Richey? Yeah, I'm serious." He held up his hands to frame the jury box and squinted. "And how do you think some venetian blinds would look up there?"

"Excuse me?" Katz said.

Gaskins lowered his hands and smiled at him. "That's what he said he was thinkin' about, right out loud. I was there – and I still couldn't believe I heard it!"

"Come on, Phil, you're just messin' with me now, right? I know he can be a little nuts, but this is off the charts nutty."

"I wish I was, Jake, but there's been so much crazy shit going on, I can almost understand why he's thinkin' about it. I don't want to talk out of school, Jake, so you'll just have to take my word for it." The Marshal blew out a gust of air and shook his head before he looked back to the jury box. "Your old buddies talked him out of the blinds, but there's plenty of other stuff no one could talk him out of."

"Like what, I'm afraid to ask," Katz asked anyhow.

"Like, when this thing starts on Monday, that whole area inside the glass is going to be ringed with my guys and MPD guys, all locked and loaded – and up on the roof, outside? – SWAT guys, all over. And – " Gaskins pointed to one corner of the ceiling behind the bench, then the other. Katz saw what looked like Magic 8 balls staring back at him and turned back to him, clueless. "Closed circuit TV cameras. We're gonna be monitoring 'em all day every day. Someone out there reaches in his pocket for a Kleenex, one of us is gonna grab his wrist before it comes out." He walked back to the opening in the glass wall. "That's about it, at least for now. No tellin' what else they'll come up with by the time your lady testifies."

Katz took one more look around to take it all in. His eyes lingered on the witness box. There was no way he could prepare Cleo for what to expect. This was going to be uncharted territory for everyone. He followed the Marshal back into the hallway. Gaskins plucked the Popeyes bag off the table and they fell in step heading back to the elevators in silence until Katz spoke. "If I had known how much trouble you were going through to get ready for this thing, there's no way I would have ever bugged you to do this, honestly, I'd like to think."

Gaskins smiled. "I don't mind doin' it, Jake – and I do mean that honestly. If nothing else, you gave me a break from thinkin' about whether we're actually gonna be able to do all the rest of the stuff the brass says we got to do somehow."

"There's more? How's that possible?"

"So there are eleven defendants in this trial, okay? No matter everything you saw in there, my boss is still so scared shitless that he's assigned one Marshal to each an' every one of 'em through the whole trial, however long it lasts."

"What's that even mean? You can't sit with them in there."

"No, but we'll be right up next to 'em everywhere else. To and from lunch, at lunch, on the bus to and from wherever they're going to be put up, in the hotel camped outside the door – everywhere but the bathroom, Jake, and we're waitin' to hear on that too, man, no lie." He thumbed the Down button on the elevator. "And that don't count babysittin' Richey and Rayful too. Richey's going to have an armed escort to and from his house every day, and round-the-clock protection there too, and Rayful's gonna get the red carpet treatment too, of course. Bus'll pick him up at the jail every day, with two phony buses to throw off whoever's supposed to be aimin' at him, motorcycle escort, sirens flashin', the whole bit. Whatever bus he's in won't hit a red light the whole way either."

The elevator came and they took it down to one. When Katz saw the metal detectors come into view, he asked "What time're you opening up for the public tomorrow?"

"Seven."

"Ugh," Katz said.

"Though that may change too, Richey gets his way."

"What's that mean?" Gaskins stopped and took a deep breath before turning to him. "Means he's talking about keepin' 'em out altogether." Katz laughed until he saw Gaskins level his gaze at him. "Wait, you're serious?"

"Oh yes I am, 'cause he is dead serious."

"That is ludicrous. What did Jay Stephens have to say about that?"

"Jay Stephens, Mr. Madden, none of them don't know anything about it yet. I heard it from one of Richey's law clerks and he only told me 'cause I thought he was havin' a nervous breakdown in the bathroom the other day. What I'm telling you is why he was." They watched each other shake their heads. "And don't you tell them I told you either."

"They won't hear it from me, Scout's honor," Katz said and shook Gaskins' hand. "Thanks for the tour."

When he got home, the red light on his answering machine was blinking. He pressed the Play button, hoping it was not from who he knew it was.

"You have . . . one message."

"Hi, Jake," he heard Cleo say, "you're out and about bright and early. Probably couldn't sleep either. Just wanted to talk to you before the big day tomorrow, so give me a call when you get back. The Marshal's number's 202-514-7790. Bye."

It took him no time to convince himself he needed a lot of time to figure out what he was going to tell her, so he grabbed the *Post*, made himself comfortable on the throne, and waited for inspiration to strike him. He took care of his business, and came back out to stare at the phone before picking up the receiver and dialing her up, hoping inspiration would find him by the time he opened his mouth.

"Jake?" he heard and pictured her lying in bed, half-asleep, happy to finally hear his voice.

"I am," he said.

"Jesus Christ! Where the fuck have you been?" The picture went black.

"I was actually out at the courthouse, getting a tour of what you're going to be dealing with when you get up on the stand."

"Oh wow. Sorry I snapped. I'm just a little wired, especially after what the guys here told me what's goin' on down there."

"What'd they tell you?"

"Cops're pretty much going to be sitttin' in everyone's lap – and they're puttin' up a bulletproof shield? I get it, absolutely, but that kinda gets your attention, you know?"

"I do, but it's all to protect you and everyone else in there, so it's a good thing, right? They say anything else?"

"If they did, I didn't hear it. I think my brain shut off after 'bulletproof'. What'd you see?"

Inspiration finally arrived and told him it was pointless to rattle her even more by going into any of the rest of it. "That's pretty much it. And by the time you testify, hopefully everything will have mellowed out and it'll be business as usual."

"Business as usual is exactly what I'm afraid of, Jake – Rayful's business."

"I get it, Cleo, I do," he said, as sincerely as he could. "Just remember, they're going to protect you as much as they can wherever you are." He heard her sigh and wished he was there to put his arms around her, kiss her on the forehead, and tell her to her face that everything was going to be all right.

"I just need you to tell me everything that's going on during the trial, whatever you see, whatever you hear, whatever you read, good or bad. Just tell it like it is, okay? Promise me you will."

"I will, Cleo, absolutely," he said so sincerely that he almost convinced himself he wasn't bullshitting both of them.

29

Four days of jury selection gave Katz the chance to figure out how to keep his promise to Cleo, and his sanity. Some of it turned out to be by design, some by serendipity, but all of it was welcome, eventually. The design part started when he asked LaVerne on Monday if she'd like a little time away from her desk every day to go over to the courthouse and take a few notes on what was happening, starting today. She was out the door as soon as the words left his lips. Two hours later, he looked up to see she was back in his doorway, and fuming.

"Let me just tell you what I've been thinkin' ever since I got stuck waitin' in that security line, okay? If I gotta stand in line for an hour just to get in somewhere, it's gonna be Best Buy or Woodie's or someplace I can at least walk away with somethin' I want, not a damn courthouse."

"I am so sorry. Did you ever get in?"

"The building, yeah, but by the time I got up to the fourth floor, the line to the courtroom was all the way down the hall, Jake! I took one look, turned around, and came right back down the same elevator."

That night, he called his new best friend Phil to see if he could arrange something. On Tuesday, when LaVerne skipped the line, waved a sheet of Jake Katz, Esq. letterhead naming her his representative at the Marshal at the door, and followed him to the seat marked "Reserved" in the front row, it stopped being a problem.

The serendipity started when Harry called him right after he called Gaskins. "Jake, were you over there today? I didn't see you." Katz stuck to his time-honored Harry playbook: Step 1: Say nothing more than absolutely necessary. Step 2: If Step 1 doesn't work, say nothing at all. Step 3: If Step 2 doesn't work, hang up. "No, I wasn't."

"It was a zoo, man," Harry said, then proceeded to tell him what he already knew. The glass, the cops, the cameras, the lawyers. Harry waited for a response. Katz deployed Step 2. But just before he got to enjoy Step 3, Harry threw him a curve. "So, listen, any chance you might want to tag team with me down there?"

"What do you mean?" Katz asked, always suspicious of anything Harry said that sounded remotely promising.

"I go one day, you go the next maybe?" Katz rewrote the playbook on the spot. Step 2.5: Dissemble. "Why would I want to go at all?" he asked.

"Come on, Jake, you can't shit a shitter. We're in the same position, man."

"What're you talking about, Harry?"

"Cooperators. We're both dealin' with 'em, okay? It ain't a secret anymore." Katz wouldn't be surprised if Harry really did know by now, but he knew who he was dealing with, so he slipped the punch.

315

"I don't even know where to start with that, Harry, so I'm not even going to try. But I am a little curious to see it for myself, so what suits your busy schedule?"

They worked it out so Harry would cover Monday and Wednesdays, he'd take Tuesdays and Thursdays, and they'd talk about Fridays. LaVerne would fill in for him if he couldn't make it, and everyone was happy. *For now*, he warned himself. *Keep your guard up.*

Wednesday afternoon, Harry told him jury selection was still going on, but if everyone behaved, he thought they'd get it done Thursday. Katz waited till a little after 2 on Thursday just to hedge his bets, but when he came into the courtroom, the bench was empty and the only people in front of the glass were the defendants and about three times as many armed uniforms staring at them from every wall and most of the well. He walked over to a Marshal he didn't recognize and asked him where everyone else was. "Chambers," he said. "Jury shit."

Katz nodded and took a look at the gallery. Every seat was filled, a few people chatting, a few more staring aimlessly, even more dozing. He took his reserved seat and looked down the row. He thought he remembered a few of the faces closest to the defendants from some of the photos Hutchison and Madden had passed around over the last few weeks, but the only one he was sure of was Bootsie. Her red turban was the liveliest thing in the room.

Katz couldn't put a name to anyone else, but trying to guess who was who on the other side of the glass and who was back here kept him occupied until the door behind

316

the bench swung open and a flotilla of lawyers streamed through, followed by the courtroom staff. When the clerk saw everyone in their places, he called out "Order in the court, all rise." Katz stood up and watched the folks down the row from him get up a lot more slowly than everyone else. Richey emerged in a few seconds, his long-time limp more marked than Katz remembered. When he took his seat, the clerk said "Court is now in session, The Honorable Charles R. Richey presiding. Please be seated." Katz watched Richey put on his big black-framed glasses, flip a folder open, and scan it closely.

He looked older and shorter than Katz remembered, but once he realized the Scientology case was ten years ago now, he cut him some slack. All in all, he was a pretty well preserved specimen for what Katz figured was his late 60s. His hair was shorter too – and whiter – and Katz didn't recall his hairline being quite that high, but when Richey finally looked up and grimly surveyed the spectacle in front of him, he looked as ready as anyone could to face whatever was going to play out in front of him in the weeks ahead.

"Ladies and gentlemen," he said in his flat Midwestern accent, "I am very happy to announce that we have a jury." He nodded to a bailiff at the door that led back to his chambers and the jury room. The bailiff opened it and Katz watched the line of jurors who were going to decide the defendants' fate – and maybe risk their own – file into the courtroom. Each of them was black. Ten were men and two were women, almost a perfect match to the defendants' nine men and two women – Niecey and

Armaretta. All of them looked middle-aged or older. Their footsteps across the tile were the only sound. When they were in their seats, Richey turned to them.

"Ladies and gentlemen of the jury, I just want to say in open court what I told you back in my chambers. I sincerely thank you for your willingness to serve in this case, especially in light of the great disruption that your time here might cause you over what I expect will be a matter of several weeks, if not months." A few of them managed nods or weak smiles but the rest were probably too busy listening to the voices screaming in their own heads to show any response at all.

Richey turned to look out at the gallery. "Please know that over the past four days, I have excused more than one hundred jurors for a variety of reasons. As you may know, the number of lawyers involved in the selection process dictated that we use wireless microphones but, as I promised the members of the press here when we began, you'll be able to pick up transcripts of those discussions later today at the Public Information Office down the hall." He turned to the tables to his right.

"Counsel, I know a number of you have motions and objections you wish to make on the record, so who wants to be heard first?" Billy Murphy got up from the table closest to Richey and stepped to the lectern.

"Your Honor," he said. "I wish to note my objection on the record to your refusal to grant our many requests for a change of venue. As you well know, Judge, I do not believe that Mr. Edmond can get a fair trial in the

318

District of Columbia by any stretch of the imagination. All Your Honor has to do is take a look around this courtroom to see the many so-called safeguards you have put in place to protect the jury and witnesses from the alleged threat you believe the defendants pose to their safety. How could any member of this jury feel anything other than that you already believe these defendants are dangerous and guilty of the crimes the government has charged them with? Your Honor, I move that you grant us this request at this time to ensure that Mr. Edmond and his fellow defendants receive the fair trial guaranteed them by the United States Constitution."

"Motion denied."

"Further, Your Honor," Murphy said without skipping a beat, "these jurors read the newspapers. They see the steady drumbeat of articles in the *Washington Post* purporting to link Mr. Edmond and all the rest of the defendants to all manner of criminal activity. They see the TV news, they hear the radio bombarding them with the government's charges. How can you reasonably expect any of these fine people to not be affected by all this prejudicial publicity? Your Honor, I move for a change of venue on those grounds as well."

"Motion denied."

"Your Honor, this entirely unusual and unorthodox method of selecting these jurors is also unconstitutional. To begin with, we do not even know their names so we have no independent way of learning anything about them, who they know, or what their backgrounds are, other than what they've told us. What kind of safeguard is that for these people who may be deprived of their liberty, perhaps for the rest of their lives? We need to be assured that these jurors are capable of rending the fair and impartial verdict the law requires. The procedures Your Honor has put in place guarantee anything but. Your Honor, for all of these reasons, we move that you dismiss this jury."

"That motion is also denied."

"Thank you, Your Honor." Murphy took his seat. "Who's next?" Richey asked.

Katz recognized the lawyer who came to the lectern. Leroy Nesbitt was a force Katz did not look forward to reckoning with any time they squared off in the courtroom when he was an AUSA. They each stood about five-eight, but Nesbitt was more of a presence, maybe because he had about twenty pounds on him, but more likely because of how he dazzled a jury. Like Harry, his dapper wardrobe always seemed to make an impression, but his real advantage lay in the way he talked to them. His deep voice and studious demeanor drew them in, but his folksy friendliness almost guaranteed that at least one of them would see it his way in the end. He was a show horse and a work horse, a combination that made him tough to beat, even if you had the facts and the law on your side.

"Your Honor," he said, "defendant Tony Lewis makes the same motions Mr. Murphy just made on behalf of Mr. Edmond, and further moves to dismiss the jury for one other reason. You told us just before we came out here that all of us needed to confer with each other about any

320

final challenges to any juror in front of the jury, but, your Honor, that creates the appearance that any challenge any individual lawyer wants to make to any juror will be seen as being made on behalf of the group. I know you are aware that each of our clients must be judged separately during the trial, Judge, but your requirement that we all confer before any of us challenges a juror tars us all with the same brush and will create a feeling in that juror's mind, if he or she is retained, that all of us were out to get him, if you will. Your Honor, I hope you understand the gravity of this problem and grant this motion to dismiss."

"I do understand, Mr. Nesbitt," Richey said. "Your motion is denied."

One after the other they came before him, advising him of their concurrence in all the previous motions and offering new variations on the same themes, only longer. On and on it went till Katz totally tuned it out, like everyone else drifting off behind the glass. The only constant was Richey's denial. Katz remembered Silbert telling him that Richey usually went out of his way to be nice to lawyers on both sides because he was a trial lawyer himself. *He must've gotten over that*, Katz thought. He sounded like he already had it with all of them and the trial hadn't even started. When the last lawyer sat, Richey looked at his watch and Katz glanced at the clock over his head. 4:05.

"Thank you, gentlemen, ladies," Richey said. "I think given the lateness of the hour, we ought to adjourn for the day. I also think it would be best for all concerned if we gave everyone the weekend to take care of any

321

necessary business before we get started, so we are going to adjourn until 9:30 Monday morning, when Mr. Madden will present the government's opening statement. Marshals, please arrange for the jurors to be sequestered tonight, after you've taken them home to pick up their clothes and taken care of whatever child care needs they might have." He looked at the prosecutors, then the defense. "Anything further today? Anyone?"

No lawyer raised a hand. But a juror did, one of the older black men in the back row. Richey fell back in his chair and waved at the bailiff to find out what he wanted. The juror leaned over the side rail to whisper in the bailiff's ear. When he was done, the bailiff walked behind the bench and whispered in Richey's ear. Richey sat forward, put his arms on his desk, and dipped his head for a long moment before he forced himself to look back out on the courtroom.

"We're back in recess," he sighed. "Bailiff, please take the jury out."

When the door closed behind them, Richey stood up and banged the gavel. "Ladies and gentlemen," he said to the lawyers, "I need you back in chambers." Katz watched them file out behind him, stunned by the first thought that leaped to his mind. There was no confusion this time, no bitterness about the money he wouldn't be making, only gratitude: *Thank you, Petty, thank you for sparing me all this aggravation*, he heard himself say, *and everything else that's got to be coming.*

322

30

One thing that came was worse than even Katz's most dismal expectations. He wasn't surprised by a lot of what happened over the next few weeks – more threats to witnesses, Deborah Phillips' refusal to testify after the government's screw-up at the grand jury, every lawyer's constant objections, the unending war of words between Madden and Murphy, and most of all, Richey's instant freakout about every bit of all of the above – but what soared way past the limits of his imagination was when Richey finally decided to do what Marshal Gaskins had told him he just might: keep the public from seeing any more of it.

Richey had been having more than his share of trouble keeping jurors in the box even after he dismissed the guy who raised his hand that first day. He replaced three more in the next two weeks. The first one said it was because he recognized someone in the audience, presumably not his priest. The second one left after one of the defense lawyers said that "a distant relative" of his had been spotted in the audience, and the third was gone after two other lawyers said they knew the street where he lived.

Other judges had done novel things to protect jurors even beyond what Richey had already done, like having them watch the trial on closed-circuit TV from somewhere else, or closing the courtroom for a specific witness, and that's what Katz expected to hear when – courtesy of George Washington's silver countenance staring at him from LaVerne's palm right after Harry called "Heads!" over the speaker phone – he was there to see him start to read from a prepared statement last Friday. But he was wrong.

"The potential consequences of somebody in the audience from the general public recognizing one of the jurors or vice versa are simply too serious and the remedies available to the Court, such as perhaps having to declare a mistrial, are too extreme," Richey read. "The Court sees no other alternative than closing the trial to the general public. The media will act as their surrogate."

This time, Richey's freakout was nothing compared to the lawyers', inside the courtroom and out. James Robertson called it "outrageous" and asked anyone who would listen "Whatever happened to a free country?" A lawyer for the Public Defender Service put it another way: "Can you imagine your son going to jail for the rest of his life and not being able to watch the proceedings?"

The government and the defense had no problem taking a side, and for a change, it was the same one. Within hours, they both filed emergency appeals with the Federal Court of Appeals, urging it to overturn the order. On Saturday, Richey filed his own argument, pronouncing it "astounding" the prosecution was appealing because the Justice Department's own guidelines allowed a courtroom to be closed in extreme circumstances.

The Court of Appeals wasted no time telling him it begged to differ. Three days after Richey issued his ruling, Chief Judge Wald issued her court's unanimous decision overturning it. His order, she wrote, was "far broader in scope than most, and longer in duration than any previously condoned partial disclosure." After politely scolding him for a few more paragraphs, she ended by pointing out what was obvious even to Katz all along. The media, she said, "is not a substitute for the public's right to see the proceedings for itself. Indeed, excluding the public but not the press may create the erroneous perception that the courtroom is open only to particular members of the public."

The trial started up again on Tuesday but it took less than a day for Katz to think Richey might have been right after all. The key government witness that day was Kathy Sellers, yet another cooperating witness the government turned. Katz heard her tell how she picked up crack cocaine from a lot of the defendants' homes, saw Jerry Millington and James Antonio Jones give directions to runners, watched the runners sell the coke on Morton and Orleans, and witnessed Bootsie run the thousands of dollars they collected through a money-counting machine at her daughter Rachelle's house. Everyone in the gallery was riveted, and maybe a little dismayed, when she said she did it all for $800 a week, about what a mid-level bureaucrat made without nearly as much effort.

Wednesday morning, Katz woke up to WTOP radio telling him that Sellers' mother's house on Morton Street caught fire a little around one a.m., right after she heard glass breaking, then a pop-pop-pop. Neighbors saw flames on the ground floor and called the Fire Department. They got her out and put out the fire before it did a lot of damage, but it was on the news because an unknown person apparently started it by throwing a beer bottle filled with gasoline through the front window. The only good thing about it was that it happened after he called Cleo to give her his daily update. Even though Wednesday was Harry's day, he decided to go back over to see for himself if Sellers would come back for cross-examination – and hope he could pick up some kernel of good news to tell Cleo later.

When he got to the side door of the courthouse, he saw Bruce Johnson and a cameraman barrel past him and turn the corner to the front of the building on Constitution. He followed them to see what was up, and when he saw a line of suits and uniforms fanned out behind a podium bearing a half-dozen microphones, he knew instantly and waited for Jay Stephens to make his way to it. He started by reciting the facts of what happened on Morton Street last night, then immediately proceeded to cover the ass of everyone on the podium, most prominently his own. "I want to remind everyone that every witness in this case has been offered police protection. Last night, we saw the consequences of what might happen if they refuse it," he said. Katz didn't need to hear more, so he made his way back up to the fourth floor.

The first thing he saw in the courtroom was Harry reading the paper in the back row, an empty chair right beside him. Katz longingly eyed the *Reserved* sign in the front row, but once he played out the grief that was sure to follow when Harry saw him sit there, he manned up, edged down the row, and took the seat next to him. Harry lifted his head to give him a perfunctory nod before it registered who he was nodding at. "Katz!" he said, extending his hand. "Hey, this ain't your day, man!"

Katz gave him a short shake. "I know, but after last night, I thought she might be a good one to see."

"Uh huh," Harry said. "Or maybe see how they're gonna rough up *your* client?"

Katz didn't like the sound of that. He'd told Harry Cleo was his client but never let him know she'd flipped. So did someone else tell him? Or was he just fishing? Katz still had the scars from Harry grilling him at the Khaalis trial, so he tried to come up with an answer that wouldn't lead to more questions.

"What are you talking about, Harry?" was the best he could do. Harry gave him the stink eye but before he could say anything, the bailiff bailed him out. He opened the door behind the bench and everyone filed through – except the jury. When Richey took his seat, Katz thought he looked ten years older than last week.

"Ladies and gentlemen," he said, "as you're probably aware, there was an incident last night at the home of our first witness, Miss Sellers. Counsel and I have been back in chambers awhile talking about how we ought to handle it here today." He glanced at the defense tables, then at the prosecutors. "I'm sure someone will be quick to correct me if I'm wrong, but I want to put my understanding of what we agreed to on the record before she appears." He slipped his glasses on and read from a yellow legal pad in his hands.

"First, all parties agree that we have a duty to keep the jury from hearing any questions or testimony that may even remotely pertain to last night's incident. Per our discussion, I have told Miss Sellers that she is not to mention the incident during her testimony, whether she is asked about it or not. I assure you all that she has assured me she will not. In addition, counsel who will be examining her on cross and re-direct today have also assured me that they will not ask her about it. Counsel, I ask you to please repeat that assurance now for the record."

Katz watched each of them stand and make their recitals. When Hutchison stood, he saw another lawyer he didn't remember seeing before, sitting at a smaller table perpendicular to the side of the prosecution table nearest the bench. Then it occurred to him. He was Sellers' lawyer and that was where Katz was going to be sitting when it was Cleo's turn to talk. He ratcheted up his attention, but was immediately distracted by someone at his left nudging his arm. He turned to see him point at Marshal Gaskins, standing in the aisle and nodding his head back to the hallway. Katz muttered a quick bye to Harry, then followed the Marshal out and back towards the elevators.

"What's up, Phil?" he said, but Gaskins waved him off and neither of them said another thing until they'd walked past the elevator they rode up on before the trial started around a corner to a door marked "Maintenance Only". The Marshal turned to look at him, then reached into his pocket and pulled out a sealed envelope with a

United States Marshals Service logo, but no addressee. "What's that?" Katz asked.

"It's something you ought to read, but you can't tell anyone where you got it, okay?"

"Okay," Katz said, genuinely baffled.

"Okay then," Gaskins said and handed him the envelope. "I'll be back by the elevator, makin' sure nobody comes around. When you're done, you tuck that away and come on by so we can walk and talk a little." He patted Katz on the shoulder and left him alone. Katz watched him turn the corner before he ripped the side of the envelope open and slid whatever was inside out. The FBI letterhead caught his attention first. By the time he finished reading what followed "I Charles M. Anderson, Special Agent, FBI, do hereby swear," it was the last thing on his mind.

"On or about October 1, 1989," Agent Anderson wrote, "I received information from other special agents of the Federal Bureau of Investigation that a confidential source who has provided information to the FBI for approximately four years and who is responsible for numerous arrests, indictments, convictions, and seizures, and who has never been known to provide unreliable information, advised that $30,000.00 was available to anyone who would kill Cleopatra Salome Smythe."

Katz felt dizzy until he realized he'd been holding his breath the whole time he was reading, then sucked in a gulp of air and steadied himself. He re-read the paragraph one more time, then put the memo back into the envelope, and slid it into the inside left pocket of his suit jacket. When he came around the corner, Gaskins walked ahead of him back to the main hallway and headed back towards the courtroom. Katz waited a few seconds, then followed him, catching up just before they got to the main elevators.

"Well hi, Marshal," he said with a grin he hoped wasn't too phony. Gaskins nodded to him. "So how did Agent Anderson come to file this?" Katz said breezily, like he was asking his pal Phil if he caught last week's Redskins game.

"To back up Richey's order to close the trial last week," Gaskins smiled back.

"That is some serious shit," Katz said, coughing up a dry chuckle. "You hear anything more since then?"

"Nope, but that's probably enough, I figure. I just wanted to make sure you know what Mr. Madden and them already know." He smiled again and poked Katz' chest. "So don't let them bullshit you about just how safe and secure you and your client are, because you ain't, you hear?" He turned before Katz could answer, and went back into the courtroom. Katz stood there a moment before he headed back down the hall, lost in thought the whole time.

What should he tell Cleo? Or should he not tell her anything at all? The Marshals guarding her had to know what was in Agent Anderson's memo, so nothing Katz could say would make a bit of difference to whatever they were already doing to keep her safe. All it would do was freak her out, and there was enough of that going around already. Plus, it might cause her to go the Deborah Phillips route and refuse to testify altogether, which meant Lorton, or worse. So saying nothing was the best thing for her, he decided, and it was merely a happy coincidence that ducking the fireworks that was sure to follow him saying anything was the best thing for him too. He kept believing that all the way back to his office, until he couldn't keep ignoring the nagging thought that all that made sense only if the Marshals guarding Cleo really did know what the note said, so he asked LaVerne to dial Marshal Kravitz.

"Take me out to the ball game," he heard when he picked up his phone.

"Is that code for something?" Katz asked.

"No," Kravitz laughed. "Wheel of Fortune. I just wanted them to know I knew it."

Katz laughed. "You sound like one big happy family."

"We figure out how to pass the time okay, I guess. So you want to talk to her?"

"I want to talk to you first. Are you somewhere she can't hear you?"

The line went quiet until he heard a door close. "I am now. What's up?"

"Does she know about the $30,000 bounty on her head?"

"Christ!" Kravitz muttered. "How do you know about it?"

"I overheard something about it in the courtroom today. Does she know about it?"

"Hell, no," Kravitz said, "and don't tell her either. Madden said enough people're gettin' spooked, they can't afford to lose her. He doesn't want anything on her mind but her testimony."

"You got no worries about me. How about Kathy Sellers' mom's house? Does she know about that?"

"No, she doesn't see any newspapers and we keep her away from the TV news and pull the radio from the room every time we bring her somewhere new. She can listen to tapes and CDs on a boom box kind of thing, but that's it. She really knows nothin' about nothin' going on down at the courthouse."

"That's very reassuring. Thank you, really."

"You want to talk to her?" As much as he wanted to hear her voice, it took Katz only a second to figure out he could wait. "No, just call me regular time tonight. No sense making her curious about why I'm calling now."

"Okay then. Talk to you tonight." Katz hung up and felt nothing but exhaustion. He glanced at his watch. 11:50 and gassed already. He had to start jogging again, or at least walking, but even thinking about it was tiring, so he settled for falling back into his chair and stretching his legs onto the desk. It wouldn't be the first time he had sleep for lunch, but it seemed to be happening more these days.

The sound of the buzzer scared the shit out of him. When his eyes sprung open, they saw LaVerne in the doorway. "Oh, Jake, I am so sorry. I didn't know you was sackin' out."

He slid his feet off the desk and pulled his hands down his face. "I didn't either. "Who is it?"

"Mr. Hutchison."

"Put him through." he said. At the buzz, he picked up the phone. "Aren't you supposed to be in court?"

"Lunch break," Hutchison said.

Katz looked at his watch. 12:09. He pulled his hand down his face. "Okay, so what's up?"

"We need to set up a final get-together with you and your client. She's next."

31

"Next" turned out to be eight days later because of unforeseen delays that all of them should have foreseen by now. Billy Murphy's continuing objections to pretty much everything the government presented or planned to present were first and foremost, as usual, but he was now scaling new heights of absurdity. He demanded that not one, not two, but three witnesses undergo psychiatric evaluations because they were each so mentally ill they tried to kill themselves. He accused another witness of filing fraudulent tax returns that hid her mother's numbers operation. He asked a police officer to stop calling men and women "males" and "females" because not only were those terms degrading, they "could mean another species."

When Katz found himself at a urinal next to Madden during a recess, he asked him if he thought Cleo had a shot at getting called before Halloween. "Maybe, if Richey can figure out how to get the appeals court to let him stuff a sock down Murphy's throat," Madden said. "He did put his foot down on one thing though. Murphy told him he wanted Friday off so he and this young babe he supposedly just married could have a honeymoon weekend. Richey told him 'She's not that hard up. Denied!'"

Finally, on Wednesday the 18th, the last witness before Cleo was excused. When Madden asked for a recess till the following Monday to prepare her, Richey shook his head.

"Mr. Murphy has given you plenty of time to get her ready, Mr. Madden." We'll resume at 2:00 tomorrow afternoon." He banged his gavel, stood up, and pointed the business end at Madden. "Use your time wisely."

That night, Katz joined Madden, Hutchison, and Cleo to run through their questions and her answers one last time. They were back at the Mayflower, on the top floor this time. When he squeezed Cleo's hand after shaking theirs, it seemed ten degrees cooler. He pulled himself close to her and murmured quietly "Do you want to talk, alone?"

"Let's get this over with first," she muttered back. Katz nodded, pulled a kitchenette chair next to her, took a seat, and flashed as genuine a phony smile as he could muster. "Gentlemen, you're on."

"Ms. Smythe," Madden said, "you know what we're going to ask you and we know what you're going to tell us. We've gone over all of it, so you're not going to hear any surprises from us, okay? I just want to hit the highlights of what we plan to ask you tomorrow, and then on Sunday night, we'll go over what we plan to ask you on Monday, and so on until we finish, okay?"

"And when's that going to be?"

"That's not totally within our control," Madden said. "Any lawyer for any defendant can object to anything we ask."

"And have, and will," Hutchison said.

"But you're going to object to all their objecting, right?" Cleo asked.

"Just like we've been doing every day," Madden said.

"And Jake? Can he object too?"

"He can talk to us, but we have to make the objection." Cleo looked at Katz. "I'll be sitting right next to them," he said. "Shouldn't be a problem."

Madden reached into his bag and pulled out a yellow legal pad. Cleo reached into her bag and pulled out a lighter and a soft pack of Kools. She slid a cigarette out, then shook the pack and watched one more fall into her hand. She crumpled up the empty pack and showed it to Madden and Hutchison. "Okay, so unless you or your wardens out there want to run down and get me another one of these, I'm good for about twenty minutes, tops." She flipped the crumple onto the low table between them and lit up. When Hutchison opened his mouth, she held up a hand. "I know I can't light up in there. Trust me, I'll be fine tomorrow. But now? Go, just go."

"Okay," Madden said. "We're going to start with when you came to D.C., what brought you here, where you worked before you met Rayful, and how you came to meet him. Should be pretty straightforward stuff."

"A couple of things," Katz said. "First, she didn't start out as Cleo Smythe, right? Should you get that out in the open right off the bat, rather than have them bring it up and make it sound like something shady? 'That's not even your real name, is it?' might make the jury doubt everything they hear from her."

"That's a good point, Mr. Katz," Madden said, jotting a note on his pad. "I'll take care of that right up front. Anything else?"

"Yeah. One of the places she worked was Archibald's, the topless place? There may be a few jurors who're gonna think that's a den of iniquity or God knows what else. Maybe she can just say 'I worked a few odd jobs, like waitressing' and let it go at that." Madden and Hutchison looked at each other. Katz wasn't sure what was really going through either of their heads, but he hoped they got back to his question. Hutchison did first.

"If we don't say anything and Murphy brings it up, they might think we were trying to hide it, and that's not good either."

Cleo rubbed out her cigarette. "If he brings it up," she said, "I'll tell him the truth – I hated it and only did it for the money until I could find something else."

"Works for me," Madden said.

Cleo lit the last one up. "Margaret Ann will be on her best behavior, don't worry," she said and spun her free hand. "Can we pick up the pace a little? I might need a carton at this rate."

Madden looked down at his pad. "Okay, moving on. You met Rayful at the Florida Grill. He was a big tipper. You became friendly. He gave you his beeper number but you didn't call him, then he pulled you over on Connecticut Avenue one day with Tony Lewis." He looked up. "Anything on any of that?" Cleo swallowed a drag, crossed her legs, and gave him another spin cycle.

"Okay. Then I'm going to ask you to look at some pictures and verify some people, and some things too – like Rayful, Tony Lewis, the Porsche." He bent down and reached into his briefcase. "I know what they look like," Cleo said. "Keep going."

"All right, then we get to you working for Rayful in Arlington." Cleo shot to her feet, choked out a cough and ripped the cigarette from her mouth, her cheeks bright red. "What the fuck?" she finally hacked out. "Who told you that?" As cold as she was before, Katz thought, she was that hot and more now. Her eyes flamed.

"You told us, Cleo," Madden reminded her. "You said you leased an apartment for him in Crystal City, at the Buchanan House, you brought bags of money in and out, all that. Do I have it right? I have the lease right here if –" The color drained from Cleo's cheeks as fast as it rose. She took a deep pull on the Kool, and turned away from them, her free hand shielding her eyes. Katz got up and laid a hand on her back. She turned away from him to send a billow of smoke hurrying to the wall behind them.

"You okay?" he whispered. She dropped her hand and Katz waited while she took in a deep gulp of air, eyes closed, trembling. "I just – I didn't know where he was going with that – that's all," she said.

"You want to take a few minutes?" he asked. She nodded a quick yes. He turned back to Madden and

Hutchison, sitting still and quiet, like any move might trigger another blast. "Can we have a few minutes?" he asked. Cleo whipped around and waved her cigarette at them. "And a few packs too?"

"Yeah, sure, of course," Madden said. "Take as much time as you need." He turned to Hutchison. "Would you mind going down to the lobby and getting her the cigarettes?" Hutchison headed for the door. Katz laid a hand on Cleo's shoulder and squeezed it softly. "You want to take a couple minutes to get yourself together? I'll see what I can do to get this over with asap." She patted his hand and gave him a very weak smile, then headed back to the bathroom. When the door closed behind her, Katz motioned to Madden to follow him back to the door to the hallway.

"I don't know how much more of this is going to be productive," Katz said.

"I'm thinking the same thing."

"And I wish I could tell you why she freaked, but I really don't know."

Madden ran a hand through his hair. "Maybe it just hit her that tomorrow's the day she actually starts testifying face to face against a bunch of guys she knows would like nothing more than to see her dead – and do the job themselves. That would make anyone freak."

"That'd do it for me."

Hutchison came back through the door, two cartons of Kools cradled in his right arm. "This should hold her for a while," he said.

"Salvation!" they heard Cleo crow, and turned to see her coming from the bathroom, arms stretched out to him. When Hutchison handed her the cartons, she started to rip one open, then stopped. "Are we still going?" she asked Madden. He shook his head no.

"I think the best thing we can do now is make sure you get a good night's sleep. Your testimony's not till two, so how about we pick you up at noon and have lunch with Mr. Katz in my office? If anything comes to anyone overnight, we can talk about it then, okay?"

When Katz turned to Cleo, all he saw was relief. "I think that's a great idea," he said.

"Okay, then," Madden said and reached his hand out to Cleo. "Ms. Smythe, thank you for enduring all this. I hope I don't need me to tell you this by now, but you are in good hands. The Marshals will continue to take care of you tonight and every night till the trial's over, and Ron and I and Mr. Katz will take care of you at the courthouse for however long it takes, trust me."

Katz was fine with that speech right up to "trust me". He thought back to all the leaks, Billy's unexpected visit to his office, Harry ducking his questions about whether he was representing anyone, even Marshal Gaskins handing him the envelope, and wondered if he – and, more importantly, Cleo – could really trust anyone anymore.

When he heard himself say "Cleo, all you need to worry about is telling the truth," he even doubted himself.

True or not, Cleo bought it. She took Madden's hand in both of hers. "Thank you, Mr. Madden. I may not always show it, but I appreciate everything you're doing to keep me safe."

Madden turned to Katz. "Can we drop you somewhere?"

"No, thanks. I want to talk to my client a little bit longer. I will see you at lunch."

"See you then," Madden said and went out the door. Before Hutchison pulled it shut behind them, he popped his head back into the room. "When you're through, let the Marshal know and he'll get a cab to pick you up in the basement."

"Ten-four," Katz said and waited till the door clicked shut before he turned to Cleo. She fell into his arms. He squeezed her tight and they clung to each other, rocking slowly without a word until he heard her say something lost in his lapel. He pulled his head back to see a mat of blond hair. He patted it back in place, then ran his hand down her wet cheek to lift her chin. The pain in her face somehow made her even more beautiful. She looked up into his eyes for a flicker of a moment, then buried her face in his tie.

"God, what a fucking mess I've made of everything," she said with more anguish than Katz had ever heard spill out of anyone in his life. He rocked with her gently. "It's almost over, Cleo. You can get there from here."

She raised her head just enough to shake it, then looked up at him. "And where is that, Jake? Where am I going, huh? And who am I going to be when I get there? Margaret Ann? Cleo? Somebody else?" He had no answers but it didn't matter because she wasn't done. "Christ, how did I even get *here*? The only thing I ever really wanted in my life was to get out of goddamned Williamsburg – and how'd that work out? Shit! So stupid. Everything else, I just rolled with, fell into, let happen, whatever, because I didn't have a clue what was good for me, what I wanted out of my freaking life. And the sad joke is I still don't know!"

He wrapped his arms around her shoulders and hugged her to his chest. In a few seconds, he whispered in her ear. "You've got a fresh start now, Cleo. It may not've come in the way you wanted, but you've got it. Freedom, money, a clean break from your past, a new life, it's all yours. Not many people ever have the chance to start all over. You do."

She grabbed his lapels, lifted her head, and locked her eyes on his, the smile on her lips at war with the rest of her face. "Jake, there's only one truly good thing that's ever happened to me since I left Williamsburg," she said. "You."

Katz was always quick to duck any compliments coming his way, not so much from humility – true or false – but mostly because he didn't want to build himself up too high just in case everything came crashing down later. *If you don't give me all the credit, you won't give me all the blame* was his working mantra, honed by a lifetime of reversals in his career, the courts, his love life, sometimes all of them at once.

"Cleo —" was all he got out before she put a finger on his lips to shush him. "Quiet. I need to say this and you need to hear it. Since the day they busted me, you have been the only person in my corner. And I have been nothing but a pain in your ass. Don't deny it!"

"You're my client, Cleo. You're supposed to be a pain in the ass."

"Let me finish. You asked me a couple of times why I didn't want to go into witness protection, change my name, go someplace else, start all over again — and every time I gave you some bullshit reason, because I couldn't even be honest with myself about the real reason." A cold chill quivered Katz' spine a split second before his brain told him that magic words were coming, words he'd only heard once in his life from someone who was not his parent. When Lisa said them to him, he repeated them because that was what you were supposed to do. But look how that turned out. *Maybe this time you actually ought to think before you say anything,* he thought, but she wasn't letting him think.

"The real reason, Jake, is I don't want to leave you. No one — not my mother, my father, even Ray — has ever looked out for me the way you have."

He tried to put off the inevitable the only way he knew how. "You know I'm paid to do that, right?" She punched him in the chest.

"Nice try, but I'm not buying it. You've shown me how you feel – and I'm not just talking about what I know you're thinking about – but all the times you've looked out for me, protected me, cared for me, like no one else ever has. Jake – "

"Cleo – "

"I love you, Jake." When he heard the words this time, whatever words were coming to his own lips fluttered away, forgotten forever. Now he said what he knew he had to say, but with more certainty than he'd said anything, ever.

"I love you too, Cleo. We will get through this. Together." When he kissed her, it was with more urgency than he'd done anything ever too.

32

Katz was as surprised by Cleo's demeanor at lunch as he was by her outburst the night before. She was as calm, committed, and confident as anyone facing multiple days of giving turncoat testimony in a criminal felony case could be. Katz guessed the reason might be the same one that explained his own uncharacteristically good mood, but that didn't explain why Madden and Hutchison seemed just as upbeat. Maybe a good vibe was contagious, but he doubted that Madden was nudging Hutchison's hand off his thigh like he was Cleo's. It was like he was in ninth grade again, except for the part about a girl touching him.

Cleo even let Madden show her the photos of all her ex-co-conspirators this time, lifting her hand long enough to point out everyone by name, and answering all the questions she wouldn't let him finish last night about her work for Edmond in Crystal City. At twenty to two, Madden threw Hutchison a look that said "You got anything else?" When Hutchison shook his head no, Madden looked from Katz to Cleo. "Either of you want to go over anything?"

When they said "No" in unison, Madden got to his feet. "Mr. Katz, we'll give you a minute to talk to your client, then we'll take her up with us. We'll see you in the courtroom." When Hutchison closed the door behind them, Katz waited to make sure he wasn't coming back before he stretched his arm out to pull Cleo close.

"Anything we need to talk about?" he asked. She nestled into his shoulder. "Not unless you've changed your mind about anything," she murmured.

"I was talking about your testimony."

She ran an arm under his jacket, squeezing him tight. "I'm not," she said. So much to talk about." She lifted her ice blue eyes to his. "So much to live for. For a change."

He kissed her forehead. "Like Curt Gowdy used to say, 'Your future's all ahead of you.'"

"God," she groaned, "what am I getting myself into?" Katz got up, took her by the hand, and walked her slowly to the door. "First things first. Go out there and do your job. Stay cool and – above all – *non illegitimi carborundum*."

"Non what?"

"Don't let the bastards grind you down. You know what the truth is, so don't let them rattle you up there. Just keep your focus and let the three of us do the arguing for you. That's what we're paid for." He reached for the doorknob but she grabbed his hand and held it to her cheek. The ice in her eyes was melting.

"Jake –," she started but he put a finger on her chin so he wouldn't smudge her lipstick. "Cleo, put everything out of your mind – even me – until Richey excuses you. Just answer the questions truthfully as best you know how and everything else will take care of itself. When it's all over, we'll get on with the rest of our lives starting that second, I promise."

She smiled, took a very deep breath, and took a step back. "So how do I look?"

Katz took in her ivory suit, the light blue and gray paisley silk scarf that draped around the thick collar of a navy blue turtleneck that gathered in a loose knot between her breasts, and the classy white heels that gave even more shape to her legs, but it really didn't matter that she looked terrific. He would have given her the same answer, no matter what he saw.

"Perfect," he said. "You'll wow them." He pulled the door open. Madden reached his hand out to Cleo. "It's about that time, Ms. Smythe. Let's not keep his honor waiting."

Katz waited to hear the elevator ding and the doors close before following them up. In a minute, he was waving his letterhead at the Marshal in the hallway. He plucked the Reserved sign from his usual seat and walked down the row to the Marshal parked in the glass doorway to the courtroom. When the Marshal turned his sleepy gaze to him, Katz handed him the sign. The Marshal moved himself to blink. "And you're giving me this because?" he asked.

"Because I won't need it for a few days." He pointed to the courtroom. "I'll be in there."

"Says who?"

"Says Mr. Madden, the AUSA trying this thing." The Marshal slowly turned his head around to take in the courtroom. The only people there were a clerk, a court reporter, and the bailiff. He turned back to Katz even more slowly. "I'm going to have to hear it from him, and he ain't there."

"He's expecting me, I guarantee you. As a matter of fact, the show won't even start till I'm there, which means the later it starts, the later it's going to finish, you catch my drift?" Katz waited for some glimmer of understanding, but when it didn't arrive, he said "He's probably back with the judge. Can you just ask the bailiff to let him know I'm here?"

"Hold on," the Marshal said, and turned to wave at the bailiff to come over. When he got close, he yelled "Can you check with them back there to see if Mr." – he turned to Katz, who recited his name – "Katz is supposed to be in the cage today?"

The bailiff gave him a thumbs up and disappeared through the door to Richey's offices. The Marshal sat himself back down and Katz killed time checking out who else was in the gallery. It was already filled, thanks no doubt to Cleo's much-anticipated appearance. The usual faces, and in Bootsie's case, hat – this one a tall Robin Hood-style green cap with a gold feather bobbing over it – were just behind him, with more press types than usual in the back rows. In the back corner at the left, Katz noticed someone standing and feathering a pencil over a large sketch pad propped against his hip.

"Hey, Katz," he heard, and turned to see the Marshal beckoning him. "They say you're okay to come in now." Just as he squeezed past him, a familiar voice boomed out behind him. "Katz! Where the hell are you goin'?" He turned to see Wallace grinning at him from just inside the door to the hallway.

"I'll be right there," Katz told the Marshal and followed Wallace back into the hall. They joined in a soul shake.

"So what are you doing here?" Katz asked him.

"Oh man, I had to come today, you know, see the headliner. And you?"

Katz laughed. "That's why I'm here too." Wallace started to smile, then stopped. He threw Katz a quizzical look. "Were you headin' up front when I saw you?"

"I was."

"And why is that?"

"The headliner's my client."

All the pleasure that glowed in Wallace's face a second ago disappeared, replaced by what Katz took for confusion.

"She's the one they assigned to me after we had that dinner at Marrocco's," he said. "You remember, the night you gave me Rayful Edmond 101." The words seemed to hit Wallace like they were bricks. He seemed to stagger for

349

a moment, but Katz was more focused on how pale he suddenly looked.

"Cleo Smythe," Wallace finally said, pronouncing it right. "She's your client?"

"Yeah. Cleopatra Salome Smythe, to be precise. I'm going to be sitting up at the prosecution table with Madden and Hutchison for as long as she –"

"Are you – " Wallace cut him off, then stopped like he was having a stroke. Katz didn't know what to make of it, but his mind flashed back to the last time he remembered seeing Wallace, just before Cleo testified to the grand jury. "You knew I was representing her. You saw her with me in the lawyers' room outside the grand jury."

"I saw you, man, but I didn't see her. Believe me on that! If I did, this is what you'd've seen then. Jesus Christ!" Wallace looked more agitated than Katz could remember, and that was saying a lot. They almost came to blows at Brenda Queen's autopsy after the riots and Katz thought he'd seen him at his worst when he lost his Detective badge, but what made this time worse was he had no idea why he was so distressed.

"Do you know her?" he asked. Wallace strode away from him, then turned back and drew closer, his face drawn taut and dark now, but he couldn't bring himself to speak.

"Tom, what's up? What is going on?" Wallace pointed his index fingers at him. Katz watched them shake.

350

"Your client, Jake, is bad news. Very bad news."

"I know, Tom. She's no angel. I get that."
Whatever Wallace was trying to say back to him stuck in
his throat. Katz wanted to wrap an arm around him and tell
him everything was all right, but he knew it wasn't. He
waited for Wallace to draw his hands down his face and
square his shoulders, then strained to hear the words he
forced out. "You know what? I can't do this now, here,
whatever. We need to be able to sit down somewhere and
have a long talk."

"Okay. You want to have dinner? Tonight? Get
whatever this is off your – "

"Yeah, you know what," Wallace said, "let's do
that. I'll let the lady at your office know where and when."
He headed for the elevators.

"Hey, make it late," Katz called after him. "I don't
know when they're going to be done with her tonight."

Wallace punched the elevator button. The doors
opened immediately. He stepped on, then turned back to
Katz and reached over to push a button. "She has a lot to
talk about, man," he said, "and so do we. See you tonight."
Katz watched the doors close between them. He spent a
hopeless minute trying to decipher the undecipherable
before he remembered he was due in the courtroom. He
hustled back in, but now it seemed like the second most
important thing he'd do today.

33

Katz always felt like he was an actor on a stage every time he tried a case, but this time the wall of glass made him feel like a fish in an aquarium, except everyone on the other side was not so much admiring him as wondering why he was there. He sat down at the laminated walnut table appended to the prosecutors' table and busied himself with his papers until the door behind him swung open for Cleo, followed by Madden and Hutchison, then a phalanx of defendants and lawyers. The steely look on her face softened only when her eyes met his.

Madden directed her to the seat closest to him. Once she sat down, Katz followed her eyes to Rayful's impossibly young face. He was the first one in his seat, slouching and staring at her blankly before giving her a nod and as thin a smile as his broad mouth allowed. Katz turned to see Cleo turn back to him, no weakness apparent in her resolve. He reached over to rest his hand on her forearm.

"You okay?" he asked. She let out a deep breath.

"I will be the second it's over with. That's what you said, right?"

"That's what I said," he smiled back. He felt a hand on his shoulder and looked up to see Madden.

"Welcome to the party, Jake."

"Anything more I need to know?" Katz asked.

"Nope." Madden tipped his head to the throng across the well. "The only thing you missed back there was a lot of hot-dogging and you can imagine how well that went over with his honor."

Katz watched them take their seats, Billy Murphy in the first chair at the table nearest the bench, the rest strung out beside and behind him. When Murphy turned to check out the newcomer, he broke into a wide smile, then got up and walked to Katz, hand extended. "Mr. Katz, I thought I might see you here before this thing was over."

You knew damn well exactly when you'd see me here, Katz thought, but he said "Well, I didn't want to disappoint you, so here I am."

"I'm looking forward to what your client has to say," Murphy said.

"I'm sure you are," Katz said, "and I'm looking forward to what you have to ask her."

Murphy smiled and waved him off. "Nothing you haven't prepped her for, I'm sure. It'll be a walk in the park for all of us." Katz heard the door behind him swing open and the crowd behind the glass rustle to its feet. Richey came through without a glance at him or anyone else and teetered his way up to his seat.

"Court is now in session," the clerk called out. "The Honorable Charles R. Richey presiding. Please be seated." Billy tapped him on the shoulder and headed back to his chair. "We're ready for your next witness, Mr. Madden," Richey said.

"The government calls Cleo Smythe, Your Honor."
Katz watched Cleo step to her seat and take the oath, her "I
do" firm and loud. Madden approached her, pad in hand,
and the game was on.

Per the game plan, he walked her through her name
change first, then the reason she came to D.C., how she met
Rayful at the Florida Grill, and how he waved her over
from his Porsche that day on Connecticut Avenue. Katz
expected objections to every answer, but heard none until
she identified a picture of Tony Lewis as the driver, and
Leroy Nesbitt leapt to his feet.

"I object, Your Honor. She just stated that she
thought Tony Lewis was driving. Now she says it
definitely was him. I object and ask that the prior
testimony be stricken."

"Overruled," Richey said, never taking his gaze
away from Madden. Nesbitt sat back down. When
Madden moved to admit photos of Edmond and Lewis,
Murphy got to his feet.

"Objection, Your Honor," he said, "Rule 403."
Katz knew it by heart. Rule 403 of the Federal Rules of
Evidence allowed a judge to exclude evidence if its
"probative value" was substantially outweighed by a
laundry list of factors that were detrimental to a defendant
or might confuse a jury.

"Overruled," Richey said, his eyes still locked on
Madden. Katz pulled his legal pad to him. He drew a line
down the middle of the sheet. At the top of the left side, he

scribbled "Objections". At the top of the right, he wrote "Sustained". He made two slashes under the left heading, then heard Madden ask Cleo about how long she paid the rent for the apartment at the Buchanan House.

"Ray and I paid the rent – "

"Objection, Your Honor," Murphy said. "Not responsive." Katz added a slash.

"Overruled," Richey said.

"Your Honor, may we approach?" Murphy asked.

"No," Richey said.

"Can the Court instruct the witness to answer only the questions that the United States Attorney actually asks?" "Yes," Richey said. He turned to Madden with open palms but without a word, then waved him to proceed. Katz gave Murphy that one and slashed to the right.

"Now, before we move on," Madden said, "I ask you to look around the courtroom." Cleo looked at the defense tables. "Do you see the people you mentioned, Mr. Edmond and Mr. Lewis seated in the courtroom, and, if you do, take your time and please let us know where they are seated and the items of clothing they are wearing." Cleo pointed to Tony Lewis first, in a chair two down from Rayful. "Mr. Lewis is seated right there and has a white striped shirt on and Rayful is seated next to his attorney, Mr. Murphy."

"You have to tell us what row and what he is wearing, please," Madden said.

"First row," Cleo said, "white shirt."

"May the record reflect the identification of both Mr. Edmond and Mr. Lewis."

Richey looked at Murphy. "No objection," he said. Nesbitt shook his head no. Katz put his pen down. "The Court hears no objection," Richey said. "So identified." The pen stayed down until Madden got to the Vegas trip.

"Ms. Smythe, what were the circumstances that led you to take the trip?" he asked.

"Rayful was taking a group of people to the fight."

"Objection. Calls for speculation," Murphy called out from his seat. "Overruled," Richey called out from his.

"And how did it happen that you went?" Madden asked. "Where did you get the ticket?"

"Rayful told me to meet him at American Airlines." James Robertson objected this time.

"Objection to the use of Mr. Edmond as Rayful," he said.

Richey turned to Cleo. "Is that how you knew him?" he asked. "That is how I knew him," she said. "Overruled."

"Did you see him purchase the tickets for the flight?" Madden asked.

"I did not see him purchase them, no."

"Did he tell you about purchasing them?"

"Objection," Murphy said. "Leading."
"Overruled."

"Can you name some of the people who you knew to be affiliated with Mr. Edmond who were in Las Vegas with you?"

"Tony Lewis, Fila Bob, Big Ray – his father – Bootsie, Constance Perry – his mother – that's all I recall." Katz was watching her intently but his mind was seeing Wallace's trembling fingers point at him again and hearing his constricted words: "She's bad news, Jake, very bad news." *That was a pretty select group of people traveling to Vegas to party with Ray*, he thought. Now Cleo's face came back into focus. *Why were you part of it? Were you bad news? Are you still?*

Madden walked back to the table and picked up the photograph of Cleo that Hutchison had shown him back in his office at DOJ.

"Can you identify the persons with you in this picture?" Katz heard Madden ask, but if she answered, he didn't hear it. His mind was still deep in a Milky Way-sized swirl of speculation about what so rattled Wallace and what Cleo had to do with it. He found himself focusing on her eyes, *the windows of the soul*, someone

357

said, trying and failing to divine the answer to a question he didn't even know yet. Madden's voice brought him back to the here and now.

"Do you know how much that piece of Gucci luggage that Mr. Lewis is holding cost?" A chorus of objections filled the court. Murphy and Nesbitt, of course, but three other lawyers were on their feet too.

"There are all kinds of places to buy suitcases, Your Honor," Nesbitt said.

"Overruled," Richey said and turned to Cleo. "Answer it, please."

"If it was authentic, and I am quite sure that one was – " The same five lawyers jumped back up, howling their objections again. "Judge," Murphy said, "would you advise the witness not to make assumptions that – "

"Overruled."

"May counsel approach the bench, your – " Murphy got out before Richey told him "No" and turned to Cleo. "You may answer." Katz marked his scorecard and counted the slashes, then checked his watch. Twelve objections in a little more than an hour, not counting however many he zoned on while he was away, and all but one overruled. A good day for the prosecution. So far. Madden and Hutchison huddled for a minute, which was evidently longer than Richey was willing to sit still for this late in the day because he said "Mr. Madden, do you think this might be a good time to break for the day?" Madden took the cue.

"That'd be fine, Your Honor."

"Ms. Smythe," Richey told her, "you may step down." He waited for her to take a seat next to Hutchison before he turned to the jury. "I will see you all back here at ten a.m. sharp. Have a good evening."

He banged his gavel and everyone stood until he disappeared through the door. Once the Marshals escorted the other side out and the bailiff closed the door behind them, Katz came to Cleo's end of the table and knelt next to her. "You were great," he said. "Unbelievably great."

"I didn't feel so great, man. I could feel them all looking – like they were shooting lightning bolts at me or something. I wouldn't even look over there 'cause I was afraid I'd lose it."

"I couldn't tell a thing, Cleo," Katz said. "You looked like a person who was confident she was telling the truth, period." While Madden and Hutchison offered their congratulations, Katz tried to figure out how he could bail on tonight's meeting, but was coming up short on plausible excuses until Madden rescued him.

"So here's what Ron and I are thinking. Because of all the objections, we didn't get halfway through what we already talked about last night, so we think that maybe we should take the night off, let Ms. Smythe get a good night's sleep, and regroup at the courtroom a little before nine just in case anyone has had a brainstorm about anything. What do you think?"

Katz looked to Cleo and hoped his raised eyebrows and shrug didn't give away the frantic signals his brain was sending her way. "Sounds good to me," Cleo said, "I'm wiped."

Katz pushed his luck. "Are you sure? If there's anything we need to talk about – "

"It can wait till tomorrow morning," she said. "I could hit the hay right now, honest to God."

"Okay then," Katz said to Madden. "I will see you all a little before nine." He shook hands all around, with an added squeeze for Cleo, before he watched them leave. By the time he hit the hallway, *She has a lot to talk about, man, and so do we* was the only thing filling his head. He always looked forward to his dinners with Wallace, but he looked forward to this one with nothing but dread.

34

At eight o'clock, Katz slowed his walk to an amble as he made his way down the Southwest waterfront towards the Channel Inn. Boats of all sizes and colors bobbed from piers down the marina to his right. The Washington Channel flowed from the Tidal Basin behind him into the Anacostia about a mile ahead, but the marina stretched only a couple hundred yards. A few restaurants and a fish market were the only places to go there, but the rare opportunity to see boats and water up close made the waterfront one of those rare D.C. venues that attracted more locals than tourists.

The waterfront scene was also rare because blacks filled its restaurants as much as, if not more than whites. Katz strained to think of anyplace else anywhere near downtown that could make that claim. He remembered Harry used to eat, drink, and dance – often – at a place called Foxtrappe up near Dupont Circle, but that was as long gone as their relationship was. Now, outside of Ben's and the Florida Avenue Grill, he couldn't think of one.

When he came to the Channel Inn, he went to the restaurant check-in counter to ask if Mr. Wallace had arrived yet. A pretty lady with long, ironed brown hair told him he hadn't, but suggested he check the lounge down the hall. All the way down, Katz hoped that whatever was on Wallace's mind hadn't been serious enough to send him back to the booze. He was happy he didn't see him there and headed back up the hall, just in time to see him come through the doors on the Maine Avenue side of the lobby.

They caught eyes and Wallace waited for him at the entrance to the restaurant. His face was as grim as it'd been earlier, but the squint of his eyes suggested something else had been added to the mix.

"Were you down the Engine Room 'cause you thought I might be in there?" he asked.

Katz gestured to the woman smiling at them behind the counter. "Excuse me, but I'm sure the witness will testify that she suggested I go down there to see if you might be waiting for me."

"Guilty," she smiled. "Are you ready to eat now?" Katz looked at Wallace and took the flatlined response back as consent. "We're ready."

She hoisted two thick menus under her arm and led them to a table by the window. Katz counted way too many people at the tables around them, then noticed an empty one against the mahogany wall across the room. "Can we sit there instead? Missed the sunset anyhow." She led them over and left them alone with their menus. Neither of them picked one up.

"Tom," Katz said. "It's just us now. Here, alone. There's not going to be any better time. What is going on?" Wallace turned to stare at the mahogany. The waiter brought them water and a basket of bread. Wallace grabbed the glass and downed half of it before putting it back down and looking back at Katz.

"I gather it's about Cleo, right?" Katz asked.

"It is about Cleo – and Schein."

Katz didn't see that coming. "Schein? What's he got to do with it?"

"I'm not totally sure what it's got to do with him, but I need to tell you something about the way he died – the way he really died."

"You told me it was an overdose. How much worse can it be?"

"A lot worse."

The waiter came back. "Gentlemen, let me tell you about – " Wallace held up a large hand. "Give us some time, man. A lot of time." The waiter paused, then saw the wisdom of leaving without a word. Katz hadn't taken his eyes off Wallace.

"Schein was murdered, man," Wallace said. "That's all you need to know."

Katz felt like he was pushed off a plane without a chute. "What?" he said loud enough to draw stares, then dialed it down. "You told me it was an overdose! When did you find out it was murder?"

"I knew it all along, Jake. I just couldn't bring myself to tell you."

"How do you know it was murder?"

"I found the body, okay? Believe me, it was murder. Don't ask me how or I will start drinkin' again, right here, right now, trust me."

"So why wasn't anyone ever charged?"

"Because we don't know who did it – yet."

Katz pushed back in his seat. His hands gripped the edge of the table like they were nailed there. "I can't believe you kept this from me all this time, and why the hell are you telling me now?"

"Because I just found out Ms. Smythe was your client!" Wallace pounded a fist on the table. More heads turned their way, but neither one of them cared. "That's the only reason you're hearin' this! I was gonna take it to my grave until I saw her with you today."

"So, what are you telling me?" Katz lowered his voice. "That she killed him? You just said you don't know who killed him." Wallace started to say something, then stopped and pushed back from the table. "I can't sit here and talk about this, man, not here. You hungry, you go ahead have your dinner, but I gotta get some air." He pushed his chair back and headed for the exit.

Katz felt his head was about to blast off from his neck. He pulled out his wallet and threw a ten on the table, then got up and followed Wallace out into the night, not sure he even wanted to catch up until he saw him stop at the end of the marina, past all the boats, and turn to face the channel. Katz walked into his field of vision. "Tom. Let me hear it, all of it, whatever it is. It's the only way either one of us is ever going to get past it." Until Wallace spoke, the only sound was water gently lapping against the concrete wharf. Wind stirred the blossoms on the trees behind him.

"I gotta start at the beginning," he said. "That's the only way any of this is going to make any sense."

"Okay. I'm listening. Go."

"I don't know when you got off the rehab train with him, but you know it never took with him, right?" Wallace said. Katz nodded. "Well, the last time he was in one of those joints, maybe two, three years ago, he just up and disappeared from the place. Nobody went lookin' for him – but one night, there's this bust out in Chantilly or somewhere out in the sticks in Virginia, and Schein's one of the dudes they bring in."

"That I didn't know."

"Okay. And did you know your client Ms. Smythe was busted that night too?"

"No. For what?"

"I'm getting there, but let's stick with Schein a minute. He was in some diner out there and told a guy he could score some coke for him, so they go out to the parking lot to make the deal and – the guy's undercover DEA."

"Christ," Katz said, "typical shit Schein luck."

"Yeah, but they don't nail him on the spot. The guy makes the buy and they trail him home and he doesn't come back out, goes to sleep, whatever, but they stake him out and the next night, he drives into D.C."

"To Morton Street?"

"No," Wallace said, "your client's house. Fifth Street Northeast up near E, do I have it right?"

Katz nodded, eager for Wallace to cut to the chase. "Why'd he go there?"

"Because she was runnin' him and a bunch of other small-time goobers out there, tryin' to get Rayful into Virginia," Wallace said. "And that's when she got busted. Conspiracy to sell interstate, mostly as a holding charge, until they could get her on other shit." Katz remembered glancing through her priors the day Petty gave him her file to see if she'd ever been convicted of anything. She hadn't. "But they didn't," he said.

"Nope. Not even on the conspiracy."

"Why?"

"Bad search warrant." Wallace shook his head at the memory. "Didn't say Fifth Street Northeast, just Fifth Street – no Northeast, Northwest, Southeast, no anything – so her lawyer got the judge to throw it out."

It only took Katz a second to figure out why she needed a new lawyer when she was busted this time – no one in Rayful's stable was going to let her turn state's evidence – and less than another second to realize that meant she knew she was going to turn all along. She just needed Katz to make the best deal he could. So was she just using him then? And now? He refocused.

"So what happened with Schein?"

"I didn't put two and two together till I wound up with him in the interrogation room. Schein must've been goin' through the same changes 'cause he says 'You look familiar to me' and I stop and really look at him for the first time and I say the same thing and then he says 'You're the cop at the Coliseum!' And then it hits me an' I say 'An' you're his fat friend!'"

That night at the D.C. Coliseum came rushing back to Katz. Smokey Robinson. Flip Wilson. An all-star revue. Katz was with MPD then, but he was there as a fan and took Schein with him for free, thanks to some lame contest Katz won on WOL. They were the only white guys there and a crowd of brothers started pushing into them in the middle of the floor. They tried to push through it till Schein yelled out someone'd hocked his wallet. Katz tried to get it back before a dude cracked a wooden folding chair over his head and sent him to the floor. He somehow got up and started flailing at the guy until Wallace pulled him off and got both of them out of there. He'd never forgotten it and now he knew Wallace and Schein never did either.

"'Man, that must've been twenty years ago' I tell him," Wallace said. "'You remember that, your brain ain't fried yet.' He says 'Yeah, well bein' scared shitless you're about to die is somethin' you don't forget.' The guy was funny. Fat and fucked-up, but funny too." He shook his head like he didn't know whether to laugh or cry, exactly how Katz used to feel when it came to Schein. "Then it was just a matter of tellin' him what was what and how he could stay out of the slammer, and he jumped right on it." He leveled wet eyes at Katz. "Man, I think about it still, how I put him in that spot. It's on me, I know that, but I was tryin' to help him, get him out from under his charges, that's all. Never in a million years thought it'd come to –" He let the rest stay inside him.

Katz knew exactly how he felt. "Tom, Schein and I smoked weed for the first time together. I told you that and I told you how many times I've tortured myself about whether he'd've ended up like he did if we'd never touched the stuff. Maybe he wouldn't have, but you know what? You and me were just two of a million contributing factors. It was Schein who decided to do all of it, all the shit that wound up killing him. That's harsh, I know, but it's the only way I can live with it." A light rain started falling. Katz turned up his coat collar. Wallace didn't seem to notice.

"How did he die, Tom?" Katz asked. "Tell me the truth, the whole truth."

"I told you, man. He was murdered." Katz remembered what the Black Muslims did to James Price in prison after they got the word he was going to rat out the other animals who killed Hamaas Khaalis' family in 1973. They carved up his balls with a knife and shoved a screwdriver up his ass before strangling him with their shoelaces.

368

"You can get murdered a lot of ways, Tom."

"Yeah, you can, but that's somethin' you'll never hear from me, man. You ask again, this conversation's over." *Knowing how he died isn't going to bring him back,* Katz told himself. *Let it go.*

"Then at least tell me why he was murdered."

"Because they caught him wearin' the wire."

Katz' brain went into spin cycle. *Cleo said she knew what Rayful did to rats. Is this how she knew? Did she know it first hand?* "How'd they find out he was wearing it?"

"Like I told you at dinner that night, they got people everywhere, man – MPD, DEA, everywhere."

Katz worked hard to put all the pieces in place. "And you think Cleo Smythe had something to do with his murder?" he made himself ask.

"I told you I don't know that," Wallace said, "for sure."

"But you think it."

"I'm not the lawyer, man. I don't have the fucking evidence you all need – but I do know that she was Schein's connection to Rayful, I do know that he wore a wire, and I do know that he wound up fucking dead. So you connect the dots and you tell me if you think she had something to do with it, okay?"

The rain picked up. Wallace pulled his sport jacket up over his head. Katz tucked his hands in his pockets and kept his head down as they double-timed back to the lobby of the Inn. They watched the rain fall down harder but Katz' mind was elsewhere. It only came back to the here and now when Wallace put a hand on his shoulder. "Jake, man, I am so sorry to lay this on you and I swear to God I never ever would have until – " He threw up his hands.

"I got it, man. I'll – " he started, but stopped. He didn't know what he'd do. Get to the bottom of it? See what he could get out of Cleo? Did he really want to? Thunder boomed outside the doors. They both turned to see rain hitting the concrete like machine gun fire.

"Your car in the garage?" Katz asked.

"No, I walked. It's ten minutes from here. I'll wait it out." Katz took one more look at the water crashing down. "You might be here till Tuesday. I'm in the garage. Let me drop you off."

When they pulled out, the rain attacked the car hard and loud. Katz put the wipers on high and cranked up the Nova's noisy air conditioning to clear the windshield. The ceiling cloth fell and dangled between them. Wallace told him something, but Katz couldn't hear him, so Wallace pointed to the right. In a block, Wallace reached over to turn the AC down.

"You gotta make a right on Fourth," he yelled. "Next block!" Katz made the right and realized he'd never been anywhere in Southeast past the restaurants on Capitol

Hill. A sign told him Fort McNair was just ahead. Now he had a vague sense of where he was. Fort McNair housed the National War College and that sat right on the Channel across from Hains Point, a jut of land he'd jogged around and even golfed on before he decided his clubs'd be more useful as kindling. Wallace directed him left on Canal Street, then right on O. At a cluster of garden apartments, he told him to pull over.

"This is as close as you can drop me," he said. "I'll make it from here." He reached a hand over. Katz shook it and Wallace pushed the door open. The rain had eased to a torrent. He turned back to Katz. "Don't think about Schein dead, man. Think of him the way you always did."

He slapped the door shut, pulled his coat back up over his head, and ran into the complex.

Fat, stoned, and happy, Katz thought. Wallace disappeared in the darkness. *I'll never think of him that way again.*

35

Katz didn't plan to stare at his ceiling at 4:57 a.m., but the million questions clanging in his brain gave him no choice. Okay, Wallace did a pretty good job of connecting dots between Cleo and Schein, but those were only the dots he could see – or thought he saw. But besides Rayful Edmond, who really knew how many dots were out there and how they were connected? If Wallace or anyone else in law enforcement knew enough to find even probable cause, wouldn't they would have arrested Cleo for Schein's murder, if only to have another bargaining chip to pressure her into wearing the wire? And even if Cleo did have a connection to Schein, did that mean she killed him? Why not any of the enforcers Rayful paid to do whatever happened to Schein and God knows how many others? And should he tell Madden what Wallace told him? But had he really told him anything?

He rolled over and closed his eyes, satisfied he'd made his case. But was that his brain talking or his heart, or an even lower part of his anatomy? Was he really closing his eyes to the possibility that Cleo might have had a hand in Schein's death just because he didn't want it to be true, no matter what the evidence said? And why was he siding with her anyhow over the guy who was probably his best friend ever, whom he'd shed tears over at his funeral? She was just a woman he really knew next to nothing about, except that she was a major player in Rayful's operation. And beautiful. And he was in love with her.

He flopped over onto his back again, eyes riveted on a ceiling he'd never found so fascinating. Out of the muddle swirling through his head, one other thing he knew about her took center stage: She was his client and as long as she was, he had a duty to defend her and hold the government to its bargain – how did the rules put it? – "zealously and diligently."

He forced his eyes shut and inside a minute, he was running through a hotel somewhere, dressed in the brown robe and cowl he always wore, but running, up and down stairs, leaping from balcony to balcony. The bobbies were drawing closer, screaming at him, holding their nightsticks high, but he got away just in the nick of time, every time. And there was Cleo on a balcony far, far away from him, but now her name was Juliet. She waved her arms and wailed for him to rescue her, but it was so far and an endless abyss yawned below. He grabbed a thick cord hanging from nowhere and swung into the chasm, the bobbies railing from the balcony he leaped from as he soared through the air until he felt himself falling without a chute into oblivion.

His eyes jumped open and focused on the clock. 7:22. He was exhausted from all that running and jumping but forced himself to stagger to the shower. By 8:15, he was out the door and heading for his car before he stopped. The sky had cleared from the night before and the air was crisp and cool. He was happy to remember the world could actually be a pleasant place if you let it, so he turned around and walked to the courthouse, slowly, to make that forgotten feeling linger as long as he could.

The feeling was long forgotten by the time he watched Cleo walk into the courtroom a few minutes before nine, and seeing her didn't bring it back. If she saw any shadow of doubt in his eyes, she hid it well, flashing him the same dazzling smile he'd grown to love, and squeezing his shoulder lightly as she made her way past him to her seat. He knew he should want to connect every dot between her and Schein, between her and himself, between her and the truth, but he also felt the sudden grip of a fear he remembered feeling only once before, a long time ago, when his dad disappeared. Finding out exactly why and how he did was a thing he desperately wanted to know – but not know either. If he'd found out that Sam been killed doing something heroic, it would have measured up to the vision he'd always had of him and he would have carried it high, a badge of honor, forever. But if he had died because he was involved in any of the *shondas* – the disgraces – that were whispered after he disappeared, he would have given his own life not to know. Looking back today, through the prism of all the evils and troubles he'd come to know life could bring, he was glad he'd been spared the burden of knowing even a fleck of anything that might reveal his father's story. Watching Cleo harden her face at the sight of the full gallery, the same tug not to know pulled at him, but this time it was no match for his lust to know everything about it.

Madden took the chair closest to Katz, Hutchison at his other side. "So," he said, "we're going to pick up with the Vegas trip, then move on to her paying for Rayful's cars, then start in on the wiretaps."

"Sounds good," Katz said. "And by the time they finish objecting, we can break for Thanksgiving." He turned to Cleo. "Anything else come to you we ought to talk about?"

"No. You?"

"No," he said with what he hoped was the right tone of nonchalance, "just keep telling the truth and everything will take care of itself." Cleo sighed and nodded at him. Richey entered and they stood and waited for him to climb back onto the bench. After a few seconds of paper shuffling, he gestured to Cleo to take the stand again.

"You are still under oath, Ms. Smythe," he reminded her.

"I know, Your Honor," she said. Richey looked at Madden.

"Whenever you're ready, counselor."

Round two started at a quick pace, but it didn't last long. Madden managed to walk Cleo through three pictures of her with different members of Rayful's crowd at a Gucci store in Vegas before Murphy's first objection. Katz pulled his scorepad close and started a new inning.

"Overruled," Richey said and Katz drew his first slash of the day. By the time Madden got done walking her through paying for Edmond's Jag and Range Rover, hauling bags of money to L.A., and getting busted in February, the score for Objections had climbed to 23. Sustaineds were still at 1.

"Now, Ms. Smythe," Madden said, "I'd like to show you Government's Exhibits 412-A and 412-B. Do you recognize them?" When Cleo said she did, Madden handed her a small clear plastic box.

"Would you open up what is contained in Exhibit 412-A and tell me what you see?" Cleo opened it up and looked at it. "It's a tape with my initials on it," she said.

"What about this transcript that you have in front of you that is Government 412-B?" Madden asked. "Do you recognize that particular copy?"

"Yes I do," Cleo said. "It has my initials on it and the date that I read it."

"Have you had occasion to listen to the tape recording and review the transcript?"

"Yes, I have."

"Is the transcript an accurate transcription of what is contained on Government's Exhibit 412-A?"

"Yes, it is."

"And have you had the opportunity to listen carefully to the tape recording itself?"

"I have."

"And were you present at the time that the tape recording was made?"

"Yes, I was."

"Is it a fair and accurate recording of what was said during that conversation?"

"Yes."

"And can you state who the conversation was with?"

"Rayful Edmond the third." Katz took a quick glance at Edmond. Slouching in his chair, head resting on his left hand, he looked like someone waiting for his number to be called at the DMV.

Madden turned to Richey. "Your Honor, at this time I move into evidence Government's Exhibit 412-A and 412-B and ask that it be played as an aid to the jury." In a second, the score was 24-1. "Your Honor, I ask that it be published to the jury at this time."

"Ladies and gentlemen of the jury," Richey said, "this would be the appropriate time to put on your headphones. The Marshals will give you help if you need it." Katz watched them put them on while he put on his own. The first thing he heard was a man's voice. "This is Special Agent – SA – Charles M. Anderson." Katz remembered he was the agent who signed the affidavit Marshal Gaskins gave him about the $30,000 bounty on Cleo's head. "Today's date is February 27, 1989, and this is going to be Cleo Smythe receiving a call from Rayful Edmond, at 945-3350. Hold on for the time." Katz heard some beeps, a telephone ring, and a pickup. "At the tone, the time will be . . . two twenty eight . . . pm . . . and twenty seconds." He heard more beeping and ringing before another pickup.

"Hello," Cleo said, kind of hesitantly.

"Yeah. What's up?" a man's voice on the other end said.

It only took Katz a second to remember this was the call she put on speaker for him the day the plumber came. The whole scene roared back to him, especially the fear that gripped him so tight he couldn't breathe. *It was then, not now,* he reminded himself and pushed out a long exhale between pursed lips. If Cleo remembered Katz was there, she didn't show it. He was not surprised. The rest of the call lasted about three or four minutes, all of it about the Range Rover. Nothing they said was of any legal consequence, but Katz knew Madden was playing it just to bolster Cleo's credibility by showing how tight she and Rayful were. Madden picked up another box and handed it to Cleo.

"Ms. Smythe, I'd now like to show you Government's Exhibits 413-A and 413-B. Do you recognize them?"

"Yes."

"Would you open up what is contained in Exhibit 413-A and look at it?"

When Katz was an AUSA, he loved the precision of laying the foundation for a piece of evidence almost more than the payoff of getting it admitted. It didn't matter if it was a document, like it was back then, or a tape like now, it was the ceremony of applying the ancient rules of evidence that made him feel like a worthy member of the legal fraternity. But now, he was as bored by it as everyone else in the courtroom, except Madden. He had a case to build so he pressed on: Two more tapes of Cleo and Rayful about the Range Rover, one with Rachelle about dumping anything that might tie them to Rayful, one with Jerry Millington about Dave McCraw getting busted, and all of them broken up by lawyers arguing about accuracy, unintelligibility, hearsay, relevance. When Richey finally called the lunch recess, Katz never remembered looking forward to a meal in the court cafeteria so much. Madden and Hutchison sat down to join him while a female Marshal escorted Cleo to the ladies' room.

"So," Madden asked him, "how'd we do?"

"Let's just say it was somewhat less than riveting."

"We had to get it all on the record, man," Hutchison said.

"I know," Katz said, "but the jury's tuning out. You may need to get to the good stuff soon."

"Her and Bootsie on the tape's next," Madden said. "That's the best we got."

"That should keep them awake," Katz allowed, "if Billy and the rest of them stop objecting every five seconds."

"There is one other thing," Hutchison said. "The three oh twos." Cleo pulled out a chair and joined them. "What's a 302?" she asked.

"It's an FBI report," Katz said. "Usually their report on a witness interview. If there's anything that might remotely show a defendant's innocent, the Government has to give it to the defense before they cross-examine the person they interviewed – you, in this case."

"That's true," Madden said, "but in this case, the 302's not your statement. It's the inventory of the stuff the FBI seized when they went through your house after they arrested you."

Cleo went white. "Are you serious?"

"I'm afraid so. We've held on to it as long as we legally could, but since they're going to start cross-examining you tomorrow, we have to give it to them today. The law says they're entitled to see anything we have that might exculpate you."

"Holy goddamn Christ!" Cleo said. "And let me guess. They can ask me anything they want about it!"

"Not anything," Hutchison said, "we can object to anything that's not relevant or – "

He stopped short when a waitress came into the room, a smile on her face and a pencil in her hand.

"Hello there," she said. "What can I get you folks today?" Cleo shot up, sending her chair tumbling back onto the linoleum. The door to the room swung open, the lady Marshal in the doorway, a hand on the Glock on her hip. "What's going on?" she asked.

"I don't feel good," Cleo said. "Can you take me somewhere to lie down for a few minutes?" The Marshal looked to Madden, who gave her a short nod back. "I'll come get her in a half hour or so. Just let me know where she is."

Cleo headed for the door, shaking her head and muttering dark thoughts. Katz took a step with her, but before he could say a thing, she shook him off and disappeared through the door. The Marshal closed it behind them.

"Any idea what that was all about?" Madden asked Katz.

"None."

"She's got immunity and witness protection," Hutchison said. "What's she got to worry about?"

"That's a good question," Katz said. "I wish I had an answer."

Cleo didn't give him one when they got back together just before court resumed, so he just let her be in the judge's hallway to the court and joined the lawyers' parley at the bench before Richey called court back in session. Murphy was holding forth on a document he'd just given the clerk.

"Judge, this morning, when we came back from a break, we found waiting on the defense table an FBI 302 report concerning the search of Ms. Smythe's home last February."

The clerk said handed it to Richey.

"Your honor," Murphy said, "this statement is the inventory of the search of her home. It includes, among other things, assorted phone books, assorted photographs, and various material possessions, including a dollar bill or, I should say dollar *bills* with white residue on them. A dollar bill, Your Honor, for the Court's information, is used by cocaine users as a tube to snort the powder from glass or some other smooth surface into their nostrils."

"Into the what?" Richey asked.

"Into the nostrils," Murphy said. "In other words, it's used like a straw from the nose to the cocaine powder, and when it's used like that, it has a residue of cocaine left on it, and we want to know whether or not the government had the cocaine on those dollar bills analyzed, because that is powerful evidence that Ms. Smythe was using cocaine herself."

Katz flashed on Hutchison interrogating Cleo at the Mayflower about whether she was a user – and her denying it. "Your Honor," he said, "my client does not use cocaine."

Murphy grinned at him. "Mr. Katz is protecting his client like a good lawyer's supposed to, Your Honor, but my question is to Mr. Madden: Did the government

analyze that residue?" He didn't wait for the answer before he turned back to Richey. "In addition, Judge, there were two file drawers of records that Ms. Smythe kept, and we have evidence that these records were of her own cocaine –
"

Robertson grabbed his elbow and Murphy stopped. "Well, don't let me put it on the record just yet, because I don't want to say it in front of the government, Judge. It's part of our defense. They'll find out soon enough, but not now."

He held the inventory out to Richey like he wanted him to take it but when Richey didn't, Murphy must have felt he couldn't hold back any more. He walked closer to the bench and further from Robertson.

"Judge, with this inventory, we're in a much better position to tell the Court that Ms. Smythe will testify that she kept excellent records of the names of her cocaine sources and her cocaine customers. She also kept records of her financial dealings, and records about a safe deposit box, and we're entitled to look at all that because it's relevant to our defense."

Madden and Murphy started arguing about whether Richey had already issued a ruling that precluded Murphy from seeing the inventory but Katz was listening to his brain ask him again if he knew who his client really was and what she really did. He managed to return to the real world in time to hear Murphy read to Richey from the inventory.

"Judge, she had a suitcase containing drug paraphernalia. She had a Ziploc bag with white residue. She had numerous cigarette papers, which indicates that she smokes marijuana, and she had plastic packing paper, which indicates that she was in some kind of drug packaging operation. Plus safe deposit boxes and credit cards. Your Honor, we want to know where those boxes were and how many of them there were, because they're essential to our theory of defense, which I would like to proffer for the Court, because without a proffer in the record, the Court won't be able to ascertain the relevancy of these materials."

Madden reminded Richey again that Murphy only had a right to see the inventory, not the items inventoried. "I will hold my ruling in abeyance," Richey said. "Let's proceed, Mr. Murphy."

"Your Honor," Murphy said, "my motion needs to be addressed now." "All right," Richey said. "It's denied." He turned to the clerk. "Let's get Ms. Smythe back on the stand and the jury back in the room. Gentlemen, ladies," he said to the lawyers, "please return to your neutral corners." Back at their table, Katz asked Madden "Did you know she had all this stuff?"

"I did," he said, "but I didn't see the need to tell you once she agreed to cooperate. Did she ever tell you she was running her own operation?"

"No," Katz said. "You heard what she told you and Hutchison when you were prepping her. She wasn't, and she never told me anything different."

"The good news is Murphy let us know what's coming," Hutchison said, "so we can deal with it on re-direct." He nodded to the door and they all watched Cleo come through and take her seat on the stand again, looking for all the world as composed as she was going to have to be, especially when Murphy started in on her. Until then, she was in good hands.

Madden broke her conversations with Bootsie into nine segments and paused after each segment to have Cleo – and, more importantly, the jurors – look at pictures of the people she was talking to so they'd put a face with a name. He asked Cleo to fill in the missing details about all of their roles in the operation so they could remember one more time who did what. He asked her to clarify how much money and how much drugs she was talking about to underscore the mammoth amounts of both. He only let the jury read the transcript pages of a segment while it was being played so they wouldn't get distracted. Katz knew what Madden knew: The more time the government spends on something, the more important a jury thinks it is, so Cleo's testimony was going to be the most important thing of all. It was a masterful performance even before he came to the grand finale.

"Now, Your Honor, I'd like the jury to hear segment nine, Ms. Smythe's conversation with Ms. Perry at Pier Seven Restaurant in Washington, D.C. on March 23, 1989 at approximately 11:15 a.m."

"Objection!" Murphy called out. "Mr. Madden is testifying, Your Honor, and he's assuming facts that aren't in – "

"Denied," Richey said.

Katz knew exactly what was coming. He'd heard the tape more than once. But this was the first time the jury would. If they understood what they were hearing, they'd have no choice: They had to convict. But if they didn't grasp what Bootsie was telling them, or worse, if even only one of them was going to let Rayful Edmond walk, no matter what, the case was doomed and so was Cleo. And maybe, he couldn't help but think, so was he.

Your Honor," he heard Madden say, "from pages thirty-eight to forty-three, whenever you feel it appropriate."

"All right, let's go," Richey said. They all put their headphones back on and Katz heard Bootsie's voice roll off the tape.

"So, Cleo, you okay with Toni these days?" He remembered that Toni was Art Reynolds' wife.

"Yeah, right," Cleo answered. "You know what it is, Bootsie? She has always wanted to be in the position that I'm in. She couldn't understand why Ray would trust me and talk to me and be friendly with me and not let her do more. She wanted to be on the inside."

"That's right," Bootsie said. "And what tickled me was Art's talkin' about when he's gonna buy the car from Rayful for her. What is he gonna buy it with?"

"I know!" Cleo said. "When Art was sayin' that, I'm thinkin' they already owe Rayful twenty thousand dollars – how in the world can he get a seventy thousand dollar car? And you know that Toni has some kind of degree, but they don't know anything about the street or the people out in it and they think just 'cause they got college degrees, they can talk to people any way they want to and they think everybody else is stupid."

A man's voice came though the headphones. "Ladies" he asked, "are you ready to order?" The waiter.

"I want the jumbo shrimp cocktail," Bootsie said, "but can you give me enough so it's a meal? It's all I want."

"You know what?" Cleo said. "That sounds good to me too."

In a few seconds, Bootsie picked up the conversation. "What you said 'bout Toni? You got that exactly right. That's why Rayful has you doin' what you do. Here's the way I look at it, Cleo. She knows that you take care of Ray's business, you do a lot of things for him –"

"A *lot* of things," Cleo said, "and a lot more than she's ever done – or would ever do, Bootsie. You know that. She was very envious of me, Bootsie. That's all I'm saying, and that makes me mad!

"You know what it is, at bottom? She's probably tryin' to find out whether you was seeing Rayful, see?"

"People can still never believe that Rayful and me're just friends."

"That's what I tell 'em, but Toni an' all these young boys, they see him with a white girl, you know they gonna start thinkin' somethin'."

"But see, Bootsie," Cleo said, then stopped. Katz could picture her trying to get herself together enough to keep going. "The boys, they know better than to insult me 'cause Rayful's already set 'em straight about me, you know what I'm sayin'? 'Cause they always – none of 'em ever treated me with any disrespect because they see the way I carry myself. I never gave 'em the opportunity to – "

"An' that is the thing, Cleo," Bootsie said. "That is the thing that counts."

"Shrimp cocktails, ladies?" the waiter interrupted. After some clanking and tinkling, Cleo said "Hey, so listen, Bootsie, how is Niecey holding up? See, that's one reason I wanted to talk to you, find out what happened."

"Minor is the police," Bootsie said. "He set her up, set Dave up."

"Has he always been the police?"

"No, here's what we think. They was stealing stuff off Rayful, okay, Dave workin' on one end and Minor workin' on the other over here in Southeast, an' he got busted, and they probably put him on the spot, you know, sayin', 'hey, you gotta give us somebody or you can lose your job and you can go to jail and all that,' so he set up Dave. Now the first time, some guy who was the real police, undercover police, he goes up to Dave and sells him an ounce, okay? And Dave brings the stuff out to Minor,

388

and Minor tells him he was police and Dave say, 'Oh Jesus, this is it'. But that lawyer you set us up with out there in Virginia, what's his name?"

"Whiteside?" Cleo asked. Katz remembered that was who he told her to call. "That guy?"

"That's the guy. He was trying to cut a deal for 'em, but a couple days later, Dave went back to the hotel – because Minor set him up – and that's when they grabbed him." A pause lasted until Bootsie talked again. "Dave always wanted to be the big deal."

"And, you know, he tried to make Ray think I was takin' the money," Cleo said.

"I know," Bootsie said, "an' I told him 'they're the ones that're doing it,' but Ray had so much confidence in him and he loved Niecey so much he didn't think either of 'em'd do anything like that." After another pause when it sounded like they were lighting up, Bootsie went on.

"Yeah, but there's worse," she said. "And Niecey, you know, she wouldn't've done anything behind Rayful's back, but she was overwhelmed by Dave. You saw 'em, you know what I'm talkin' about. Lord, I could not believe a man could turn a woman's head like that. Cleo, she put Dave's mother, everybody, before me and everybody else. And then she bought that car, and now the police have it – and then they had a check in the house for nineteen thousand dollars. Tell me why would you leave a check in the house for that amount? And have it in Dave's name? Shit!"

"She ain't gonna get that back," Cleo said.

"Hell, no, she ain't! If she'd listened to Rayful –
that boy, I don't know if it's ESP or what – but the Lord
has been with him and anything he tell you to do, if you do
the opposite, something always happen."

Katz heard the waiter's voice again, then Bootsie
saying "We're done. You can take 'em."

"They were so good," Cleo said.

"Did you leave room for dessert?" the waiter said.

"I think I'm filled up," Bootsie said. "Maybe just
some coffee to wash it down."

"Me too," Cleo said.

"But what you was sayin' about Toni?" Bootsie said
a few seconds later. "Dave was the same way. He wanted
to be a master all the time, but sometimes you just have to
step back."

"You remember that time Ray wanted to know if I
told anybody who wasn't there about that thing?" Cleo
asked. "I didn't tell nobody."

Katz hadn't heard that part of the tape since long
before Wallace told him about how Schein really died.
Now that he had an idea about what "that thing" might be,
he prayed he was wrong.

"I know you didn't," Bootsie said, "an' that's the way it should be. If nobody don't know, can't nobody tell nothin'. That's the way I look at it."

"And least of all would I want Dave or any of them to know what I did or where I did it," Cleo said.

"I tell you, I know," Bootsie said. "You know, I remember when Rayniece was holding the stuff for them, you know, and then she got rid of it." Katz did remember what was coming now and he pressed fingers to each headphone, waiting to hear it as clearly as he could. If a juror took it as a cue to listen good now too, that was fine with him. Bootsie went on.

"An' that was because she said she didn't want everybody runnin' through her house and everything. And I can understand that. But, Dave, he was there but he don't know how to run things there so I was runnin' things, you know, this and that, an' I knew Dave was stealing, 'cause one night one of the girls he was runnin' say 'no they just kin' crumbs or the dust they have left. Ray said they ʜ have it.' So I said, just testin' 'em, you know, 'well I ᶠ everybody's getting some, I can get me some too.' ǥave me some in a bag and I'm not telling you no ᴠas yea big. Now if they gave that to me, Cleo, ʲnk they had for themselves, you know, not ˢs going to go back and tell Rayful they ᵃntly. Every night. And they gave it ᶜorner to sell and then Jerry and ᵃid Dave gave it to him. An' ʰis, up and down. But see, ʰis if it wasn't his?"

"You know I worry about Rayful, Bootsie," Cleo cut in, almost like she was trying to change the conversation, Katz thought, but he knew it was too little too late. Katz looked down at his notepad before he stole a look at Cleo, who met his eyes with a blank stare. Katz swiveled his chair back towards the jury. He panned each member's face, trying to imagine what they'd look like at the end of the tape.

"We all worry, child," Bootsie said. "Do like I do, all you can do is pray. You know, Ray say if he could do it all over again, he would do some things different. But see, it all started with his daddy. If his daddy had never started him, he'd'a never got into all this. A long time ago, I used to do some small stuff, like I used to sell pills and stuff and Rayful would go around with me and he'd take my money home, and like when he started out, it was like he was doing hand to hand on the corner and they was selling and getting it from Big Ray. And then, it just got too big, and he just up and went out on his own."

The waiter's voice came back. "I'll just leave this here," he said, then he must have seen something that made him say "I'm sorry, I didn't mean to intrude." Katz heard what must have been a purse snapping, then Cleo saying "Please, Bootsie. It's on me." Then the tape clicked off.

Madden paused, ostensibly to look over his questions, but also, Katz knew, to let all the damning words from Rayful's own mother sink a little deeper into each juror. Hutchison scribbled something on his pad, then turned it to him, beaming the first smile Katz ever saw o his face.

"Fucking devastating!!" he read. Katz nodded his agreement, then turned slowly to look at Bootsie, in her usual seat and sporting her usual unusual headgear, this one a dark blue number with a white flower pinned to its right side and a light blue veil falling just below her eyes. Like everyone else on the other side of the glass, she didn't hear what they just heard on this side. Seeing her sit so proud and stoic, Katz wondered whether she remembered what she said that day, and whether she knew that if anything was going to convince the jury to put her son away for the rest of her life, it was the words they just heard come out of her own mouth. Billy Murphy brought his attention back to this side of the glass.

"Judge, move for a mistrial," he said. "It's impossible for this jury not to give credence to this testimony no matter what you do, and it isn't supported by anything that Mr. Madden has put into the record concerning my client, Rayful Edmond the Third. There's not a scintilla of evidence this woman was around for anything he said or that she has personal knowledge or any other kind of knowledge."

"Mr. Murphy – " Richey cut in to no avail.

"Second, Judge, I think that for the first time the Court is really able to hear what we have been arguing in our motions to strike some of this preposterous evidence. These tapes are full of gossip, third-, fourth-, and fifth-hand hearsay, and there's no way to tell from the tapes whether or not the speakers are speaking from personal knowledge or whether they're speaking from that fourth- or fifth-hand knowledge."

"Mr. – "

"We complained about that before the tapes were admitted," Murphy roared on, "and we renew our complaint again. We made timely objection to these tapes, and I move for a mistrial on the grounds that they are not admissible either as co-conspirator statements made in furtherance of the conspiracy or on any other theory. It's just gossip."

"Are you through, Mr. Murphy?" Richey asked.

"Yes, Your Honor."

"All right," Richey said. "Motions are denied. Thank you." He turned to Madden. "Do you have any further questions for Ms. Smythe?"

"Your honor," Madden said, "I believe the Government will be able to reserve its further questions for Ms. Smythe on re-direct."

"All right," Richey said and turned back to Murphy. "Mr. Murphy, you can start your cross-examination tomorrow morning. Nine-thirty sharp." He banged his gavel. "This Court's in recess till then."

When the door to chambers closed behind him, Katz stepped over to the witness stand and reached his hand out to Cleo. She took it and climbed down, her eyes on the front defense table the whole time. Rayful made a point of letting his eyes linger on hers, then turned his back and followed Billy and a Marshal out of the courtroom. Madden greeted her at the table.

"Ms. Smythe, you did a terrific job up there today. Very impressive."

"I'm glad you're happy."

"You're not?" he asked. "You should be."

"Mr. Madden, what I am is beat. Do we have to get together tonight or can I just lay down till nine thirty tomorrow?"

"Can we have an early dinner in your room?" Madden asked. "It'll be quick, I promise." Cleo groaned. "It's important, Cleo," Katz said. "Murphy tipped his hand about what he plans to ask you about tomorrow, so we can just zero in on that. I promise you, we'll be gone right after dinner and you can get into your jammies and nod out even before Jeopardy comes on."

"Fine. Just get up there as soon as you can. The quicker you come, the quicker you'll go. I've fucking had it." When the Marshal closed the door behind her, Madden turned to Katz. "Your client was tremendous today, Mr. Katz. She did us a world of good."

"I'm as happy as you are, believe me," Katz said. What he didn't say was what they all were thinking. *If Billy Murphy carves her up tomorrow, today won't mean shit.*

36

From his seat in the well the next morning, Katz had an unobstructed look at what everyone in the courtroom and the packed gallery had no choice but to look at: Bootsie, or more precisely, the hat she chose to wear for the first time today, the day of the main event, the cross-examination that would determine whether her son spent the rest of his life in the free world or in a cage. A milliner might have been able to describe it just so, but the best Katz could come up with was it looked like the love child of a cross-species three-way. The hat itself was a rounded leopard-skin number, but it was graced with a long brown feather on one side and an even longer gold plume on the other, and under it all sat Bootsie, less Estelle Jefferson today than Queen of the Valkyries, jaw set, eyes afire. If she was sending a message that she was ready for a battle royale, Katz got it loud and clear. She might as well have been wearing a sword and shield.

He scanned the room. Every seat was filled. He didn't see Harry in the chair they usually shared, but he did see another familiar face nod at him from the rear wall. Katz nodded back to Wallace, then wagged a finger back and forth between them, jerked a thumb towards the hallway, and pointed to his watch. He took Wallace's thumbs-up for an OK to what he hoped he took as "Let's talk out there later."

Katz turned to check out the jurors, but the stony looks he got back only made him more uneasy about what Murphy had in store for them today, and that made him remember something else just as unpleasant: What passed for dinner with Cleo last night. She wasn't happy with anything or anybody – Madden and Hutchison because they sandbagged her on the 302s, Richey because he let Murphy go on and on, Murphy because he was Murphy, and Katz because he didn't protect her from any of them. No one could make her focus on the day that lay ahead, so the prosecutors excused themselves before dessert and Katz didn't make it to the crust of his key lime pie before Cleo excused him too. When he caught up to Madden and Hutchison on the sidewalk hailing a cab, they all tried to assure each other that she'd be fine after a good night's sleep but looking at their faces approaching him now, they looked even less convinced than he felt. Madden planted his briefcase on the table with a heavy thud.

"Good morning, Mr. Katz. Have you had a chance to take your client's temperature this morning?"

"I have not," Katz said, tipping his head to the door behind him. "The Marshals told me they'd let me know when she showed up." Hutchison looked at the clock over the bench. "It's nine twenty-two," he said. "Maybe you ought to check on – " The door behind them swung open. Marshal Gaskins came through first, then Cleo. Katz stood to greet her, but before he could say a thing, she asked Madden "Can I talk to Jake back here for a minute?"

"Sure. Anything I ought to know about?"

"No. I just need to talk to my lawyer a second."

"Go right ahead," Madden said, "but when you see Richey, it's show time." Cleo nodded and Katz followed her back through the door. The clerk and the court reporter stopped their chat by the door to Richey's chambers long enough to look at them, then went back to it.

"You squared away for today?" Katz asked. "Ready to go the distance?"

"That's not why I wanted to talk to you, Jake. I don't want you to say anything, I just want to say I'm sorry – again – for being such an asshole last night." Her eyes welled up with tears and she fished a tissue out of her pocketbook to dab them away.

"Cleo, forget about last night. Forget about everything except what you're doing up there today."

"No chance I'm forgetting that," she said, stuffing the tissue back in her bag and shaking her head.

"Cleo, if you just tell it like it is, just like we've gone over and over and over, you'll do great."

"Yeah, but –." Katz put his hands on her shoulders. "We've been over this. Short and sweet, right? He asks you a question, you answer it, period. No speeches, no explanations, not a syllable more than you have to, just like we talked about, okay?"

She shook her head yes, then no. "It's just – there's a lot riding on this. Everything you guys've told me about him tells me he can fuck me up in a heartbeat. And fucking up today means fucking up my whole life. It's a lot to deal with, Jake." Before Wallace had told him about her connection with Schein, he'd've given her a hug, kiss away the tears welling back into her eyes, tell her everything would be all right, but now all he wanted to do was think of something, anything that would calm her down, get her to focus. Desperation delivered a trick he remembered from his AUSA days that also reminded him how long it'd been since he'd been in court for a real live trial, not just a plea bargain.

"Okay, listen, if I pull my tie up like this," he said, pushing up the knot, "you bring whatever sentence you're saying to a full stop as soon as you can, then shut up and take a deep breath, okay?" She started to answer until Katz saw Richey step out of his chambers and escorted her back into the courtroom. In a minute, the clerk, the reporter, and Richey followed. In two minutes, Cleo was sworn in, seated, and watching Murphy approach her, the cover of his black leather binder flipped open to show Cleo, Katz, and anyone else paying attention a handwritten list of questions that filled the top sheet of a thick legal pad. Katz felt like a kid at the top of a roller coaster. He knew what Cleo felt like. Murphy smiled at her just enough to give Katz a gleam of the gold tooth.

"Ms. Smythe," he said, "you're originally from Virginia, is that right?"

"It is."

"And what part of Virginia?"

Madden bolted to his feet. "Objection, relevance." Richey looked at him as quizzically as Katz did.

"Overruled," he said but Madden stayed on his feet. "Security, Your Honor," he said.

"She doesn't live there any more, Judge," Murphy said.

"I don't know where she lives," Richey said, "but it really doesn't make any difference, does it, Mr. Madden? The Court has ruled. Proceed, Mr. Murphy."

Madden sat back down. Hutchison pushed a note in front of Katz. "2 can play this game," he read. Katz nodded he got it, but now he hoped the trial would end by New Year's.

"So, again, Ms. Smythe, where did you live in Virginia?"

"Williamsburg."

"And did you move to the D.C. area directly from Williamsburg?"

"Yes."

"And how long ago was that?"

"About five years ago. Actually, it'll be –." Katz leaned forward to catch her eye, then pushed his tie up, hard. "Five years is right." Hutchison looked Katz' way, but he ignored him.

"And you claim to have met Rayful Edmond the Third about three years ago, is that right?" Murphy asked.

"Yes."

"And so when you claim to have met him, he was just twenty-one years old and you were twenty, is that correct?"

"I don't know how old he was."

"Well, if he's twenty-four now, he was twenty-one then, wasn't he?"

"If you say so." Murphy turned to the jury. "Well, these are simple questions, Ms. Smythe," he said before turning back to her, "and you understand that you're under oath, don't you? So I want full and complete answers – "

Madden got to his feet again. "Objection to the speech, Your Honor."

"Objection sustained."

"I'll rephrase the question," Murphy said. "If he's twenty-four now, how old was he when you met him?"

"Objection to a fact not in evidence," Madden called out, barely back in his chair.

"Sustained." Murphy turned to Madden, no smile, no gleam now.

"Is the government willing to stipulate that Mr. Edmond is twenty-four years old so we can move on to something important?" Madden stood up and looked at Richey.

"No, Your Honor."

Murphy turned to Richey. "Okay, I'll proffer, Judge. He's twenty-four years old."

"Objection."

"All right," Richey said. "I've ruled. Let's move on." Murphy spent a few seconds looking down at his pad, more to settle himself down than figure out what to ask, Katz thought.

"Now, Ms. Smythe, you were pulled over and busted by the FBI on February 21, 1989, weren't you?"

"Yes."

"And you were busted because Charles Lewis set up a buy of cocaine with you – "

Madden leapt to his feet. "Objection, Your Honor! Relevance."

" – and an undercover FBI agent, isn't that correct?" Murphy yelled over him.

"No, it's not, I –," Cleo said before she saw Katz practically choking himself.

"May we approach the bench?" Madden asked. Richey waved them forward with a sigh. Katz leaned in to Hutchison. "What's the deal?" he whispered. "Who's Charles Lewis? Is he related to Tony Lewis?"

Hutchison pulled his chair closer to Katz. "He's a buddy of the Mayor. That's all I can tell you. He's got nothing to do with Tony Lewis."

Katz flashed back to his conversation with Wallace at Marrocco's about a high D.C. official. A million questions piled up in his brain but he filed them when Madden waved them both up to join him. When they got there, Madden told Richey, "Your Honor, I've asked Mr. Katz to join us because, as Ms. Smythe's attorney, he should have a chance to hear what Mr. Murphy is alleging about his client and respond to it."

"Fine," Richey said. "Welcome to the party, Mr. Katz. So please let us know where you're going with all this, Mr. Murphy, I beg you."

"Your Honor, as I said, we're going to show that she was the head of a large-scale cocaine operation and was the head of that corporation – "

"No, Mr. Murphy," Richey said, "you are not going to drag names of corporations that haven't been charged with anything into this trial, so I'm going to sustain the government's objection."

"Your Honor, the name is essential to establishing the fact that at all times Ms. Smythe was operating on her own and that she was not involved in cocaine activities on behalf of Rayful Edmond the Third as she claims. Disclosing the name will let us establish the full scope of her cocaine activity and show that she has committed perjury – in your courtroom, Judge – by false testimony that she wasn't involved in any cocaine activities other than with my client. And I would proffer, Your Honor, that the people involved in her cocaine network are dealing in multi-kilogram quantities of cocaine, and further, Judge, that the reason she's concealing all of this is because she does not want to face Continuing Criminal Enterprise charges."

Katz remembered Hutchison peppering Cleo with the same questions, but he wasn't appreciating how good their prep was as much as worrying about whether she lied to them about not running her own show and, if she did, what else she would – or did – lie about. Her words from the plea bargain discussions slammed into his mind one more time. *I never fucking killed anyone!* He hoped it was true, he wanted it to be true, but it didn't keep the seed of doubt Wallace planted in his head from taking firmer root.

"I'm not foreclosing your defense, Mr. Murphy," he heard Richey say, "but I am inclined to sustain the government's objection."

"But, with all deference, Judge, you are foreclosing it. The Court is violating – unintentionally, I want to be clear, but violating nonetheless – my client's Sixth Amendment right to confront this witness because, as the Court knows, the Government has made a deal with this woman that's part of the consideration for why she's testifying. The Government has proffered that she was simply a courier for my client. We don't believe that for a minute, Your Honor, given the information we have collected about Ms. Smythe. We want to show she's pulled the wool over the government's eyes about this."

404

The lawyer in Katz knew he should hope Richey would sustain Madden's objection, but the rest of him prayed he'd let Murphy dig down deep and pull up the truth about who Cleo really was and what she really did, root and all, any way he could. His prayers were answered.

"Mr. Madden," Richey said, "I'm going to permit this line of inquiry. Mr. Murphy, you may proceed."

"Thank you, Your Honor." Murphy waited at the lectern for Katz and the prosecutors to take their seats before he looked to Cleo. "Now, Ms. Smythe," he said, "you had your own cocaine operation going, didn't you?"

"No, I did not."

"And when you were busted on February 21st, you immediately became a police informant, isn't that correct?"

"Not immediately."

"But lickety-split, just as soon as you and Mr. Katz here could get everything you wanted out of the government, right?"

"Objection," Madden called out.

"Sustained," Richey called back. Murphy flipped to the next page of his pad and walked back to Rayful's side before turning back to Cleo.

"Now you're familiar with street terms, aren't you, Ms. Smythe?" Murphy asked.

"Yes."

"What's the street term for police informant? Is it snitcher?"

"Yes," Cleo said. Murphy turned to the jury.

"Stool pigeon?" he asked.

"Yes."

"Judas?"

"Yes."

"Songbird?"

"Yes."

"And after you got busted, Ms. Smythe, you got Mr. Katz here as your court-appointed lawyer, didn't you?"

"Yes."

"How many minutes after you got busted did you talk to Mr. Katz, Ms. Smythe?"

"It wasn't minutes," Cleo said. "It was the next morning."

"And did you talk to an FBI agent at that time?"

"No."

"Did you talk to a government lawyer at that time?"

"I didn't, not then. Mr. Katz did."

"But you authorized Mr. Katz to negotiate for you with the government, is that right?"

"Yes sir."

"And as a result of Mr. Katz's negotiation on your authority, your behalf, you made a plea bargain with the government, didn't you?"

"Yes sir."

Murphy picked a sheaf of papers off his desk with his left hand and held it over his head. "And there's a written plea bargain agreement that resulted from that, correct?"

"Yes sir."

"And you've had a chance to read that agreement, haven't you?"

"Yes sir."

"I'd like to ask you about some terms in it, Ms. Smythe, and ask you if you understand them, all right?

"Yes sir."

Murphy walked over to Madden and showed him the agreement. Madden compared the exhibit stamp on it with the stamp on his own copy and nodded. Murphy walked to Cleo, flipped the agreement open to one of the last pages, and laid it on the rail of the stand. "So let me ask you if you understand these terms, Ms. Smythe. There on the bottom of the page, right above where you signed it, what does it say?"

"I have read this agreement and carefully reviewed every part of it with my attorney. I understand it and I voluntarily agree to it."

"And did you witness Mr. Katz and Mr. Madden's signing there right below you?"

"I did."

"Now above that, do you see the word 'perjury'?"

"I do."

Murphy walked past Katz to the jury. "Ms. Smythe, I'd like you to tell the ladies and gentlemen of the jury what you believe perjury is."

"False statements," Cleo said.

"To whom?" Murphy asked.

"To anyone," she replied.

"So that would include the ladies and gentlemen of this jury then, wouldn't it?"

"That's correct."

"Now the agreement you signed also uses other terms in that same paragraph, doesn't it? Go ahead, you can look through it to see if I'm right. It uses 'false statement' and 'lie' doesn't it, as I recall."

"Yes."

"And you know what a lie is, don't you?"

"Of course."

"It's when you deliberately tell somebody an untruth, correct? Like when you commit perjury before a grand jury or a jury at a trial, you're lying to them, right?"

"Right."

"So now that we know you know what you signed your name to, Ms. Smythe, I want you to think again about that time you told Mr. Madden you went up to Tony Lewis' apartment at the Buchanan House in Alexandria, I think it was. Do I have that right?" The next fifteen minutes of Murphy's performance focused on every detail of Cleo's account of that visit to the grand jury. He picked every nit and made mountains of every molehill – "Well, was it three million dollars or more than three million? How did you know anyhow? Did you take the time to count every bill?" – but Cleo was up to the challenge, as short and as sweet as anyone could be under Murphy's siege. Madden and Hutchison made no objections to his questions, but objected to all of his speeches. Things came to a head after Cleo grew tired of his constant questioning about forgetting specific dates and gave him an answer that was more tart than sweet.

"Well, if you know the date, Mr. Murphy," she said, "why don't you help me out?"

"I want the truth, Ms. Smythe. I don't want to help you the way you've been led so far."

Madden jumped up. "Objection to the speech."

"Sustained."

"Ask that it be stricken and counsel admonished."

Murphy yelped like he was in pain. "Your Honor! May we approach?"

At the bench, Katz and everyone else in the room heard Murphy's frustration spew out. "Judge, I find Mr. Madden's continuing objections and his schoolboy running to the teacher to be absolutely, amazingly unconscionable! The substance of his argument is always the same: 'Ouch, that hurts!'"

"Your Honor," Madden said only a little quieter, "the prosecution only wants Mr. Murphy to abide by the rules this Court has set, repeatedly: No roaming around the well of the court, no preening, no putting on a show for the jury." Murphy laughed.

"What he's really objecting to, Judge, is the jury doubting his precious prized witness – and if that isn't what he's complaining of, then grits ain't groceries. Everything he said is unsupported by law."

Richey held up his hands before anyone could get in the next lick. "Nobody's going to do anything now but me, Mr. Murphy. I realize this is a big moment for you and, apparently, it's one of the highlights of this case, but you are going to have to abide by the rules we have established for this trial. You are going to speak from the lectern. You're not going to roam the well of the courtroom. You are not to make remarks to the jury and the government may make objections as appropriate, and I will rule, and you will abide by them."

Madden started to talk, but now it was Murphy's turn to talk over someone. "Your Honor, the prosecution's strategy seems to be to make any kind of objection that will disrupt the flow of what I'm doing. You've heard them all, Judge. Objecting to my asking where she lived, objecting to asking how old my client is, it's grade school stuff. If that isn't petty, Your Honor, my name isn't Bill Murphy. I'm just asking you to make sure that if they want to disrupt my cross-examination, they do it fair and square, that's all."

"Mr. Murphy," Richey said, "this court has bent over backwards to make sure this trial is fair and square. I have given you broad leeway to present your cross-examination and your case as you see fit. No judge on this court could have been any fairer to you and your client, so when I hear you say that the government has been petty in making objections to your behavior that I have sustained, Mr. Murphy, it is aggravating in the extreme – as is, I may add, your public criticism of me for insisting that you follow the rules of this court."

"I have not criticized you publicly, Your Honor."

"Oh yes you have. I've heard it and other people have heard it and reported it to me, and I've got it right in my office."

"No, Judge – "

"You've accused me of engaging in busy work and complained that I ought to let you speak on your feet like you were trained to do. I know that you have, Mr. Murphy, because it's been reported in the press."

"Judge, the only thing I have said to the press about you is that even though we have frequent disagreements, I have great respect for the Court. Anything beyond that is just not true." Richey had kept his cool throughout the trial way more than Katz expected, but he was running hot now.

"It's in my office, Mr. Murphy. Would you like me to go get it right now?"

"Judge, if you're going to go on press reports, then indict Jay Stephens, would you please, for his illegal conduct and unethical conduct before the trial."

"I have nothing to do with Mr. Stephens,"

"If you're going to go by the press, let's go by the press. They can make up all the stories they want, but, despite everything they're saying, they know we're winning, Judge." Richey went wide-eyed and Katz winced. He didn't know if Murphy was trying some kind of mental ju-jitsu to get Richey to say something Murphy could use on appeal, but he was sure Richey wasn't going to tolerate whatever it was. He braced himself for what he knew was coming. Full-on rage. Pounding the bench. A harangue of epic proportions. He was wrong.

412

"Mr. Murphy," Richey asked, "do you honestly think you're going to lose this case in front of this jury?"

Katz was stunned. He knew he told Cleo that just one 'Not Guilty' vote could hang the jury, but that was just to make her focus. He never really believed any of them could actually find Edmond innocent after seeing and hearing the mountain of evidence the government presented. Eyewitnesses, informers, tapes, documents, pictures – was it all for nothing? And what would that mean for Cleo? Her deal depended on Rayful being convicted. What would the government do with her if he wasn't? Katz forced himself to concentrate on the words coming out of Murphy's mouth before he had to confront the question of what it might mean for him.

"Judge, you don't mean to ask that question, do you?"

Richey seemed to realize he'd just said what he said out loud. He tried to regroup. "No," he said, "I don't ask that in all seriousness, Mr. Murphy, but I'm not going to tolerate you disrupting this trial any more than you already have. If you feel confident in your defense, then you act like the gentleman you are."

"At all times, Judge," Murphy said, "thank you." Richey waved them all away. "All right," he said, "let's resume, please."

Katz locked eyes with Cleo on his way back to the table and gave his tie a pre-emptory tug. If she was anywhere near as alarmed as he was, he wasn't shocked she

413

didn't show it. Murphy walked to the lectern between the lawyers' tables and waited for everyone to take their seats before flipping to the next sheet in his folder. "Now, Ms. Smythe, on the night you were busted, you were holding one kilogram of cocaine, is that right?"

"Yes."

"And you were planning to sell that cocaine that night, weren't you?"

"Yes."

"You sold a lot of cocaine this year, didn't you, Ms. Smythe?"

"Yes."

"And in 1988 too, right?"

"I don't remember."

"You don't remember if you sold any cocaine in 1988?," Murphy asked, apparently incredulous. "Is that your testimony, Ms. Smythe?"

"I don't remember when I sold it, Mr. Murphy."

"But you told the grand jury you sold cocaine in 1988, kilos of it, in fact." Murphy held up a transcript. "Were you lying then or are you lying now, Ms. Smythe?"

"If that's what I told the grand jury, it's true. I just didn't remember the date is all."

"Maybe it's understandable you have problems remembering dates, Ms. Smythe, but when your memory somehow fails you about selling *kilos* of cocaine, that's truly unbe – "

"Objection, Your Honor," Madden said. "Another speech." Before Richey could sustain it, Murphy said "I'll re-phrase, Your Honor. So, Ms. Smythe, *why* do you have no problem remembering a lot of trivial details, but so much trouble remembering you sold kilos of cocaine in 1988" – he looked at Madden – "question mark."

"I told you I was not clear about the date," Cleo said. Murphy managed to restrain himself from making a comment, but Katz knew the arch of his eyebrow and the shake of his head spoke volumes to the jury.

"Tell us the truth, Ms. Smythe, you were running your own game, your own gang, weren't you?"

Katz remembered Hutchison blazing questions at her about whether she dealt drugs on her own, but even he didn't accuse her of having her own gang. Katz braced himself for the answer but Madden spared him. "Objection," he said. "The witness is not on trial, Your Honor."

"Sustained."

"Ms. Smythe," Murphy said, "please take a look at page three of your agreement with the government and when you get there, would you please read paragraph seven to the jury?"

415

"The United States," Cleo read, "agrees that, other than the offenses for which Ms. Smythe will be charged, as mentioned in paragraph one, and other than crimes of violence, she will not be charged with any violations of federal or state law about which the United States Attorney's Office for the District of Columbia was aware prior to her cooperation." She looked up at Murphy as placid as she could be. Katz gripped the arms of his chair, waiting for Murphy's question, but even more for Cleo's answer.

"Have you committed any crimes of violence, Ms. Smythe?"

"Not that I'm aware of, Mr. Murphy." Katz scanned her face for any inkling of deception, unsure if he was scared to find it or hoping he would, certain only he wanted to know one way or the other. He found no sign of anything. Murphy pressed her.

"Not that you're aware of," he repeated, "Is that your testimony, Ms. Smythe?"

"Objection, Your Honor," Madden said, "asked and answered." "Sustained."

"Well then, let me put it a different way," Murphy said. "Didn't you in fact kill someone for doing just what you're doing here today, Ms. Smythe?" Madden and Katz jumped to their feet.

"Objection! No foundation, Your Honor!" Katz got in first. Madden barely let him finish. "We object to Mr.

416

Murphy introducing facts that are not in evidence solely to inflame the jury with such a preposterous allegation!"

"The objection is sustained," Richey said and pointed his gavel at Murphy. "You are walking a very dangerous line here, Mr. Murphy."

"May we approach, Judge?"

"You may not. Continue your examination within the bounds established by this Court and the law, please." Murphy approached anyway, Madden and Katz right behind.

"Your Honor, with all due respect," Murphy said, "I'm just trying to find out how big the witness' crimes were that the government agreed to wash away. If they were serious offenses that go to the trustworthiness of her testimony, my client has a right to ask about them under the Sixth Amendment. Murder is the most venal crime of them all, Your Honor."

Madden beat Katz to the punch this time. "Judge, there is not one scintilla of evidence in the record or in any of the documents the government provided Mr. Murphy about this outrageous accusation. This is sheer inflammatory speculation on Mr. Murphy's part."

"The objections are sustained, Mr. Murphy," Richey said. "Move on, I implore you."

Katz headed back to his table and looked at Cleo. Her face was tighter and whiter than he'd ever seen it. She gave him a flicker of an inscrutable glance before she

moved her eyes to Murphy. He took his seat and heard
Murphy's voice but he was too focused on the questions he
was asking himself to hear whatever he was asking Cleo.
*Of all the crimes of violence he could pick, why did he pick
that one? Was he just planting another seed with the jury
or did he know something? And if he did, who told him?*
The answer to that one was obvious, he knew, watching
Rayful look vacantly at Cleo. *But did that mean Murphy
was just trying to distance his client from another crime?
Or was it true?* He tried not to think the unthinkable but
couldn't. He turned back to see if he could draw a hint
from Wallace's face but couldn't do that either. He was
gone.

37

In another ten minutes, they were all gone, to lunch. Katz spent half of it fruitlessly looking for Wallace and the other half listening to Madden, Hutchison, and Cleo bitch about Murphy, which was an even bigger waste of time, but one he welcomed because it kept him from thinking about why he was looking for Wallace.

When Cleo got back on the stand at quarter to two, Katz tensed himself to hear Murphy find a different way to start where he left off, but he didn't. He went after her again on her alleged coke gang, but didn't get a minute into it before he earned another objection. The surprise was it came from the defense table.

Murphy had just asked Cleo where one of the conversations she taped took place.

"At Jerry Millington and Rachelle's house," she said.

"And was Jerry part of your crew?"

Joseph Conte, Millington's attorney, sprang to his feet. "Objection, Your Honor."

Richey overruled that one but not many more. The closer Murphy got to tying their clients to Cleo's supposed operation, the more their lawyers objected, and the more Richey sustained them. If Katz felt Murphy was under siege from everyone in the courtroom, Murphy must have felt it even more. A half hour later he confirmed it. The latest chorus of Madden's "Objection!" and Richey's

"Sustained." still hung in the air when Murphy slammed his binder on the lectern and threw up his hands.

"That's it!" he yelled. "Judge, they're not allowing me to get her to answer questions that will show my client is innocent of the charges the Government has levied against him and – with all deference, Your Honor – you're aiding and abetting them every step of the way."

Madden stood up. "And we object to that too, Your Honor," he said. "One more speech."

"Sustained."

"Of course it is, Judge, of course it is," Murphy said. He snapped his binder shut and threw his hands wide. "Billy Murphy surrenders, Judge. You win. I have no further questions for this witness." He took his seat next to Rayful, whose face showed concern for the first time all trial. James Robertson jumped from his chair at Edmond's other side and asked for a short recess to "confer" with Mr. Murphy. Richey gave them five minutes and left the courtroom while the two of them conferred with each other and every other member of the defense team, sometimes all at once. In ten minutes, Katz saw Robertson nod to a Marshal at the door back to Richey's chambers. In another ten minutes, Richey called them back to order, his face redder than when he left.

Murphy was at the lectern, somehow looking different to Katz, apparently trying for something on the order of contrite. "Your Honor," he said softly, "I apologize for my outburst. It's been a long few days for

420

everyone, but I have had a conversation with my client and he's asked me to continue my questioning of Ms. Smythe, so with the Court's indulgence, I'd like to resume my questions."

Richey did not indulge him. "You withdrew, Mr. Murphy!"

"If it please the Court – " Murphy started but Richey cut him dead.

"The Court is not pleased," he said. "Your request is denied." He turned to the defense table. "Who's next?"

Diane Lepley, Mangie Sutton's attorney, raised her hand and stepped to Murphy's side at the lectern. Murphy glanced at her, turned to Richey and opened his mouth, then thought better of it, and took his seat.

Over the next few hours, Lepley, Elise Haldane, and Cynthia Lobo each took a whack at shaking Cleo's testimony – and accusing her of running her own operation – but none of them mentioned anything remotely violent, or got anything more than Cleo's sweet and short reply, with nary a yank on Katz' tie. The most noteworthy thing to Katz had nothing to do with her testimony: It was the first time he'd ever seen three women in a row examine a witness in a criminal trial anywhere. At 3:37 p.m., after Madden decided "No further questions, Your Honor" was the appropriate amount of re-direct, and after almost three full days of testimony spanning four calendar days, Richey uttered the words that Cleo and Katz had been waiting for since she took the stand.

"Ms. Smythe, you may be excused." Cleo stepped down and followed a Marshal out the door without a look back at Katz.

"I think this is a good time to end our day," Richey said. "We'll resume at nine-thirty tomorrow morning."

When he disappeared through the door, Madden turned to give Katz a hearty handshake. "Mr. Katz, I can't say it was a pleasure, but thank you for everything you've done up here. You were terrific."

"And your client was spectacular," Hutchison said.

"Thank you both," Katz said, "and best of luck the rest of the way, for everyone's sake."

"Here's hoping, and if they do the right thing," Madden said, nodding at the jury filing out, "I'll be back in touch on the witness protection thing pronto."

"I'll look forward to that," Katz said, even if he didn't. He took in the view one more time, then packed his bag up and left, looking forward to an unhurried walk back to his office. But when every step seemed to bring another thought he didn't want to think, he picked up the pace. At the steps to the landing of his building, he saw LaVerne come through the door at the top. She gave him a double-take, then took a quick look at her watch. "I didn't think you were coming back," she said.

"I didn't either, but they got done with her quicker than I expected."

"Well, that's good," she said, but something in his face must have told her maybe it wasn't. "Isn't it?" He wasn't sure how to answer that. "Jake, is everything okay?"

That stumped him too. "I'm not sure, to tell you the truth," he finally said. "The only thing I know for sure is she's done and that's good enough for now." He headed up the steps.

"You want me to come back up?"

"No, I'm just going to dump my stuff and go home and lie down until sometime tomorrow. Or next month, we'll see."

"Okay, see you tomorrow – Oh, I just left you a message from Mr. Wallace. Jake, answer me somethin'."

"What?"

"You know any black men that ain't angry?"

Katz scrambled up the stairs and called Wallace from her desk.

"Detective Wallace."

"Tom, this is Jake."

"Hold on a minute," Katz heard, followed by a chair rolling back and a door closing before Wallace came back on the line. "Listen, I know you wanted to talk to me, but I couldn't stick around after Richey okayed your objection to

Murphy's question about her killing someone for doing what she was doing. I just couldn't."

"Tom, I had to object. I'm her lawyer."

"What?" Wallace said. "Jake, no, I wasn't pissed at you. I was pissed at whoever told Murphy what I told you about Schein." Katz breathed a sigh of relief. One of the thousand thoughts he'd been tormenting himself with was whether Wallace did somehow get the word to Murphy to ask Cleo that question. He never came up with a good answer why he would, other than to satisfy his own curiosity, but before he could come up with something to say, Wallace continued.

"And, I know that's pretty lame, Jake, because how can I get pissed at someone for leakin' something when I did it too, but I swear that I only told you after you told me you were her lawyer, after holding it in for over a goddamned year. I would never tell a fucking real live defendant's lawyer anything ever, you need to know that."

"Tom, don't beat yourself up over this. It had to be Rayful who told him, right?"

"Yeah, he's the obvious choice, but then the cop in me starts thinkin' that maybe he wouldn't've told Murphy anything about a killing he had anything to do with – like probably ordering it. And then, of course, I start thinkin' about all the leaks springing out of this place, and I think, hmm, maybe someone here told him. They been givin' him inside shit all along, why not now?"

424

"Tom, I am so sorry to hear how you're tormenting yourself. It's exactly what I've been going through, thinking about Cleo and Schein, over and over and over."

"Me too, Jake, trust me. I don't have to tell you that, do I?"

"No, man, you don't. But now it's on me to get her to tell me what really happened, somehow, someday, one way or the other. And when she does, I will tell you, trust me."

38

After Cleo stepped down, Katz sat in the gallery less and less, and each time he did show up, fewer people were back there with him than the time before. The only seats occupied every day were the ones Bootsie and a rotating cast of Edmond's aunts, uncles, and cousins filled faithfully, at least until Richey moved them to seats at the far end of the row after he spotted Rayful mouthing something to a ten-year-old cousin.

Over the next few weeks, there were a few moments of drama – like a bomb scare that cleared the courthouse – or surprise – like when Katz learned Edmond had been moved to Quantico because the D.C. Jail guards were treating him like he was Bobby Brown – but otherwise the trial seemed to be running out of steam, a show where everyone in the room was just waiting for the final curtain to come down. Even Cleo seemed to be losing interest. Their phone calls were short, and they spent more time in person talking about how much to bet on Final Jeopardy than anything to do with the case. The only question both of them had about the trial was one neither of them could answer: When is it going to be over? Finally, on December 1, Madden began his closing statement, the first scene of the final act.

"This has been a very long trial," he told the jury. Katz did the quick math. Picking them started almost three months ago. "And I know we have presented a mountain of evidence to you over that time, so the first thing I want you to know is I am not going to re-cap all of it for you now." Madden smiled but none of the jurors did. Katz knew there was no way to know what any of them was thinking so he promised himself not to waste time trying to decipher the undecipherable. "I am, however, going to try to pull together the key evidence you've heard so that, by the time I sit down, you will be convinced, well beyond any reasonable doubt, that Rayful Edmond the Third and every other one of these defendants are guilty of every one of the crimes they have been charged with.

"First of all, the evidence demonstrates – beyond *any* shadow of doubt – that Mr. Edmond was the President and the Chief Executive Officer of one of the biggest business operations in the Washington, D.C. metropolitan area. He ran an illegitimate business that was as well organized and well run as any legitimate corporation, there can be no doubt about that."

One by one, he pointed at each of the other defendants and described their roles. "There's James Antonio Jones, Mr. Edmond's Vice-President for enforcement, if you will. That's Jerry Millington, his Vice-President for the operations you heard witnesses describe at length." When he finished pinpointing each of them, he laid out how they all worked together to make the business hum.

"You heard witnesses describe their first-hand knowledge of every step in the process, every link in the chain, every element of every transaction from beginning to end. You may not remember all the testimony, or all the documents, or all the tapes, but you saw and heard how it all added up, from buying the cocaine from Melvin Butler, Mr. Edmond's supplier in Los Angeles, to bringing it

427

across the country in planes, forty-foot moving vans, trucks of all sizes, and cars, to arrive here in Washington, D.C., where Mr. Edmond's employees carefully weighed it and packaged it into amounts that other employees – including young children – would sell on the street, and not just Morton Street, not just the streets of Washington, D.C., but the streets of Maryland and Virginia too. This was a national operation of unprecedented scope and size in and around the Nation's Capital."

Katz watched Madden study his notebook to make sure they had time to think about everything they just heard him say. "Mr. Edmond's enterprise was an incredibly well run business," he went on, "and just like K-Mart or Sears or Macy's, it knew its customers' tastes, so it would buy and package a wide variety of ever-changing products to cater to them. And to insure employee loyalty as well as customer loyalty, Mr. Edmond provided benefits to everyone who worked for him that were as good as any company in corporate America, like salaries high enough for Mr. Lewis to buy himself the hundreds of pairs of shoes you heard about, and big fine cars – including, I'm sure you remember this, a red Jaguar with gold wheels for the CEO himself – and many other perks, like lawyers, real estate agents, and trips to Las Vegas and California. And the gifts Mr. Edmond lavished on his employees including not just the cars and the clothes, but jewelry of all kinds – rings, earrings, necklaces, bracelets, watches.

"And all of it, everything, was substantiated by documents, the testimony of cooperating witnesses, and wiretaps where his own lieutenants told you just *how* guilty he was of these crimes. Every tape you listened to talked about cocaine – every one! Whether it was about Mr. Lewis buying it or Mr. Millington packaging it or Mr. Jones killing people over it, Mr. Edmond's cocaine enterprise was at the heart of every conversation you heard. This was a major, major drug trafficking operation. You can have no doubt about that either. "

When Madden flipped a page, Katz finally turned to look at the jury. He'd spent the last two nights with Madden and Hutchison, helping them hone every paragraph, every word, every pause. The courtroom was dead quiet as Madden dove in for the kill.

"And on top of all of this," he said, "on top of everything I have summarized, everything you saw, everything you heard, everyone who implicated Mr. Edmond in every facet of this enterprise, one piece of evidence that I have not yet even mentioned stands out above them all, the most important, the most telling piece of evidence we presented to you: The conversation that Mr. Edmond's own mother, Constance Perry, 'Bootsie' Perry, you've heard her called throughout this trial, had with Ms. Smythe at the Pier Seven Restaurant that Sunday morning.

"I have no doubt you remember it, but let me remind you of the key parts, the most damning parts of what she said specifically about Mr. Edmond – her son! – to Ms. Smythe. I'm quoting now. 'See, it all started with his daddy,' she said. 'If his daddy had never started him, he'd've never got into all this. A long time ago, like I used to do some small stuff, like I used to sell pills and stuff and

429

Rayful would go around with me and he'd take my money home and like when he started out, it was like he was doing hand to hand on the corner and they was selling and getting it from Big Ray. And then, it just got too big, and he just up and went out on his own.'" The silence was deafening now. "Ladies and gentlemen, ask yourselves, as Mr. Hutchison and I did many times: Why would she lie about members of her own family, her husband, her son? Your answer will be, must be, the same as ours: She wouldn't. Of course she wouldn't."

He looked down at his notebook and read from it again. "'It just got too big, and he just up and went out on his own.'" He looked up and scanned the jury from one end to the other. "Ladies and gentlemen of the jury, the Government asks that you find Mr. Edmond and his fellow defendants guilty of each of the felonies with which they have been charged. Thank you for your attention, today and throughout the trial."

Katz expected Murphy to get up next, but Robertson was at the lectern before Madden was back in his seat, shaking his head in exasperation. "Ladies and gentlemen," he said, "let me begin right now by saying something I did not plan to say first thing to you today, but it's something that I simply have to point out because Mr. Madden conveniently forgot to point it out in his remarks. He did a very thorough job of reminding you of all the testimony and all the wiretaps you heard, but for some reason, he forgot to mention whose mouths every word you heard was coming from. Informers, to be polite. To not be so polite: Turncoats. Stoolies. Snitches. Squealers. Judases."

By the time he got to "Stoolies," Katz knew that this was exactly what he planned to say. "You can call them whatever you like, the point is that every one of them was lying to you for just one reason. They were lying to save their own," he paused, "selves, to be polite, because the Government was going to throw their – selves – in prison for a very long time unless they testified just like the Government wanted them to do. You heard Ms. Smythe, their supposed star witness. She started cooperating with them the very next day after she was caught running her own operation. And why did she do it? You know why. To save her – self. That is the one and only reason she cooperated, informed, squealed, snitched, and told these lies to your face, period. So she could stick these crimes on Mr. Edmond and the rest of these defendants and walk back into the free world with a new name and God knows what else the Government is giving her for her false testimony."

Robertson walked to the jury box and rested both hands on the rail. He took his time looking at every one of the twelve rapt faces looking back at him. "Now, I know you know what the Bible says about bearing false witness. It's in the Ten Commandments, isn't it? Number nine, right above 'Thou shalt not covet thy neighbor's wife,' am I right? It's even comes before that, doesn't it?" Katz saw two of the women nod they knew it did. "Thou shalt not bear false witness against thy neighbor," Robertson said, more righteous than any rabbi Katz had ever heard. "And that's what Cleo Smythe and Kathy Sellers and Deborah

431

Phillips and all of these deceivers have been doing, right in front of you, bearing false witness against Rayful Edmond and all of these gentlemen behind me, and, even worse, they expect you to buy it! Hook, line, and sinker!" He shook his head at the shame of it all, all the way back to the lectern.

"I'm getting near the end here, ladies and gentlemen," Robertson finally said, "so please try and stick with me just a little bit more. What I want to do in my final moments before you is to ask you to ask yourselves about something that you have not directly seen or heard because you have been sequestered so long, but that you have seen played out in front of you in this courtroom since the day this trial started. The question I want you to think about is this: Why have Mr. Madden and Mr. Hutchison's boss, Mr. Jay Stephens, and people in the Metropolitan Police Department, and God knows where else in the government of the District of Columbia, systemically leaked things to the press over the past twelve weeks to create a hanging atmosphere for this trial and try to enrage the honorable judge presiding over it, Judge Richey, against Mr. Edmond?"

Katz looked at Richey, who seemed no more peeved than usual, then to Madden to see if he might object, which almost never happened during a closing argument unless a lawyer made a wildly outrageous statement that was totally unsupported by anything a jury might have heard during the case. Katz wasn't surprised that Madden didn't move a muscle to defend his boss, probably because he knew it was true – and even more

432

probably, because he was happy to let him twist slowly in the wind.

After Robertson took his seat, all the other defendants' attorneys took their turns at trying to bat away what Madden – and their co-counsel – said about their clients' guilt, but when they were done, Madden rebutted them by only making a few minor corrections. When he rested after less than two minutes, his real message was one he didn't say: Those guys didn't lay a glove on me.

At 9:30 the next morning, Richey began to instruct the jury about every element of every crime that every defendant was charged with. At 12:30, Katz was hit by the thought that the instructions were taking longer than pretty much any trial he'd ever prosecuted. At 2:17, he finally got the chance to stand and watch the jury file out to begin deliberating the fate of the defendants. It was only when the chill air outside the courthouse hit him at 2:22 that he realized they were deciding Cleo's and his too.

39

The ring of his phone blared him awake a little before seven. "Jesus Christ!" he barked into the receiver. "Do you know what fucking time it is?" His disposition did not improve when he realized it was also Monday.

"Jake, I'm sorry," he heard Cleo say. "I just saw the article on the front page of the Metro section and freaked out!"

"What article?" he asked, hoping this was just a really vivid dream – or nightmare, depending on her answer. "Do you have the paper there?" A look at the clock flicking to 6:58 confirmed this was real life.

"Cleo, I'm still in bed. Should I go get it?"

"No, it's short," she said. "Listen. 'The jurors in the cocaine conspiracy trial of Rayful Edmond the Third deliberated yesterday for the third day without reaching a verdict. But in a dramatic development, they asked the judge in a note if they could find that Edmond had violated more drug laws than needed to convict him of the most serious charge.' That's good, isn't it?"

She had Katz' full attention now. "Is that it?" he asked.

"No. 'James Robertson said that the note gave some indication of which direction they're leaning, but added "I hope I'm wrong." Edmond has been charged with a continuing criminal enterprise,' blah, blah, blah, 'which means, Richey instructed the jurors, that they must find that he is guilty of conspiracy to distribute cocaine and violated at least two other federal drug laws. In their note, the jurors asked if they could list more than five violations on their verdict form. Richey said he will instruct the jurors today that they can.' That's it. I'm no lawyer, Jake, but that sounds to me like they think he's even more guilty than he needs to be for them to send him away forever."

That's what it sounded like to Katz too but he didn't want to read too much into it. "It does sound good, but they just might be looking at all their options. It doesn't necessarily mean all twelve of them agree on any one of them yet."

"Shit, Jake. I was looking for a little bit more of a pick-me-up than that."

"Cleo, you woke me up before seven o'clock. Let me pick myself up first."

"Wish I could do that," she giggled. Now himself was picking up all on its own. Before he could figure out what to say back, she said "I really can't wait to see you, Jake."

"I can come by today," he said. "I can bring in some lunch."

"I don't mean like that, Jake," she said. "I don't want to play gin rummy or watch game shows with you — and the Marshals! I just want you and me to be alone together, like normal people. I just want this goddamn thing to be over with once and for all so we can get on with the rest of our lives."

The "we" and "our" didn't have the same oomph they would have before his talk with Wallace that night on the wharf. "It shouldn't be long now, Cleo," he said. "We'll figure all that out as soon as they come back."

"Promise?"

"Promise."

"Okay, if that's the best I can do, I'll settle for tuna."

"Excuse me?"

"For lunch" she said, "with a side of Katz."

LaVerne poked her head into his office a little more than an hour later.

"You're in bright and early on a Monday," she said. He saw no point in telling her that if Cleo hadn't woken him up, he'd still be sleeping. "You know me," he said. "Up and at 'em."

"You see that Redskin game yesterday?" He also saw no point in telling her he didn't, but he did remember seeing the headline in the *Post* when he was looking for the article Cleo read to him.

"Yeah, great win," he said, "29-10."

"Never mind that. You see that boy A.J. Johnson?"

Katz had no idea who A. J. Johnson was but he if he was in for another dime, he was in for the dollar. "Yeah, wow, he was so good."

"And cute too. You see him when he took off his helmet? Mm-mm! That is one good-lookin' young black man."

Katz decided it was time to fold. "I have a question for you," he said.

"Shoot."

"You know where I can get a decent tuna sandwich around here?"

"What?! Antonio's finally give you heartburn or somethin'?"

"I'm meeting Cleo for lunch. She wants tuna."

"I will get right on it. What do you – " The phone ringing on her desk cut her short. She held up a finger and went to get it. "If it's Harry," Katz called out, "I'm still home. And I'm sick. And it's terminal, so no need to call back."

"Jake Katz's office," she said, then "One minute please." She punched a button and Katz' phone rang. "It's Mr. Madden," she said and hung up.

"Good morning, Charlie. What's up?"

"You might want to get over here, like now."

"Okay, your office?"

"No, the courtroom. The clerk just called. The jury's coming back, with a verdict."

"Oh Christ! When?"

"Ten thirty's what she told me but if you can get over here in the next fifteen minutes, I'll get the Marshals to let you sit with us." "I'll be there in ten," Katz said and hung up the phone. "The jury's coming back!" he yelled to LaVerne, then threw on his jacket, grabbed his briefcase, and ran down the steps. Ten minutes later, he was back in front of the glass with Hutchison.

"So where's Madden?" he asked.

Hutchison rolled his eyes. "He had to meet with Stephens, go over the post-game festivities." After Katz squinted at him, he elaborated. "Who's going to say what if we win, who's going to say what if we lose."

"I bet I can guess who's grabbing the mike if you win, and what he's going to tell Madden to say if you lose."

"Here he comes," Hutchison said, nodding to the doorway to the side doorway. "Can't wait to hear." Madden dropped his briefcase on the table and shook both of their hands. "So?" Hutchison asked.

"Let's just say it's not going to be pleasant no matter what happens."

"Guy can take the joy out of Christmas," Hutchison said, shaking his head. Now Madden changed the subject. He nodded to the gallery. "Looks like a full house."

Katz turned to see every seat behind them filled and every wall around them packed, the buzz of chatter loud enough to penetrate the glass. Bootsie and her brood were back in their seats behind the defense table, but everyone else was standing. The local TV and Post reporters he recognized were arrayed along the back wall, no doubt poised to run to the hallway to scoop each other as soon as Richey read the verdicts. When the people in front started to sit, Katz turned to see the jurors filing into the box. Richey came through the door next and his clerk stepped to his post. "This court is now in session," his voice boomed, "the Honorable Charles R. Richey presiding. Please be seated."

Richey wasted no time getting down to business. "Mr. Foreman," he asked, "does the jury have a verdict?"

An elderly black man previously known only as Juror Number Five stood up in the front row, a large manila envelope in his hands. "We do, Your Honor," he said, holding the envelope up. Richey turned to Marshal Gaskins at the door back to chambers.

"Marshal, would you please bring the envelope to me?"

When he had it, he opened it and slid out a sheaf of paper. Katz had never seen such a thick stack of verdict forms, but he'd never tried a case with eleven defendants facing multiple counts either. He watched Richey slowly turn over page after page, the flipping of the sheets inaudible over the pounding in his temples. Finally, Richey turned the papers back over and looked to the defense tables. "Will the defendants please rise?" Niecey let go of Dave's hand and they all stood.

"Rayful Edmond," Richey read without a glance at him, "the jury finds you guilty of Count One, engaging in a criminal continuing enterprise under 21 United States Code sections 848(b) and 853. The jury finds you guilty of Count Two, conspiracy to distribute and possess with intent to distribute more than five kilograms of cocaine and more than fifty kilograms of cocaine base under 21 USC section 846."

Katz pulled out his pad, scribbled Edmond's initials in the margin, and wrote two Gs next to them. He looked at Edmond to see if he was still as blasé as he'd been every other day, but he was dead serious now, his only motion a blink when each verdict was read. *Probably adding up the years*, Katz thought.

"The jury finds you guilty of Count Five, unlawfully employing a person under eighteen years of age under 21 USC section 845(b)," Richey continued. "The jury finds you guilty of Count Eleven, participating in interstate travel in aid of racketeering under 18 USC 1952(a)." He turned the sheet over. "And the jury finds you guilty of Counts Fourteen, Fifteen, Sixteen, and Eighteen, the unlawful use of a communications facility under 21 USC section 843(b)."

Richey turned that sheet over and continued to read without pausing or lifting his eyes. His voice was loud, clear, and flat, like he was reciting the steps of an owner's manual he'd read a thousand times before. "Melvin Butler, you are guilty of conspiracy to distribute and possess with intent to distribute more than five kilograms of cocaine and more than fifty grams of cocaine base under 21 USC 846."

The defendants and the counts droned on and every slash Katz slashed was left of the dividing line until Richey said – with no change in monotone – the jury found James Antonio Jones not guilty of intent to distribute cocaine. By the time Richey came to the end of all eleven defendants, almost half an hour after he started, that was still the only NG Katz had written. He counted up the ones on the left. Thirty-four. Richey flipped over the pile of sheets and turned to the jury box.

"Mr. Foreman, were these verdicts unanimous?"

"They were, Your Honor," Juror Five answered.

Murphy jumped to his feet. "Judge," he said, "the defense asks that you poll each juror as to each count against each of these defendants." Richey shook his head. "I'm not going to do that, Mr. Murphy," he said, turning back to the jury box, "but I will ask each of you to stand in turn and affirm – or deny – that, except for the count where you found Mr. Jones not guilty, you voted to convict every defendant of all of the crimes I just read. Juror number one, do you affirm, with that exception, that you voted to convict each of the defendants of the crimes they were charged with?"

"I do, Your Honor," he said. The rest followed in turn. The second they were done, Katz heard a bustle behind him and turned to see a scrum of reporters pushing each other through the door. He heard Richey say the trial was adjourned and thank the jurors for their service but couldn't take his eyes off Bootsie consoling a child in each arm, tears running down her cheeks, turning her head back and forth so violently Katz thought she was trying to shake what she'd just seen and heard out of her mind forever. He turned to the defense table, where Edmond hugged Robertson, then Murphy, and exchanged a variety of soul shakes and hugs with everyone else, before Marshal Gaskins placed the cuffs on his wrists and led him out the door to the holding cell. A slap on Katz' shoulder got his attention.

Madden had his hand out and they shook, hard. "Thanks for all the help, Jake. Couldn't have done it without you or your client and that's the truth."

"You guys did a great job," Katz said, now shaking Hutchison's hand. Madden put a hand on his arm and leaned in close to make himself heard over the hubbub behind them. "No rush, but I do need to know what your client wants, and sooner's better than later, for everyone."

"I know," Katz yelled into his ear, "and I will get you the answer as soon as I get it." Madden nodded and grabbed his briefcase.

"Going to see the show?" he asked.

"I'll leave you to it," Katz said. Ten minutes later, he was in his office. LaVerne wasn't, but the While You Were Out pad on the front lip of her desk told him Cleo had called and, for the first time in a long time, gave him a number he could actually call back.

"Jake?" she answered, with more energy in that syllable than he'd heard from her over the last three months combined.

"It's me. Congratulations!"

"I know! I heard it from the Marshals! It's great news, right?"

"It absolutely is, Cleo. But do they know you're calling?"

"Absolutely. They told me to. 'School's out now', that's what Julie said."

"Julie?"

"Sorry, Marshal Bykovsky. I told you, we've all kind of bonded here."

"Well, she's right. Everyone was convicted of every count, except for James Jones, who got off on a small one."

"Oh my God! I didn't want to believe it till I heard it straight from you. I am freaking big time!"

"It's just what we were hoping for, Cleo. Couldn't be any better."

"So can we celebrate?"

"I don't know," Katz said. "You might have to check with Julie on – "

"She said we could, here for now."

"Where's here?" Katz heard her say something to someone before she came back on the line. "Sorry, just wanted to make sure I wouldn't get detention the last day. We're at the Holiday Inn on Rhode Island, near Scott Circle?"

"Okay, and did Julie tell you just how we're going to celebrate?"

"You can bring something in," she said. "There's a really good Chinese place right around the block on 16th."

"Oh man, carryout Chinese at the Holiday Inn? You really know how to party. Okay, tell me what you want."

"You got a pen?"

"Why do I need a pen? How much are you planning to eat?"

"It's not just for me. You're bringing in for Julie and Dennis and Johnnie Lee too. We all have something to celebrate." Katz figured Dennis was Kravitz and Johnnie Lee was the guy in the hall at the Mayflower, but he didn't care about any of that. "Any chance we can have some alone time after the herd clears out?"

444

"Why do you think you're buying them dinner?" she said quietly. "That's the price of them eating it somewhere else." Katz pulled a pen and paper to him.

"Tell me what they want."

41

Katz' new friend Johnnie Lee met him in the lobby and took a few bags off his hands. Katz followed him into the elevator and watched him push 2. "Congratulations on the verdicts, Mr. Katz. You have a very happy client."

"And she has a very happy lawyer." Katz waited for the doors to close, then waited some more. When he reached over to punch the lit 2 button again, the doors began to slide shut slowly. Johnnie Lee shook his head and clucked a chuckle. "They know, man. They play with your head."

"Long way from the Mayflower."

"We've been in worse. You're better off not knowing, believe me." When the elevator bounced to a stop, Johnnie Lee led him down the hall, pushed open 210, and nodded to Katz to go in first. Kravitz was sipping a beer in the kitchen area and grabbed a bag from him.

"All right!" Julie said and jumped out of a chair across from the room. "Cleo!" she yelled to her left, "dinner's here! And oh yeah – your lawyer!" Cleo came running around the corner and weaved her way through the traffic to Katz just as he dropped his bag on the counter. She threw her arms around him, pinning his to his sides, and squeezed him tight before she looked up, her eyes more alive with something he wouldn't let himself name than he'd ever seen before.

"All my clients are like this," he told Kravitz with as much of a shrug as he could muster. Kravitz raised his bottle to him with a big grin and drained it. In less than a minute, everyone had their food boxes in front of them and bottles of Tsingtao raised high.

"To truth, justice, and the American way," Kravitz said.

"And going home!" Cleo said.

They all drank till Katz raised his bottle again. "And a giant thank-you to all of you for taking such good care of Cleo."

"Amen to that," Cleo said. "I feel like we've been through a war together, no kidding! Thank you! Thank you! Thank you!" she said to each of them. They all hugged and exchanged cheek kisses before Dennis said "Well, okay, we'll get out of your hair now. Mr. Katz, thanks for dinner. Cleo, call my room when you're ready. One of us'll be down the hall just in case."

Katz watched them file out the door, not quite sure if that was a wink he got from Julie until she turned back at the door and gave Cleo one he couldn't mistake. When the door closed behind them, he gave Cleo a quizzical look.

"Down the hall? What happened to camped at the door?" She walked to him and held him tight. Her breasts pushed into him and he couldn't help but push back a little lower.

"I was a model prisoner, Jake," she said softly. "Tonight's the first time I ever asked for anything, so . . ." They kissed each other long and hard until Cleo came up

447

for air first. "I missed you, Jake. I'm so glad you're here and I'm so glad that trial is over and I'm so glad the jury did what it did, I can't even believe it's all real."

"You still need to figure out one more thing, you know."

"No I don't, Jake. I know what I want."

"Okay. So what is it?"

"You," she said. "I'd rather have you than whatever money they give me to go into witness protection. If I have to give you up, it's not worth it, period." Katz gave into the moment and kissed her again and again until the whirlwind of questions swirling through his brain about what he really wanted made him stop. The sight of Chinese food over her shoulder gave him a chance to regroup.

"Let's talk about it over dinner," he said and scooped up the boxes and their beers. She fished chopsticks, forks, and napkins out of the bag, grabbed some paper plates, and led him to the couch. He dug into his Kung Pao Shrimp and tasted her Stir-Fried Bok Choy With Ginger And Garlic before going back to where he wasn't sure he really wanted to go.

"Cleo, I'm flattered, and you know I want the same thing," he said as convincingly as he could, "but you know it's a lot more complicated than that. You stay here, you're taking your life in your hands every day, every hour. People who are not happy with you know where you live, and that's just for openers."

Cleo swallowed her bite. "So here's something you maybe haven't thought about, okay? I've lived my whole life living in fear of somebody, starting with my own daddy dearest."

"I know, but –" Katz got out but she wasn't done. She pointed a chopstick at him. "*And* ever since I started working for Rayful, my life's been on the line every day, not just from the cops but his guys too! Now the cops don't want me and everyone with Rayful's going to be locked away for a long, long time – that's what you told me, counselor, right?"

"Right, but – "

"So the way I look it, I'm way ahead of where I was. It's not complicated, Jake, it's pretty simple. If you're here, I want to be here. I've had plenty of time to think about it over the past umpteen weeks, you know? I'm a big girl. I know all the pros and cons. I'll take my chances – with you."

She stuffed down a monster wad of cabbage for emphasis. They watched each other finish their bites. Katz knew he had nothing left to say until and unless he got her to open up about Schein or – he found himself truly hoping – convince him she had no idea what he was talking about. But this wasn't the time. They both seemed to have even more pressing things in mind. Cleo wiped her mouth with a napkin, then reached over to dab his before falling to her knees in front of him and pulling his face down to hers with both hands. She licked his lips and smiled.

"I'm getting to like Kung Pao," she said and they locked into a hot wet mess of a kiss. Her hands slid down Katz' shirt to his fly and caressed him into as much of a full and upright position as he could manage. She bent down and kissed him there, then pushed herself up off his knees. "Finish your shrimp, Jake," she smiled, then wagged a finger at his bulge, "and you just hold your horses, mister. I'll let you know when I'm ready to see you." She blew him a kiss and let him enjoy her walking away and softly pushing the bedroom door shut without a glance back.

He rearranged himself as best he could, then scarfed down his shrimp until he heard some familiar music throb at him from behind her door. He spent a few seconds trying to place it before the door swung open, her beckoning finger the only part of her he could see before the lights went out behind her. "You can come in now, Jake," he heard. Now there was no mistaking the hot pulse of *Little Red Corvette*. When he cleared the door, Cleo was nowhere to be seen, but a light sliced at him through the frame of the door to what he guessed was the bathroom. "Make yourself comfortable," he heard. He resisted the impulse to release his huddled mass yearning to be free, and contented himself with kicking off his shoes and lying on the bed.

"You comfortable?"

"Most of me," he said.

"Then close your eyes." A second after he did, he heard the door pop open, then sensed a change in the darkness. "Okay, open 'em."

When he did, he turned to see Cleo spinning past him to the foot of the bed, just barely visible in the bathroom light coming through the crack of the closed door. It took a second for his eyes to adjust, but when they did, they feasted on the sight of her swaying to the music, a very short white negligee keeping time to the backbeat, something else white and silky hiding her eyes. In another second, he realized she was putting on her show, just for him. Prince crooned right on cue.

> *And honey I say*
> *Little red Corvette*
> *Baby you're much too fast*
> *Little red Corvette*
> *You need a love that's gonna last*

She spun to the right, then to the left so he could get a 360 view of the most gorgeous, sexy sight he'd ever seen in the full-length mirror she'd set behind her. He never appreciated a performance more and he pushed himself down the bed to let her know just how much he did. She lifted the veil from her head to reveal another one right below it. "You like?" she asked.

"What's not to like?" he answered. Her sweet smile improved the view. "My own private Archibald's," he whispered.

"Just for you," she whispered back and took off the second veil. Prince faded out and Bruce faded in. *I'm on Fire*. "Wow, a mix tape," Katz said. "Very high production values."

451

Hey little girl is your daddy home
Did he go away and leave you all alone
I got a bad desire
I'm on fire

She came to him and buried his face between her breasts, rocking them both to the music, then went to her knees. She kept her eyes fixed on his while she undid his belt, unzipped him, and finally freed him. He watched her stroke him, then lick him, then swallow him.

"Jesus God," he said. "No wonder they loved you at Archibald's."

She slapped his thigh. He laid back and pulled her up to her knees over him, then returned the favor before she straddled his dick and took him in. They came together in a rush of heat and moans, but rocked in place till Bruce was done, then rolled to the side and uncoupled. Katz started to drift off but came back to life when he felt a breast slide across his face. His eyes popped open to see Cleo reaching across him for an ash tray and a pack of Kools. He smothered himself in both breasts on her way back and she let him linger until his tongue flicked her nipple once too often.

"God, that tickles!" she yelped. "I'll keep that in mind," he smiled. She piled the pillows up behind her, lit up, and puffed a stream of smoke away from him.

"That was very nice," she said.

"I couldn't agree more." Hall and Oates' *You Make My Dreams Come True* started punching out of the tape

452

recorder on the side table. "How much music did you record?"

"Hour and a half, give or take."

"So an hour and twenty minutes still to go?" he laughed.

"The night is young," she smiled.

"I appreciate your confidence."

"So did you get it?" she asked. Katz' face must've told her he didn't. "The dance," she said. "Did you get it?"

"I'm not sure what I'm supposed to – "

"Think of my name." Katz didn't even know which name to think of. *Cleo? Smythe? Margaret Ann?* "My middle name!" she said, wide-eyed now. "Salome? In the Bible?"

"There was a Salome in the Bible?"

"What!? Yes! The dance of the seven veils? It's in Mark – and Matthew!"

"Ah, my people didn't get that far. Sorry. Fill me in."

She took another drag and shook her head. "Herod – he was a King of the Romans? – he had this beautiful girl – *Salome?* – dance in veils at this big party and he was so wowed by her, he told her he'd give her whatever she asked for. So she asked her mother what she should ask for and she wound up telling him give me the head of John the Baptist on a platter, which he did, ugh."

Now Katz shook his head. "Wow, your people's stories are so much better than ours. Okay, we parted the sea and all that, but coming back from the dead, turning water to wine, now this? You guys took it to another level. Very impressive."

She laughed and stubbed out her cigarette, then snuggled in close to him. "You do, you know," she whispered in his ear.

"Do what?" he asked. She made a fist around his growing cock. "You make-a my dreams come true." This time around, there was a lot less licking and tickling and a lot more pounding away. Katz finished before Darryl did. Cleo broke the tape as soon as Salt-N-Pepa pushed it real good. When she caught her breath, she rolled to him and reached down to him again. "There's still an hour and ten minutes left," she laughed. He grabbed her hand before she could feel he was still dead on arrival.

"Turn that goddamned machine off," he said. She laughed, pushed it off, and pulled the Kools box to her. She lit up and took a long drag, and they both watched her smoke dissolve into the darkness. She snorted a laugh and shook her head. "Well, this has been one hell of a day."

Katz saw his opening and took it. "So, anything about what the jury did you want to talk about?"

454

"God no! All I need to know is what you already told me. There's no possibility of any of them being on the street anytime again ever, that's what you said, right?"

"That is what I said, but you didn't let me finish. There is maybe just a teeny little asterisk."

"Oh, Jesus Christ," she said, choking on the smoke, "here we go. Just how fucking teeny?"

"Really fucking teeny, and it's only an issue if one of them cooperates, like you did."

"Little late to wear a wire, isn't it?"

"Yeah, but it's not too late to start pointing fingers at everyone else to get yourself a Get Out Of Jail Free card, or at least shorten your sentence."

"So what's that mean?"

"It means that if someone does decide to cooperate, and if the Government decides to use the evidence they get from him in the next trial, and if what he provides helps convict some bad guys, *and* if the Government asks Richey to cut his sentence, *and* if Richey agrees to do it, then whoever he is could be out on the street sooner than we think."

Cleo held her inhale in while she mulled that over a while, then blew it out. "That's a lot of ands and ifs."

"It is, but it's still possible." She nodded she got it, then stubbed out her Kool and shook her head. "I appreciate you letting me know all that, Jake, but I'll still take my chances." She threw him a quizzical look. "You're good with that, right?"

"Absolutely." Katz picked up her hand and kissed it. She didn't look any less quizzical.

"You're sure?" she asked. "Is there something I should know?" He held on to her hand and leaned on an elbow, facing her.

"No, but there are one or two things I'd like to know."

"O-kay. What?"

"When Murphy was cross-examining you, what was he talking about when he said you were running your own coke operation?"

"That was total bullshit, Jake," she said.

"So you didn't set up a corporation to run it?"

"Oh for sure I did. It was such a big coke operation, I absolutely had to." She laughed. "Jake, that was for the goddamned nail salon I told you about way back, at Lorton."

"Ah, okay," Katz said, genuinely enlightened. "So do I get another question?"

"Sure," she said, "but that doesn't mean I answer it."

"When he brought up an informant being murdered, Madden objected and you never got to answer –"

She sat bolt upright and held the sheet to her chest. "And I ain't going to now either," she said, as fiery as she was loving a minute ago.

"Cleo, if we're going to make this work, we have to be honest with each – "

"Jesus Effing Christ, Jake!" She exploded out of bed, wrapped the sheet around her, grabbed the Kools and the lighter, stomped out of the room, and slammed the door. Katz managed to get his pants back on before she roared back in.

"The judge didn't make me answer, but now you will, is that the deal? Whose fucking side are you on, Jake?"

"Yours. Ours. Listen, I'm going to tell you a secret, okay? One I kept from you for your own good."

"Who the fuck cares?" she said and turned to the wall.

"I don't give a shit if you care," Katz said. "I'm telling you anyhow. Before you ever testified, maybe a month, six weeks ago, who the hell can remember now, one of the Marshals told me someone put a thirty thousand dollar bounty on your head to keep you from testifying."

"That is more total bullshit!"

"It isn't bullshit, Cleo. It was in an FBI agent's affidavit I read with my own eyes. It's the goddamned truth!"

"Right!" she muttered but the look on her face when she dropped into the chair next to the mirror told him she knew he wasn't lying. He took a seat on the edge of the bed across from her and waited a minute for the temperature to lower before he spoke again.

"I didn't want you to freak out and be too scared to give the testimony that would keep you out of jail. I wanted you – I wanted us – to have a shot at a life where you could be Cleo Smythe or Margaret Ann Mahoney or whoever you want to be without worrying about who might be around the next corner. So I didn't tell you, until now, when you're out of harm's way."

"Except for that teeny tiny little asterisk," she grunted.

"You're right," he said, "but even with all those ands and ifs, you're a million times safer than you were before you testified." He stood up and spread his arms. "Cleo, it's your life that's on the line, so how you live it is totally your call. But if your life's going to include me, I need to know the truth, whatever it is." She dropped her head and stared at the carpet before she looked back to him, those eyes weaker than he'd ever seen before.

"Confession's good for the soul, I hear," Katz said. "That's gotta be in the Bible somewhere." She glared at him. "*Now* he's the big fucking Biblical scholar." She shook her head, shook a Kool out of the pack in her hand, lit up, and sucked down about a quarter-inch worth of hot orange ember before she looked at him and held up the index finger of her left hand.

"One time. I am going to tell you this one time and I am never going to talk about it again, may God strike me down dead. You ever bring this up again, ask a question, raise an eyebrow, whatever, we are done right then and there. Am I making myself clear enough?"

"You are," Katz said and waited to hear the story that would bind him to her or drive them apart forever. There was no point now in wanting it to be a happy ending or fearing it would be the worst horror story he ever heard. Now he just needed to know. The room was dead quiet and dark everywhere except where the Kool was. Another glow lit up Cleo's face. She swallowed the smoke, then turned to him.

"You need to know how it was for me when I started working for Rayful. Right from the get-go, they all thought he was banging me and that was the only reason he kept moving me up the ladder, giving me shit to sell he wasn't giving them, making them report to me, whatever, the details didn't matter, the truth didn't matter, and they all let him know what they thought."

"I remember you talking about it with Bootsie," Katz said quietly, "on the tape."

"I never banged him, I never did him in any way, shape, or form. We were friends and then we were business partners and that was all we were, ever." She stopped and he waited for her to go wherever she was going however she wanted to get there.

"Ray was hearing it all the time, way more than I was, 'cause none of them ever had the balls to say it to my face, so the first thing he did was to give me new turf out in Virginia – outside of D.C., outside of Maryland – where I could develop my own networks and my own customers without having to deal with all those assholes. And that worked for a while." Katz clung to 'for a while,' praying to God that Ray moved her from Virginia, away from anywhere near Schein.

"But then it didn't," she said and took on a new, bitchy voice. "'Oh, the only reason you're givin' her all that is you're tryin' to make yo' white girlfriend happy, uh huh'." She shook her head in disgust. "So one night," she said, "Tony calls on the beeper, and tells me Ray wants to have dinner with me, at Morton's in Crystal City. It was like eight o'clock and I said 'I already ate, how about tomorrow night?' and he comes back on the phone and says 'No, he needs to talk to you tonight. Nine o'clock.' and he hangs up. So I went and we have this private dining room all to ourselves, and Ray orders this big steak I take like a sliver of and we drink a little wine, and then he tells me 'the only way this shit is gonna stop is if you prove yourself.' I say 'What do you mean?' He says 'Make your bones, like the Mafia.' 'Like are you telling me I got to kill somebody?' I say. Ray gives me this look I'll never forget. 'Not just somebody,' he says, 'somebody white.' Katz

460

clutched the side of the bed and held his breath, cursing God and Ray.

"'What white guy am I gonna kill?' I ask him. He says 'You know that guy you're running out there?' I gotta back up," she said but Katz was already way ahead of her. He felt like he was a drill driving head first into the core of the earth, and gaining speed. "Once Ray knew he could trust me and wanted me to branch out, he hooked me up with this fat slob, a guy who used to show up on Morton like every other night to buy stuff he was selling out of the basement in his *parents' house* somewhere in the hoity-toity end of Arlington up near McLean, unbelievable!"

She shook her head at the memory, then looked at Katz, wide-eyed. "You remember that night right before I testified when I freaked out about Madden saying I worked for Ray in Arlington? This is what I thought he was talking about, not Crystal City. I didn't even know Crystal City was Arlington. And the records they grabbed that were in the 302s or whatever they are, I was so scared there was something in there that Murphy would latch onto to show he was part of this bullshit gang he kept going on about! Jake, you with me?"

"Yeah," he barely managed to push out. She held up her hands. "Hey, you asked. I know the story. I don't need to tell it."

Yes you do, Katz thought. He rotated his index finger. "Keep going."

"Okay, so back at the dinner, Ray tells me this guy is wearing a wire – remember I told you I knew what they do to people who wear a wire? This is *how* I knew. I say 'Ray I can't kill this guy, I can't kill anyone!' He says you don't have to be the one to actually kill him. You just step up and stick him first, the other guys'll do the rest. I'm like nauseous even thinking about it but I say yes 'cause when it came right down to it, I didn't have a choice. It was me or him at this point." Katz cleared his throat and held up his hand, the room starting to spin to hell with him. He grasped at his last straw.

"Did you even know the guy's name?" he asked.

"Fuck no! What difference does it make anyhow? There had be tons of fat white slobs dealing drugs in Virginia." He held on to that straw for the second it took her to jerk it away. "Wait, hold on. I remember what we used to call him. Shitball. Mostly because he looked like one, but it had something to do with his real name too. Anyhow, let me fucking finish telling this goddamned thing already, okay?" But Katz had stopped listening. He heard words – house on Morton, ripped the fucking wire off, her knife bouncing off the shitball's chest, guys on him like wolves, she can't watch – but nothing made sense any more except the sick joke the universe played on him, making him solve a jigsaw puzzle he didn't even know he was a piece in. More and more words spilled out of Cleo, but now, worst of all, the dark overlord of the cosmos was letting them make sense again.

"We split up in two cars," she said. "I was in the decoy – this cop was right on us! – but when we got up on

U Street somewhere, we all bolted in different directions like it was a Chinese fire drill gone crazy, you know, and he didn't get any of us!" She smiled and shook her head like she was remembering good times, but then she leveled her gaze at Katz, who was having trouble keeping her in focus. He tasted shrimp and vegetables again and something a lot more foul coming up from deep within.

"But Ray was right, Jake. Next day he told me they found the guy with his head barely hanging on to his neck and he gave me a fucking high five and that was it. None of those fuckers ever gave me one more piece of shit about –" Katz thought his brain would explode but his stomach did first. He lurched the three steps to the bathroom, fell to his knees, and spewed everything into the bowl so hard the water splashed his vomit back into his face. He heard her say something behind him but couldn't make it out over his dry heaves until they finally stopped an eternity later.

"Oh my God, honey!" he heard behind him. "Are you okay?"

"Close the door please," he croaked. He waited to hear the door click behind him before he reached for the toilet paper, wiped what he'd spewed up off the toilet seat, flushed most of it down, then all of it on a second try, and pushed himself off the seat to his feet. He edged to the sink and rubbed hot water on his face until he couldn't feel anything but flesh, wiped himself dry with a towel hanging over the shower rod, and forced himself to look in the mirror. He heard a light knock on the door, then watched it swing open behind him.

"Jake, how are you, sweetie?" He'd never seen that look on Cleo's face before, or on the other face that shimmered in the glass between them like the ghost he was, and in that second, Katz knew he'd never be able to see her face again without seeing Schein's. He dropped his head and whispered to himself. *Sorry, buddy. So sorry.*

Cleo's hand was on his back. "Wow, what was that?" she asked him softly. Katz kept his eyes on the sink and shook his head.

"Must've been something I ate." He spit out whatever was left in his mouth and turned on the water and watched it swirl down the drain before he turned to give her a weak smile and an even weaker pat on the shoulder. "I'm real sorry, Cleo, but I need to go." She let him go past and followed him into the bedroom. He sat on the side of the bed and started pulling on his socks.

"Jake, it's not even eight thirty," Cleo said. "Why don't you lay down and give yourself some time to get over it? I'll make you some tea or something." He started buttoning his shirt and stood up before he answered her.

"I appreciate that, Cleo, but if I'm going to heave again, I'm doing it in my own toilet. I am so sorry." He tucked his shirt into his pants, slipped into his shoes, threw his jacket and tie over his arm, and avoided anything approaching eye contact with her until they got to the front door. He caressed her troubled face, then blew her a kiss, and pulled the door open.

"I'll call you tomorrow to see how you're doing," she said. Katz nodded.

"I love you," she said.

"Love you too," Katz made himself say and pulled the door shut behind him.

But I can never forgive you.

He looked down the hall at Johnnie Lee sleeping in a chair next to the elevator, then turned to see the door to the stairway just behind him. He looked back to her door.

"Goodbye, Cleo," he said, and took the steps down and out of her life.

42

Even before Katz pushed through the door to Rhode Island, his mind was reeling from trying to calculate everything he needed to do next. The temperature must've dropped five degrees from the time he got to the hotel, but the brisk air helped him focus, so he kept his jacket off and hoped he wouldn't freeze to death before he figured out what he had to do. By the time he got the two blocks down to Mass Av, he knew he wasn't heading home anymore. By the time he got to his office thirteen blocks and three flights up later, he had a plan. No moment of clarity had leaped out at him like it did when he knew he had to end his marriage and head to law school, but he knew he had to write four letters, then let the chips fall where they would.

When he threw his coat over LaVerne's chair and bellied up to her typewriter, he saw the time on the clock. 8:54. Forty-five minutes ago, he was in the throes of sexual ecstasy. A half-hour before that, he was scarfing down some excellent Kung Pao Shrimp. Now he was trying to salvage his career and maybe his life.

He addressed four envelopes by hand, then rolled a sheet of letterhead and a carbon into the typewriter and addressed the first letter to Richey. He'd never withdrawn as anyone's lawyer before and he had no idea what the protocol was, so he just got to the point.

Dear Judge Richey,

This is to notify you that, effectively immediately, I am withdrawing as Cleo Smythe's attorney in the U.S. v. Edmond trial.

Sincerely, Jake Katz

cc: Charles Madden, U.S. Attorneys' Office

He pulled the letter out and signed it.

The second letter was to Madden. After telling him he'd resigned as Cleo's lawyer per the enclosed copy of the letter to Richey, he typed:

My last request on her behalf is that you place her in witness protection for both her personal and economic security. I ask that you give her the maximum sum of money you can to convince her to take the deal.

His fingers hovered over the keys for a minute while he mulled the lawyerly way of saying "Please also think about how it will look if anything happens to her and the press finds out you were asked to up the ante, but didn't," before he realized that Madden would figure that out all by himself anyhow. He signed the letter and threw it on the first one, but he knew the next one would take a little more time and thought, so he grabbed a pen and pad to scratch out a draft first. When he was done, he dug up the address and was surprised to learn the Bar's Office of Disciplinary Counsel was one of his neighbors on Fifth Street. He read it over one more time before he typed it.

Dear Sir:

I am Jacob Katz, Bar No. 355511. I practice law at 410 5th St., N.W. I am writing to inform you that I violated Rule 1.7(b)(4) by having sexual relations with my client Cleopatra Salome Smythe on two occasions while I was representing her as a cooperating witness in the case of U.S. v. Rayful Edmond III, Cr. No. 89-162 (D.D.C.).

I have terminated my professional relationship with Ms. Smythe today and have also notified Judge Charles Richey and the United States Attorney's Office of that fact today. I will accept whatever sanctions you believe are appropriate in this matter. Please contact me at the above address or phone number at any time.

Sincerely,

Jacob Katz, Esq.

He signed it and tossed it on the pile, then looked at the clock. 11:11.

He yearned to lie down and let the day end already but he knew he didn't want to wake up looking forward to writing the last letter, so he grabbed the pad and pen and retreated to the more comfy chair behind his desk. No letterhead or typewriter would be needed for this one, so he settled himself in and took his time writing it out. Four crumples later, he was ready to send it. By the time he slid all four letters down the mail drop and pushed himself down the steps, he'd already received one bit of mercy. It was finally tomorrow.

March 3, 1990

43

Katz knew he'd remember the rest of the way if he could just find Fort McNair. The last and only time he'd been to Wallace's place, he'd been distracted by a torrential rain but even more by the bomb Wallace had planted in his brain about Cleo maybe having something to do with Schein's death. Tonight was clear and that bomb had gone off, so Katz had no excuse for not finding his way, other than his preoccupation with two questions he'd had ever since Wallace called him Thursday and asked if he'd like to come over for dinner Saturday night: Why, and why now?

The fort appeared dead ahead and in less than five minutes, Katz buzzed the intercom at the gates to Wallace's condo community and heard a click granting him entrance to the grounds. Finding Wallace's unit stopped being a problem when Katz saw him waving and smiling from the sidewalk up ahead on the left. They gave each other the half hug and Katz followed Wallace up three steps to a landing and through his front door.

"Welcome to my humble abode," Wallace said. Katz took a look around. The kitchen was to his right, with what looked like a small dining room behind it. A short hallway that ended in a closed door was in front of him, and a den down a short flight of steps was to his left.

"This is nice, Tom. You own it?"

"Tryin' to. Bank mostly does now. You hungry?"

"Absolutely."

"Good." Wallace pointed to the two-liter Coke bottle on the counter. "Grab that, will you?" He turned to pull an ice tray out of the freezer on top of the fridge, then nodded to Katz to follow him down the stairs. A bucket of KFC sat in the middle of a coffee table, alongside a roll of Bounty and two settings of paper plates, plastic forks, and plastic cups on the side of the table facing an entertainment console. Wallace picked up a remote and turned on the TV sitting on top of the console, then picked up another remote to fire up the VCR sitting on the cable box next to it.

"Have a seat, man. I got some top-flight entertainment for you tonight. You're going to see somethin' ain't nobody without a FBI clearance has ever seen. I called you the day I got it 'cause I knew you'd be – what do they call it? – an appreciative audience." Wallace pointed Katz to a seat on the couch across from the console and sat down next to him.

"Okay, you know our Mayor For Life is finally gettin' his, right?" Katz remembered reading a few days ago that Barry's trial date had been set for sometime in June. Five of the counts were for using coke and three were for telling the grand jury he didn't.

"I do."

"And you know the FBI videotaped him the night they busted him?"

"Right."

"Well, you're about to see the world premiere." Wallace pressed Play and Katz saw grainy black-and-white

472

images of Barry and a woman standing inside what looked like a hotel room. The angle was from somewhere below them and white letters superimposed on the screen told him it was 20:25:35 on 01-18-90.

"Jesus! Do they know you have this?" Wallace paused the tape and stared at him.

"Jake, I'm 'they', okay? Don't worry about any of that, all right?"

Katz threw up his arms. "Fine. Sorry. I'm a lawyer. I can't help it."

"Just watch. I got it cued up to the best part." He started the tape again. Barry and the woman were chatting about something Katz couldn't hear and his mind drifted back to the only time he remembered Barry's name coming up during the Edmond trial. When Murphy asked Cleo if she knew him, she told him "I've never ridden in his limo."

Katz watched Barry light up something in his mouth with two hands, then saw a herd of men rumble past the camera and over a bed to grab him. Katz couldn't read the lettering on the back of one of their jackets, but guessed it spelled DEA. Another man followed the herd and Katz could make out shouts of "FBI!" and "Don't move!" before he saw Barry come back into view, with one of the DEA guys telling him to put his hands on the wall. Katz couldn't see the woman anymore, but he could hear she was frantic. "What is going on here?" he heard over and over until someone said "Get the woman out of here."

473

"Damn, I'll be damned," Katz heard Barry say. "I get tricked like this, damn." He asked what he was being arrested for. An agent told him it was for violating the narcotics laws of the District of Columbia. "That bitch was the one who got me in a set-up," Katz thought Barry said.

"Pay attention to what I'm telling you," the agent said but Barry's mind was apparently fixed on just one thing.

"That was a set-up, goddamn it, a fucking set-up," he muttered. "Goddamn, I shouldn'ta come up here." The agent started to read him his rights but even that didn't get his attention. "Goddamn, that was a set-up."

"You have a right to see a lawyer – "

"Shit! I'll be goddamned!"

"You have a right to stop answering at any time."

"Goddamn bitch set me up, Goddamn!"

"Mayor, do you understand your rights?"

"Yeah," he said, "got me set up, ain't that a bitch?"

Wallace hit Stop.

"Wow!" was all Katz could say.

"That fucker is going away for a long time," Wallace said.

"Did he get his coke from Rayful?"

"DEA's still runnin' that down. Right now it looks like his shit was comin' from the Virgin Islands, not L.A., but, whatever, it's all comin' somewhere out of Colombia anyhow."

"It'd be unbelievable," Katz said, "if I didn't just see it."

Wallace threw the remote on the table and pulled the lid off the KFC bucket. He grabbed a breast and pushed the tub to Katz. Katz grabbed another breast and they both dug in till Wallace tore a sheet off the Bounty roll and wiped his mouth. "So, you hear back from anybody yet?"

"Nothing from Richey or Madden, which I expected, and the Bar sent me a letter saying they'd get back to me, but they haven't yet, so I guess I'm just going to be in limbo for a while." He hadn't told Wallace about the other letter, so he just let it go at that.

"What do you think they're going to do to you?" Wallace asked between bites.

"I really don't know. Outside of what they did to Harry, I don't know too much about how they do what they do."

Wallace cracked a sharp laugh. "You can't go by him, man. From what you told me, he did worse things before breakfast any goddamn day than you did in your whole life. And – you turned yourself in. Probably what I shoulda done."

Katz knew exactly what he was talking about. When they first met, working on Brenda Queen's murder back in '68, Wallace took it on himself to go to Memphis to check out an angle without telling anyone at MPD. He wound up being demoted from Detective until the brass brought him back up during Khaalis' siege.

"You got your badge back," Katz said. "Eventually."

Wallace swallowed a bite. "Yeah, nine years eventually. Pretty sure your situation's gonna work itself out a little quicker, you bein' white an' all – and, oh yeah, sober too." They touched their cups and ate some more before Wallace leaned back and turned to Katz. "After that night, you ever see Cleo again?"

"Nope."

"Ever hear from her?"

"Nope."

"Know what happened to her and the witness protection thing?"

"That would be another nope. I told you I didn't hear back from Madden and no, I didn't call him either."

"So you got no idea if she's still around here or – "

"She could be anywhere, man. I just don't know and I'm trying not to think about it anymore either." They held each other's gaze for a second before Wallace extended his fist to him and they tapped knuckles. "I give you respect, man. Had to be hard to give that up, I will say that, no matter what she did. That was one fine-looking woman." Katz watched a kaleidoscope of pictures flit through his head.

"Still is, I bet," he said.

* * *

The next morning, Cleo took a long last drag of her Salem and impaled it in the sand urn next to the bench. She yawned and stretched, then went into the ladies' room and knocked on the door of the handicapped stall at the back.

"How's it going, hon?" she asked. "You need any help?"

"No, I think I'm fine," she heard. "I'm just putting on the new ones."

"You sure you don't need help?" After a few grunts and rustles behind the door, she heard "No, I just need one more minute, that's all." Cleo knew that meant five minutes, at least. "Okay, I'll be back in two. Take your time."

"All right."

Cleo turned to look in the mirror at the face she was finally getting used to. The dull brown contacts looking back at her were still strange but when she pulled her scrunchie tight on the short shank of jet black hair hanging behind her, she thought *This ponytail is growing on me* before she winced at the accidental pun, then winced again at the second chin that was growing too. Sitting in her car for the two-and-a-half hours it took to drive to and from Rocky Mount every weekend wasn't helping, but laying around that motor hotel across from the pottery factory five nights a week was even worse. Her immediate solution was to get away from the mirror and light up another one out in the hall, but a glare of sunlight through the front doors changed her mind. She tugged her coat belt around her tight and stepped into the cold air outside. A Volvo pulled into the circular drive and stopped just past her. One of the valets scrambled around the front of the car, traded a paper stub for the owner's keys, and drove it into a space maybe ten yards away.

Cleo followed the car's path, then angled over to a bench that sat just inside a cluster of oaks and pines facing the still green grass stretching away from her. She reached into her pocketbook for what she always did when she sat there, a folded piece of yellow paper peeking at her from behind the Salems. She'd memorized every crease, word, smudge, and dot a long time ago so she didn't need to pull it out to remember what it said, but she couldn't help herself from holding the only piece of Jake she still had, one more time.

> Cleo, this is the toughest letter I've ever had to write but we both need to move on, and we need to do it now, so I'm just going to get to the point. Effective right now, I'm no longer your lawyer. I've let Madden know, and I've asked him to try and get you as much money as he can, but regardless of how much he gets, you <u>need</u> to go into witness protection, because you need to be

someplace else for your own safety and peace of mind. If you stay here, your life will be in jeopardy every day, and if anything would ever happen to you, I couldn't live knowing I was the reason for it. I've already lived through that with one person I loved, and I won't do it again.

I wish I could convince myself that if we went somewhere else, we'd be happy as long as we have each other. But I can't. You need to start over, fresh, with the whole world in front of you, without anything – or anyone – that might lead someone to think you might have once lived in D.C. and start asking questions you can't answer.

I am so sorry things couldn't work out between us but believe me when I say I wish you all the best. Take good care of yourself. You've earned it. Jake

If anyone else had written her that letter, she would say it was total b.s., but she believed everything he wrote because she knew who he was. Her heart broke for both of them.

She folded the note up, slipped it back into the bag, and headed back to the building. She'd fought for the extra money just like Jake asked her to, but mostly as a bargaining chip to get what she really wanted more. When she finally said she'd take the $207,106 and the Director of the Marshals Service agreed to let her start over so close to D.C., she could practically hear him thinking *It's her life, what the fuck do I care?*

When she got back to the bathroom, the handicapped door was still closed. "You ready now, hon?" Cleo asked.

"I can't find my keys. I don't know how I'm going to get home."

"I'll get you home, don't you worry about that. We're going to get picked up, ride home in style, I promise you. Sure you don't need help?"

"No, I have it," she heard her sigh. "Oh, I am so sorry to be such a bother. Just hold on." In a minute, Cleo heard the door lock turn and opened the door wide enough for the wheelchair to roll out. A pretty face with a sad smile looked up at her.

"What can I say? I'm not the girl I used to be."

"None of us is, dear," Cleo smiled and steered her out of the stall and through the door to the hall. "Let's get some lunch, okay?"

"Oh, we're going to have lunch? That would be good. Where are we going?"

"Just down the hall. Hang on one minute."

When they got to the stand, the receptionist greeted Cleo like the old friend she'd become in less than a month. "Ms. Majak, so good to see the two of you again. We've got you at your usual table." Cleo pushed the wheelchair to a table right next to the window and parked it so it faced the green. She took the menus from the waitress, then watched a pair of trim ladies climb out of a cart wearing billed caps, sweaters, and long pants.

"They're sports," Cleo said. "It is really chilly out there today."

Her companion watched each of them pull a putter from their bags, then turned to Cleo, a proud smile filling her face. "Did you know I used to be a championship golfer?" she asked. "Three times in a row?"

"Yes, Mrs. Mahoney," Cleo said. "I've heard that."

Postscript

This book is a work of fiction, but the crimes ascribed to Rayful Edmond and his accomplices, and the events described at the trial are all fact. Almost all of the wiretapped conversations, trial testimony, and bench conferences are taken verbatim from transcripts, with edits made only for clarity or reference to fictional events I created for the novel, most prominently Schein's death.

Jake Katz, Tom Wallace, Andy Scheingold, Charlie Madden, Ron Hutchison, Phil Gaskins, and the other Marshals are all characters I invented. A white woman who was high up in Rayful Edmond's hierarchy was a co-operating witness at the trial, but any resemblance Cleo Smythe bears to her in any other way is purely coincidental.

Rayful Edmond and every other defendant, Billy Murphy and every other defense attorney, Judge Richey, and Jay Stephens are real persons and the conversations ascribed to them in court, on wiretaps, and from behind a podium are real, with occasional edits made only to increase clarity. I also occasionally shortened or changed the time that some events occurred to keep the story moving.

I worked on the book for about three and a half years, during which the people I thank below made the work much easier. My great gratitude goes to:

- Anne Brewer, for her outstanding editorial skills;

- Bill Miller, the Public Information Officer of the D.C. United States Attorney's Office and his staff, for their exceptional willingness and ability to find and reproduce copies of the wiretap transcripts;

- John Dominguez, an Assistant United States Attorney who was one of Mr. Edmond's prosecutors at one of his trials – and is still at the D.C. U.S. Attorney's Office – for sharing his still vivid memories of the case;

- Bryant Johnson, the Records Supervisor at the United States District Court for the District of Columbia, who located the trial transcripts in the court's archives, made them available to me, and permitted me to copy them;

- Ernie McIntosh, Esq., a distinguished member of the District of Columbia Bar, who represented a defendant at Mr. Edmond's second trial, and shared both his memories of the cases and his prodigious criminal law expertise;

- Jim Lyons, Esq., another distinguished member of the D.C. Bar, who gave me valuable insights into some of the lawyers representing Mr. Edmond's co-defendants;

- Neil Trugman, Deputy Chief of the Amtrak Police Department, for sharing his knowledge about wiretaps he participated in when he was a police officer with the Metropolitan Police Department;

- Jennifer Sullivan, who provided information I found useful in developing Cleo Smythe's background;

- Liz Trupin-Pulli, for all her support, encouragement, and efforts to find me a commercial publisher; and

- Street Stars Films, May 3rd Films, Kirk Fraser, and Troy Reed for producing "The Rayful Edmond Story" (parts 1 and 2), available on YouTube.

My most heartfelt thanks go to Sandy Tevelin for her outstanding work in her continuing roles as Muse, Wife, Love Of My Life, and Executive Editor.

Rayful Edmond's incredible saga continued well after the events depicted in this book, and would be worthy of a separate novel, if it wasn't all true. In September 1990, Judge Richey sentenced him to life without parole on three counts, as well as shorter sentences on other counts, and ordered him to serve them all concurrently. Shortly after he was imprisoned at Lewisburg Federal Penitentiary, he became acquainted with Osvaldo "Chickie" Trujillo-Blanco, who was serving a sentence at the same prison. Chickie had been a key member of Colombia's Medellin drug cartel, in which his mother Griselda continued to play a prominent role. Within a year after Rayful's incarceration, he and Chickie were operating a drug enterprise behind Federal bars that was bigger than the one Edmond had operated as a free man in the District of Columbia.

In 1992, Federal law enforcement officials began recording their conversations with suppliers and dealers on the outside, and in 1996, Edmond pleaded guilty to a new drug conspiracy charge – and began informing the government about numerous other drug traffickers. His decision to cooperate was motivated by his mother's conviction on drug-trafficking charges at the second Edmond-related trial conducted by Judge Richey in 1990, which ultimately resulted in a 14-year sentence. In exchange for his fruitful cooperation, Bootsie Perry was released from prison in 1998. Edmond remains in Federal custody at an unknown location. At this writing, his release is under consideration by U.S. District Court Judge Emmet G. Sullivan.

Made in the USA
Middletown, DE
29 September 2023

39746182R10275